Praise for Kate Duignan

The New Ships is a gripping novel about lost children and a very fine portrait of family life in all its beauty and betrayal. Intricate, compelling, and deeply moving.
—Anna Smaill

Breakwater is an astonishingly polished and confident first novel.
—Rebecca Palmer, *Otago Daily Times*

Duignan's first novel proves that she is already an accomplished writer who has a good grasp on the interior lives of contemporary New Zealanders.
—Gilbert Wong, *NZ Herald*

One of the most enjoyable novels of the year.
—Chris Bourke, *North & South*

It is an impressively confident debut. With an unerring ear, she knows when to leave her characters alone and when to intervene as narrator. . . . It is the novel's great strength that it asks the reader to think about the way in which contemporary families are configured.
—Jane Stafford, *NZ Listener*

THE NEW SHIPS

Kate Duignan

Victoria University Press

TE WHARE WĀNANGA O TE ŪPOKO O TE IKA A MĀUI
VICTORIA
UNIVERSITY OF WELLINGTON

VICTORIA UNIVERSITY PRESS
Victoria University of Wellington
PO Box 600 Wellington
vup.victoria.ac.nz

ISBN 9781776561889

A catalogue record for this book is available from the
National Library of New Zealand.

Published with the assistance of a grant from

ARTS COUNCIL OF NEW ZEALAND *TOI AOTEAROA*

Printed by 1010 Printing International, China

For James

This form, this face, this life
Living to live in a world of time beyond me; let me
Resign my life for this life, my speech for that unspoken,
The awakened, lips parted, the hope, the new ships.

T S Eliot, 'Marina'

When we launched life
on the river of grief,
how vital were our arms, how ruby our blood.
With a few strokes, it seemed,
we would cross all pain,
we would soon disembark.
That didn't happen.
In the stillness of each wave we found invisible currents.
The boatmen, too, were unskilled,
their oars untested.
Investigate the matter as you will,
blame whomever, as much as you want,
but the river hasn't changed,
the raft is still the same.
Now *you* suggest what's to be done,
you tell us how to come ashore.

Faiz Ahmed Faiz, 'You Tell Us What To Do'
(trans Agha Shahid Ali)

There are mothers and fathers, Kevin, whom we barely know.
They lift us. Eventually we all shall go
into the dark furniture of the radio.

Bill Manhire, 'Kevin'

Part One

One

Rob rang from England last night.

'Peter. You poor bugger.'

His New Zealand vowels, hiding under the received pronounciation.

'Clare and I were talking about that time you two came over and stayed with us. We went to Bratton Down and saw the chalk horse, remember? Your Moira, trying to speak Italian with the tourists. She was gorgeous.'

I murmured a bland response. Rob didn't make contact in all the time my wife was ill. He knew, of course. Our mothers play Mahjong together every week. For a while I cut him slack, supposing it was the usual *mañana, mañana* that we all fall prey to, the delusion that there'll be plenty of time. Moira's cancer was incurable, and then aggressive, and still he didn't call. Even from the far side of the world, the stink of mortality we were giving off was too strong. Rob, who rowed the Sea Scouts whaler with me down the Whanganui River as an eleven-year-old, was scared shitless to talk to me while my wife was dying.

So I changed the subject.

'How's London? Aaron flies back tomorrow.'

'Jittery, to tell you the truth,' he said. 'High security

11

everywhere. Took me two hours to get on a flight to Athens last week. Tell your boy to keep a sleeping bag handy.'

'A work trip?'

'It's been a frenzy. In fact we've just bought ourselves a holiday home over in Greece, trying to slow ourselves down. Lesbos, do you know it? Cheap as chips. But the prices are going to go through the roof the minute they join the euro. Pretty little place. Views over the Aegean. Your old wine-dark, eh? You'd love it.'

'Mytilene.'

'Ah, you do know it. You know, funny thing, Peter. We were having lunch down on the waterfront back in August, one of those places that do paninis and so forth, full of local kids drinking their Nescafé. The pictures set us off and we were full of it, talking about Amsterdam, the boat and Geneviève and you, and . . .'

I heard his hesitation.

'What am I saying? This isn't the time.'

'Probably not. But you've started now.'

'We were talking about Geneviève, and about . . .'

He got stuck again.

'About Abigail,' I said.

Abigail, *wail*, *pale*, *flail*. The echoes wash up the long-distance line. When did I last say her name out loud?

'Yes. Abigail.'

It comes from the Hebrew, *Avigail*: my father is joy. Or better, perhaps: my father rejoices. The biblical Abigail was married to the wealthy Nabal, and then to King David, 'a woman of good understanding, and of a beautiful countenance', according to the Book of Samuel. I looked all that up at the time. It might have been shortened to Abby or Abi or Gail, but we always used the long form.

'So the waitress brings out the meals. I did a double

take. The girl looked just like Geneviève. For all the world. The spitting image.'

'Geneviève's dead,' I said. 'Years ago.'

'Of course. Of course.'

Then I just felt tired. I wanted to put the phone down, and I wanted to go to bed.

'She was just a young thing,' Rob was saying. 'They're all young now though, aren't they?

'Power of suggestion. You were talking about Geneviève at the time.'

'Maybe. Unnerving though. Because she had a French accent. That was the thing, a French girl waitressing over there on the scrabbly end of Greece.'

'Sure,' I said. 'Pretty French girl gets a job in Greece. What are the odds?'

But by then he'd done it, injected a breath of hope. I felt it move down into my chest. I've had some experience, over the past year, with the problem of hope. *I could do without this tonight, Robbie.*

'It made us wonder, that's all. Peter, tell me. Did you ever go back to that doctor in Lyon?'

There are many things I haven't done. Did I push Moira hard enough, forcefully enough, to try every possibile cure? There was talk back in July of new drugs coming through, experimental trials she might have joined.

'Did you press him further?'

'No, I never did do that.'

We shall not all sleep but we shall all be changed, in a moment, in the twinkling of an eye, at the last trump: for the trumpet shall sound, and the dead shall be raised incorruptible, and we shall be changed. Such extraordinary promises the minister made at Moira's funeral.

Rob's wife I suppose, has been telling Rob to call me. Has been insisting.

'You saw this girl in August,' I said. 'Vaguely familiar face, serves you coffee. Three months ago. You said nothing at the time. You didn't call. How important, really, was this?'

'Well. At the time. You were—'

I'd let the silence hang. *Useless bastard.*

'Anyway. Your boy. How's he holding up?'

'One parent left,' I said. 'Leaves him out on a limb a bit, doesn't it?'

'How old is he now?'

'Twenty-five.'

'Not a kid, thank god. I mean, imagine.'

'Not a kid.'

'Sorry. Stupid thing to say.'

It's true though. When Aaron was small, I used to wonder—don't all parents?—how I'd manage if we had to go it alone. I figured there would be a long stretch of takeaways and general degeneration, then we'd bob up and survive. What other option could there be?

'Moira liked you,' I said. 'She rated Clare, too.'

'I should have called.'

'Yes.' It gave me such a weary feeling. 'You should have.'

'Look, bring Aaron over. Come to Greece, both of you. Ouzo, ruins. The sailing's brilliant. We've got a friend with a yacht, I'll take you out. That's what he needs. Just the thing.'

Afterwards, I slept badly. The wind got up, and the branches of the unpruned ngaio scraped against the glass sliders. In the middle of the night, I went down to the study and found the golden book, a foot high and heavy as a box of files. I spread it open on the desk. *Daphnis and Chloe.* It was supposed to be a gift. In the end I kept it, and brought it back to New Zealand with me. The book

14

is easily the most valuable object in the house, although a burglar would be unlikely to notice it.

The text is in French. In 1971 I learnt whole phrases by heart to recite to Geneviève. I can't work out the sentences anymore. Chagall's lithographs tell the story: the boats beaching on the shore, lovers washing in the shrine of the nymphs, an altar, spring wine and bird-snaring. Towards the end, a double plate awash in red: a feast is laid out for all the citizens of Mytilene, where the girl is at last recognised by her high-born father, who had exposed her on a hillside as an infant. The final plate shows the wedding night, bride and groom on one side of the door, the villagers pressed against it, lamps swung high. It's a story of comic innocence, about a boy who didn't know how to make love to a girl. The prints are housed in a museum just outside of Mytilene, on Lesbos. It would be something to see those prints, it really would. It would be worth going to Rob's for that alone. *Moira would love it.*

But Moira's dead.

And now this waitress, serving tables where Chagall painted. This girl who looks like Geneviève, who must, *ipso facto*, look like Abigail.

Abigail was my daughter, born when I was twenty and Geneviève a year older. She was born on the Amstel river on a houseboat called the *Lychorida*, a former coal barge owned by a secondhand bookseller. Rob, Clare, Geneviève and I had spent an entire Amsterdam autumn sanding, hammering and caulking, and in December, we moved in.

Abigail arrived in the middle of a storm. The boat pulled on the mooring ropes and rocked on the currents. It was difficult, as births can be, but nothing went wrong and she was perfectly formed.

She died at six weeks old, at Geneviève's father's home

near Lyon. I was in Amsterdam at the time. The cause of death, according to the doctor's certificate, was acute septicaemia following on from pneumonia. The certificate has a date and a municipal seal, and is signed with an elaborate flourish by one *Docteur Gabriel Barreau*. It's a flimsy, xeroxed copy, but it looks official enough. For seventeen years I had no reason to question its veracity. The last time I saw Geneviève in Lyon she told me things that sent me back to stare fixedly at that certificate time and time again. It has now been eleven years since that meeting, and for all of those years I have found myself paralysed, neither able to seek out answers nor to put the questions from my mind.

*

When I step out of the lift, the new receptionist gives me the kind of startled half-smile that suggests she knows I belong here in spite of my jeans and Nikes, that she recognises my face but hasn't got a clue what my name is.

'Afternoon,' I say.

When I fish in my pocket I realise I've left my swipe card in the car. I mime a little hand show and gesture to the glass doors.

'Could you let me through, Rebecca?'

She looks sceptical. It's six weeks now since the towers came down. *High security everywhere.*

'Peter Collie,' I say firmly. 'I'm going through to see Richard.'

There's a subtle eye-flick to the list beside the phone, an apologetic smile, and she reaches for the button under her desk. The lock on the glass door makes a soft pop, and I'm through.

To be fair to the receptionist, she hasn't seen me here often. There have been weeks and months of absence, half-days, quarter-days at best, coming in late at night for a scrambling two hours after Moira fell asleep, or sitting on the couch beside her with the laptop warm against my thighs, *Pride and Prejudice* running on the TV while I fire off the emails needed to keep it all at bay for another twenty-four hours, another week. Keep it in a holding pattern, a hundred balls in the air, flights waiting to touch down, a flock of irritations, nothing that I could attend to or bother with, nothing that mattered. Now nine months since the oncologist showed us where the cells had metastasized to Moira's femur, sternum, skull and liver, four months since we called a halt to treatments, one month after her funeral, I am, it seems, ready to *get back to it*.

Richard, the firm's managing partner, is in his office. I go right through and stand beside the window. The harbour is a pattern of erasures and smudges.

'Peter.' Richard's voice and eyes brim with the apparent pleasure of seeing me. 'I didn't know you were in the building.'

'Just briefly,' I say. 'Dropping in.'

He tilts his head on one side and considers for a moment.

'I've been in Queenstown all week,' he says. 'Got back last night.'

'How did it go?'

'Gus made me try white water rafting. An afternoon of pure terror.'

We're laughing. How well he creates ease, easiness.

'And you, Peter. You're looking well.'

He keeps his eyes steady on me, his gaze doctor-like, wise, concerned, diagnostic. I'm almost ten years older than him, but I feel *fathered*: there's no other word for how it feels to have the full beam of Richard's attention swung round onto me.

'I've lost track. You've been with your parents in Wanganui?'

'No,' I say. 'Aaron flies out tonight. I'll head up after that.'

He closes the door, and leads me to the two red wing-chairs at the coffee table by the glass. A Hotere hangs on the wall opposite, a treasure of the firm's which has migrated around the walls over the years, from reception, to boardroom, to hallway. It's startling all over again to see it here in Richard's office and I wonder just how he managed to comandeer it for himself, the fat black cross, the white text which I've mentally fiddled with through many a long partnership meeting: LE PAPE EST MORT. Le pape, pope, papa. Mort, mortal, moribund, from the Latin, *mortalis*, one destined to die, *brotos* in the Greek. Below, a text in Māori: *E hinga atu ana he tetekura e ara mai ana he tetekura.*

Kura, which might mean school? I can't begin to unravel it. The painting brings back the taste of peppermints, the smell of coffee served at partnership meetings, the jangling silver bracelets of our secretary Natasha typing up the minutes, and gazing out at the blue, or silver, or white-whipped plane of the harbour when the discussions got bogged down.

'How's the house going?'

Richard hesitates, gauging whether I really want the switch in conversation.

'Bit by bit,' he says. 'We've found a blacksmith in Otaki. Can you believe it? He's working with us on designs for the gates. We're deciding whether to go for a plain look, or a William Morris-y kind of thing, more the late Victorian style. Excuse the technical detail.' He gives a mock grimace. 'I become very boring when you get me started on all this.'

Richard and his partner have been renovating their

Mount Victoria villa for the past five years. They have both the perfectionism and the substantial income necessary for the task.

'It's much fiddlier to do the Morris, of course.' His brow frets up, the variables of the decision clearly weighty upon him. 'I would prefer it, if he can pull it off.'

'And is he, do you think? Up to it?'

'Oh, look, the man's highly skilled. He has his own forge.'

'Do they deliver by horse and cart too?'

Richard laughs gently. Out on the water the rain is gathering, soft funnels of grey passing over the island and Oriental Bay.

'You know, I've never been to such a large funeral,' Richard says now. He stood in the back row, along with a handful of other colleagues. Throngs of people showed up. Moira's choir, who sang 'The Lord is My Shepherd' and 'Abide with Me'. Her Tuesday lunch girls. Aaron's friends from school days. People I didn't expect. Aaron's fifth-form music teacher, a tall Indian man, his hair starting to silver now. I spotted him in the back row standing beside his sister Sangeeta, a childhood friend of Moira's. Sangeeta raised her fingers in a tiny salutation as I walked back down the aisle, my left arm taking the weight of the casket. When 'Amazing Grace' struck up, the church boomed with sound. *I once was lost but now am found.*

'Yes,' I say. 'It took us by surprise.'

'That mother-in-law of yours,' he says. 'Quite a woman. You know what they say in Ireland? She'd eat you without salt.'

Claudia gave a eulogy that, as throughout Moira's life, put herself in rather more important a light than her daughter. She wore flowing blacks and a wide-brimmed black straw hat. I alternated between bitterness and relief at the way she took over as mourner-in-chief. She got her High Anglican service, with the Order for the Burial of the Dead, and I gave up on my idea to have the choir sing something from Mozart's Requiem, which Moira loved. I did put my foot down about her coffin outfit, smuggling her favourite floral dress into the funeral home after a set of devious conversations with the funeral director. Her mother wanted her in a tailored suit, and although I wondered what kind of stupid man would get between mother and daughter on the matter of clothes, I couldn't lose this one last battle. Moira and Claudia, when at their worst, would get locked into a kind of mutual stubbornness that onlookers could only shake their heads at. Moira was my wife though, and I was almost always on her side. And she did hate suits.

I'd seen Claudia at the tail-end of that long day, sitting in her armchair, the tide of visitors gone out, her youngest daughter fixing a cup of tea in the kitchen. Her face, without an audience, fell slack and grey, cheeks falling inward, her eyes sunk back into the expression of someone who is composed almost entirely of pain. She is seventy-eight. She'll never recover.

'She's a softy, really,' I say. 'I'm not sure how she's going to get through.'

Richard shakes his head. 'Such a terrible time,' he says. 'For all of you.'

Over all these months and weeks I've never worked out how to respond to platitudes. But Richard says these ordinary things with such sincerity.

He leans forward. 'How can we help?'

Now, from nowhere, I wish I could weep.

'I've been cut a lot of slack already.' My hands are waving in the air, a gesture I hope might distract him from my face, which I sense I'm not controlling well.

'You've had a few weeks at home?'

'Tidying,' I shrug. 'Sorting.'

Richard presses his lips together and puts his fingers into a steeple under his chin. 'You've needed it, Peter,' he says. 'It's not unreasonable. Although.'

Although.

A fizz erupts in my chest, and shoots down to my fingers. Both euphoria and the desire for weeping are cleaned out in a second. I'm a rabbit in a field, snapped to attention.

Richard runs his tongue along his teeth, under his lip. 'I might mention. You've always brought in major clients.' The steeple pulls apart. His palms come down flat on the glass table. 'Look, we understand what you've been going through. But when you're back on your feet, say, in the next month or two, it would be a good time to concentrate on'—his head gives a little weave, to and fro, to and fro—'client maintenance. Keeping those big names happy.'

I lick my lips.

'The bean counters are at it, then?'

It comes out rather more defensive than I intend.

'When do they ever stop?' He says it for laughs, but he looks pained, serious. 'You've been through the most awful . . . well. But it's been the best part of a year since we've had you at full capacity. That's the difficulty. To be plain.'

On the wall, the painting seems to flicker. *Tetekura, tetekura.* I want to try the word aloud. Maybe it's a transliteration? *Tetekura, petticoat, petticoat, billygoat.* What does it mean to Richard, to keep company with this painting all day? It's possible he cherishes it as I do, that he has held conversations with it and that the work is a friend occupying part of his brain, history, heart. It's equally possible that it's a piece of morbid cultural real estate hanging on his wall.

Richard follows my gaze and cranes around in his chair.

'What does it mean?' I ask. 'I've always wondered.'

'Oh. When one chief falls, another rises to take his place.'

I consider this.

'The king is dead,' I say after a while. 'Long live the king.'

'Yes.' Richard seems surprised. 'I suppose so.' The mottled beginning of a blush rises on his neck. 'When are you back from your parents'?'

The answer I am supposed to give is Monday. Monday conveys what Richard needs to hear: resurrection, focus, loyalty.

My mother's anxiety, my father's heart.

'Tuesday.'

I'd like to take a week. I'd like to spend long quiet days with my parents, and then come home via the Wairarapa, spend a night or two at our bach on the exposed, windblown tip of the coast at Castlepoint.

But Tuesday is a compromise. I'll show my face here at the office, demonstrate focus. And I'll make it a daytrip up to the bach on Wednesday. I want to show a real estate agent through, get the ball rolling on selling the place.

Richard nods.

'You're an asset, Peter. I'm on your side.'

Adrenaline again, chest to arm.

E hinga atu ana he tetekura e ara mai ana he tetekura.

Right now Aaron is in Wellington. He's ordering eggs in a café in Aro Valley, he's walking around the waterfront, he's eating toast in a house on Adams Terrace. If the earthquake hit today, if the Alpine fault made its thousand-year adjustment, I would search for Aaron first, and he would search for me.

But by the time I get to Wanganui tonight, he'll be halfway across the Pacific. If the earthquake hits after that, I don't know who will look for me. Do I sound sorry for myself? Perhaps I am. But he has to go back to London, there is nothing else for it. He is already lining up auditions for the spring.

Aaron's star is on the rise. Two years ago he amazed us by gaining entrance into a Masters in classical acting at Saint Martin's University in London on full scholarship. He spent winter at an institute in Moscow training in the Russian method, studying Chekhov, whose plays, he told us (surely in words stolen from his lecturer), just go to show that most lives are sustained from morning to night by the fabrication of self-delusions. In his final student performance, he was singled out for mention by the *Guardian*. He aspires to the Barbican, the Royal Court and the Globe. I don't think he'll come back to perform for us here any time soon, at the small theatre on the waterfront where the audience spills out onto the dock.

He is a good son, he loved his mother ferociously, and yet three months ago it took an hour down in the den talking on the phone, detailing the breakdown in Moira's body in explicit, fairly gruesome detail, to convince him that he needed to get on a plane, and immediately, and without any fixed date to return. Because Moira had already been diagnosed with, and apparently recovered from, breast cancer less than five years previously, it was immensely difficult for him to see the terminus that was swimming into view. None of us wanted to look at it straight on. But it was happening, nevertheless.

I paid for his fare in full. We just wanted him here, his kiss on her cheek, his company through the weakening afternoons. We both needed his company.

Many of the nights he has spent in Wellington have been

at a house in Aro Valley full of thespian friends, including a girl, Akenese, who is either an old friend or a new lover, or both. I've only met her once, and that was by accident when I bumped into them in Aro Café one afternoon, and we ended up having coffee there together. Akenese was deferential, or shy, or dismissive, barely spoke to me. Aaron never brought her to the hospice, nor to the funeral.

At six tonight, I'll collect him from his friend's house in Aro and drive him to the airport. I'll take the road around the bays, let him drink up the sunset over the harbour before he burrows back to London's autumn. As we weave around the Parade, I will break the news to him, in a gentle yet decisive manner, that I intend to sell the bach at Castlepoint. We'll have a half hour together at the airport and then he'll leave.

The duck grey sky closes in lower over the harbour. What would it take to delay his trip? It's a mutinous, needy thought, and it can't be done, but there it is, hard and breathy, the old mammal brain that crawls out from the nest and squawks, *stay, stay*. When Moira first got the cancer back I started devising elaborate bargains in my head: *two grand donated to charity + clean out the dark recesses of the garage = a good prognosis*. It was like negotiating with air, with fire. Whatever we demanded or wanted or willed, whatever we spent or pledged or researched, had nothing to do with it. We were at the mercy of forces well outside my power, of microscopic, relentlessly proliferating cells.

Dylan's hair is tufted up Bart Simpson style, his tie wide and yellow. He takes a couple of steps into my office and stops there, rubbing his thumb over the back of his hand, his head slightly bowed, not quite making eye contact.

'Come in.'

He sits down, crosses his ankles.

'How's your day going?' I ask. 'You winning?'

'Some winning.' He dips his head.

That solemnity. He reminds me of Moira's undertaker.

Dylan is a good lawyer, one of the more senior in the team I manage. I've paid him plenty of attention, but over the last year I've realised he's never going to make partner. He'd make the business case, just about, but there's something missing. I see parts of myself in him, this lanky, quiet thirty-five-year-old: he's funny and self-deprecating but also prone, I think, to deep self-doubt. He grew up in one of the meaner parts of Hamilton and got his degree from the University of Waikato, which in his case seems to have given rise to a gnawing inadequacy. I understand that, although it does irritate me. We're not in Tory Britain, after all, even if some of the partners from Christchurch display a fetishistic nostalgia for their old schools. Dylan grew far more relaxed around me when he found out that my father mended fridges for a living, half a lifetime ago. But even with me, he just won't assert himself. The most forceful desire I've heard him express is his wish to move his kids out of Titahi Bay before the eldest starts school next year.

I made partner at a time when the firm was in clover, before the Asian shocks set everyone back. I'd been a loyal soldier for fifteen years, a safe pair of hands. To boot, I had Richard's singular, unwavering faith in me, which must have helped tip the balance in my favour.

I like Dylan, and I want to do the same for him, but I just don't think it will be possible. What I had, and what he simply doesn't have, was the confidence to sit at the table. I don't know if I *did* have that, but I knew how to fake it, which in the end comes down to the same thing.

My mother saying, *You're just as good as any of them, Peter, don't ever forget that.* How fierce she was in her desires for me, in her desires for herself. The meticulous way she applied her makeup every day that she went to work at the library, her pride when they made her chief librarian. She downplayed it in front of Dad, but I heard it all, every ambition, every strategy.

When I speak to Dylan at performance reviews about partnership or career planning or even the amorphous *goals,* he flushes and almost by instinct starts mentioning where he has failed, some project on which he has fallen short. He sits below everyone's radar. I just don't know. I've certainly tried. I tell my colleagues at every opportunity about his tenacious, methodical mind for detail. He's a profoundly brilliant technician. When we worked on the Meridian Energy file, and came up against the question of the smelter contract, he found a way to approach the issue that none of us had ever seen before.

'Peter, I wanted to ask.'

'Fire away.'

'The bonuses this year.'

'Right,' I said. 'Let's book a time for your performance review.'

'Because, these targets?'

'Sure. We'll go through all that.'

Back in February, it was agreed by majority vote to remove discretion, making Christmas bonuses dependant on transparent criteria. All other things being equal, this translates to billable hours. It's dodgy policy, as the partners well know, one which tends to encourage a slack use of time and a creep towards padding the bill. The associates with kids at home get huffy. It doesn't let you thank the poor bastard who took on a whole lot of approved pro bono work to give the firm a good name.

'I'm about three hundred hours below the cut-off.'

This is Dylan, precisely. Every other associate in

the building has assiduously billed to the limit since the February memo and made sure by whatever means necessary that they are over the line.

I sigh, more dramatically than I mean to. He winces.

'You've been billing daily?'

'Of course.'

'Accounts don't close until December. You're six weeks away.'

He shrugs. 'It's not going to add up.'

'Right,' I say. 'Right.'

This, here, is where I stop. This is the line beyond which no manager has any business stepping. What's the big problem with the schools in Titahi Bay, anyway? If Dylan doesn't have the gumption to get his extra ten per cent this year, well, his world will not fold.

I walk over to the window and look out. The tugboats are looping a Korean tanker.

In the middle of the year, Dylan's wife got some kind of septic leg injury. He took a lot of leave then. The smell of the hospital each time you come onto the ward. The children wailing in the night. That vertiginous feeling, the droning hum in the ear, the sense of a chasm, somewhere, opening up.

'Remind me,' I say, 'who are your major clients?'

He names our two big banks, one government department and a couple of start-ups. The banks have us on a panel, screw us down on every quarter hour and occasionally threaten to shift the core work to the opposition. You don't muck around with the banks. The start-ups, on the other hand—well, the start-ups ask a great deal and have only the vaguest sense of what's involved.

The ship swings around to face forward, and the tugboats spray water in welcome.

'You've done a lot on BioCom.'

I keep my eyes out the window, so I can't see Dylan's face, and he can't see mine.

'A complicated piece of work, a lot of thinking time gone in. You want to reflect that. The big picture.'

I walk back behind my desk, move my pens around. Dylan is nodding slowly, his brow tightening up.

'Are you saying I should—'

Shut up, idiot. 'I'm saying, it's possible you haven't been accounting accurately. I'm saying you may want to make some amendments in the next period.'

For a dreadful moment, I think he's going to say something more. He gives himself a tiny shake.

'Right. We'll meet next week then.'

He clicks the door shut behind him.

The answerphone is chockablock with messages from neglected clients. I write everything down. The last message is from a woman I don't know. I'm with the all fierce, she says, we're so terribly sorry. *I'm with the awe fest.* The office. The *orifice?* Surely not. Fifth time over, the syllables fall into place. *The Orpheus.* Moira's choir. Orpheus, who went down to the underworld to fetch back his beloved wife.

It's intolerable to let Aaron go without a fixed date to see him again. I want him back here at Easter, five months away: late autumn, those crisp gold and blue days.

I get Mark from House of Travel on the line, price out some Gatwick to Auckland tickets. One other thing, I hear myself ask. How much would a flight to Athens cost? With an onward connection to Lesbos.

'We're mainly booking routes through Asia,' Mark says. 'The USA is still complicated. We could do Singapore, Hong Kong or Bangkok.'

'Whichever,' I say. 'I don't care.'

'It's coming up low season in the Greek Islands, of course. You're fine to travel in the winter?'

It'll be summer work she'll be doing at that café, for sure. That girl, *just a young thing*, will be out of there by November.

'I need to get there soon,' I say. 'Now. Immediately.'

There is rustling at the end of the line.

'The airlines can free up a seat for an emergency. I can get you on something routed through Asia probably in, let's see, the next twenty-four hours.'

'It's not an emergency.'

'It's not? Okay, but you're looking for a flight within the week?'

A beep starts up on the line, another call coming through. What did I promise Richard? Back on Monday. No, Tuesday. My mother, my father.

'The difficulty is my parents,' I say. 'My father is ill.'

'Got you,' Mark says. 'Look, that kind of situation can be considered an emergency, depending on, if you don't mind me asking, the severity. We can get you to Lesbos quickly, for sure.'

'My father's in Wanganui.'

'Sorry, who's in Greece?'

'These paintings,' I say. 'Do you know Chagall? In a museum in Mytilene.'

'When exactly do you want to travel, sir?'

'His heart is weak,' I say. 'My mother, she worries so much. I can't go to Greece, sorry, of course I can't.'

There is a long silence from Mark.

'You can't. No. All right.'

'I'm wasting your time here.' I hang up the phone and lay my head down on my desk. I don't understand why I'm not with Aaron right now. I don't know why I didn't organise to spend the day, this last day, with him.

29

Chagall's lithographs of the *Daphnis and Chloe* story were commissioned for a limited edition of the Greek romance, published as a large book in 1961 in Paris by Tériade. The only copy of this book I've ever seen is the one I own. I found it in a secondhand bookshop on Koningsplein in Amsterdam, about a month after Rob and I had fled London together, arriving with backpacks and a canvas tent and pitching it along with all the other squatters in the Vondelpark.

I found the book on a hot July day, although it didn't come into my possession until some months later. When I look back on that time, the book seems the key to everything that followed, because finding it led to the *Lychorida*, and the *Lychorida* led to Geneviève.

I remember stepping off the busy street into a dark, narrow room that silenced the rush of the crowd. Shelves rose to the yellowed ceiling. It was empty except for an elderly man seated behind a desk in the dim recesses of the shop. A reading lamp with a green shade was lit, the light pooling onto a newspaper, *The Times*, spread before him.

'Excuse me,' I said. 'Could I put my bag down for a while?'

'*Ja*,' he said, gesturing to the space beside him.

'Where are the English books?' I asked.

'There,' he said, pointing to two of the aisles. 'And there.'

I found an illustrated copy of Homer's *Iliad*. I had taken classics in my final year at Wanganui High. It was a tiny class, with only six students. My mother had encouraged me, and brought back all the extra books I asked for from the city library: Sophocles, Euripides, Ovid. At the end of that year I had laid plans to go to Auckland University. But somehow I had diverted to this other course, had taken a job in a garage, saved money for a plane fare and followed Rob to London, where I worked at a bar in Covent Garden for a year, then went on with him to Holland. In the bookshop I felt, for the first time since leaving home, a desire to return and begin study. It was this unexpected and forceful longing that was passing through me when I smelt tobacco, and became aware that the shopkeeper was behind me.

'You like that?' He held the cigarette in his hand and smoke escaped from the corners of his mouth as he spoke.

'I do,' I said, scrambling to my feet. 'But I already have a copy.'

He clenched the cigarette between his teeth and took the book from me with both hands, flipping it to look at the cover.

'Come here,' he said. 'I have something you will find interesting.'

He led me over to a glass case set against the back wall of the shop and produced a set of keys from his pocket, fumbling among them to find the correct one. He unlocked the case, and pulled from it a heavy book stored on the lowest shelf, bound in gold cloth, a foot high and almost a foot wide, as weighty as a testament from a temple.

'You like the Greeks?' he asked, and I nodded.

He closed the door, turned the key, and with two hands carried the book across to the desk. I pushed books and papers aside and he laid it flat.

'Look at this,' he said. He slid his thumbs down the side and parted it close to the middle, the pages falling open like arms.

An illustration spread across both pages, a broad wash of night-time blue. On one side a hedge of flowers exploded into yellow and red, and on the other two vaguely drawn figures gazed at one another: a woman, naked, standing beside a pool of white water, her arms raised above her head, her breasts suggested by two semicircles, and a man, also nude, his skin luminous white, reclining on one elbow by the water's edge. I lifted the page and turned it over, the letters clear and high like a child's storybook.

'It's French?'

'*Ja*. Of course.'

He shuffled off, and returned with a spotted paperback, creasing the front cover back and pointing to the text.

'Here. This is the same story in English.'

The book described the city of Mytilene on the island of Lesbos, its canals, inward-flowing sea and bridges of polished stone. *You will think when you see it that it is not so much a city as an island.* I mapped the words back and forth. The story begins with a farmer who comes across a goat suckling a foundling child, and takes the child in because he is ashamed to show less humanity than the goat: the line made me laugh aloud, and the shopkeeper sucked approvingly on his cigarette, wheeled around his chair and gestured for me to sit, moving off to rearrange piles and leaving me alone for the next hour.

It is hard to accurately recover my thoughts on first reading it. It would have been the sex that interested me first. Daphnis and Chloe, no more than teenagers, inflamed, rubbing up against each other in the fields, so wildly frustrated by their lack of knowledge that Daphnis sits and bursts into tears—*to think that any sheep knew more about love than he did*—the story could perhaps have been a balm for my own painfully felt frustrations at the time, because I had been wanting to sleep with a girl, Geneviève, whom I had met in the Vondelpark, and who had been ignoring me. I thought I might buy it for her.

'You like the book?' asked the shopkeeper.

'It's beautiful,' I said.

'One hundred guilders,' he said.

As it was, I had about half that amount in my pocket, the total savings Rob and I had between us. The shopkeeper saw me waver.

'Where do you come from?' he asked.

'New Zealand.'

'Ah!' he said. 'And I am from Zeeland. Old Zeeland.' He put a hand on his stomach, chuckling. 'For you, seventy-five.'

I probably could have kept beating him down, but I imagined Rob's face if I turned up at the Vondelpark with the book, and all our money gone.

'Pay it little by little,' said the shopkeeper. 'Until October, I'll keep it at this price for you. Do you have work, *m'n jong*?'

'Not yet,' I said. I picked up a paperback and flicked through it.

'How do you spend your time?'

I looked up. 'Walk around,' I said. 'Talk. Bike, sometimes. I went out to Monnickendam the other day.'

The shopkeeper shook his head. 'What are you going to do with your life?'

'Not sure,' I said. 'I'm interested in classics.'

'You want to become a professor?'

'Maybe,' I said. 'I don't know much about that.'

'How is this going to happen?'

'I'd have to go back to New Zealand,' I said. 'Go to university.'

'You know this city?' he said. 'You know *Mokum*, Amsterdam? Built on what, do you think?'

I shrugged, thinking: tulips, ships, girls in windows.

'On the swamp. Can you imagine how much work this takes, to build a city out of the water? For years, for hundreds of years, Holland is a place where people work, a

33

city of merchants, traders and sailors. This is who we are. not princes, not aristocrats, we are people who work, work hard to make anything, land even, out of the sea.'

He slumped down in his seat behind the desk, lit up a cigarette.

'I know how to work,' I said. 'I've worked in a garage and I've worked in pubs. I just haven't found anything here yet.'

'These kids,' he continued. 'These foreigners. Gone in the head, they do nothing, they are sleeping in the street, in the park. I don't mind so much, personally. They don't like to wash, what do I care? But what do they want? Why do they come to Amsterdam?'

'It's different here than anywhere else,' I said. 'There's more freedom.'

He pulled on his cigarette and let out a long stream of smoke. It hung on the air and I stifled a cough.

'*Ja*,' he said. 'Freedom.'

He took another drag and stared at a point just past my left shoulder.

'I'll tell you something. You need to know this. They took the people from this city, *m'n jong*.'

'Sorry?'

'Doctors, dentists, bakers, artists. Here for centuries, they have homes, jobs, our neighbours, our colleagues, they run our shops, work in our banks. Within a few months'—he flicked the fingers of one hand up into the air as if spraying water—'gone.'

His gaze stayed concentrated on the bookshelf behind me. Smoke collected in the corner of the ceiling. I scratched at my ear, shifted my weight from one foot to the other. The cat leapt up onto the desk and nuzzled into his chest.

'Amsterdam was occupied, you know.' He looked directly at me. 'Each man has to make choices. Everyone hopes for the best.'

'Our generation has problems too,' I said. I think even as I said it I was aware there was something badly off-key in the comparison.

'So.' The bookseller shook himself. 'What's this?' he pointed to the book in my hand.

'Sophocles,' I said.

'You want to read it?' he said.

'I've got no money.'

He dismissed me with a wave of his hand. 'You borrow it,' he said. 'Bring it back when you're finished. You read whatever you like.'

'Really?' I said, looking around me, wondering where I would begin.

'You have your freedom.' The bell jangled and the door opened. 'If you *kinderen* want to use it to wear the feet naked,' he said, gazing past me, nodding his head in greeting to the customer, 'well, I don't judge you.'

I curled my toes up, black and tough from the summer. 'Thanks,' I said, clutching the paperback to my chest. 'I'll bring it back tomorrow.'

'Where do you live?' he asked.

'In the Vondelpark,' I said, but I couldn't look straight at him. 'With friends.'

'I have a boat,' he said. 'It's moored on the Amstel near the Carré Theatre, between the Amstelsluizen and the Hogesluis. It will be empty from October. You and your friends, if you're willing to work and fix it up, you can live there.'

Chagall was sixty years old when he went to Lesbos to start work on the *Daphnis and Chloe* paintings. He was honeymooning with a new, Jewish wife, who followed on from an English mistress who had brought him seven years of complicated misery and an unexpected son. The mistress, Virginia, had followed on from his beloved Bella, born in his home town of Vitebsk in Russia; Bella, to whom Chagall was married for almost three decades. Bella died in her fifties when Chagall, although he didn't know it, still had forty-one years to live. The second wife seems to have been a sort of exhausted compromise. There's nothing wrong with compromise, under the circumstances, although there is a melancholy about the lovers in the lithographs, when you know all this.

The part of Chagall's biography that has always gripped me, the story I've always thought someone would make a film of one day, is his last days in France under the Vichy Government in 1941. The Chagall family have left it late to leave, almost too late. Marc and Bella have been granted visas to flee to America under the sponsorship of Solomon Guggenheim, and the art world of New York has raised funds to pay for his passage. For some weeks, he and Bella are waiting in Marseille, waiting together with his daughter Ida and her husband Michel, waiting in a cheap hotel, waiting in a town where thousands of others are waiting too, waiting for the correct papers, waiting for forged visas or real ones, waiting for instructions, waiting to be told *go now*, waiting to travel overland to Portugal and board a ship. Chagall hesitates, he doesn't want to go, because this is France, he considers himself a Frenchman now, he wants to come back one day, and so they delay departure, he and Bella, in order to apply for a re-entry passport. His and Bella's exit visas are ready, but Ida's and Michel's are not. Ida is packing a case with his paintings, planning to smuggle them out. If he leaves France, cuts himself off from her, will he ever see her again? Imagine the anxiety of this time, the terrible paralysis. He cannot bear to go, he has to go.

Then one morning he and Bella are arrested, rounded up with all the other Jews from the hotels of the city and sent to police headquarters. Somehow, through American connections, their release is arranged. The danger has become manifest, there is no option to wait any longer. He and Bella farewell their daughter, and travel west by train to the border of Spain.

Some months later Ida and Michel get out, and all four make it to America, and the collection of paintings too. Chagall goes on to lose Bella to a bad virus in New York, not to a concentration camp. He returns to Europe, and works on *Daphnis and Chloe* a decade later, under the Greek sun in Lesbos, now married to a woman who seems to have done her best to care for him, and this is a kind of restoration, a happy ending.

Shortly after I found *Daphnis and Chloe* in the bookshop, Geneviève started sleeping with me. We spent August camping beside the artificial lake in the Vondelpark, thick with scum and weed. We barely left our tent that month. We'd emerge in the evening and eat the food she gleaned from the fruit stall where she worked early mornings in the Albert Cuypstraat market, apples and walnuts, cherries and grapefruit.

When it rained the park turned to a mudbowl. We went to a squat where her Parisian friends were living, and waited it out. We would take the chance to wash, heating pots of water on the stove and bathing in the bath. Electric wires coiled down from the ceiling above, my legs wrapped around her waist, and her hair was loose, blooming into loops and whirls on the meniscus.

They were on junk, the people who stayed in that squat. We saw their tiny pupils, the track marks on their arms, the way they lay drifting in and out of consciousness under blankets in the corners of the room. Once we walked in on a young boy shooting up his girlfriend, her forearm extended, a belt tightened around her bicep. Geneviève shouted and swore at the boy, and dragged the girl outside and onto the street. She told me that she'd known the girl in Paris, that she had once been a student at the Sorbonne, that she had, two years ago, won an award for her first year of humanities studies. This shit destroys everything, said Geneviève. I hate this shit.

I still had no work. Rob managed to get a job writing for a left-wing weekly broadsheet, and also received a monthly cheque from his father. He had paid me back an amount of money I had lent him in London. There was enough to buy bread, cheese and ham to supplement the bruised fruit from the market, and enough left over to put a little down on *Daphnis and Chloe*, or to pay for a train ride out to Scheveningen and back, or to buy a secondhand shirt and hot chips at the fleamarket in Waterlooplein. There was no difficulty about anything.

Later the girl Geneviève had dragged outside died of an overdose, and the police came and raided the flat. We heard news of it at the park, and we came back a week later and saw that the landlord had boarded and padlocked the door. Somebody had painted across the boards in large red letters: HOW FOOLISHLY MAN GUARDS HIS NOTHING.

*

What if I did it, though—flew to Athens, then northeast to Mytilene? What if I wandered down through the town to the waterfront, alone, in the early morning, the Aegean pale blue, the sky soft, holding on to dawn, the boats anchored still? The girl with her French accent would be setting out the chairs and tables, getting ready for the day.

She would offer me a seat, and bring me a menu covered in plastic, and wipe her hands on a teatowel, and return to take my order. She has Geneviève's hair, hanging down loose, wavy, shades of brown and gold. Her face is a blank oval. I can't project onto it the exact variation of uncanny you'd expect.

'Who are your parents? Where were you born?'

She would turn—would have turned—thirty this year.

'You are asking me?'

I have to work out the dialogue here, but she answers the questions and I answer hers, and we rally to and fro, to and fro, until we get to the far point of what language can prove. She hunts for a photo in her pocket and lays it down on the table. The photo is a battered black-and-white print of me, bare chested, standing on the deck of the *Lychorida*, grinning, legs planted apart, facing square to the girl behind the camera, Geneviève, who is lining up this shot in the late summer of 1972, who is wearing a sunflower-yellow dress that drapes around her pregnant belly and down to her bare feet, long brown hair worn down, squinting through the viewfinder to take the photo she will later use as a bookmark in her copy of *L'Étranger*; who is now pressing down the button to capture the photo; who will take *L'Étranger* to Lyon with her two months later along with the baby, who is hot, too hot.

'That's me,' I'll say to the girl. 'Yes, that's me.'

The scene gets vague and blurry after that, but the laying down of the photo, I have it blow by blow. The photo is always the trump card, the forensic evidence.

I've had that bit for years. The Greek island setting is a tidy coincidence. I've seen our reunion play out in Amsterdam, in London, in Lyon, in Wellington. Why would Abigail come to Wellington? I have the logic for that too. I have embroidered all the details, a knock on the door one evening, an email asking to meet at a café on Oriental Parade. Someone in France has given her my name, a detail, a clue. She will come to me of her own accord, and all I have to do is stay still and pay attention. On occasion I have gone out of my way to walk past the entrances to the backpacker hostels around the city.

But, actually, I don't give a shit about this could-be daughter.

I know precisely where in France she was last seen, at six weeks old. I have the names that Geneviève gave me. I have a copy of the death certificate. There are letters that could be written, advertisements that could be taken out, even now that *Docteur Gabriel Barreau* is dead. Even though Geneviève herself is dead. I could contact the French police, I could hire a private investigator. I have taken no steps, in eleven years. I have built complicated, consoling fantasies.

The furthest I've got? Last Easter, I used Yahoo to look for versions of her name. Moira had just been given her diagnosis. I was becoming aware of the thousand useful things one could research on the World Wide Web.

Abigail Collie, the name registered on her birth certificate, was a real estate agent in Cheltenham. A PhD student in Chicago. She featured in results from an athletic meet in Illinois. Improbably, she is a lead detective in a crime fiction series that seems to have an enormous following in the USA. I searched for Abigail Barreau and found nothing at all. Abigail Barrera, the computer suggested. Abigail Barrow. Abigail Barron.

When I break for lunch there's a new girl on reception, a law student who does a few hours administration a week. I noticed her back in the winter, walking through the office from time to time, a small parade in her pinks and lime greens. Today, she's in a neon-yellow shirt that makes me blink.

'I'm Peter Collie.' I pause on my way past, offering a hand. 'I'm not sure that we've met properly.'

'Oh, but that's great!' Her eyes light up. 'There's a message for you,' she says. 'I was just working out what to do with it.'

I raise my eyebrows. 'Give it to my secretary?'

Last time I was in, my secretary was a temp from the agency.

'Well, she's gone. And there's no replacement. So anyway, you should take this.'

She tears a piece of paper from a pad and hands it to me. I'm down to volunteer at the local Community Law Centre on Tuesday night, a form of corporate tithing which I continue with in order to encourage the young ones, and in order to encourage myself. At the Centre I am reminded that beyond the relentless mental *clickity-clack* of the charge-out sheet, and the thousands of varieties of self-deception the profession offers, there are human beings of all stripes who actually need us to do the thing we do.

I fold the paper into my pocket. 'You didn't tell me your name.'

'Laura.'

She looks a few years younger than Aaron, twenty at most. She still seems some way off being tamed into corporate life. Her clothes have unexpected zips and buckles, the skirts are short and the boots chunky and coloured, everything clashing, the brash mess of it showing up her prettiness.

'It's going all right, is it?' I say. 'This must be a bit dull for you.'

'I don't mind, really,' she says. 'I've got reading to do.'

A wad of photocopies are on the desk before her.

Passages have been highlighted in pink, in blue, in yellow, and neat notes, like a border of red berries, decorate each margin.

'Final exams, is it?'

'Yeah.' She grimaces. 'Company and Partnership Law next Thursday.'

The switchboard lights up. I stand back as she attends to the call, busying myself with a paperclip, reading her papers over the edge of the desk. Her dark eyes are animated, moving constantly in the frame of her face as she speaks, as if she were a notch more awake than anyone else; her hands tap a rainstorm of characters into the keyboard as she transcribes the message.

'You're studying *Murdoch*, are you?' I say, once she's finished. 'I was involved in that. Come and chat to me about it sometime, if it's helpful.'

She has a cover of soft, barely visible down on her cheek, just above her jaw. She looks up at me now, and the fullness of her smile, unexpected, is beautiful.

'Oh, can I? That would be brilliant.'

*

We moved onto the *Lychorida* in December 1971 and Geneviève knew she was pregnant by February. When she told me, I felt that I barely knew her. We had spent three months together, and not all of that exclusively. There was a girl from San Francisco, Mary, who lived on a boat on Herengracht. I slept with Mary a couple of times. I didn't hide this from Geneviève, but we didn't discuss it directly: it was the times.

Geneviève, for her part, was close with an old friend from Paris who lived on Rozengracht, a lanky thirty-year-old who had studied sociology at the Sorbonne. I always felt that he spoke to me with a little too much enthusiasm, too much intensity. Geneviève and this Parisian would sit pressed up against each other on the couch up on deck of the boat, and he would stroke her hair. She told me it was now platonic between them, but that she had been his girlfriend in the year she first left home, and that this Parisian sociologist had, in some way, rescued her from the streets where she was, at the time, if not living then spending a great many of her days and some nights too, because she had little money and no connections in the city. I had come to realise that her first months in Paris had been a time of darkness and mere survival for her.

Geneviève had left her home in rural Lyon when it became intolerable to stay. She told me her mother had turned into a shadow who wept all the time, who was self-abnegating to the point of having no desires of her own. Geneviève had been close with her father, who had once been in the military but now worked their small farm, yet as she came towards the end of her college years she had fought bitterly with him about wanting to leave Chavanoz and live and study elsewhere, on her own. She had friends in Lyon who had been in the riots in Paris in 1968. Her father despised these people, called them communists and ranted at her about how they should be jailed. Once, he had locked her in her room for two days to prevent her seeing them. That was the last straw. She had run away, taken a train north with her friends, first to Dijon, then to Paris. For over half a year she didn't tell her father where she was living, until she arrived in Amsterdam.

Several of the girls we knew were involved with Dolle Mina over that summer. When Rob's girlfriend Clare arrived from London, some time after us, she immediately joined in with them, staging happenings to demand free and legal abortion and contraception. I remember her standing in a line of women stretching the width of Dam Square, blocking the tram lines, each woman with her top hitched up, *Baas in Eigen Buik* scrawled in thick black ink on the skin of her abdomen. Boss of my belly. Geneviève watched from the side. She seemed not ambivalent, but disengaged. I never saw her participate in any political action.

Who can say why one woman chooses to have her child and another doesn't? In any case, once she knew about the pregnancy, our conversations leapt immediately to how we were going to manage. Geneviève had worked all the time I had known her. She set off to the produce markets at Albert Cuypstraat at five in the morning, six days out of seven. She said we could expect no help from her family, that she refused to ask them for money, and she told me that I would need to find work too, immediately. She suggested I try my luck at the shipyards.

I biked along the IJ waterfront, past container ships and fishing boats. I came to an open gap and looked out at the grey water. A red barge was moored up in the slipway on the pier opposite, and towering above it in a drydock was the rusting prow of an old cargo ship, the final portion, like the head of a gnawed fish. The empty holds were bared to the sky, the overhangs of decks and cabins jutting out.

A sheet of metal that had been peeled away from the hull of the ship was winched up and swung through the air, tipping back and forth, a kite floating on a limp breeze.

The shipyard gate was open, and I walked in. The sheet of metal from the flank of the boat had been laid down on the ground. Two workers with blowtorches were breaking it up, cutting chunks out from each side, sparks hailing gold and white over their heads. Men worked in teams, filling wheelbarrows and hauling them away, sorting wires, pipes, buckets of plugs and scraps of steel into separate containers. The dismantling was orderly, efficient, rapacious. Shipdust coated the ground and swirled in the air, thick and ferrous on my tongue.

One of the cutters stood up from his work, raised his visor. '*U bent hier voor de baan?*'

I smiled, raised my hands in a shrug. '*Engels,*' I said.

'*Spreekt u Engels?*'

I nodded yes, English.

He disappeared into the building. I thought I should turn tail and leave before I was forcibly evicted, but his tone had been amiable. He returned with a tall blond man in overalls, sporting a handlebar moustache which had been neatly oiled. Despite the moustache, I could see he was close to my own age.

'You can start today?'

I blinked. 'That's right.'

'Good.' He sniffed. 'We are behind. You have experience?'

'Some.'

He peered down at me. 'English only? *Geen Nederlands?*'

'Sorry.'

'Hendrik.' He put out his hand, and we shook. 'I'll bring equipment.'

Did he take me for a metal cutter? I wanted to use a blower, to feel it knifing through solid steel. I had welded often enough in my father's workshop, but I knew that cutting required the right balance of gases, and without the ability to ask questions there was a fair risk I would cause an explosion. If they put a propane blower in my hands, I decided I would walk off.

Hendrik came out of the office with boots and a helmet.

'You're English?'

'New Zealander.'

His brow knotted up briefly. 'Not many here speak English. Talk to me if you have problems. Thomas!' He whistled to a boy on the far side of the yard. '*Spreekt u Engels?*'

The boy gestured a pinch in the air. *A little.*

Hendrik slapped his hand on my back.

'Go with him. Okay, *ja?*'

What moment can you can point to and say, Right here, this is it where it started, here is the origin of the catastrophe? If the cutter had brushed me off, if I had wheeled my bike out of the shipyard and ridden away towards Wittenburg, if I had never spoken to Hendrik, would it all have turned out differently? In the months and years that followed I thought so, and I was very bitter, in my mind, about that day.

The ship's head reared up, four stories high, a pillaged and wrecked cathedral. Two-thirds had been dismantled, but it was still a vast bulk of matter. It seemed improbable that human hands would ever unravel it.

'*Zet uw helm op.*'

The boy tapped his helmet in warning. I followed him across the gangplank and we descended through a riddle of stairs and ladders to the chambers of the lowermost level. All the doors had been taken out, and the partitions and flats above had been punched through with rough holes. Light and air poured in, the reflections richocheting off the steel at wild angles. The air vibrated with the raw clangs of hammers, an orchestra of crashes and thumps, and the echo of men's voices, high and reedy, shouting instructions.

We came to a room where the walls were lined with copper pipes. A man was standing atop a stepladder, hacking at the top layer with a handsaw.

'*Uw werk is om de leidingen naar de bak te brengen.*'

The boy looked at me expectantly.

I pulled a face, shrugged. 'Sorry,' I said.

'Okay.' He wiped his brow, irritated.

'He—' he stuck his finger up towards to the man.

I nodded enthusiastically.

'Cut.' His hand sawed in the air. 'And you'—his finger, jabbing at my chest—'like this.'

He mimed the action, lifting a pipe from the wall, hoisting it onto his shoulder and carrying it across the room to a square bin.

'*Ja?*'

Manual labour. No skill involved.

'Yes,' I said. 'I see. All right.'

After five hours' work, I took off my helmet, wiped my face dry. The locker room was dense with steam. I hoisted my feet up onto the bench and unclipped the boots. The toenail on the left foot had gone black and seamy with blood, and a red blister the size of a milk-bottle top had formed on the heel. I prodded at it, winced, stripped off the overalls and shunted my foot down into my sneaker.

Hendrik appeared with a cigarette clenched between his lips. He waved an envelope at me.

'*Betaaldag,*' he shouted. '*"Je kunt het ophalen bij het kantoor.*'

I nodded, stripped off my working gear, too tired now to bother decoding, but he grabbed my arm, insisted I follow him out into the passageway. The men, dressed in clean shirts and jeans, were lined up in front of a metal grill.

'Payday.' He opened his envelope, fanned out the notes. 'Go up and collect.'

I joined the queue, signed my name. For five hours' work, I had earned six guilders. It was enough. I could feed myself and Geneviève on this, and buy whatever the baby would need.

'Come back at eight tomorrow,' Hendrik said. 'I have

work for you all this week.'

When I left the IJ shipyard I turned back to look. Lumbering out of the dusk, the wreck was stubbornly there. There were new gaps in the hull, and the line of the bridge had visibly lowered. But the prow was ship, still ship. It held its shape against the air, defying the work of the day.

I worked in that shipyard for three months. In that time, we dismantled the rest of the ship, and started on another one as well.

*

When I walk out of my office I find Dylan and Richard standing in front of Laura's desk, heads bowed in conversation. All three startle when they see me. There is a shift in the air.

'We were talking about Dylan's Great Dane.' Richard recovers first. 'Eighty kilos of dog. That's going to take a lot of feeding, right?

'Do *you* have a dog, Peter?' Laura asks.

'We had a cat,' I say. 'We got rid of him when Moira's immune system was messed up by the chemotherapy.'

All three go doe-eyed. The abyss opening right up, there under the beige carpet squares.

'Hey,' I say. 'I've got a joke. So, Erwin Schrödinger—you know Schrödinger—he gets pulled over by the cops, right? And they search the car, you know, open up the boot, and then the officer comes back to Schrödinger, and he goes, "Ah, sir, do you know there is a dead cat in your boot?"'

Richard looks perplexed.

'And then Schrödinger goes, "Well now I do, you bastard."'

Laura's laugh, after a few seconds, is real. Richard and Dylan smile weakly.

'Theoretical physics,' I say. 'There's this box. The cat is imaginary.'

Laura bites at the corner of her lip.

'Yeah,' she says. 'Dead or alive. Depends whether you're looking.'

Her shirt is quite something, the cool glow of the yellow. Not many girls could carry off a colour like that.

'That's it,' I say. 'Yes.'

She lowers her eyes, but she's pleased. I think she's pleased.

'And how far do you have to walk the dog, Dylan?' Richard asks, angling his body towards him. 'He'd be keeping you fit, wouldn't he?'

*

Late in Geneviève's pregnancy, Hendrik, the superintendent from the shipyards, stopped by the *Lychorida* one night and sat on deck with us. We drank bottles of Amstel and Christoffel. Hendrik brought weed with him, and we shared it out amongst us and smoked. Light gusts sent the smoke whirling about our faces and drifting towards passersby on the riverbank. I remember pulling Geneviève onto my knee, running my hand over her back and round belly, and feeling, under the sweet loosening of the drug, a vast rush of satisfaction.

I knew he approved of me. He thought well of the way I worked. I had rapidly moved on from carting chunks of scrap metal to cutting away the structures of the ship with the propane blower. Often he worked at the cutting too, and then we worked alongside one another silently, intuitively. I thought of him as a model of competence. He would never lavish praise on anyone, but here he was. He had come to my home, was drinking my beer, receiving my hospitality, laughing with my friends. I was proud that

49

Geneviève was there to witness his visit, and proud that Hendrik saw me with her too, the full swell of her figure, her natural elegance and her sharp mind on display as she talked about French poetry.

*

There are hours to go until I'm due to pick up Aaron, but it's intolerable to go home. I drive round the Basin Reserve twice, and up the main arterial route to Newtown, on towards Island Bay, cresting over the hill at Athletic Park, where I pull over and stop the car.

Bulldozers are tearing into the bare ground that used to be the park, and pre-fabricated retirement units are starting to pop up. By this time next year the residents will be taking cautious walks on zimmerframes right over the pitch where Stu Wilson and Bernie Fraser pounded home to the tryline. Last spring the city council pulled down the Millard Stand, the steep, rickety frame of iron that swayed in high winds, where I had taken Aaron once or twice as a youngster. He was never much into the game, more preoccupied by running up and down the vertiginous steps than watching the match. The stand collapsed in a series of slow huffs. Each time we drove past it last August, another part had come down.

Ah, Moira. The truth is, in part it's a relief to have it over. As far back as April, the deep pain in her right leg left her unable to speak for minutes at a time, and later the cough in her lungs grew into an agony of breathlessness as if she were trying to draw air up through a wet sponge. Her terror. She knew what was happening. She wasn't brave about dying. She didn't want to do it, not well, not badly, not at all. Would I have given her an overdose of morphine if I'd had it, if she'd asked? We never spoke like that. Even when she couldn't walk or toilet herself, she had her mind, her speech, her eyesight, her hearing. She remained conscious and able to speak for much of the time until the last twenty-four hours. Only two days before the end, we watched her take nibbles of pineapple with great relish, licking the juice. She took everything that was left to her, and then it happened faster than we thought it would.

Crying felt clean in the days before she died, and the first days afterwards. I shouted and kicked at the glass every morning in the shower and the salt water and the clean water ran together. I had the brace of our people around me. At the funeral, we carried her casket out to the porch of the church and paused on the step in the face of a haka, unexpectedly performed by Aaron's school friends and some of his actor mates. The Rongotai College boys, the Lemalu twins and Tama Horomia, took up the front row. *Ka mate, ka mate, ka ora, ka ora.* I knew Claudia would be spitting about it—*What do they think this is, a rugby match?*—but for me the unity of the bodies, the force of the chant and the ceremony it put around the moment made it both unbearable and easy to carry her body onwards to the hearse, and I was grateful. Her leaving was out of my hands, it had nothing to do with me. The weeping that came on in those early days was utterly impersonal, a sort of ecstatic unbuttoning, a force that wanted only to move through my body. *He will wipe every tear from their eyes*, the Reverend had read at the funeral. *There will be no more death or mourning or crying or pain, for the old order of things has passed away.*

But here I am in the usual old order, bawling my eyes out in the car on a side street in Berhampore. And tonight Aaron goes away.

Two

I'm home, parked in the carport, fishing in the glovebox for a CD when the phone rings, his name lighting up the screen.

'Aaron?'

'Dad. You on your way?'

There is a blanket of noise in the background, the steam bursts and hubbub of a café.

'Just leaving. Are we late?'

'No, not at all. But change of plan.'

'What's that?'

'I'm down on Cuba Street.'

'You want me to pick you up there?'

'I'm having coffee with Jack Mulholland.'

I know the name. He's famous, locally, for his role in a recent Hollywood film.

'You wouldn't believe this guy.' His voice lowers. 'He's a complete starfucker. I'm getting a minute by minute account of his dinner with Scorsese.'

'Well connected.'

'He's full of it. He's an airhead. But look, I'm going to catch a lift to the airport with him.'

I've been counting on the car ride out with him. I've been imagining the conversation about selling the bach unfolding with Oriental Bay as a backdrop, the sea still and blue in the afternoon sun, the fountain playing. I'd choose something comforting and cheesy to play. The Eagles is a good bet. Aaron would tip his neck back and ham it up—*sparkling earrings, skin so brown*—then he'd get sick of it and swap it out for his high school favourite that's still kicking around in the glovebox, *Come break my chains, come help me out, living in the city ain't so bad*. He used to play that album endlessly as we drove up and down from Wanganui, the summer he was nineteen.

'Okay,' I say. 'Okay, I'll meet you there.'

'Thanks, Dad. And there's just one thing I need.'

'What's that?'

'If you can have a look—'

He breaks off and talks to someone, and when his voice returns it's thin, distracted.

'I left a letter in the lounge.'

'Right.' I slam the car door behind me, walk into the house. 'Sure. I'll fetch it.'

'It's on the table. Cream envelope, I think. Handwritten. You see?'

He's once again speaking to a person beside him. I leaf through the clutter of papers, dead flowers, cards. A great many objects have not yet been tidied away or sorted out. There is a huge red, blue and white striped bag in the corner of the room containing Moira's clothes and personal effects from the hospice which I haven't had it in me yet to open up. I tend to skirt around that part of the room.

'Where exactly?'

The phone offers clatter and laughter. His voice, talking on and on.

'Yes!' I shout. 'Hello?'

I imagine myself, a tinny voice at his elbow. There's fumbling, static, apologies.

'Sorry. You right?'

53

'Aaron, it's a muddle here. Tell me again what I'm looking for. '

'I saw it on the table, Dad. Or in the kitchen somewhere?'

The cleaner came yesterday, ran the vacuum around the dining room, scrubbed down every surface of the kitchen. There are no random letters.

'I can't see it.'

He sighs. 'Okay. Never mind. Send it on to me later.'

But here, something already opened. I slip the paper from the envelope: National Bank, the black horse thundering ahead, all the names we bestowed on him printed at the top of the page.

'Don't stress,' Aaron says. 'I have to go. See you at the airport.'

He hangs up, and I'm left with the paper in hand, the staggering figures. What kind of bank would offer a student a credit card limit of ten thousand? He hasn't reached this limit, he's a few grand shy, but below, another account, an amount that is not, on close inspection, savings to offset this but rather another debt, a personal loan of ten thousand more.

Aaron is twenty-five. I was feeding, clothing and housing him at the same age. There is no definition under which he is a child: he is free to arrange or fail to arrange his affairs as he sees fit. *20k in the red and not an asset in sight.* Profligate wastrel.

I suppose it could be worse. One or two of his classmates have fallen off the edge of the universe: Charmaine Jones, a sweet-faced girl from Newtown who used to come round and listen to Roberta Flack 'Killing Me Softly' in our lounge, is now doing time in Arohata. Vincent St John, who got knocked off his motorbike before he finished seventh form. His best mate from Rongotai College, Tama Horomia, who's had several run-ins with the law. Tama and

54

Aaron were arrested one night when they were eighteen, after a brawl of some kind broke out on Courtenay Place. I went down to the station, and the police were prepared to let Aaron come home with me, once I convinced them that I was his father. (I couldn't do anything for Tama though. The cops wouldn't release him no matter what arguments I came up with.) My god, it was a relief to have Aaron home in his bed that night, and out of that cold cell.

Through many dangers, toils and snares, I have already come. My kid has won himself a scholarship, my kid is doing fine. But there it is again, this lurch in the stomach, a sensation of dread and failure combined. *What if he does something desparate for the money?*

A few minutes later I find his other letter, his creamy envelope, ripped open, lying on top of the TV. Australian stamp, loopy handwriting. A foreign script on the stamp, Thai, perhaps, or Urdu, or Tamil. Who on earth is Aaron corresponding with? I slide the letter out an inch, two inches, but there's something so naked about the thin sheets, their faint grey lines, the black loops of the pen, that embarrassment gets the better of me and I put it back, and pull myself together into the respectful father I generally am.

*

Aaron touched down in Wellington two months ago. When he first came home, Moira was throwing herself into arrangements with what was to be her last sustained burst of energy. Once we had made the decision to abandon further rounds of treatment, and once the hospice had calibrated the right medications to bring the pain in her bones and chest under control, she seemed to rally. She had many good days around that time. There was almost a euphoria in her, a sweet clarity. She was very clear-headed about what she wanted, and what she was doing. Any visitor who came into the house over that time left with a gift: a crystal vase, a garment, a painting.

'Try it on,' she insisted from her bed, pressing a silk scarf that I had bought her some years ago onto a reluctant fellow member of the Orpheus Choir. 'It suits you. Take it. Do.'

She organised for Aaron to have a large box shipped back to London, including an album of photographs, a large canvas of a family group on Island Bay beach (which, although he won't remember, Moira worked on ceaselessly the year he started school), and a collection of glass goblets, which she had wrapped for him in great sheets of bubbled plastic.

'I drank my first whisky from one of these.' Aaron spun one round, with the baubled red, green and blue stem clenched between his fingers. 'I brought the boys home one night in fifth form, and we broke into Dad's Glenmorangie.'

I was sitting at the table, absorbed in work.

'Three quarters of a bottle.' Moira bit off a strip of Sellotape with her teeth. 'The giggling lot of you stinking like a distillery. And you thought he wouldn't know.'

Aaron looked up, surprised. 'Did you know, Dad? You never said anything.'

'Twelve-year-old top shelf single malt? Yeah, I knew.'

'We mixed it with Fanta.' Aaron set the glass down. 'Men that we were.'

'Don't even tell me,' I groaned. 'Just don't even tell me.'

'We bought those glasses in Venice,' said Moira. 'Do you remember, that day you got on the vaporetto without us?'

'Oh, I remember Venice. Many a time in the Rialto you hath rated me.'

I leant over the keyboard, tapped out a string of letters,

and erased them again. The anecdote came up every year or two. Aaron always relished the retellings, but Venice had, in fact, been difficult. Aaron went missing twice on the same day, the second incident more upsetting from our point of view. I don't know if she ever told him the full story.

'You were such a dope,' said Moira. 'Getting on the wrong boat. Do you know I knocked down a little girl trying to get to you? We were waving and yelling as the boat set off, but you'd rushed ahead without us. They shut the gates and we couldn't get on. You didn't even realise we were still standing on the jetty.'

'I figured you were right behind me. I thought you were on board.'

'In a total daydream, you were.'

'Still, Mum, calling the police. That was pretty hysterical, wasn't it? I mean, I was thirteen years old.'

'You say that now,' she said, 'but you would have been smuggled off and sold. Anyway, those police weren't doing anything useful. All tight pants and walkie-talkies. You should have seen their smiles when we asked for help. They were thrilled.'

'They got busy soon enough.'

Moira pushed a glass down into the shredded paper, stretched out her back and yawned widely. The fatigue was tremendous. She slept through the mornings and was always at her best after lunch, although the amount of time she had each day reduced as the illness got worse. I anticipated her tiredness now, and expected her to get up from the floor and wander into the bedroom, and I was ready to follow her, close the door, pour out a glass of water and help her into the bed, but she shuddered through her back and shoulders and kept on.

'They arrested me, actually.'

Aaron had laid a piece of the bubble sheet on the coffee table and was pressing his thumbs on it, systematically popping the blisters.

Moira let her hands fall still into her lap.

'They what?'

'At first they thought there was a kidnapping. That's what they were shouting when their boat pulled up alongside the vaporetto. Through the megaphone. *Rapimento! Un ragazzo inglese e' stato rapito!* "English boy kidnapped." I asked the bellboy about it at the hotel.'

Aaron has always had a good memory. At seven or eight years old he would parrot back to us not only phrases but entire exchanges, mimicking our voices with a terrible accuracy.

'We said you were lost.' Moira turned to face me. 'That was all, wasn't it, Peter? *Our son is lost*—nothing about kidnapping.'

'Quickly,' I said, 'rapidly. We could have been misinterpreted.'

'I wanted them to get a move on,' she said. 'The boat was halfway to Croatia.'

'Well,' I said, 'perhaps Giudecca.'

'Anyway, when they got on board,' said Aaron, 'they couldn't find their English boy, could they?'

The statement hung in the air. Moira's face started to work hard, her lips pressing together.

'You were such a dreamer,' she said. 'I wouldn't have trusted you to find your way home from Lambton Quay at that age.'

'They found *me*, though. I had an expensive camera. And no ticket. A dirty little Moroccan pickpocket.'

'*I* had the tickets. Of course you didn't have a ticket.'

'They pushed me to the ground and handcuffed me.'

'They did *not*!' She stood up in a rush, then seemed to

regret it, and sank down into the couch. 'You've never told me this. Aaron, why did you never tell me this?'

He smiled. 'They figured it out pretty quick. There were ladies on the boat in fur coats, shouting at the police about you, I think, how they'd seen me with you two. They let me go, started apologising. *Mi dispiace, mi dispiace.*'

His hands pinched the air in front of his face, eyes imploring, lips pursed. He was archetypal Italian.

'When we got back to the bridge everyone cheered. You were so cross.'

'They gave us prosecco.' Moira brushed off her skirt. 'I *thought* that was extravagant.' She lay back on the couch. 'But really, Aaron, did this happen?'

'"If you prick us, do we not bleed? If you tickle us, do we not laugh?" It happened. Here, Mum.'

He handed her a cushion. She shook it out lightly, placed it beneath her head, and turned to look at him.

'I don't know what to say. We never knew. Peter would have . . . well.'

The two of them looked over at me. I realised I needed to make a contribution.

'Handcuffed?' I asked. 'Really?'

'"Fair sir,"' he recited, '"you spit on me on Wednesday last, you spurned me such a day, another time you called me dog, and for these courtesies, I'll lend you thus much moneys." All sorts of things happen, Pete. All sorts.'

I can't understand why nothing came up at the time. It's true, there was a bad moment where it looked as though the Carabinieri would not accept that we were his parents: 'He is Moroccan,' stated the senior cop, his slicked hair shot with silver. 'You are not.' I'm his father, I stated over and over again, I'm his father. One of the cops held back a yellow Alsatian on a short metal chain. The men and the dog all looked at me coolly. Moira whispered a word in my ear. *Padre*, I started shouting. *Padre, padre, padre, padre.*

In the end it turned out fine. The whole thing amounted, it later seemed to me, to nothing worse than a comic, blunt, Italian-inflected version of the same confusion we ran into often enough at home. But now, to contemplate this, that they manhandled my child, treated him like a criminal, because they couldn't recognise him as the 'English boy' they were looking for? I can't wedge such a fact into the shape I have for that day. If it did happen, or if something like it happened, he weathered it. He seems to have weathered it.

On that trip I remember comparing Aaron's skin colour and newly adolescent bone structure to that of the waiters in restaurants in Hong Kong, Italy and Turkey, trying to work out if he could blend in, whether he was lighter, or darker, what the forms of his features might signify. At various stages in Aaron's life I became obsessed with categorisation. *He is Moroccan. You are not.*

You spit on me on Wednesday last. Aaron was still a pre-schooler when the police bashed and bloodied the protestors on Molesworth Street. I had supported HART quietly from the safety of my armchair, but after that I took to the streets and helped blockade traffic in Newtown for the Wellington match. In the leafy suburbs of Johannesburg and Cape Town, our four-year-old couldn't legally have lived with us. Couldn't have gone to school, or later, bought land, or voted. I had been lazy, but after Muldoon unleashed his dogs, it felt personal. The writhings of 1981 gave form to the ugly question that Moira and I had never dared put directly to each other. Would our child suffer in this part of our country, in Woburn, Khandallah, Hataitai, because of the colour of his skin? We were optimistic enough not to worry about it. In any case, what choice did we have? If you asked me now, twenty years on, I would say it went fine.

A month ago in the hospice, I quizzed Aaron again about Venice. We were standing in the kitchen, making tea in Styrofoam cups.

'You *did* have my camera on when you got on that vaporetto,' I said. 'I remember that now.'

He scooped an extra teaspoon of sugar into his tea and stirred it with the white plastic spoon.

'Do you remember how the lens cap got lost?' he said. 'And you had to find a camera shop to replace it?'

I nodded.

'Well,' he said. 'The scuffle. They pulled it off me.'

He leaned his hips back against the bench. His face was blotchy under the fluorescent lights. Things were accelerating. He had stayed on with Moira until past midnight the night before.

'Why didn't you say anything to us?' I asked.

'I don't think I really got it at the time.'

'So you reconstructed it later?'

'Don't you remember what it's like to be a kid? Things are blurry. You don't understand until you're older.'

'Handcuffing, though. That's pretty specific.'

He ran his hand around his left wrist as though rubbing away a sore.

'Maybe I added that in,' he said. 'They might have just grabbed me.'

'You did used to watch a lot of *Get Smart*.'

'Tell me this. Why do I feel like I'm on the stand, Dad?'

I looked up. He was on the brink of tears.

'I just wanted to clarify,' I said. 'I suppose it's not the time for this.'

'Mum's worse.' He blinked. 'It's going to be this week, I think.'

'Yes, perhaps. Probably.'

You are too young for this.

'I'll stay with her tonight. Get some sleep.' I fished forty dollars out of my pocket. 'Or get something to eat.'

He looked stooped, heavy, as he walked off down the hallway in his black greatcoat, the linoleum squeaking under each step, and I badly wanted a power I didn't have. I wanted to take it away from him, to relieve him of his mother's death, as if it were nothing more a difficult piece of homework.

I wanted to help, because that's what fathers do. Fix washing machines, caulk the seams. Stave off anyone and anything that could cause harm: police dogs, disease, the bitter winter cold that rises off a river.

*

Down by the slipway, the yachts bob on the slight swell. Light reflects off the underside of the fibreglass hulls, and I squint against the ferocious white. Still half an hour until I'm due at the airport. Two sailing school yachts are rafted up by the dock, the instructor out on the floating jetty, coiling rope. He catches me gazing, lifts his chin in greeting.

'Evening.'

I lift a hand, snap down my sunglasses, and scrutinise his face. I know this man. I've sailed with him. He was there when I had the accident, the last time I was on the water.

I'd been out sailing with a colleague, had a good run and wound up agreeing to join a race crew. We won the first two Sundays I went out. On my third trip, a day when the sky was charged with rain and the sea lemon-green, I hooked the kite on upside down just as we rounded the Ngauranga buoy. Shouting erupted behind me as the sail got stuck, and strangled around the forestay. We dropped out of the race, and the spinnaker had to be cut free. The skipper scooped it from the water, a drowned red blanket, and then he bore down the deck towards me, swearing.

It was this man here who stepped in and, like a horse-whisperer, spoke a few soft words that calmed the skipper down. The crew were silent as we chugged back home, sliding down alongside Kaiwharawhara to get out of the way of the race.

We crossed the inner harbour. I remember this sailor trying to cheer me up, pointing out the HMNZS *Canterbury* which was tied up at Queens Wharf that week, thousands of tonnes of white-grey metal sitting on the bouncing water. I thought about how many months it would take to dismantle such a ship. I wondered how many more years' service the *Canterbury* could be expected to give, and who it would be sold to afterwards, and at which port it would come to, eventually, once condemned.

We got back to the marina and I offered to shout the crew drinks, but I had a strong feeling the skipper didn't want me back. I never raced again after that.

The sailor's face is open, smiling. He's as stumped on the matter of names as I am. Possibly he can't place me at all.

'Breeze has dropped off.'

He finishes with the rope, lays it at his feet. His entire demeanour is that of a man who moves steadily from the centre of himself, one who would crack a chicken's neck in the backyard without flinching, pluck a body from the boiling sea with a steady arm. His head will be full of depth-soundings, isobars, tidal patterns. He will impress military-style order on his garage, and young boys who learn to sail under him will flush with triumph when they earn his brief nod of approval. I'd trust this man to put down a dog I was fond of.

He rises up to the balls of his feet, flexes his hands together and stretches.

'Not looking to buy, are you?'

He looks out to the breakwater wall. A large yacht is adorned with a sign, a phone number, the black digits half a foot high.

Beyond, on the far side of the harbour, the wharfs are stacked with tesselations of coloured packing crates, the houses spilled like confetti along the first ridgeline. The green peak of Mount Kaukau rises up and crowns the lot. At the summit, the radio antenna holds a perfect vertical line.

'It's a lovely cruiser. Going at a good price.'

'Yours?'

'Yeah, it is.'

From up there on the hill above Khandallah, you look down on all this, laid out like a temptation, the sailing boats bucking over the water, the gold strip of imported sand along the bay, the mirrored bunker of the pool, this cluster of matchstick masts that I am now standing amongst. An observer might have been marking the progress of the *Mary-Kate* that day from the hilltop as the spinnaker briefly fluttered out and sunk. A girl might have put her hand on her friend's shoulder, and pointed: *Will it capsize?* Perhaps the designated watchman aboard the *Canterbury* had watched the kite billow and fail through his binoculars, and made a note of it in the ship's logbook. There are always more people witnessing than you think.

'After something for weekend trips, are you?'

Clearly he can't for the life of him remember who I am. After all, it would be a poor show to let a cherished boat go to a man who doesn't know how to sail.

'I'll row you out for a look if you're interested.'

I chuckle, thrust my hands into my pocket.

'Yeah,' I say. 'No, probably not. I'm not looking to buy at the moment.'

'Rightio.' He turns away, hefts a coil of rope up onto the deck of the boat.

'But just out of interest,' I say, 'what would something that size go for?'

His brow furrows up, and he pushes his tongue up into the top corner of his cheek, sucking on his teeth. He walks down the jetty and stands alongside me, folds his arms and looks back across the marina.

'We've just done a refit on it. Brooks and Gatehouse instruments, new set of sails.'

He releases a small puff of air through his lips, and names a sum that makes me blink.

'Go on,' he says, spinning his finger round in an arc to indicate the path out to the marina wall. 'Take a look from the shore. You can get to it around that way.'

A boardwalk runs beneath the overhang of the Freyberg pool. Homeless teenagers have marked it out as their own with tagged legends and signs. In the shaded corner, between two pillars, are woollen blankets and a red nylon sleeping bag stained with brackish brown spots. Some kids must sleep here, listening to the demented battering of the halyards on the masts all night long. The extractor fan from the pool blows chlorinated air through my hair. In the shallows, rubbish eddies up against the rocks: a used condom, a parking ticket that no one will pay, an ice-cream stick.

I walk along the sea wall to the spiked gate that stops the kids and everyone else getting to the boats. Hold on for balance, water sloshing on either side, and look through.

She is sleek and ready to sail. She has chrome stanchions, a tall rig and her name stencilled on the bow, *Te Haunui*.

A boat like this could sail anywhere. I could advertise for experienced crew and sail across the Tasman, up the coast past Townsville, through Torres Strait, the Timor Sea, over the Indian Ocean, into the Gulf of Aden and the Red Sea, through the Suez into the Mediterranean, then on past Crete into the Aegean, to Lesbos, fetch up in Mytilene and meet Rob and Clare. At the scraggly end of Greece.

Find her. *The spitting image.* Track that girl down.

I would bring her on board the boat, bring out cold beer, a plate of figs and nuts, and get her talking on and on while I breathed in the sight of her. A fuzz of down along her jawline, animated, dark eyes.

A black shadow shifts beneath the surface of the water, a stingray the size of a tabletop, rippling like cloth.

The old shudder. *What if what if what if.* Some wrinkle in the universe. Some sleight of hand, some trick. A real girl, a woman, in fact, thirty years old, standing somewhere on the earth, walking around in her own body, *breathing.* I've never wanted to know. I still don't want to know. Would she look like Geneviève? Would she look like my mother? There's been such pleasure, such strangeness in seeing Moira's features refracted back at me in Aaron's face over the years, male and his own, and yet part of her as well.

Abigail would look like me, one supposes, she would have to. Some version of my face, some imprint of my features.

Falling, about to fall. One long swoon into the shallow water. It takes ten slow counts to clear the hot buzz in my head, and then I step deliberately along the sea wall, feeling the sailor's eyes heavy on me, trying not to crab down like someone who can't be trusted to keep his balance on one leg, let alone on the deck of a pitching boat.

The truth is, if I owned the big cruiser, I would just

trundle her about the bathtub of the harbour from time to time. I'm not much of a sailor, just a sketchy amateur who tried his hand at Sea Scouts as a boy.

It was Rob's dad who taught me the basics of sailing, who showed up early every Saturday morning at the Sea Scouts hall and took us out in threes and fours, hauling the sails up the pole on the old whalers, more or less indestructible ex-naval rowboats from before the First World War. In fact, there was a great deal of rowing involved, and packing sails into bags, and learning the knots. I don't remember how I got into it in the first place. We didn't know anyone who owned a boat. Rob's father bought a trailer sailer later on, when we were about fifteen, and took us once for Cokes inside the clubrooms, which confirmed to me that they were as rich as kings.

When Aaron came home, I would take him out on it. We'd go exploring down towards the harbour heads, and sit at anchor and boil up a cup of tea off the coast of Eastbourne. It'd be worth having a yacht for that alone, even if the boat did nothing until then but sit on her mooring and grow mussels.

*

There's a subplot in *Daphnis and Chloe* where rich young boys from the north of the island take a pleasure yacht down the coast of Lesbos. Their mooring rope is stolen from them by a peasant, and so they make do with a green withy. It's not from Latin or Greek, *withy*, and I've never come across the word in any other context, but it's clear enough in the story what it means. Some length of plant material, a vine, a rope woven from willow or flax. There are various animals in the story of *Daphnis and Chloe*, and they too have their part to play. On shore, the boys unleash their hunting dogs, a herd of goats are startled and come down to the seashore, where, finding no food, they eat the green withy, and so while the boys are away hunting, the yacht is set adrift by the swell and the wind. *And the backwash of the waves lifted it up and carried it out to sea.*

Well, as we all know, one thing leads to another in this life. The rich young boys have their revenge. They come back in the next season and abduct Chloe as she tends her goats. It's this scene that Chagall chose to paint for the book, the girl an arch of yellow, her brown hair long and loose, her breasts full like all the women in his lithographs, swooning into the arms of her abductor at the centre of the scene. He put no resistance into her body.

Marc Chagall was born in Vitebsk, in landlocked Belarus. The sea can't have been any part of his upbringing. Perhaps if it he had grown up on the coast he might have been drawn to paint the scene where the untethered yacht is swept out to sea, wave-battered and wind-knocked, the dismayed boys on the shore waving their fists in futility, embarrassed by their elementary mistake.

*

The smell of coffee fills the airport walkway.

'Aaron,' I say loudly.

He looks up this time, raises his eyebrows in greeting, pulls away from the newspaper.

'All right?' I put my hand on his shoulder. 'You're checked in?'

'Yeah.' He's scowling, instantly. 'The poxy man at the counter made me pay excess. I was only six kilos over.'

'Poxy indeed.' I pull a face in sympathy. 'How much did that cost?'

'A hundred bucks.'

'Damn,' I say. 'You probably should have shipped it.'

'I need that stuff. Doesn't matter.'

It does bloody well so, I want to say. *You can't afford a brass razoo.*

'Well. You'll have a coffee?' I tip my head towards the café counter, decked out in fake mahogany.

'No, I've had two. You go.'

'A juice? How about something to eat? One of those muffins?'

'Go on, then. A sweet one. Chocolate and raspberry.'

The barista, a dark-haired girl with a vine of leaves tattooed around her bicep, takes far too long with each cup, fiddling with the jug, holding back the milk froth, delicately snapping on the plastic lid. I resist the urge to drum my fingers on the counter, aware of the clock driving us forward. When I come back he's buried in an article. I pass over the plastic-wrapped muffin and pull up a stool beside him.

'Cowboys,' he points to the page, shaking his head. 'Criminals.'

'What's that?'

'They're dropping food packages on Afghanistan.'

'That doesn't sound so bad. The UN?'

He shakes his head. 'The Americans.'

'All right. A little perverse.'

'They're giving them peanut *butter*—'

'Well, there you go. It's strategic. The Taliban might acquire a taste.'

He offers a weak smile.

'The packages are wrapped in bright yellow plastic,' he starts to read, 'the same colour as unexploded cluster bombs that have fallen in the same area.'

He slides the paper over to me. Side by side the two objects could easily be confused, the instructions on both printed in the same typeface. We help you, we kill you, we feed you, we bomb you, we are your enemy, we are your friend. You do not know what we will rain down on you next. The trick gift, the messages scrambled.

'Details,' I say. 'It's all in the details.'

He bites into the muffin, crumbs spilling out over the bench. Within half an hour, he will be on the far side of the security checks, walking through the first of innumerable passageways which will channel him all the way to London.

'I'm heading up to Wanganui tonight.'

He takes a second, tremendous bite, still eating like a teenager.

'Grandad looked a wreck when I was up there,' he says. 'He's not well, is he?'

'His heart's playing up. I've thought about bringing them down to live with me,' I say, 'in Wellington.'

Aaron shifts about on his stool. Throughout the months of Moira's illness, I kept the decisions to myself, contacted the necessary services, informed him after the fact about what I had put in place. I do not, on the whole, confide my troubles in him.

'It would suit me, I think,' I carry on. 'The house is empty. I'm not sure I like it so empty.'

He appears to be listening intently.

'But they'd miss Wanganui,' I say. 'I don't know what's best, to tell you the truth. I worry about them.'

It's an abandonment, a gush of speech, as though he were Moira, as though he were my equal and not my child, a flighty boy who runs up debts.

He presses his lips together, considers, and then speaks.

'Dad?'

'Yes?'

'I've got some good news. I just heard back about some auditions I did in September. I've got a part for early next year.'

I take a breath. So, we will revert to role: his accomplishments, parental praise, our—no, *my*, singular—pride in him. 'Good. Superb.'

'It's a big deal, actually. It's going on tour. London, Edinburgh.'

'You've broken in. That's great, Aaron. What's the play?'

'*Shopping and Fucking.*'

'Sorry?'

'That's the name of the play.'

'How blunt.'

'It's not meant for third-form girls from Marsden. Listen, Nana's got this idea that she's going to come over and see it.'

'What? In London?'

'Have you spoken to her recently? She's on fire. She's gone manic.'

Each of the three of us, it would seem, has our own way of unravelling.

'Who's she going to London with?'

'She wants to come on her own, I think. The play would be a bit of a shocker for her.'

'There is no chance,' I pronounce, 'of Claudia going to London.'

He raises an eyebrow. 'You think? The thing is, she can't stay with me.'

'No. That wouldn't work.'

'It's my flatmate, Ahmed. He's Pakistani. She'd call him a wog. Worse, probably. Old bat.'

It still surprises me that Aaron laughs off his grandmother's casual, circa-1930s Timaru racism. It's true that there's no real animus in it, just the verbal tics of a lifetime. *You'd have to guess she's had a touch of the tar brush*, she'll say whenever Angela D'Audney comes on to

71

read the news. *I had an Island boy in to do the garden last week*. Dago, Sambo, Ching-chong, they've all slipped out at one time or another. Her own roots count for nothing. She talks about the Micks and Paddies. I remember her giving Aaron a twenty-dollar note when he was on his way out to town as a teenager, *I don't want to see you jewing off your friends*.

It always made Moira cringe in mortification, but Aaron's approach—perhaps his defence—has been to milk it for humour. My son and I have shared many, many laughs behind my mother-in-law's back. Mocking her has always been a reliable pact of ours.

Now Aaron raises himself up on the stool, starts to play to his gallery.

'Claudia goes on the Tube: Aaron, I will not step foot inside that *machine*!'

He raises his voice to a high, trembling pitch in a fair imitation of his grandmother, brown eyes squeezing towards tears. A few seats along, a pair of young women catch the sound and turn to face us. We have become a spectacle.

Poor, undone Claudia. There's no way she could travel to London. But she will miss him so much. Why shouldn't she have this flutter of hope?

'When does it start, this *Shopping and Fucking*?' I ask. 'It's not a musical, I take it?'

He smirks, as if to say, *Go on, say it again, Dad*. It cheers me up that the name of this play is something of an event for him, in spite of Aramoana, Columbine, Bin Laden.

'Late February.'

'And what's it about?'

'Well, shopping, for one thing. The urge to buy stuff. Credit cards at their limit.'

Including yours, I think.

'Who do you play?'

'Rent boy. I get arse-fucked on stage.'

His face is blank and easy. If he is trying to get me here, he has. I can't deny the flutter about my heart.

'How brutal.'

He shrugs. 'It's not rape. It's consensual. Well, sort of.'

A cart slides out from the terminal with three trolleys of luggage in tow. It runs across the tarmac, green plastic canopies fluttering like a toy train.

'Right. And how much do they pay you to do this?'

His face, when I look back, has hardened.

'And how much do they pay you to do this?' His eyes fix me in place. 'What are you saying, Pete?'

It's a slow, furious drawl. There was something unfortunate in the timing of the question, I appreciate that. And I do have some kind of reaction to the thought of him acting this out. Being acted upon. But this rage, this sarcasm, surely this is too much?

'You always want to know what we're *worth*.'

Where is he coming from? I cannot catch his sense.

'That's not what I meant. I just want to know that you're being treated fairly.'

'Fairly?' He raises an eyebrow. 'Yeah, because the world's so fair.'

'Aaron, I . . .' But I don't know what to say.

'I can look after myself.' He sounds as though he's marching off to his first day at school.

'Of course.'

I lay my hand on his shoulder. He looks down at it, coughs, and shakes his head in a gesture of exquisite contempt. My son is an actor, I remind myself. It is in his nature to exaggerate. And I do not know, right now, how genuine or deep this anger is, what it refers back to, what it signifies, what it predicts for our future. Moira is gone, and it is here, upon us, the test I have prepared for his whole life, and yet we are, I fear, badly underprepared.

'On tour, eh?'

He raises his eyebrows in confirmation.

'Well, you deserve it. You've worked hard for it.'

His face softens.

'Aaron, look. We're already on the topic. You know your mother wanted you to have some money. We both did. Do.'

He holds himself like a statue. Only the light flare of his nostrils gives him away.

'I'm putting the Castlepoint bach on the market,' I say. 'The money will come to you when it sells.'

There is no point now in coming at the matter any other way. For a moment, watching him gaze down at the picture in the paper as though absorbed, I can almost believe that he will take the news at face value, the pragmatic decision that it is.

'It'll be your decision, of course, what you do with it.'

'Dad, that bach,' he says, into the newspaper, 'is worth a packet more than what Mum was talking about.'

'That's true.'

He plants his palms on the bench. 'So I don't get it, Pete. Why the fire sale?'

I shrug. Do I need to justify my financial dealings to my insolvent child? I want the place sold. I want shot of it.

He puts his dukes up, mimes a left hook to my jaw. I almost flinch.

'Great,' I say. 'That helps.'

His hands hang at his sides and he sighs. 'You're *cleansing*,' he says. 'Getting rid of all the evidence she was ever here. Mum loved that place. It was part of her. She painted there. She wouldn't want it sold. Not yet.'

'I honestly don't think she'd care too much.'

Aaron stares at me, his face twitching. He seems to be undergoing some kind of internal battle. When he speaks at last, his voice is low and careful.

'You know, you didn't understand her,' he says. 'You didn't really get Moira at all.'

It doesn't hit home, because I did understand her. I understood, for instance, that the person Moira loved with her greatest devotion, clarity and constancy, was him. Aaron, and then me. It was never stated, but that is how it was. Which was fine, all in all. I also understood that she wanted him to have some money, as do I. Let the living administer the affairs of the living.

'It's just a bach, Ronny,' I say.

He gazes through the window at the tarmac. When he was a kid, I would take hold of his wrist when he stared off like that, try to make him attend.

'Just four walls and a roof,' I say. 'Not much of a roof actually, come to that.'

When he turns back around all I can see is his tiredness. His smile, false-bright, creases up the corners of his eyes. Ten years from now those lines will be etched in.

'And me?' He crosses his arms over his chest. 'I'm all oxygen, carbon and a bit of hydrogen. You going to break me up into pieces too, sell me off?'

'I'm talking about a house. Material property. Don't fudge logic.'

'Nothing fudgy at all, Pete. Just following your line of thought through.'

His face. The exhaustion in it.

'I don't need your money,' he is saying. 'I don't want it.'

'I've already decided.' I can hear my voice, louder than I should be, louder than I want to be. 'The sale is happening, this is what I'm telling you. This is not a consultation.'

'Yeah, I got it.' He stands and sets his backpack onto the bench. 'Watch this, will you? I'm going for a walk.'

The misery of fighting with a child at the wrong time. Today of all days, I want to be able to avoid quarrels and to set a tone. Since Aaron was a baby I've enacted over and over again that basic gesture of parenthood, the effort to arrest myself in my least adult moments, halt the rage, the irritation, get past the way the boy can needle up a hot provocation in my brain. I've succeeded, often, and then again and again I've failed. Such a familiar, hard failure to swallow today when all I wanted was for him to leave with a sense of steadiness and the ground under his feet, with the door to the house left wide open for his return. He has no fixed plans for a return visit. In half an hour he'll jet off into the big blue. I've botched it.

Aaron takes his theatrics too far; he takes everything to heart. He takes, and he takes, and he takes.

Sometimes, after we fight, he goes into a sulk for days or weeks. I suppose he'll retreat there now, and I might not hear much from him for a week or two. It has always been his mother who has travelled to that subterranean place to call him back. She has cajoled him back from almost wilful fosterings of pain, also from some big drinking sessions that worry her. Worried her.

Moira. Who will go down to call for you now? Eurydice had her rockstar husband with his songs to melt the earth, to make the prison walls bend. A musical genius with a vast hubris, *I can bring back the dead*. And then, as if the calculus of the natural order could shift simply under the force of one man's longing, it happens, grace cracks like lightning, *yes*. She can go home.

On Moira's last day, I was rubbing ointment into her hands, pressing on the knuckles and fingerbones through the loose bag of her skin. She was emaciated to the point of being unrecognisable. Her signals back to me came like a failing morse code, a stutter of small squeezes, the electrical impulses of the brain firing more and more faintly. The ointment smelled of roses and beeswax, and I kept catching the smell of it under my fingernails over the next few days, felt myself blank back to that room, those hours. Would the dead be returned to us in the state they left? What use would that be?

Did Orpheus reckon on that, that he might get her back wrecked? Did he consider, before he set off with his consuming stupid mania, what a few weeks of hell might do to a body? See, there's the sticking point, with all that putting on of incorruptible flesh and changing in the twinkling of an eye: how to undo what has been done in time?

That's me, the guy with all the questions. I'm no Orpheus.

My name trumpeted through the air.

'Peter. There you are!' Claudia stops. 'Oh, don't tell me!'

Up and down the coffee bar, heads turn.

'Would you *believe* it!'

She drops her handbag to the ground, stacks her hands onto her generous hips. Beside her stands a woman dressed in black, white hair cropped close about her ears.

'Too late,' Claudia proclaims. 'Wretched, wretched traffic. Didn't I say? Didn't I *say* we should have gone through Hataitai?'

Looking neither to the right nor the left, I stand up, take hold of her arm and shepherd my mother-in-law over to the side of the walkway.

'You're fine.' I am as sensible and placating as a news-reader. 'He's gone for a walk. He'll be back any moment.'

Claudia collapses on a stool. She tilts her head forward

to offer me her cheek, which I kiss, powdered, soft as a worn sheet. The elfin woman reaches us.

'I don't think you've met Margaret,' Claudia says. 'My second cousin.'

'I'm sorry.' She offers her hand. 'I met your wife just once, but she made a strong impression. It's a terrible loss.'

'It's been marvellous, connecting with Margaret again.' Claudia lays a hand on my arm, speaks in a stage whisper. 'She's talked me into going to Europe.'

'She has?' I say. 'A strange time for wanderlust, Claudia?'

'It's a tour,' she says. 'It's all laid on, lovely accommodation, everything organised. Italy and France. Late medieval art. We leave late February.'

Margaret looks highly plausible. An organised tour under her command might be possible for Claudia, if she were at her best. But Aaron has diagnosed her accurately; she is burning too high.

'I'd like you to come,' she says.

'I'm sorry?'

'With us. On the tour. You will, won't you, Peter? Margaret is the guide, you see.'

'Ah. Well, I'm sure it will be fascinating.' I look in Margaret's direction and she accepts the compliment with a nod. 'It's good of you to ask, but no, I don't think so.'

'Why on earth not?'

'Well, Claudia, I have a great deal of work on, first of all, and there's the question of my parents' health, and'— *But why*, I think, *am I explaining this?*—'basically, I don't want to go to Europe this summer. I can hardly think of anything I'd like less.'

'Something to look forward to. Take your mind off things.'

'Actually my mind will be on things for quite some time, and I would rather sit it out in the comfort of my own home than in some frenzied *piazza*.'

'It's just what you need.'

Moira had the same tenacity as her mother, but a far more delicate way of going about things.

'You think you know what I need? I do not need to go to *Italy*, Claudia. I do not, now, or in the foreseeable future, have any need, or any desire, or any wish, to go to France. I don't need to go to Germany or Holland or Portugal. Or anywhere else on your itinerary. And I certainly don't need to go to fucking *Greece* and drink bad coffee in Lesbos. Or Mytilene, or whatever it's called. What a waste of time and money.'

Claudia pulls back and stares at me.

'Greece,' she says at last. 'Who's talking about Greece?'

'If I may interrupt,' says Margaret, 'I do have someone else keen for the place. I'll probably be able to reimburse you in full.'

'Claudia. Is Margaret telling me that you've paid for my place on the trip?'

She keeps her eyes on me. After a moment, she reaches to steady herself against the bench and raises herself up from the stool. The gesture feels planned, a performance of old age.

'I didn't want to be alone.'

'It's a tour,' I say. 'There'll be an entire group.'

'No one who knew my daughter.'

'No. Probably not.'

'Who will I talk to?'

'The bus driver. The concierge. Plenty of people.'

'Mock all you like,' she says, turning back to me, 'but at a time like this you want family. You've always been my favourite son-in-law.'

Claudia only resorts to flattery when she is on a losing streak.

'We can spend time together here,' I say. 'We can speak of Moira as much as you like, on the phone or in person.'

'Ah, but what about Aaron's play?' she says, easing her way back onto the stool, her eyes brightening. 'You'll come to London for that. You have to.'

'I don't think,' I say, selecting the words with care, 'that Aaron's play will be quite your thing.'

'He told me it's full of buggery,' she says, 'but I don't care about that. Moira would go. And she'd want you to as well, you know she would.'

A pair of high priests, the two of them, heaving open the inerrant Word of the Lord and silencing all rational argument. *She's dead!* I want to shout. Moira has no dreams, wants, hopes. *Would you please stop summoning her?*

'Speak up, Peter. What are you saying?'

'London's not on the agenda either,' I say. 'I am not going to Europe. There is nothing in Europe for me.'

'Well don't blame me,' she says darkly, 'if one day—'

'Look who we have here,' I say, cutting her off mid-prophecy. 'The man himself.'

Aaron swoops down on his grandmother like a parrot in his red hoodie, and pecks her on her cheek.

'My darling.' She fumbles to clasp his hand in hers. 'We thought we'd missed you.'

'Not a chance.' He twists up his shopping bag, which seems to have a hoard of purchases in it. Goods he will pay for five times over in interest. 'I wouldn't have boarded without seeing you, Nana.'

He presents his back to me, studiously avoiding my eye.

'Margaret—' Claudia beckons to her friend, brings her forward into the pool of Aaron's attention. 'This is him. My grandson.' She holds his hand up in the air as though he is her prize, her Olympic victory.

Margaret and Aaron bow slightly to one another, a keen amusement running between them in a current.

'It's eleven o'clock,' I say. 'We ought to get you on the plane.'

He looks at me for the first time.

'Here.' I hand him the creamy envelope. 'I found it.'

He startles, and his hand darts out, snatchy.

'Thanks, Dad.'

A wide, winning smile, the envelope pressed like a winning Lotto ticket to his chest.

At the gate, Claudia holds Aaron for a long minute, making big exhalations. When she finally pulls back, they are both in tears.

He fishes in the shopping bag and holds something out to me, a CD wrapped in plastic.

'Here,' he says. 'I got you something.'

'What's all this about?'

'Tupac.'

Every Christmas, every birthday, Aaron buys me music. His music. I want to take him in my arms and hold him to me. When such gestures became too difficult, I cannot remember. I pat his back fiercely, squeeze his arm. He does not quite look me in the eye. I lift the CD up in the air, shake it like a tambourine.

'I'll listen on the way home.'

'Crank it up loud,' he says. 'You need to hear the words.'

The cover shows the naked, tattooed torso and face of a black man, his arms crossed or held behind his back, face turned to the side.

'Where's he from?' I ask.

'LA. But, actually, he's dead. Drive-by shooting. Years back.'

'Geez.' I peer at the dates on the back. 'Clever guy. Songs from beyond the grave.'

'Well. His studio, you know.'

'Parental Advisory,' I read.

'I think you'll handle it.'

'Thanks, Aaron. Really.'

'And Dad?'

'Yeah?'

'Try not to worry about everything so much, okay?'

Then I do hug him, and he lets me.

He nods, and hoists his small backpack onto his shoulders. '*Adios, amigos.*'

His grandmother pushes forward for another kiss, his face held between both palms.

'Go well,' I say, softly. Whether he hears or not, I can't quite tell. At the metal detector, he hoists his crimson hood up to cover his hair, and snaps his fingers at us in salute.

Three

In the middle of the night, in my parents' bungalow, I place Mozart's Requiem on the stereo. I turn it down to one notch above silence and huddle up to one of the speakers.

Fac eas, Domine, de morte
transire ad vitam

Grant them, O Lord, to pass from death to life.

Crossing the bridge at Pauatahanui, smears of red-gold light reflected in the black water. Aaron's hip hop pattering on, *these broken wings da da da dum dum come and heal me da da dum*, racing the freight train along the flats between Otaki and Levin. Just out of Bulls, two ambulances wailing past.

Moira loved the Requiem. Her choir performed it three years ago. I really would have liked to have heard some of it at the funeral. It was soft of me to let Claudia so completely have her way.

Quand olim Abrahae promisisti

Here where the line breaks, falling and pouring over and over again, like a sheet of water racing itself down the rock face. As Thou did promise—*promisiti* at the centre of the fugue, split across four notes.

Et semini ejus

It's very literal here, the Latin. Abraham's *semini*, seed, semen: milky, sticky ejaculate from which the countless multitudes descended.

My father appears in the doorway, his outline black against the hallway light, all billowing pyjamas and bandy legs.

'Dad. Damn, sorry.'

'You're all right,' he says. 'Go on.'

I haul up onto the couch, and he sits beside me, picks up his pack of Rothmans from the arm. The flame of the lighter shows up the ridgelines of his face. I hear his ribs lift with each breath. My father suffers from low iron, bowel complaints and a dicky heart. He takes all the pills he is told to, has given up butter and full cream milk, but when it comes to tobacco he refuses to listen to any of us.

'That's lovely. One of Mum's. Beethoven, is it?'

'Mozart. Moira loved it.'

He shakes his head and coughs, lays a hand on my knee.

'Gee,' he sighs. 'She was a good girl though.'

'She was.'

'Don't know how she put up with you, to be honest.'

My father's stuck to this line for twenty-three years.

'We wanted to come to the funeral,' he says. 'You know that, don't you?'

I place my hand over his for a moment, patting.

My parents loved Moira deeply, but I'd ruled out the funeral and I know they'd been relieved. It was too much. They haven't had a night away from home in over a year. I wouldn't have coped with looking after them that day, their enormous frailty and need.

'Go get us a cuppa, would you?'

'Rightio.'

The jug's roar bounces off the low ceiling. I pull out the smallest of the nesting tables and set out the cups. Dad's flicked the heater back on and he's fiddling with the footstool, trying to get it in position, while I oversee the business with the teapot.

'Aaron'll be on the ground in Hong Kong by now.'

'Isn't that something?' Dad shakes his head in wonder. 'You see, Peter, when you went to London, which would have been in 19—'

He's interrupted by a string of coughs, by spits of phlegm forming at the corners of his mouth, by the complexities of retrieving his handkerchief from the pyjama pocket.

'1970—' Hacking like a consumptive. He takes a drag on his cigarette to calm the airways, then slurps his tea and looks blank.

'1970,' I prompt.

'Yes. When you took that plane to London, and this is August of 1970 that I'm talking about here.'

I wouldn't be surprised if he could give me the departure time and flight number too.

'Now, that aeroplane there took three days to get to London.'

I nod my head slowly. 'Things have improved.'

'But, what I want to know.' His lecturing finger comes out, tapping the arm of the sofa. 'Is how is it that they can carry enough fuel in a jumbo jet to get them those kinds of distances?'

'Well, the 747. It was a breakthrough plane. Highly efficient engine, big wing area.'

'Remarkable. How do they come up with these things?'

'I don't know. Back of an envelope?'

'But it's something, isn't it. To think that ordinary men like you or me might set about designing an aeroplane.'

'I guess so. It's something you'd learn over time, Dad, same as fixing gadgets.'

'Smart men.' He's shaking his head doggedly now. 'You've got a bit of that in you. You understand all that.'

There it goes, the classic feint. My father's deference to my 'smarts', to my higher education, has irritated me my whole adult life.

'Well, you understand the principles too.' I make a wing of my palm, slide the other hand alternately under and over it in turn. 'Airflow around the wing causes lift and drag.'

'Right,' he says. 'Wind, and so on.'

Dad rubs his feet one over the other in his thick socks. Before I was born, he had the little toe on his right foot sliced off by the engine of a washing machine, which fell off a shelf in his workshop. I used to sit on the floor by the fire when he sat here just like this, and rub my fingers over the healed nub. In my child's mind, it had been a clean cut, and I imagined him picking up the tiny piece of flesh and cradling it in his palm like a kernel of corn, like the first tooth I lost, which gave me terrific shudders when it fell out and I got to look at it whole, a part of the body separate from the body.

'Not wind, Dad.' But am I actually doing this, badgering my eighty-three-year-old father about aerodynamics at 4am? 'Because, think about it, how would you fly on a still day? The aeroplane moves through the air. The speed comes from the plane.'

'You wouldn't want to meditate over it too much, would you, when you're up there.'

Aaron, in the middle of the air.

'Aaron was chomping at the bit to get back to London.'

'You'll miss him.' He fixes his rheumy blue eyes on me.

Bloody Dad and his bloody instinct for getting to the bloody heart.

'I'm going to buy him a flight home,' I say. 'Get him back here at Easter.'

He settles back against the chair and crosses his arms. I carry the teacups out to the kitchen bench. When I look around, his white head has fallen back against the sofa and his mouth is softly open. This is what you will look like before they close your mouth finally. When you fall. *He tetekura.*

I could stay here for a week, a fortnight, with my mother and father, could just fall out of the world and sit and drink tea in this room with the roses in the carpet if it weren't for Richard's dangerous kindness yesterday afternoon. The empty secretary's desk. The receptionist's scepticism.

'What do I do about the big clients, Dad?' I whisper from the kitchen. 'Got some tricks for keeping them happy?'

The snores come in rhythm, a catch in each breath. Outside, a faint wash of indigo has come into the sky.

I slip the Requiem back in its sleeve, flick the heater off.

'Let's get you back to bed.'

He jolts awake at my touch.

'Does he want to come back?'

I blink.

'Aaron,' he says. 'Does he want to come home again, so soon?'

Outside, a starling starts up in the pear tree.

'Bed, Dad.' I'm taking a firm tone. 'Time for bed.'

Geneviève and I used to talk a great deal about our parents. Hers were younger than mine. Her father was in the French military, young enough to be sent to Algeria in the 1950s when he was still in his early thirties.

She told me once about the day he came home from that war, how her mother had woken her early, carrying into her bedroom a brand new dress still in the box. They rode the tram together into Lyon. She remembered holding her mother's hand. She remembered the way her mother stared out the window. There were crowds on the streets. We are going to pick up your father, her mother said. He had been gone for over a year by then. Geneviève was ten years old, and the questions burned in her chest. Is the war over? Her mother said it was. Did we win? I don't know, her mother answered, and then she said, France has lost Algeria, and Geneviève had wondered at this, that a country might lose a land as one might lose a coat, a scarf, an umbrella. When she saw him, he swept her up and kissed her, and they had gone together to a café, and although she was only eleven, she had been allowed a glass of wine that day.

Geneviève was immensely fond of her father, I think, in spite of the way things had gone between them. When she told me stories like this I understood that, living in Amsterdam, she missed him, that she felt the absence of both her parents, athough she wouldn't have said that. I missed my mother and father too, acutely at times. They were much further away than hers by distance but I had the comfort of monthly phone calls, which I made from a pay phone in Dam Square. The line was always full of echoes and clicks, as if I were speaking to them from underwater or from outer space, and I would lean against the glass and look out at the morning blur of trams and bikes rattling over the cobblestones, and hear my mother's voice spooling out to me from the exact spot where I knew she would be sitting down at the telephone table in the hallway, the dimpled glass of the front door casting yellow evening light over the roses on the carpet, the print of Joseph and Jesus working in the woodshop together by candlelight hanging on the wall above her head.

Geneviève never phoned her parents. She didn't even phone to tell them about Abigail's birth, although letters were sent back and forth. Mostly, it was her father who wrote. She read the letters aloud to me, translating as she went. In these letters, he was constantly cajoling, or pleading, or ordering her to come home. *You are my child*, he wrote. *I want what's best for you.* Geneviève snorted. *Il est pisse-froid mon père,* she said. He's a cold bastard.

Morning sun cuts in at the lounge window, banks of white cloud piling up on the horizon. My mother prepares tea and clatters about in the cupboards.

'Why don't you stay.' She pours from the pot, trembling. 'Stay the rest of the week.'

On the front page of the newspaper, the sinking share market and a background piece on the Taliban.

'There'll be cherry tomatoes from the greenhouse in a fortnight. Stay until they're ready, Peter.'

I put my hand over hers, the skin so powdery.

On the second page, a spate of grisly murders in Auckland and a small piece about a delegation from the Hokianga who are preparing to depart for Europe, for France. They are going to Lyon, then Paris. It's the word Lyon that catches my eye.

'Gosh,' I say. 'How medieval.'

'What's that?'

'Bishop Pompallier.'

'I saw that. It's the Catholics, isn't it,' my mother says. 'The Catholics and the Maoris.'

'His descendants,' I read aloud, 'knew very little about the bishop's life until we began our inquiries. It seems fitting to bring him back.'

'"Him",' my mother says. 'Sentimental claptrap. Why don't they say the body?'

'Not much of that either, I'd imagine. A handful of bones at best. Buried a hundred-and-thirty years ago.'

'Where?' she asks.

'Paris. Puteaux Cemetery. But born in Lyon.'

'Pretty bizarre, if you ask me. Grave-robbing.'

'I'll make sure you're spared the indignity.'

'I hope we're all spared that kind of carry on. Like a circus.'

'Well, no one'll be digging Moira up.'

'Moira's safe from everything now.'

This is just the kind of perverse consolation my mother likes to nurse. When Dad was diagnosed with the heart condition she told everyone that at least if he went that way it would be 'quick and tidy'. Like sweeping dust into the rubbish bin. It makes me wonder if it's the secretions of the dying that she's most afraid of, all their runniness and smells. She's opting for a good clean cremation for herself, and she approved of Moira choosing the same.

'Rob called from London yesterday.'

'Oh, but I'm seeing his mother tomorrow!' Mum's hands fly to her cheeks. 'I'll tell her. How is he?'

'He's bought a house in Greece. In Mytilene.'

There's this waitress, Mum.

'Good lord. What would they want to live over there for?'

I can see Lesbos clearly, tucked in against the Turkish coast like a chunk come loose, some sixty or seventy kilometres south from the Dardanelles and Gallipoli. *There is no difference between the Johnnies and the Mehmets to us where they lie side by side here in this country of ours.* If I went to Rob's place we could take a trip to those ANZAC battlefields.

'Not live. A holiday house.'

'I thought they had one of those in Cornwall.'

'They do. It's another one.'

She falls quiet. For twenty-two years my mother was in charge of the mortgage. Each payday there was a distribution of the minute remainder into envelopes for grocery money, for the electricity, for money towards my school shoes. They could no more have imagined buying a holiday house than flying to the moon.

'Will they be back for a visit, do you think? You know Lizzie's daughter.'

I hum vaguely.

'Rob's niece. Lizzie's daughter. Didn't Rob say? She's having a baby.'

'Oh, Lizzie,' I say. 'The beautiful Liz. Still married to her cheese baron?'

I'd had a crush on Rob's older sister through most of secondary school.

'So the baby will be the first great-grandchild. Nine grandchildren.'

The fingers on her left hand start to tap against the table, into which I read, fairly or otherwise, reproach, disappointment. My mother has one grandchild from one son. Such statistics are important to the seventy-plus crowd.

She has two grandchildren.

Dam Square, trams, bikes, snow in the sky, in the dark, the street lights blazing. After the police had come to the boat, I'd picked the best time to call that I could, early morning back home. Twisting the coiled cord of the phone around and around my fingers. Mum, are you sitting down? I checked that Dad was in the house. Even then I wanted the job to be taken out of my hands. Septicaemia, Mum—*miamum*. The echo on the line. Blood poisoning—*soning*. Are you okay Mum—*kaymam*. No, nothing anyone could do.

Wancoddo. Wancoddo. Wancoddo.

I have never spoken to her about the possibilities Geneviève raised with me when we met in Lyon in 1989. I don't think I even mentioned our meeting. This is out of concern for my mother. It's been the responsible thing to do. Mum suffers anxiety, there's a certain fragility to her mind. Why would anyone trouble her? If this waitress in

91

Mytilene, her dark eyes, is impossible to shake out of my own mind, why would I want to plant that image in my mother's head? It would only distress her.

'Why don't I come get you in a couple of weeks' time?' I say to Mum when at last she's got her feet up in the lounge. 'Bring you two down for a holiday in the city. We'd plan it all out, make it easy.'

'It's a lot of bother for you.'

'It's not a bother at all. That guest room downstairs is all kitted out, ensuite, everything you need. Come for a few days.'

'What would we do with ourselves in Wellington?'

'Plenty. I'll take you to see what they've done at Oriental Bay. I was down there last night. Tonnes of golden sand. You'd think it was Hawaii. Take you out for a drive to Lyall Bay.'

'Your dad always loved Lyall Bay.'

'I know he did. Chocolate ice creams on the parade. Just the thing.'

'He's not too steady, you know, Peter. He's doesn't last well.'

Last July, Moira, Mum, Dad and I went walking together in the afternoon down the riverbank. The ordinariness of it, dank woody smells of the path and the river silver through the trees. The quick-fading winter sunset.

'When did he last get his bloods done?' I ask.

'He doesn't like the new nurse. Says she's bossy and her breath smells bad.'

'Cantankerous old bugger. He has to get it done. What about the specialist?'

Mum pulls out a slim black leather diary, filled with spidery pencilled notes. That little book, I sense, is holding the whole enterprise together.

'He's to go to the hospital at the end of November.'

'Should I come along?' I ask. 'Do you think I need to talk to the doctors?'

She pours another tea and doesn't answer, which in the lexicon I have learnt since earliest childhood means *Christ yes please come and help.*

The Requiem so quiet I almost can't hear it. My parents' carpet, when you lie on it, with your head hard up against the speaker, smells of cat piss. They haven't had a cat for years.

Kyrie, eleison

Christe, eleison

Kyrie, eleison

It's 1am in Wanganui, midday in London. Aaron should be home by now. Unless, that is, he's been diverted off by jumpy British customs authorities to a small, white, camera-encrusted room deep in Heathrow Airport. His New Zealand passport, his English name with Hebrew origins, Aaron Collie—please let these details have worked in his favour, please don't let them ask about his Pakistani flatmate. These are difficult days. *Jittery*, Rob said. *High security everywhere.*

The phone rings, on and on, bleating into his hallway in Mile End. I let it go for several minutes. I could call his mobile, but he'll get snippy at the idea that I'd search him out like that, for no good reason. Best to shoot off a tiny, unintrusive bullet of parental concern. *Touchdown? Call when you can.*

Back on the floor, I start to slip away, seeing white jet trails writing on the blue, and I imagine, or dream, of the group of priests, nuns and elders travelling to raise Bishop Pompallier's remains, exhumed from the Parisian grave in which they have lain for a hundred-and-thirty years.

The clergy accompany them high through the cold air of thirty-five-thousand feet, the bones travelling at a speed Pompallier could never have known.

In sleep, it becomes my own father we are bringing home in that small casket, his remains as light as a cat's, the bones of his bandy legs laid flat, his pyjamas rolled into a neat ball.

Mors stupebit et natura,
cum resurget creatura

Death and nature will be astounded: *stupebit*, from *stupeo*, stupefied, silenced, stunned. Death dumbstruck, as all creation rises again.

On Monday afternoon I pack plastic bags of vegetables into the boot.

'Are you sure?' my mother says. 'You won't stay just one more night?'

'I need to get back to work. I'm going to Castlepoint later in the week. I'm putting the bach on the market.'

'You've got to get on. I know you do.'

I have the Mozart in my hand. 'Can I take this?'

'Of course, take it.'

Dad is ahead at the end of the driveway, running a leaf of the camellia bush between thumb and finger.

'You get him down to the blood clinic,' I say. 'Give the nurse peppermints. Give him peppermints. Whatever it takes.'

When we reach the curb, Mum offers me her cheek, and her fingers press into my shoulders, a clutch and a release.

'Bye, love.'

'Come whenever you like.' Dad wanders over and pats my shoulder. 'Your mother keeps that bed made up for you.'

I start the engine, draw the window down. My father

leans in, curling his fingers over the door.

'It's going all right for you, the motorcar?'

'Yes,' I say. 'Never have any trouble with it.'

'Cheerio then, Peter.'

He taps the roof of the Legacy twice in benediction. I circle around at the end of the street and drive back past them, hands still fluttering.

Four

Although it's been hard to stay motivated this year, although for many months now I have found it hard to see why any of the files I am involved with matter in the slightest, I don't forget, ever, unlike some of my colleagues who were born into the professional class, that much of what has made my life sound and comfortable is the effect of a good career: on the psyche, on the body, how it holds you together, and *income*, the way the money keeps coming in, ending the late-night anxiety attacks, the humiliation of pretending you have in reach many things you do not have in reach, the constant figuring and figuring, which I still remember from Amsterdam and the early years of Aaron's life while I studied for my degree.

It's not for everyone. Moira railed against the working week, asked me constantly if I would give it all up and go off-piste with her in some form or another. But I watched her flailing around, and I didn't envy her. For every day of joy her painting gave her, the doubt made her miserable for three. I often thought she just didn't have enough to do. And she, of course, ate well while she painted, our house was warm while she painted, our son wanted for nothing while she painted. Before too long I think it became her worst fear that I might in fact give it up, the lawyering, which only resulted in a redoubling of her efforts to 'check in' and to 'give me an off-ramp'. *If there's something you really want to do, we can make space for that. I can always teach*, she said at thirty-five, which was something she'd trained to do half a lifetime ago. *We'll get by.* Well, we wouldn't have got by at all, although that wasn't the main point. By my mid-thirties, I was baffled by her suggestions. She might as well have been speaking Russian.

So I show up on Tuesday morning, I attend as best I can to the business that needs attending to. Sometime in the afternoon Dylan's timesheets cross my desk. *The big picture. You'd want to reflect that.* What did I expect would happen?

A smarter lawyer would have tallied up an extra hour or two a day, at most. *A smarter lawyer wouldn't need to be told.* Dylan, brazen and daft as a teenager stuffing goods down his jacket-front, has billed BioCom for great chunks of extra time. Five hours on a Monday, eight on a Wednesday, another eight on a Friday. Twenty-seven hours on these clients across a single week, when they've been running an average of four.

I pick up the phone, dial his extension, put it down again. Dylan's desk is in an open plan, and neither a conversation nor a summons to my office would be private enough.

A simple white sheet of paper, the unmistakeable numbers printed in black ink, the loopy swirls of his signature. I could have scribbled *See me*, and sent them back to him. I could have made the sheet into a beautiful dart, glided it over to the rubbish bin.

But what if he's actually done the hours? Dylan's technical mind, his love of detail. I wouldn't put it past him to have stayed on past midnight all week, reading the files over in case he'd missed anything.

BioCom will be puzzled, they might kvetch a little, but they'll undoubtedly pay. I have nothing left in me for client maintenance, for coddling and schmoozing and sweet-talking the banks. Christmas is in sight now, and everything will go quiet over summer. Come late January, with Aaron re-established in London, myself orientated to this new life and establishing, I suppose, some kind of routine for myself, I will be able to write off the last year of distracted work like a bad debt. There's tidy little magic on offer here that will fend off those who tot up the figures until then.

This giddy, reckless feeling, like unleashing a dog onto a hare. *You started this*, I told myself, *so now you see it through.* I countersign, send them to accounts. Let it unfold.

I find Richard in the kitchen. I think if I'm perfectly honest, I went looking for him. I somehow want him to know that I'm in the building, feet under the desk, cracking on. He leans up against the Formica bench, pours himself a filter coffee in a company mug. It surprises me that a man of such fastidious tastes in most areas of life can put up with that coffee, which tastes like stewed batwing to me.

'How'd your trip go?' he asks. 'How are your parents?'

'Holding it together,' I say. 'Old age, though, it's not for the faint-hearted. How are yours?'

Richard's mother, he once told me, had polio as a child, and was left with a bad limp on one side and difficulty with her lungs. In spite of this damage, Richard was the youngest of five children. She was obviously a woman of great drive, which he has inherited. Richard made partner with the firm at thirty years old. He's a wildly capable lawyer, and I imagine he'll take silk at some stage. I really do admire him.

'They're away on safari.'

'They're where?'

'In Africa. Kenya.'

'Good lord. How intrepid.'

Richard shrugs. 'They've always been like that. My older sister's gone with them this time.'

My own mother won't come three hundred kilometres by road to Wellington.

'How's Aaron?' He takes a chocolate biscuit from a plate sitting on the benchtop, nibbles at it.

'Gone back to London.'

It troubles me that Aaron hasn't bothered to answer my texts, nor to send a quick email to say he's arrived safely. I don't know why such simple courtesies are beyond him.

'Good for him. Hey, there's drinks on Thursday at Shed 5. If you feel up to it. We're welcoming the summer clerks.'

Laura appears at my office door just after three, all bashfulness and hesitation, asking me for a time to meet—*I was wondering if maybe perhaps sometime we could.*

'Great. Shall we do it now?' I say.

She brightens right up at that, and runs off to get her notes. These days all the statutes are available to look up on the computer, although that way I often find myself lost inside the screes of text. I still prefer to open up the hard volumes in the library, flick the thin paper back and forth.

I don't have time, right now, to find the book we need. I bring the Companies Act 1993 up on the screen. *Murdoch* was a small but engaging case for our team when it first went to trial five years ago, and one that became significant when it ended up going all the way to the Court of Appeal and setting precedent. I'm not a litigator, but I had some input. The case rested on the question of reckless trading, and the nature of the test that would determine it. When Laura returns, I go into some detail with her on the arguments that were put to the lower court, where it was initially ruled that the test must be subjective, an enquiry into the states of mind of the directors of the company.

'But, do you see?' I say. 'That was overturned. Now, imagine you are a company director. In the end, your subjective judgement about how reckless or cautious your actions are is not relevant. What matters is the way in which your business is run, your modus operandi, and whether or not that puts the business at risk of serious loss.'

Laura is concentrating hard, her lips lightly pursed, elbow on the table, chin resting on her palm. She is wearing a lilac blouse, and around her necklace hangs some kind of painted clay ring, blue, with flowers, some kind of sweet gypsy piece you mind find at an open-air market.

'The road to hell is paved with good intentions.' Her brow raises.

Well, that makes me smile. 'Pretty much. Or, at least, good intentions don't matter if your practices are manifestly unsound.'

She asks about what substantial risk would mean, and by the end of half an hour, she's arrived at a good understanding of the case.

It's always cheered me up, coaching the students. I make time for it as often as possible, especially over the summer when the clerks come in. Sometimes the ones I've mentored come back to me around exam season, and I help them again then. I remember one cold August a few years back, turning up at seven in the morning several mornings in a row to get a spell with a young guy who had clerked for me the previous summer, a keen skier by the name of Perry. He would come in after every weekend with his face sunburnt, his ski-goggle marks making him look like a raccoon. He was an exceptionally talented young lawyer. Last I heard he'd headed overseas. He's the kind we need, the kind you really do hope will come back one day.

When we're done, Laura stands up and makes to leave. 'I have one more question,' she says.

'Sure.'

'You volunteer at the Law Centre, don't you?'

'I do. In fact I'm heading there'—I check my watch—'in a couple of hours.'

'Really? You are?' She lights up, then seems to quiet herself. 'That's good. I'm curious, you know, about it.'

'Come with me,' I said. 'Sit in on some interviews. You'd learn a lot. And not just about the law, either.'

'Sure. One day, maybe.' I hold the door open for her, and she turns around. The collar on her blouse is slightly caught up, asymmetrical. It's like a flinch or a hiccup in me, the desire to reach forward and correct it.

'Thanks for your help,' she says. 'I appreciate it.'

'A pleasure, Laura. Truly.'

The last client at the Community Law Centre is pale-skinned, the architecture of his face delicate, almost goblin. His name is Matthew and he has been caught in the downpour. He tells me he is twenty-four, although I would have guessed him younger. His dirty-blond curls drip water. From the moment he takes a seat in the interview room, he fixes his eyes on me and won't be shaken off.

'The charge is assault,' he says, splaying his fingers on the desk. 'My first question to you is whether they are likely to make anything of the fact that I've been arrested in protests before.'

The boy feels his own importance keenly.

'Have you ever been offered police diversion?'

'Yeah. I've used that up.'

'Tell me what happened.'

'We were protesting at the American Embassy. About Afghanistan. There was a small group of us, nine or ten, and we planned to stay through the night. We were threading flowers through the fence. The guards were just watching us until it got dark, when they started telling us to move back, right back off the pavement.'

'Security guards?'

'Yes. I climbed the fence, wanting to put some flowers up where they couldn't reach, and that's when the guard came out of the compound, and told me to come down. He was right below me as I was coming down and he put his hand on my leg, and I got a fright and kicked him, harder than I meant to, and that's when his jaw got broken.'

'And you fell down?'

He shrugged. 'I managed to stick a bunch of carnations up there first.'

'Fine,' I say. 'Perhaps we should talk through the process. Your first appearance is Monday?'

'Ten o'clock.'

'So first thing that day you talk to the duty lawyer at court. They'll represent you at that initial hearing—'

'Actually.' A tiny spray of water from his flicking hair lands on the back of my hand. 'I'm going to defend myself.'

'Well,' I say. 'That may not be wise. It's not as simple as it seems.'

'In fact'—he shakes his head again—'I don't really want to negotiate about that. I have some things I want to say to the court. I just want you to advise me on the charges.'

'The first hearing will be purely procedural. It won't do any harm to have a lawyer manage that early part for you. And it may be highly detrimental to do otherwise.'

'As I said, I will be defending myself.'

He looks at me, steady. He's contemplating a broad plain where he is charging, beautiful and noble, out to a magnificent death. The point he wishes to make will be buried in court records, while he will be left with a criminal conviction for assault.

'You might be able to make a technical argument that that side of the fence was a public area.'

'I'm not really interested in an argument that rests on technicalities.'

I lean back in the chair, put the pen down and hoist my palms up behind my head.

'Is your family rich, Matthew? Do they have influence, connections?'

He pulls his chin in, astonished.

'What are you saying?'

'Perhaps you feel impervious to the law.'

His face grows hot, a blush that seems to start at the roots of his wet hair and shades his whole face in an instant.

'I understand your cause,' I say. 'But sometimes you have to be practical.'

'They're bombing the shit out of Afghanistan. I don't want the arguments to rest on technicalities. I want to give the court the full picture. I'm going to get some publicity. I've got a friend who's a journalist, she's going to come along.'

'You're twenty-four?' I glance down at the paperwork.

'Yes,' he says.

'And. So. Twenty-four. You want to travel? You want to apply for jobs? Tell me, how's that going to work out with this on your record? You're a blessed fool. You know you can do jail time for assault, don't you?'

'Fool.' He rolls the word slowly around in his mouth.

'You don't have a clue what you're taking on here. What you're suggesting is foolish.'

Matthew pushes the chair back and stands up.

'You're out of line. I want to see someone else.'

At the door he turns around.

103

'Men like you,' he says, 'you don't take any risks, do you? You sit there in your suit and tell me to play it safe, keep my head down. I have a right to protest. I have a legal right to go to the American Embassy and tell them what they're doing is immoral. They're bombing hospitals. Do you have any idea? The people should know. The people should hear that.'

He will deliver a similar speech before the District Court judge at the list hearing tomorrow morning, which will cause a laconic lift of an eyebrow, and will result in his case being put forward to the last possible hearing date, with strict bail conditions imposed in the interim. He is an irritant, this golden boy, a mote of dust that the great circulating blood and oxygen systems of the state will wash over and clean out in a single pulse.

'I'm sorry,' I say. 'I may have overstepped the mark. You're a fine young man. I hope you make your point.'

I'm gesturing with my hands. They are waving about, white and venous and wild in the corner of my vision, and I'm on my feet, face to face with him, and he's shrinking back, irritated, his head slowly describing a nod, of affirmation or pity, which, I'm not sure, and then he leaves the room, and my hands drop, exhausted, to my side.

I finish up the paperwork, and take it out to the little office room to be filed.

The rain is still drumming down, the last of the light gathered up, pressing through the grey cloud in a blaze of pink, red tail-lights of cars and buses smeared up and down Courtenay Place.

What I need at this junction is a drink. The cheap Irish bar on the far side of the road is steamed up, full of men in jeans and rugby shirts. I take my beer out to a cast-iron table beneath the balcony and relish the burn of alcohol in the throat, sheets of water falling just past the overhang.

The bartender scoops up the empty with one finger, holding four glasses at once, a dirty chandelier in the grey light. He is a wrinkled wizard in a black leather waistcoat, his hair tied back in a lank ponytail, a packet of cigarettes rolled into the sleeve of his T-shirt.

'Another one?'

I nod, slide a ten-dollar note out of my wallet and hand it to him.

'I don't suppose you could spare a cigarette?'

He raises an eyebrow, and puts the glasses down.

'Rough day, was it?'

I shrug.

'Everyone cracks with a beer in front of them.' He opens the packet, passes me his lighter. 'I tell the punters to get home if they really want to quit.'

'I'm sure that's true.' I wonder if he has a contract with the Ministry of Health. 'Although I haven't smoked for twenty years.'

'Jesus,' he says. 'What, you just lost the winning lottery ticket?'

'Yeah.' I exhale. 'Something like that.'

'Sorry to hear it.'

He shakes his head, picks up the glasses.

'Get that down you.'

The wizard plonks the beer down in front of me, sloshing a little on the paper coaster. He fishes in his pocket, lays the ten dollar note back down.

'On the house, mate. Hope your luck turns.'

'Yeah? Cheers.'

The wizard's white fingers briefly on the table. His fingernails unexpectedly manicured, squared off. Two rings.

'Irony is, my wife died of lung cancer,' I say.

The wizard looks up from wiping the table beside me.

'Did she smoke, then?'

'No. Not at all.'

'There you go. Right as rain.'

I blow a stream of smoke out into the damp air. Charity drinks, easy banter. You often get a bit of love in a pub like this, the grimy, cheap type. It's the kind of pub my father drank in, the kind where you can nurse a fag and a beer for an hour or two, even if you're on your own, without a lick of shame.

I still don't know if I did the right thing by Moira. In her last month, there were new drugs on the horizon, experimental treatments, trials we might have signed up to. She asked my opinion, and I told her it was deeply personal, it was about her body, and I asked her how she felt about renegotiating hope. That surprised her, I think, my lack of answers. Why wasn't I more directive? Why didn't I just insist, *Yes, you must*, you must try anything, everything? I saw it as her choice, one of the last major choices she would get to make, and I didn't want to take that from her. It does haunt me, though. If I had taken her in hand, if I had said, *This is what you need to do*, could I have saved her? There's always a chance, however vanishingly small.

Someone from the glass towers at the north end of town is going to walk past on the pavement any minute, spot me drinking here and conclude that I've gone to the dogs. *Just resting*, I would want to tell them. *Just gathering my strength.*

I sometimes think about that late, unexpected son of Marc Chagall's, born to him in his fifties. When Bella died, Chagall turned his paintings to the wall and howled on the floor and wished to die. A year later he took up with with his English housekeeper, Virginia, who arrived in his house with a little girl of her own by her Scottish husband, from whom she was separated. Some time went by, a year perhaps, and suddenly, there was a baby.

They named him David. The mother was still married to her Scotsman and so the boy was named McNeil for him, and not Chagall, because by then they were living in France, and that was the law.

In the end Virginia left Chagall for a Belgian man. She took her daughter with her, and David too.

It seems to have been a terribly painful period of Chagall's life, this insult, this infidelity. He writes to his friends that *dark life has opened up for me a grave more bitter than Bella's grave.* He hopes he has the strength to tell Virginia to stay away, despite his love for her, and his rage too, *over my son whom she takes away with her own daughter.*

When he sat down on Lesbos a few years later to paint the fat babies in the *Daphnis and Chloe* lithographs, did he have his last child in mind? They are awkward plump splotches of pink, the two exposed babies in the book, unnaturally flaccid, stretched out with necks craned back each beneath the animal which, in that cold night, in that vast abandonment, has ambled up to shelter, warm and feed them. The boy, Daphnis, suckles from a goat, and the girl, Chloe, from a ewe. The shepherd looks down at the sheep, his red cloak like a hot heart, his arms cradling an empty space where the child will soon be taken up. *He saw the ewe behaving like a human being offering her teats to the baby so that it could drink all the milk it wanted, while the baby, which was not even crying, greedily applied first to one teat and then to another a mouth shining with cleanliness, for the ewe was in the habit of licking its face with her tongue when it had had enough.* The shepherd takes the baby home to his wife, where, as in all these stories, he tells her *to treat the baby as her daughter and bring it up as if it were her own, without letting anyone know the truth.*

None of the biographies of Chagall say anything about whether the Belgian man turned out to be a good stepfather, nor whether David loved him or resented him. Perhaps they found each other mutually incomprehensible. Which is common enough among fathers and sons everywhere, after all.

Back at the house, I ring the airline. I punch endless buttons to get past the auto-recordings, until a woman with a nasal voice confirms that SP 76 landed at Heathrow as scheduled on Saturday evening, local time. Aaron has been on the ground in London for two and a half days. There's no need for me to be too alarmed. Jetlag can wreak havoc with your energy, and he has a great deal to catch up on. I suppose he's not thinking much about home right now at all. And if his old man's spending his evenings getting drunk and teary in a bar at the scrag-end of Courtenay Place, well, that's hardly his problem, is it?

Five

On the way to Castlepoint yesterday I stopped at an internet café to check for emails one last time before I went down to the coast, where there would be no communications.

The room stank of damp carpet and the mouse pad was a DB coaster. I handed over three dollars in gold coins and received a piece of paper with a code on it. The inbox was empty. I whacked my open hand against the side of the monitor, willing a message to slide in from the ether while I watched. The owner, reading the TAB pages, raised his eyebrows.

Then I cleared the home answer machine from my mobile, although I'd checked it only two hours earlier. There was one new message: a breathy, silent caller who said nothing for a full ten seconds, which saw my hopes rise until Moira's cousin's nine-year-old daughter collected herself and asked in a bright, sharp voice if she could interview me for her school project.

In the end, I called Rob from the last petrol station before the Castlepoint turn-off.

'Peter!' he roared. 'You booked a ticket yet?'

A sheep truck rattled past on the main road, the smell of the animals rank on the cold air.

'I need a favour.'

I gave him Aaron's address in the East End. I could hear

him frowning down the line.

'How long has it been?'

'It's five days since he left.'

'What time of day would you expect him to be in?'

'Early morning?'

'Feel like a copper though, don't I?'

Rob's fake cockney. He tried that on an actual bobby who showed up at our flat in Earl's Court on a blue-skied autumn day in 1971, wanting to question Clare.

'She ain't here, guv,' Rob had said.

It was the day after Mayday, when riots had taken place outside the American Embassy at Grovesner Square in support of the massive demonstrations in Washington, DC. Clare, active in a number of political groups and involved in feminist, situationist and anti-Vietnam War actions almost every weekend, had led a group of women at the front of the demonstration who had attempted to crash through the police line. She came home bruised around her legs and arms, her knee smashed and swollen. The cops had used a baton on her. She was defiant, bright-eyed, excited.

'Out Mile End way.' There was an echoey quality to Rob's voice down the mobile phone. 'I haven't been there in years. It's all Bangaloreans out there, isn't it?'

'Think of it as an adventure,' I said. 'Broaden your horizons.'

'Strange times, I'm telling you. Everyone's on edge.' There was a long pause and I thought I'd lost the connection. 'There's a bad feeling in the air. A pair of Paki kids were beaten up in Hammersmith last night.'

'Rob, I'm asking you to go to Bethnal Green, not Saudi Arabia.'

'That's you speaking from your southern metropolis, is it? They'd report it in the *Evening Post* if a Muslim arrived in Wellington. I'll check on your boy tomorrow, right? I'll take him out for breakfast. You know he's just sleeping, don't you?'

'Could well be.'

We both fell silent. A campervan grumbled past on the road, a Harley Davidson, a Toyota ute.

'D'you know anyone in New York?' Rob asked.

'Not really,' I said. 'Friends of friends. But Moira's friend is a lawyer in Washington, DC. She reckons they'll be running the airports like a police state now. Random searches, detention without charge.'

'Well, of course they will. What else would they do? Look, you'd be grateful if that was you getting on a plane at JFK.'

'Unless, of course, you were the one being detained.'

'Detained for what?'

'Well, precisely. Having the wrong accent, the wrong passport, the wrong friends.' The wrong skin colour, the features a shade too Middle Eastern, dear god, don't let Aaron get it in his head to pass through the US anytime soon.

'You're living in a bubble, Pete. You're speaking in complete theoreticals. Scotland Yard is now saying these Al-Qaeda have cells in Birmingham and Leeds. *Birmingham.* You think about sending your kids on the Tube to school everyday with Alfuckingqaeda running training schools just a few hours upcountry.'

I'd felt sick, sick at heart, sick all night and all the following day, after Aaron woke me at 2am to tell me. But I watched Aaron grow excitable, go out drinking with his friends and come back to the hospice full of theories. The CIA-trained Bin Laden in Afghanistan. They funded the *mujahideen* in the first place. I heard something in his tone that could only be called glee. It was the same glee that came through from the online commentary in the

Guardian. America's hubris. Reap the whirlwind. *Had it coming.* When Aaron quoted me some statistic about more people dying in the Six-Day War than in the towers, I wanted to say, each death is immeasurable. No, I just wanted to shake him. This is not a gift to you, I wanted to say. This is not a spectacle.

'I'll be out of range for a day.' I checked my watch, counted hours back and forth. 'You won't be able to get hold of me.'

'Won't need to,' said Rob. 'Your boy can report back to you. I'll take him over to Borough Market, get black pudding, bacon and eggs into him. Uncle Rob's special. Best thing for the jetlag.'

I had a vision of Aaron leaning his mouth into a bacon butty under the shadow of Southwark Cathedral, and the relief in my shoulders was palpable. Rob hates, above all things, to feel useless. But this thing, this he can do.

'D'you reckon you'd pick him up a new phone?' I asked. 'Put some credit on it?'

'Done and dusted. Leave it with me.'

When the bobby came to our door in London in 1971, I'd walked calmly to Clare's room and helped her out the window and down the fire escape. I don't remember feeling afraid. I heard the cop downstairs asking Rob if he supported terrorists.

Would we have used that word? Clare was certainly excited about the Angry Brigade, and as each new bomb went off that autumn—at the Miss World competition at Biba, at the houses of cabinet ministers—our flat would be full of heated argument, and she would always defend their actions. I suspected, and I still suspect, that some of the more serious and quiet politicos who used to come to our flat late at night were actively involved.

In April, after the bomb went off at the Home Secretary's house, Clare made a poster on a sheet of yellow cardboard, with a long quote from Raoul Vaneigem written in block capitals, and pinned it up on the inside door of the toilet, which made for a point of brightness in a cold basement room where the window was permanently wedged open. I must have read it over a hundred times. 'The point here is not to make an apology for terrorism, but to recognise it as an action— the most pitiful action and at the same time the most noble—which is capable of disrupting and thus exposing the self-regulating mechanisms of the hierarchical social community. Inscribed in the logic of an unlivable society, murder thus conceived can only appear as the concave form of the *gift*.' In the end I got sick of looking at those words every time I sat on the john, and I took it down and put up a poster of Sonny and Cher.

Last month, on the thirteenth, the fourteenth and the fifteenth of September, I lay awake at night imagining the same thing everyone else imagined: what would I have said to Moira, what would I have said to Aaron, if I had been on that flight, crouching in the toilet, making that phone call? *I love you, I am going to die.* I did love her, and she was going to die. I didn't need planes dropping out of the sky to remember that.

Did Clare's friends set those bombs, at the fashion shop, at the minister's house? I still don't know the truth. We were kids, and we talked all kinds of rubbish. As it turned out, the Angry Brigade were inept, or perplexed, or gentle, or lucky. No one died.

I think actual violence would have been beyond the pale for Clare. Even her conviction for incitement at the Mayday riots was probably unsafe. It wasn't in her blood to fight dirty. Her family were a revelation to me. Liberal intellectuals, deeply enmeshed with the ruling class of England, they were part of the left-wing establishment. Her grandfather was a Lord, wrote books. Her life with Rob has turned out as anyone might have expected, with a large house in Richmond, children educated at private schools. Rob himself was the surprising part of the equation, the no-name boy from the colonies. When we were growing up, Rob's dad was manager of the Tip Top bread factory and had a stint on the Wanganui City Council, which made Rob elite in our neighbourhood. I can't imagine these achievements cut much mustard with the Rochfords of Thames Ditton, and I bet her parents made quiet objections. Clare would have looked them in the eye and then gone ahead and married him.

*

'Pretty spot.'

Hamish the realtor's hair is blowing about in the wind. He looks to have come fresh from sleep, alarmingly bohemian for a Thursday morning in rural Wairarapa.

'I sold a tidy little Lockwood down the road a month ago.'

A yawn ripples under his speech. He leans against his four-wheel drive, squinting into the sun, wearing jeans and an Icebreaker. I am not convinced.

'Based down in Wellington, are you?'

'That's right.'

I flick the latch of the gate open, and allow him to pass through first.

'Come up often?'

Hamish does not have a gift for easy banter.

'No,' I say, 'I don't really. Hence the sale.'

'Tidy little house. Had it long?'

'Twenty years. Go on through,' I say, turning the fat key in the front door. 'Take a look around.'

In the living area, I pull the curtains open and try the sliding doors, which open out onto the big section and the view of the sea. The door hiccups on the runner and stops, stuck. Hamish moves through the rooms making his calculations, while I shunt the door back and forth on its runner. When at last I jerk it open, the wind rushes in. Streamers of cobwebs wave in the eaves.

'This is what'll sell it,' Hamish says, stopping in front of the open door and looking out at the great scoop of the bay between Castle Rock and the lighthouse. 'Huge section, and the view.'

His left hand comes up to shade his eyes. But I'm staring at his right arm hanging down at his side now, because— *how did I not notice this immediately?*—there's no hand. The sleeve cuff is empty.

'Ah, yeah.' He lifts up the bung arm level with his shoulder. Halfway between elbow and wrist, the grey merino sleeve flops down. Hamish squeezes the gap with his other hand. 'That's right, I'm a one-armed bandit.'

'I didn't mean to—'

'Old joke,' he says. 'Don't worry. I used to be in forestry. Had to give that up, so now this.'

It's impossible not to wince. A chainsaw, a chipper? I really don't want to know, but there's a glint in Hamish's eye, as though he'd like to give me the full story, see if he can make the townie blanch.

'Well, real estate's a good wicket,' I say. 'And safe.'

And with that, we seem to have made friends. We step down together onto the section. There should obviously be decking here, outside these doors, and I do think it's a shame we never built it.

'How're the neighbours?' He hikes off down the sloping

section to the fence on the southern boundary and peers over.

'We see a couple of horses from time to time. Grazing land. Must belong to someone.'

'Yeah?' He clicks his tongue and shakes his head. 'Gee, you didn't try and buy it?'

'No, not really.'

He whistles. 'It would've made for a very tidy package, the two properties.' He keeps his arms crossed.

'Why don't you find out if it's available, then? Make a selling point out of it.'

He frowns. 'Sure, mate.'

But no one wants to be told how to do their job.

'You going to show me the shed?'

Moira called it a studio. It sits near the fenceline in the southwest corner, and has housed, over the years, all the crud that came out with us and never made it back. She organised it as a place to paint some years back, and got me to put a window in and make some minor repairs to the roof. Last time I looked, which was probably a few years ago, the detritus of the beach house, the golf clubs and bikes, the old toastie sandwich maker and piles of *Listener*s had started to take over again, and Moira's painting equipment was hemmed into a small corner.

'There's not much to see. It's full of junk.'

'No problem. I'll just get an idea.'

But in fact, the studio floor is bare and wide and the light rushes in to fill it. Our old furniture and broken toys have been stacked up in the corner and draped over with a white sheet. There's a single canvas, three feet high, propped up on the easel in the middle of the room. We are both arrested.

The painting is of a nude man sitting in a white wicker chair. The skin is pink around the face, yellowish-white

116

on the body. He is posed with one ankle propped up on his knee, his groin exposed, purple cock dropping over the bundle of the testicles. There are the rose-marks of his nipples, a pelt of black chest hair, a mound of weight on the stomach. He rests his hands squarely on his thighs and gazes out, confident, confrontational, this man with a full head of grey hair, dark drooping eyes and thin lips. My face, I think: this is me.

'Bit of an eyeful.' Hamish stays at a distance.

'My wife'—I crouch down, look in at the picture, try to make sure, to verify, but at short range the image dissolves into streaks and I cannot make it out—'painted.'

'This?'

'Yes,' I say, standing up. 'It would seem so.'

The background looks like the sitting room of the bach: the blank white wall, polished floorboards. The wicker chair the figure is seated in comes from our bedroom.

'Starkers, eh?' Hamish steps forward. 'You'd want a sunny day for that.'

But I never sat for this painting. I'm almost certain that I've never sat around naked in the bach. And when I look closer, it dissolves into a stranger, some other man. I have no idea who this is.

The painting is neither romantic nor erotic, nor crude. Hamish has, in fact, selected the right word: *stark*. Here it is, the wretchedness and glory of the body, a bald scoop of hip and balls, a pattern of veins raised in the hand, the comedy of grey hair at the ears. He will cross the waters in this skin, aching, eating, fucking, sleeping, raging on. This is the man, halfway through. Hamish slides his eyes between the painting and my face. He looks at me and grins.

'Did she do you justice?'

Of course it's me. Who else could it be?

'So as you can see,' I say, pushing the door open, 'it's just a shed.'

Hamish takes the cue, and we step out. I tug out a clump of ragwort beside the door before bolting it shut and seeing him off the property.

*

Two years ago, Moira and I took our first, our only, kayaking trip. It was Moira's idea. She bought maps of Pelorus Sound and waved pamphlets around in the kitchen.

'They hire SeaBear, Norski and Southern Light,' she said. 'What do you think the difference is?'

I'd been running on adrenaline at work for weeks and months, caught up in a file that kept delivering surprises. It was work that I loved: representing one of the good guys, a zippy new company who were making a fortune in data-mining until they crashed into the Privacy Commission; a knotty, intellectually complex set of problems; a team of super-smart young solicitors to busy at it with. I'd hoped it would be wrapped up by Christmas. Waitangi Day came and went and we were still at it. By March, everyone was starting to droop. I developed a shooting pain in my neck. Moira massaged my shoulders, said if I didn't have a holiday soon I'd be risking my health.

'It'll be peaceful,' she said. 'And great exercise.'

I foresaw rain, headwinds, damp sleeping bags, meals of surprise peas and instant mashed potatoes, and forced chumminess with Scandinavians who would be paddling themselves to Nelson and back.

'I'm too old,' I groaned. 'What about a nice B&B in Martinborough?'

She pressed her fingers in circles at my temples. Moira rarely went at an argument directly. Her modus operandi was to pretend she didn't care that much. When she wanted something and risked not getting it, a slight, almost imperceptible layer of lightness would be added to her words, gestures, movements. I think perhaps she infinitely deferred disappointment in me by simply refusing to feel it. Moira knew how to protect herself in very practical ways. When necessary, she placed herself like a piece of china on a shelf just slightly out of reach.

We took the trip at Easter, the full moon high over the ferry as we nosed past Allports Island and in to Picton. The weather stayed clear, and there were no Scandinavians, not another soul in the trinity of sea, sky and peninsula that we inhabited for those three days. We paddled from bay to bay inscribing a small loop around one inlet of the Sound. At each night's camp we could see a clear line back to the place we had come from. The morning started with blue light and birdsong, standing barefoot on the damp grass with dark hills sentinel around us. We drank our coffee huddled in jackets. The light came on by gradations, and when the sun licked yellow over the sea and the bush divided into its many greens, we buckled the hatches down and pushed the boats out. For hour upon hour, I had Moira's head and torso in view in the front seat of the kayak, her red lifejacket, the hair at the back of her neck scooped up into her khaki cap. She steered, while I did the grunt work in the back.

'They call them divorce canoes,' she laughed.

But we didn't quarrel. In fact the days on water seemed like a microcosm of our marriage at its best. We were our easy selves, the tasks parcelled out and completed in rhythm. All we had to do each day was shift ourselves and all our small cargo across the waterway. We moved in lockstep from waking to sleep. Our arms grew sore, we were a little sunburnt, the bag of pistachios fell in the water, the wind came up and we had to knuckle into it for an hour: these small problems made us happy. We talked, but not much, and even in that wide empty place we had our way of drawing a veil over what each of us held private. That has always seemed to me one of the commendable things about our life together.

On the last day we ate at a rocky beach with the boats drawn up on a thin wedge of sand. There were seals in the water, their black whiskery snouts breaking the surface to consider us in our wetskirts and lifejackets, our peanut butter sandwiches. A pair of oystercatchers emerged from the bush and started to patrol around our kayaks.

'What about animals?' I asked. 'Would you ever paint animals?'

She laughed. 'I could work the dog shows. Nice little business. Captive market.'

'Could be great. You'd make a bit, doing that. But no, I was thinking of Don Binney and his birds. Gauguin, all those horses and dogs.'

She shrugged. 'It's not really a subject for me.'

'Go back to landscapes.' I waved my arm around. 'You were great at that.'

'It bores me,' she said. 'Empty landscapes.'

'But people,' I said. 'The human figure.'

'Yes. That's what I do. That's all I want to do.'

One of the birds was repeating its keening cry, over and over. I wondered if we had stumbled into their nesting area.

'You're very clear-headed about your painting. I really don't understand why you're not at school.'

For years she had been floating the notion of going to art school, but without ever actually applying. Her dithering drove me batty.

She threw a crust out.

'I'd have to give up the Orpheus. And my Tuesday lunches with the girls.'

120

I pulled a face at her. 'You can't be serious. That's not the reason.'

She picked up a stick and started scratching at a rock with it.

'You know how I am,' she said. 'I paint for myself. I couldn't bear to be around all those kids, eighteen and brilliant, reading French theory and falling over themselves to impress people.'

'Eighteen and brilliant?'

It wasn't worth fighting over. We boiled water for tea, and I broke a bar of chocolate into a dozen squares. When the seals disappeared around the corner, I stood up. The clouds were starting to come over, and it was time to paddle the final stretch back to the dock at Elaine Bay.

*

My body and face, some representation of it, painted from memory. Is it possible for a painter to do that? And how long ago? Her last visit to the bach was in April, a crystalline week in early autumn. The oncologist had offered a final course of treatment, but by then our hopes had started to feel fragile. Moira had wanted a few days alone. Time she needed, I presumed, for an inner reckoning.

She usually chatted away to me about her projects, brought finished pieces back to show me, asked my opinion. I have never known her to paint a nude, male or female. This, she kept secret. Too difficult to speak of, perhaps, and best left to speak for itself, eloquent and complete, now that she is no longer here to defend it. Would I have objected? I like to think not, but perhaps she knew me better than to ask.

The first weekend we ever stayed at the bach, twenty years ago, old friends of Moira's came to join us with their

121

boys, five and seven, whippet-thin and scarpering over the rocks as we walked up to the lighthouse in the wind, half demented by the expanse of things, and all of us calling, constantly reining them in, fearful for their rocketing bodies and scattered sense up there on the rim of cliffs. The old Māori name for the place means sky of racing clouds, which is about right. The weather station here records the highest wind speeds in the country. It was always gusting out there on the beach in those early holidays, the exhaustion of being out in it, the kids screaming whenever the sand blew into their eyes.

We probably should have bought property over on the other coast, Waikanae or Otaki, to be honest. When a southerly kicks in on that side of the island, it gets cold and the rain pelts, but there's the entire Wellington headland buttressed against it. At Castlepoint, there's nothing. If you take a ruler and draw a line on the map from the lighthouse due south, the first land your pen will hit is the Ross Ice Shelf. We've had more than a couple of nights when we've been kept awake with a very real fear that the roof will blow off.

Aaron was almost five that first weekend we came, well past toddling, but Moira would not let me put him down although he writhed and whinged. I carried him all the way up the steps, while the older boys swooped in and pecked at his nose, and brought him stones to play with. By the time we came in at sunset, he was drunk with love, refusing to eat or bathe or play unless one of the older boys was nearby. When he turned his wide, smeary grin on them, they were smitten, and we left all three asleep in a single bed in the back room, limbs entangled.

That night, and every time we stayed, Moira left the blinds in the bedroom open. The lighthouse beam lashed over us all night. We still hoped, at that time, to fall pregnant. Possibility hovered over us each time we made love. The light beam itself, stroking her skin, might have been some sort of impregnating god, a visitation.

It wasn't clear why we were having such trouble. Moira, obviously, had conceived before, although perhaps that too had been the work of a shapeshifting god. Aaron's father left almost no trace of his identity.

Aaron had just started school when Moira sat him up on the kitchen bench in the middle of preparing dinner and started to tell him that while in most cases Dad and Mum make the baby together, in his case that wasn't true.

'Moira?' I said. 'Is this wise?'

She charged on. His dad was different—yes, I think she used that loaded, clingy, sappy word—his was a *special* kind of dad.

I was washing lettuce in the sink, appalled at the initiative she was taking without warning. I flicked water from my hands and looked up to brown eyes, staring at me, oblivious to his mother who added phrase after phrase. *Love*, she repeated, *love you, love you,* pouring the word out in absurd quantities.

'. . . so much, Aaron,' she finished, 'Daddy and me, both.'

I came across and lifted him up to me. He pressed his hands to my chest and pegged himself outwards so he could keep looking at my face. He ran his fingers through the thick of my beard, considering.

'Did Grandad do it?'

'Do what, son?'

'Help Mum make me?'

I could feel Moira's anxiety boiling out across the room.

'Not your Grandad.'

He understood this much then: a male of some sort was responsible. I took a deep breath, decided to give him something concrete.

'It was a man called Mark.' That was all we knew. All I knew.

'Mark.' He was concentrating hard.

'But I'm your dad, Aaron,' I said. 'We're just your same old Mum and Dad.'

'Philip says I got born in a jungle.'

'Philip says what? Who is Philip?'

'His kindy friend,' Moira said quietly.

'And what exactly does Philip say?'

'My dad must be a boonga and I got born in a jungle.'

'You were born in the Hutt Hospital,' I said firmly. 'We wrapped you up in a blanket and brought you home.'

'I don't want to go to a different house.'

'You don't have to,' I said. 'Nothing's changed.'

I had never intended to lie about Aaron, but I didn't realise, until he was born, just how obvious it would be that he wasn't my biological child. When my parents first laid eyes on him, they resorted to an extreme version of their natural politeness and refused to notice the colour of his skin for two months. They meant it kindly, but it was an alarming revelation of their limitations. Claudia, on the other hand, yelped.

'Black as the ace of spades!' she said. 'Did you not think to give us a bit more warning, Moira?'

She collected him up in her arms, inspected his ears, fingers, toes, the healing stub of his navel.

'He's perfect,' she pronounced. 'He's our own little man.'

But where do any of us come from? Histories that branch back along two, then four, then eight lines, then sixteen lines.

Claudia's grandfather was a Tipperary labourer who

124

joined the goldrush to Perth at the age of seventeen. He crossed the Tasman to Westport, married the half-Jewish barmaid at the local watering hole and fathered eight children upon her in quick succession. The eldest of these was Claudia's mother, who comes across in the family stories as a steely-minded social climber. She trained as a teacher, moved to the east coast, married out of her class and worked hard to eliminate all marks of where she'd come from. Her husband traced his lineage from the *Randolph*, one of the first four ships of Canterbury settlers that arrived in the South Island in 1850. Claudia and her sisters were brought up Anglican and sent to private boarding schools in Christchurch.

My father grew up thinking of himself as Scottish. His lot—highland shepherds to start off with, probably—lived just north of the border in Berwick. His grandparents came out under the shadow of some kind of financial disgrace, with Dad's father a six-year-old boy at the time, lucky, from the sound of it, to survive a bad journey with sickness running rife onboard the ship.

Mum's father had roots in Ulster. His father, one Samuel Mason, came out as a teenager with the British army and fought in the Waikato under Cameron. He was shot at, but survived, and when the war ended George Grey awarded him land near Cambridge. My grandfather was born to Samuel late, when he was pushing fifty, and by a second wife. After Samuel's death, the land and the wealth from the farm all went to the first family. My mother, who thinks of herself as fallen gentry, more or less, still speaks bitterly about the Cambridge cousins. 'That farm should have been fairly split,' she says. 'It was outright theft.'

All these details that I know about my family and about Moira's, what does it add up to? Data, anecdotes, false nostalgia. Mostly, in these parts, we forget about the past and get on with it, the here and now. Which seems sensible, and for this I am basically grateful. Samuel Mason's relatives back in Ulster are no doubt still marching on the Twelfth, whipping themselves into a frenzy of patriotism over the Battle of the Boyne. What use is it really to linger on victories, old injuries?

When Aaron as a teenager heard about the family grievance in Cambridge, he pointed out that the family land had been taken from Tainui only two generations previously, a small part of the three million acres in the Waikato confiscated in the wake of the war. It's an irony which I hadn't thought of, and which I now consider pointing out to my mother whenever the complaint arises. But I know she wouldn't have a bar of that line of thinking.

Her dad ended up working on the railways and married a Galway girl from Wanganui. Mum was the first baby to be born at the new maternity ward in Palmerston North.

The DNA was for fair skin on all sides. And then Aaron showed up.

I guessed him Spanish when he was a child, or Filipino. Then, as his face filled out in adolescence, somewhere closer to home, a boy from the South Pacific; but the more I peered at him, the less I could see. Generally, he's taken to be Māori. His eyes could be his mother's—moist, darkest brown—and his height comes from her side too, but his skin, the planes of his cheekbones, some parts of his personality and intelligence—his extraordinary memory, for instance—come from a man who has no idea at all what he has given, what he has made.

Six weeks before I met Moira, before we were any kind of item, she went to Perth for her first holiday abroad in the company of a girlfriend, and came back pregnant.

Surely he had left some clue, I asked her? She insisted that she had no real memory of the man's face, although

126

they had talked for a long time in the bar. He was a joker. He'd had her in stitches with stories of small towns in the north where he'd worked as a schoolteacher. He'd read her palm, cupped her hand in his, kissed the pad of each finger in turn. After this, her narrative became vague, ending in the morning with a wiry old farmer yelling at them to get their clothes on and get the fuck out of the back of his ute. The man had a trace of an accent, she said, and she'd thought he might have been South American. His first name, Mark, that single drumbeat syllable, common as sparrows, gave nothing away.

Mistakes happen, and yet the profound muddle in her head suggests to me that Moira must have become vacuously drunk, to the point that her consent could not possibly have been a clear matter.

In any case, by the time he arrived the baby was long awaited, and wanted, utterly. For years we hoped for more children. I pictured three or four, enough seats around the table to make me feel like a real *paterfamilias*. As a child I had been tremendously jealous of all my friends with siblings, four brothers and a sister in the case of Tommy who lived two doors down. His family more or less adopted me as a seventh. That kind of abundance has always seemed beautiful to me. But by the time Aaron was starting school, it was becoming clear that he would be our only one.

I'm not sure how even our closest friends understood our family. But how does one see anybody else's marriage, or children?

Moira's mother construed me as a magnanimous rescuer, as a man who, having made a single grand gesture, might expect to sit back and be thanked at regular intervals. For the first few years, she showered Moira with anxious messages to the effect that she should 'look after me' and 'not push her luck'. Claudia told her off, for instance, about the Saturdays when I took care of toddling Aaron while she went off to paint, or took a walk up Mount Kaukau. Moira and I laughed at all this; laughter was my way of assuring us both that there was nothing fragile or exhaustible about my commitment. It wasn't just Claudia. When I walked out with Aaron in the city, strangers—older couples—gave me a particular look, sometimes a nod, which I learnt to anticipate. Once I was sitting on a park bench in the Botanic Garden watching Aaron, maybe five, chasing and feeding crusts to the moulty ducks in the duck pond, when an older lady in a knee-length blue coat and heels handed him a peach, and said to me, *sotto voce*, that she had 'fostered children myself ten years ago'. She watched him entice a duck into gobbling a piece of bread from his palm and said, 'They come on so nicely once they're given a bit of stability.'

So that was there each time we went out to face the world, a fundamental presumption that I was doing some kind of loving charity to the child. I bridled and, with the exception of the duck pond lady, rarely bothered to explain myself and Aaron. But if I'm honest, I would say that an unguarded part of myself fell slightly in love with this idea, right from the early days, when I pushed the baby pram around the hills early in the morning so Moira could get an extra hour of sleep. I allowed myself the extra shimmer of nobility. I think it's fair to say I was rewarded, praised, applauded, more than most fathers.

Stella, Moira's sister who now works as a doctor in Seattle, was an involved aunt through Aaron's childhood. He used to stay with her in the school holidays; she must have been barely twenty at the time. She was living in a shared flat in Ponsonby, in her first year at med school. It's a little surprising now to think that we trusted him to her, young as he was, but I suppose we thought they were sensible types, those doctors-in-training. There's only twelve years between Stella and Aaron, and they've stayed close. He came home from Auckland once with a clutch of Polaroids that Stella and her friend Sangeeta had taken of the three of them at Takapuna Beach, and I remember thinking that he looked like the little brother of the group, getting his bunny-eared fingers into the frame, pulling faces.

Stella got married, and eventually moved with her husband to Washington State. Her interest and energy for Aaron fell away, as is natural enough. Her connection with Moira seemed to weaken too. There were ten years between them, and sometimes it felt like more. When I saw Stella at the funeral, it was the first time in years that I'd spoken to her.

I've wondered sometimes if she knows more than she let on. Stella was just a kid when Aaron was born, in standard six, wearing her too-big uniform at the private girls' school in Woburn which Claudia and Maurice sent their daughters to. Stella and Sangeeta were always swirling in and out of the driveway on their Raleigh Twentys whenever we'd come to visit, then they'd run inside and beg to hold the baby for a bit. There was a fair bit of whispering and giggling. God knows what Stella made of me in those days: not quite a husband to her sister, not quite a father to her nephew. On the day we made it legal at the registry office, Stella held the bunch of wilting irises, and got down on her hands and kness to follow crawling Aaron around on the floor of the restaurant afterwards, fishing objects out of his mouth, while Moira, for once, had a few champagnes and let someone else mind the baby.

*

Aaron was born five weeks early, but he was a surprisingly good weight and a capable feeder. The midwives were delighted, and Moira seemed to know exactly what to do. I watched her slip out of bed to his side before I even heard his cry.

She took him everywhere with her, wheeled him in his pram to the back of the flat when she hung out the washing, saying that he could do with the sunshine on his skin. He was five weeks old before she ventured out of the house alone; when she returned, and heard him grizzling lightly in his cot, she dropped her coat where she stood and rushed through, plucking him out and whispering apologies.

A week later, she left him with me once again while she went to the doctor. He cried hard, his tiny body stiff with rage. I drew a bath and got in, swaying him back and forth in the water.

In the steamy bathroom, clutching a fat slippery eel of an infant, I experienced a queasy overlap of time past and time present. I held his head out of the water with one hand, my finger pressed into the folds of his neck, and tapped at the bones of his chest.

'He had a bath last night.'

I startled. Moira was in the doorway.

'I know,' I said. 'But it calms him down.'

'So does walking,' she said. 'Why didn't you take him out in the pram?'

'It's cold outside. And I wanted a bath. Is there a problem?'

She reached out for Aaron. I released him, and she lifted him up and nuzzled the crown of his head.

'You should use the baby bath,' she said. 'And you shouldn't get in. What if you lost your hold on him?'

I sank back, letting my knees fall open. Moira reached for a towel and wrapped it around him.

'Peter, how long have you had him in there?' Her voice was light, but there was something forced in it. 'His skin is all wrinkled.'

'It's *water*,' I said, sitting up, sloshing water over the sides. 'For God's sake, Moira, you're acting like an Elizabethan with a morbid fear of washing. Pass the boy here, and get in with me yourself. Go on, I'll run some more hot water.'

She frowned, bent down with the baby balanced awkwardly on her hip, and picked up the talcum powder from under the sink.

'Where are his clothes?'

'In the hall,' I said. 'On the floor.'

'How long did he sleep?'

'He didn't,' I said. 'He was bawling.'

'You didn't even try?'

'He gave a good impression of being tortured by the KGB. Hence the bath. I do have some idea what I'm doing, you know.'

'How?'

'I took care of Abigail,' I said, 'a great deal.'

'That was different,' she said.

I had given few details to Moira about that time. I hardly ever had a reason to say Abigail's name aloud.

'*How* exactly do you suppose it was different?' I said

'You were living on a houseboat. You told me it was chaotic, people were stoned all the time. Did you even have a bath?'

'We had a shower and a bucket,' I said, 'and we didn't find it such a drama to use it.'

'I'm trying to keep him in a routine. You know that.'

'Fine,' I said. 'Do it your way.' I draped the streaming facecloth over my forehead. 'He's your son.'

Moira left the room, curtly shut the door after her, and

131

my stomach lurched with regret. I wrapped a towel around my waist and followed. She had the baby down on the floor in the lounge and was sprinkling him haphazardly with the powder, as though shaking icing sugar onto a cake.

'I'm sorry,' I said. 'That was unfair.'

'Who the hell are you, if you're not his father?'

Her face flushed red, furious, close to tears. I knelt down beside her and rubbed her shoulders.

'I'm trying to do the best thing for him,' she continued. 'I'm doing my best. I don't always know what's right, but I'm trying.'

I coiled my arms around her and squeezed, agreeing over and over again, *Yes, you are doing your best.* The essential thing was to keep out of the way. Whatever teaching, hormone or evolutionary tic had given her this energy for him, I wanted it to carry on its work undisturbed. She was tired, she was a little overwhelmed, but she was entirely focussed on the baby and it was a relief to see her take charge of his needs.

*

The few short weeks of Abigail's infancy were a churn of worry, exhaustion, rage. Geneviève did not take to it, to any of it. It was as if something had snapped in her.

Through late pregnancy she had grown radiant, her movements slow and languid. She floated around the boat in long cotton dresses at the dog-day end of summer, gravid and reading novels, Voltaire, Tolstoy, Camus. Her wide figure became a sort of political mascot on the boat, because we found that we couldn't talk in entirely abstract ways about the futures we predicted for the world without imagining this particular person who would inherit it. We talked as though the baby would belong, in a sense, to everyone: Clare, Rob, the seven of us who lived on the

Lychorida, our friends, our entire generation. We had broken the prison of the nuclear family.

'My father says a woman on her own with a child is like a roof with holes.'

Geneviève was reading a letter from home.

'You're not on your own.'

'Papa thinks I am. In his eyes.'

I understood what she was saying. I was a boy her father had never met, who came from a spit of land on the far side of the world. I wasn't French, I wasn't Catholic, I wasn't married to her. I didn't have any money, or the kind of family name that counted in these parts of the world. We didn't care about any of it.

Geneviève was particularly beautiful in that time, her face full, her hair lush, and not just to me, either. She had always attracted people, and now both men and women drew near to her, fell all over themselves to perform small acts of service for her. Her Parisian sociologist slunk off, and we didn't see him any longer. I wanted her madly. We had more sex in those final two months of her pregnancy than we'd had in the time since we met. We both felt optimistic, drunk on our powers. The child validated everything: our love, our life on the boat, the revolution in values we were attempting to live.

Birth shocked her. In retrospect, I don't understand why we weren't in a hospital. We didn't even have electricity on the boat. The way she looked at me after it was all done. She lay on her side and wept. It took hours until she was capable of holding the baby, and then the midwife left, and there we were with this vast responsibility, and I think suddenly we both felt like children, a long way from home.

*

It would be fair to say that my wife didn't have the easiest of personalities. There was, very often, a picky, anxious edge to her mood. *You're like a bear with a sore head*, she'd say to Aaron as he sulked and stormed through adolescence, but the truth was she glowered around the house just as often. Her irritation came on strongly when she was painting, or getting ready to paint, but those weren't the only times. In that mood, she'd snap at me for tiny things, going through the grocery bags with a view to finding fault: why did you buy the red cod, you know the blue cod tastes better. A tray of twenty eggs, what on earth do we need twenty eggs for? *They were just fucking cheaper.* It was wearying, but I didn't take the bait. I could sometimes soothe her by rubbing her shoulders, or wrapping my arms around her. Once in a while she would apologise. That was always gratifying.

Well, we all get tightly wound at times, there's nothing unusual about that. With Moira, it felt as though there was an ongoing busy churn in her mind, a preoccupation that kept the pressure on even when I thought she might finally relax. She worried constantly about Aaron. *Do you think he's all right? Do you think he's happy?* At times he was, and of course, at times he wasn't, but Moira's fretfulness was always there, clouding the air.

I don't truly understand what drove it. I've wondered if it was some doubt about *me* that kept her on edge. As if she couldn't quite bring herself to trust that the bond we'd forged would hold, even when all the evidence suggested we were a permanent couple: our names on the joint mortgage; pleasure in one another's company; desire, and cheerful, warm sex as often as we both wanted.

She told me once or twice about a boyfriend she'd had in secondary school. She had fallen, she said, violently and frighteningly in love, as had he. The affair was clandestine, largely conducted at night, in a music room which they locked themselves into. After several wildly happy and erotic months together he broke it off without warning or reason, the shock of which reduced her, in her own words, into such an abject state that she took to staking out the suburban house where he lived with his parents and sister. Moira had spent a month of winter evenings in her car, parked across the road, watching the figures move behind the curtains, and the lights turning on and off in the rooms as the family moved around the house and prepared for bed. She had imagined herself bursting through the front door, shouting insults at this boy in front of everyone. She had imagined smashing his bedroom window with a rock. Some nights she sat, wrapped in a blanket, listening beneath his window while he practised piano. *Look at me*, she wanted to scream into the darkness, *can't you see me.* Surely he would come outside and cross the road, she thought, surely he would notice the same car parked there every night. But he never did.

I wondered about Moira telling me this story. Her aching girlhood self crouched beneath that window with the piano notes playing in the dark. I heard in it a cry for reassurance: Peter, tell me you'll stay. Tell me you're not that kind of man.

*

Castle Rock rears up, a hundred-foot-high chunk of geological uplift, grassy steep ascent on one side, crumbling sandstone cliffs sheer down to the sea on the other. I haven't climbed it in years but I have an urge to get up to the top today, before leaving. The path across the farmland inscribes a long flat semicircle above the beach. The white and purple daisies run wild at this time of year, and the yellow lupins are giving off their heady smell in the morning heat.

At the base of the hill the going gets tougher. It's a fifty-degree, maybe sixty, incline, trudging the steps cut by footfall into the clay. Orpheus, scrambling up wet rock and sodden earth, breathing hard on the steep slopes, the air foul and thick. Did the journey take hours or days? Somewhere, in any case, the path at last broaden out, grey light pricking at the eyeballs. There is a whiff of grass and sea, birdsong. An hour later, or a minute, he sees it, broad day, forcing in through a shaft above.

The thrill of that, the relief, the thing so nearly achieved. What a man. What a hero. He must have had that feeling, pride: how could he not, to have descended that far— *She's gone so quiet, no footsteps, no breath?*—to have melted their hearts, and led her back step by step—*Has she tripped?*—to have brought her this far, just a few steps now from the light—*Ah, there you are, my love.*

If you asked me what it feels like, now that she's gone, I'd say the feeling is closest to fear. That's unexpected. After all, what do I have to fear now? But it boils in my stomach in exactly that way. There have been moments when her voice and face have been so definite, so present, have felt so completely to have come from outside and not of my own manufacturing that electricity has shot through me like an alarm: *she's here, she's here!*

In the first few weeks she flashed through me, irritable or calm, busy or quiet, always unpredictable. That's calcifying now. In the dim light before dawn this morning I lay in my sleeping bag on the couch, and tried to remember how she looked when she was amused by something. I couldn't quite get the shape of her mouth.

The pressure of her head against my collarbone in bed. The high notes of her laughter. I'm not sure I do remember, not exactly.

Scraps of sound, a dog barking below on the sands, a seagull shrieking.

Your face, Eurydice.

Fweeeet.

But she's gone.

Philip says I got born in a jungle. There were a few conversations with Aaron around that time, after which his curiosity seemed to fade away. Was he satisfied, or did he just suppress the questions? I had no answers, so for my part I saw no point in keeping on bringing it up. *You are who you are.* That was my line, and I said it often down the years.

Aaron had been an awkward, slightly lonely kid at eleven and twelve. In his first term at Rongotai College, he fell in with a bunch of Pacific Island kids. Moira and I watched him reinvent himself, changing his way of speaking, his demeanour, his musical tastes. He grew to be completely at ease with those boys, going to their houses, bringing them back to ours. On the whole we thought they were good kids, and we were pleased to see him happy and fitting in. I couldn't even tell you exactly where some of them came from. There were a bunch of Tongan kids. The Lemalu twins are Samoan, and Tama's a Māori boy from the Waikato.

It was a real treat to meet up with those boys again at the funeral. I'm glad he keeps up with them. They've stuck by him, they truly have. That girl he's been seeing, Akenese, perhaps she's a sister or a cousin of one of them.

Once, when Aaron was mooching around on the trampoline with some of those school mates, I was up at the top of the garden trimming the yellow rosebush. I heard his voice drift up, *Yeah, my real dad's Rarotongan.* I didn't know, I still don't, whether Moira had told him more than she'd told me, whether he'd arrived at that conclusion on his own, whether it was just pure, urgent invention. In any case, watching him latch on to those boys just as he was growing into manhood was enough to put my questions to rest.

By the time I get down off the hill, the sun is low in the sky. It takes an hour to drive back up to Masterton from the beach, the road cutting up through the river valley. The poplars are silver in the late breeze and the paddocks a hot green, soil drenched with the late spring wet. The lambs are fat, those that have survived the first kill. Beside each farm is a blossom tree, a magnolia, a scatter of daffodils.

Halfway up the valley, a low, constant hum starts up from the boot of the car. A few kilometres on it turns into a terrific rattle. I've stashed Moira's portrait back there, wrapped in a white sheet like the victim of a crime, pouches, skin-blotches and all. Something mechanical has come loose and I need to get it seen to. The man in the painting is trying to tap a message out. Both things true at once, I guess.

Two kilometres north of Carterton, a text pings in. It's Rob: *Call me.*

It will be early morning at Borough Market. Fish in ice buckets, glassy-eyed. Venison, vegetables, artisan sourdough. I suppose they'll Tube it over to London Bridge, unless Rob has picked him up in the car.

I pull over outside a bakery in the township, and hit dial. The sky streaks gold. The boy inside is closing up for the day, pulling out trays of buns and doughnuts.

'Rob's phone.' A woman's voice.

Where to start?

'Clare. It's Peter.'

There's a pause so long that I think we may have been cut off.

'Oh! Rob's not here.'

I haven't spoken with Clare in years. The improbability of it, her voice ricocheting from whatever spot in London she's standing on down to me inside this car, driving through this town I have no reason to be in, except that it's on the way to Wellington.

'Are you with Aaron?' I say. 'Are you at the market?'

I can hear her breathing.

'You haven't spoken to Rob?'

'I've been out of range. Is he with you?'

'Rob went to the East End yesterday. He didn't find Aaron. I'm sorry.'

There's a dullness in the brain, a sense of something sliding off.

'Ah. I see.'

'I should let him talk to you himself.'

Clare, it's me! How many hours, how many days, have we spent together? She was present for Abigail's birth. After everything was over in Amsterdam, we had sex, just once, on the floor at my flat in Earl's Court, when she was only days away from trial for her part in the Mayday riots, and we all thought they would lock her up in Wormwood Scrubs for a decade or more. Rob couldn't handle it and had taken off to Scotland and told her it was all over. I never told him about that time and I bet she didn't either. It was a mistake and a betrayal, an awkward banging down on the beery carpet, and we knew it the minute it was over. We've been polite and careful with each other ever since but I can't forget that afternoon. *I think you are qualified to tell me what you know about Aaron.*

'Out with it,' I say. 'Please?'

'Just. He said there was nothing there.'

139

'Okay. How do you mean?'

'In the flat. There was nothing there. His flatmate—'

'Ahmed, you mean? Pakistani guy?'

'I wasn't with them. Look, Rob's ten minutes away. He's getting his hair cut.'

Deep breath.

'How are you?' I say. 'How are you going anyway, Clare?' Take it one sentence at a time. Keep her talking, keep her on the line.

'I'm actually in the middle of'—she pauses—'right now I'm trying to—'

'Lesbos,' I say. 'You guys got a place, I hear.'

'Oh, it's bliss.'

'Rob mentioned a waitress.'

Which is not what I want to talk about at all.

'Peter, it was uncanny. Her face. Her name was Lisette. She said she was from Toulouse.'

Humming, zinging in my ears, a blood-flush.

'Ha,' I laugh. 'What nostalgic old things we are.'

'I think you should phone this place and ask to speak to that girl.'

'What did she look like? Blond, dark?'

Who did she look like?

There's a long pause.

'Actually don't answer that, Clare. Can we get back to Aaron? What do you mean, *nothing there?*'

'The café was right on the waterfront in Mytilene. I think it was called Kapos. Kipos? You could find a number, I'm sure.'

I hold the phone to my ear with my chin, and turn the car out onto the main street. It doesn't long to get back on the open road, the fields flickering green on either side.

'Do you mean Aaron's stuff was gone, or everything in the house was gone?'

'He must have moved flats, that's all. They seem to want to change everything all the time, don't they? They get bored so easily, the kids. Were we like that?'

We wanted to change everything.

'Come over to Greece. Rob's dying to get you out on a yacht.'

'Ah, well. It's a long way.'

'Go out for a grappa, poke around the ruins. Go on, say you'll come.'

'I'm not sure I'm in the right space, to be honest.'

That shuts her up. Sometimes the psychobabble comes in handy.

'Oh god. I didn't even. Moira. I'm sorry.'

'Yes.'

'Did she suffer badly?'

'Ah, well. Cancer, you know.'

But of course she knows. Her father, five years ago.

'She had a lot of morphine,' I say. 'The nurses were very good. We managed.'

There have been few people I have been able to talk to about Moira's last day. Clare, I suddenly realise, could hear it all.

'Here's Rob now.'

There's a crackle and a shift on the line. Rob gets straight to business, recounting the events of the morning. He'd driven out to Mile End, buzzed on the flat intercom, and a man—Middle Eastern type, friendly enough, could have been Ahmed, he'd missed the name—had let him up to have a look around. There was a great deal of confusion in their conversation because the man had thought Rob wanted to rent the spare room.

'So once he gets what I'm asking, he tells me Aaron comes in last Saturday morning, sleeps all day, goes out all night and turns up looking pretty marginal at sparrow fart on Sunday. They have a chat, right? Your man Ahmed goes off to work, comes back that evening and sees the room is stripped out, few boxes in the corner, and a note saying Aaron'll be back in a couple of days to clear it out. Cheque to cover two weeks' rent, which he was bitching about because the contract said three weeks' notice, and he reckons there are phone bills outstanding, line's been cut off, these sort of problems. I dished him out a bit of cash so that's all sorted.'

'Were the boxes still there?'

'Nah, gone. A couple of days later, just like he said, and he left the key. Your boy's gone and vanished himself fairly properly. He really said nothing to you before leaving?'

'That chat,' I say, 'when Aaron spoke with Ahmed. What was it about?'

'I asked him that. He was vague, you know, noncommittal on the details.'

'I thought they were pretty much friends. Aaron talked about him. Did you get a feeling?'

'He was a bit on the cagey side, but I don't think he knows anything. Probably put the wind up him, an old codger like me showing up and sniffing round.'

'Well, right now this is my last known sighting of him. It would be useful to have some more details.'

'You want me to go back? I can do that.'

'Good god, Rob, what do you *know*? What did Ahmed say?'

'Pete. Settle. Don't lose your grip, mate.'

'You're telling me everything? Honestly?'

'That's all I've got, my friend. Clare's at my elbow here. She wants a word again.'

A crackle, a transfer.

'Peter, I'm sure he's fine. It'll be a misunderstanding, that's all. Try to get some sleep. Where are you right now?'

Out the car window, to the west, the Tararuas are a wall, a blue-grey, rain-drenched mountain range between the two coasts of the island.

'He's twenty-five,' I say. 'No need to panic.'

'You know him best,' she says. 'Is this like him, would you say?'

'It's not unprecedented,' I say. 'We don't always know his plans. Although he's certainly never shifted flat and not told us. Not told Moira, I mean. It was Moira he would mainly speak to. I heard most of his news—'

'Secondhand?' she said.

'Yes. Secondhand would be a fair way to put it.'

'So it's hard to say what the pattern now would be?'

'It is hard to say.'

*

One afternoon in November, after I had been working in the shipyards for six weeks, Hendrik sought me out in the locker room just after we'd knocked off from our shift. The room was steamy and loudly hushed by a dozen showers running, and the lights were burning yellow through the haze. I was taking off my boots, and he sat beside me on the bench, hoisted one foot up, and began to unlace his own.

Abigail could only have been a week old at the time. Clare was back at the boat with her and Geneviève, and I remember wanting to get home to them, to see how they were, to take them milk and food.

'There's five of you living on the *woonboot*, *ja?*' asked Hendrik.

I nodded.

It was bitterly cold, and dark already at four. The days had closed in hard and fast since the start of the month.

'Okay,' said Hendrik.

'You looking for somewhere to live?' I asked.

Hendrik laughed out loud. He pulled off his left boot, set it on the ground, and began unlacing the other.

'*Bent u de baas?*'

'Am I the boss?

'Of the boat? Could you clear it? Be alone there?'

'What for?'

Hendrik pulled up, sniffed, and pulled his fingers over his moustache.

'Small pay here, *ja*?'

I shrugged. 'Pretty average,' I said.

'If ever you need money,' he said, 'and think you can clear the *woonboat* for two days, you tell me.'

I removed my socks, didn't look at him.

'You're talking to the wrong guy.'

'Fine,' he said. 'If you change your mind, you know where I am.'

He pulled his right boot off his foot, unpeeled his socks and tucked them into the shoes, picked both up in one hand, and walked barefoot behind the partition to his locker.

Geneviève's tears had begun the morning of the birth and became constant. She wept in the morning, and in the afternoon, and in the evening. Water pouring down her face. At first, I tried action. I urged her to sit up, to get dressed, to eat and drink, to walk up onto the deck and get sunlight. She managed these things, obediently, but they made little difference.

Clare took charge of everything. She managed washing, food, ointments, made herbal teas, she soothed the baby when it turned red and hard and screamed. The rest of the company on the boat drifted off, or offered the most mild and off-hand interest in what was happening, which was predictable, I suppose. Then Clare had to go back to London.

I remember looking for someone to watch over Abigail one night when Geneviève was asleep, and I wanted to go and buy food. They were drinking up on deck, and finally I realised that the least impaired person was a bearded Irishman who had arrived only days before, whose name I didn't even know. I deposited Abigail in his arms, wrapped up in a heavy blanket, and went out on my bicycle. When I came back, the Irishman had gone off, and the baby had been laid down in a washing basket beside the rubbish bin, her blanket missing. Her skin was cool to the touch, and she was shivering. I understood in that moment that we could not continue to live on the boat, that I had to do something to get us off the *Lychorida*. The city was awash with hippies who now, in the grip of winter, all wanted to get out of the Vondelpark and under shelter. There was a housing crisis in Amsterdam, and no cheap rents to be had anywhere. Out of the central city, in the suburbs of Jordaan and Oud-Zuid, there were tidy houses, leafy streets, with one- and two-bedroom flats going for fifty guilders a week. But my shipyard wage would fall short.

I think it was around this time that I called my father and asked him for money. It was the first time I had done this in the three years I had been away from New Zealand. I knew my parents had little to spare, and that anything they could give me would shrink hopelessly under the exchange rate. I didn't want to bring them shame or anxiety.

My mother had a thousand questions. How is she feeding? What does she weigh? What's her routine? How does she sleep?

Will you send photographs? my father asked.

I told them everything I could about Abigail, editing judiciously.

145

I'll get you something, son, my father said. It'll take me a few weeks, but I'll get you something. Weeks? I said. Really?

I'm sorry, he said. It's the best I can do.

Mary, the girl from San Francisco who lived on Herengracht, used to come down on the days I went to work. She helped with Abigail after Clare left, and we became close again for a while. It was a confusing time. Geneviève was, if anything, getting worse. She wasn't eating well, she had entire days in bed. I thought she would be best to go home, for the meantime, to stay with her parents in Lyon. Geneviève was reluctant. *Don't send me to that house alone.* It was impossible for me to leave Amsterdam, because of the work in the shipyards. I did need to work. That was one thing. I was very concerned about money at that time, about ensuring there was enough money.

From this distance, thirty years later, I could say that I was young, and that I made the best decisions I could. That might even be true.

Then the day before the train, the baby developed a temperature, and Geneviève argued strenuously that she should stay in Amsterdam. But by then there was no choice. I rode the tram with them to Centraal Station, and told her to get a doctor as soon as they arrived. Tell your mother, she needs a doctor, I said. Tell your father. Just get her to a doctor.

I once told Aaron that there had been a child. She was my sister, he said, and I agreed, although I hadn't thought of it that way. He had such a ravenous hunger for family, for more people of his own. He badgered me with questions for weeks, and I found that exhausting. I largely regretted that I had brought it up.

Moira knew the whole story. There were some details

I never went into. She was supportive when I went to visit Geneviève in Lyon in 1989. I appreciated that, and afterwards I was relieved to come back to where she and Aaron were staying in Venice.

I have given them my full concentration, all my love and care, for twenty-five years. That's something to be proud of, I think.

*

I have names but no contact details for Aaron's friends in London. That seems like a fault now, although I'm not sure Moira would know much more if she were here. But there is the flat in Aro Valley, the actors, the girl Akenese. Tama, if I had any way of tracking him down. There's that starfucker Mulholland who gave him a lift to the airport. Each of those people can be tracked down and spoken to. Aaron has told someone what he's doing.

That creamy envelope I had in my pocket at the airport. I should have kept it back from him and read every word.

The known facts are that he has very little money. That his grief, as I have observed it, has not shown up in unpredictable behaviour. If anything, he has seemed steadier in himself. I never saw him hungover in his entire three months with us. He was gracious and cordial with the guests on the day of the funeral, and he seemed to focus, after that, on catching up with old friends. He took our car up to Khandallah several times, where I suppose some buddy from school days must have moved back in with his parents.

The twist down from the summit of the Rimutakas, and then the bouncing foothills. Just past Upper Hutt, a name from the UK swims into mind. Because Aaron has, in fact, done this once before. Shortly after he arrived in England four years ago, long before any of us had mobile phones, he vanished for two weeks and his flatmates didn't know where he'd gone. When he called us at last, he told Moira he'd gone into 'lockdown', that he'd been recovering from a particularly gruelling set of rehearsals, that although he was very sorry we had been worried, we shouldn't have been. He had been holed up out in Essex, in Colchester, staying with a woman in his class whose name was Emily Shelton, or perhaps Emily Skeller, or Emily Keillor. I recall that she was older than Aaron, in her thirties, and that her parents had died in a dreadful car crash and left her the house. The truly salient piece of information was that her father was a Liberal member of the House of Lords, which means, first, that it will be easy to seek her out even with such vague facts, and second, that Clare's family will almost certainly have a connection.

I arrive home in the dark. Inside, the red, blue and white striped bag of Moira's possessions is in the way. For half an hour, I move around it, turning on the lights, shifting the dirty plates and glasses to the sink, crossing between the dining room and the kitchen. I make a cup of tea and slurp it down in front of the television. A BBC correspondent reports from a stretch of desert near the border of Pakistan. There are grey-gold hills in the background and the man's shadow is short on the ground. The US Special Forces are in Kandahar, Afghanistan. An estimated thirty or forty civilians were killed by bombs falling overnight on the village of Chowkar-Karez. A woman has been widowed by the explosion, her six children killed.

Later, I fetch the portrait from the boot of the car, propping it up on a chair, pulling aside the white sheet. It is remarkable, in fact, what Moira has achieved with it. She has produced something that out-punches all her other efforts. The painting makes demands on the viewer. It must have taken the best part of her last energies to complete.

Mozart's Requiem on the stereo. Wine to settle the blood.

I lift Moira's bag to the centre of the room, undo the zip and kneel, penitent, then tip forward, head first.

libera eas de ore leonis
ne absorbeat eas tartarus
ne cadant in obscurum

Deliver them from the mouth of the lion. Each time I rise up for air, I am admonished by the painting, my own face, this hard stare. I am prostrated, I am speaking Moira's name over and over, the incense of her sweat floats up, and if there is any priest, any minister, it is this naked man, myself, watching in judgement, in forgiveness, in mercy.

I cannot bear to have him in the house. Later I will lodge him back in the boot of the car, hide him under the cloth.

May hell not swallow them up. I do not believe in the dead, I do not believe in any place where they reside, I do not believe I can do anything for them, but my prayer goes up anyway: Moira, Geneviève. Abigail. *May they not fall into darkness.*

Aaron. Somewhere on this globe of light. You have my full attention now.

Six

When Aaron was thirteen, we lost him in Venice twice in one day. The day before this happened, I had left the pair of them alone and travelled north by train to France in order to meet with Geneviève. I had not seen her since the time of Abigail's death.

Venice was wet that April, and the sky and sea had stayed hard grey for days. The lobby of the hotel where we were staying in San Zaccaria flooded, and the staff set up a boardwalk from the foot of the steps to the main doors, and swept brackish water out with brooms. Moira, Aaron and I sat on the mezzanine level with coffees and Coke, watching the patrons balance along the board, and it all seemed comic, part of the lovely improbability of the city.

The morning I came back to Italy from Lyon the rain at last let up, the sky was blue, and we went to visit the little Guggenheim art gallery. Moira listened to the commentary through the headphones and considered each picture in turn, while Aaron and I stood in the courtyard watching the boats slide down the Canal Grande. Aaron was young enough to giggle at the erect bronze cock of the naked man on horseback, pointing largely and directly at the water. Moira wandered out and informed us that this piece of the statue was detachable, that, indeed, for many years it had been taken out each Sunday in deference to the Bishop of Venice, whose route to mass at San Marco took him past the statue; these facts Moira relayed to us from behind her headphones, her voice raised a notch more than the usual speaking volume, her hands demonstrating the 'detachable' nature of the object with an unscrewing motion that caused Aaron to stagger off with his head in his hands, his mortification not entirely hammed up, I think. Moira winked at me and went to look at the graves of Peggy Guggenheim's dogs.

On the way back from Lyon I had woken at 3am in the belly of the train, listening to the *clack-clack-clack* of the wheels and the rise and fall of sleepers' breath from the bunks above. I walked down the carriage to wash my face under the cold tap in the toilet, and saw the light cracking over the lake at Stresa.

Moira had met me on the platform at Santa Lucia, put her hands on my cheeks, looked at me rather seriously with her wide brown eyes, and said that I had done a fine thing.

'You don't even know what happened,' I said.

'It was an act of kindness to go.'

I might have felt ashamed when she said that, but I was only relieved to be back with her.

Aaron was ahead of us. He was wearing the white Adidas baseball cap I'd bought him on the way through LAX. He fiddled with it, tipping the brim back, then down, then swivelling it away to one side. He yanked it off, smoothed his hair and placed it back lightly up on the crown, perched like a cockatoo's crest. His walk developed a little groove to go with this look, hands pushed into his pockets so his shoulders hunched up, a tiny, deniable lift of the chin to greet the hawkers, Nigerian or Senegalese, who stood waiting beside their blankets of fake Gucci and Ralph Lauren goods, watching my son walk past with no expression in their eyes.

'Our last day.' I'd smiled at Moira. 'What do you say we go see something a bit more modern?'

It was on the way back from the Guggenheim that Aaron boarded the vaporetto without us. It was early afternoon by the time we recovered him and were accompanied to the police station to fill out forms in triplicate. The senior police officer with silver hair and wire-rimmed glasses scrutinised our passports. *The boy is Moroccan. You are not.* The younger officer put a bottle of prosecco into Moira's hands, and she was flustered by this and looked at me with alarm, and I shrugged up my shoulders. *Prego, prego!* The senior officer smiled and shouted and waved us out of the station. (Aaron's wrists, were they red or sore? If so, he never mentioned it. I don't remember seeing any marks on him.)

We sat down at last to a meal in a cheap-end restaurant near San Marco, wedged into a booth beside a mirrored wall. Aaron launched into a detailed description of an episode of *Miami Vice* he had watched while I was away, his shoulders and hands full of expression. Moira turned away and called over to the bar.

'*Garçon!*'

'*Cameriere*,' I mouthed. 'You're not in Paris.'

'Save your sanctimony.' She pulled a red lipstick from her pocket and ran it over her lips.

A carafe of red wine came, and a caramel pudding which Aaron tucked in to. The waiter seemed to be Italian, but when I glanced past the serving counter, the cooks were Chinese.

'Dad, boats are private property, right? The cops aren't just allowed to board your boat.'

Aaron had removed his cap at the table. His face was doubled in the mirror, both pairs of eyes bright with the question. Was he talking about the TV show, or his own rescue from the water? I wasn't sure.

'Yes,' I said. 'No. That's right.'

'But if,' he said, 'they had to arrest you at sea, they could. How, though?'

'With a faster boat, I suppose. Force and speed. How do the police catch anyone?'

The waiter hovered with a latte. I tapped the table in front of me, and he reached over to set it down. His hair was thick and curled at the nape.

'*Vino?*' The waiter picked up the empty carafe.

'*Sì, certo,*' said Moira.

He returned and topped up her glass before placing the carafe squarely between us. Moira glanced at him, the tip of her tongue touching the corner of her lip. With each passing day in Italy she had more openly started to enjoy the little frissons between men and women, an element of the culture which in New Zealand, she said, was 'terminally repressed'.

'Dad?'

'Yes, Aaron.'

'I was thinking, when we get to London.' With his fork he pushed the last glob of caramel to the edge of the plate.

I hummed.

'Because it's English-speaking, you know.'

'Being England.'

He looked up, smiled weakly.

'So can we go to the movies?'

'Movies? Sure.'

'A lot, I mean? You know, rather than the whole art and famous oldy things crap.'

Our horribly spoiled boy. The arithmetic was on me before I could stop it: the two-thousand-dollar airfare, the train tickets, the upgrade to two-bedroom hotel rooms so he could have his privacy, and we ours. He was here

153

because his mother had argued strenuously that we should 'expose him to Europe' while he still 'had all his senses open'. I had been all for leaving him with his grandparents in Wanganui to have his senses exposed to the thrills and surprises of provincial New Zealand, BMX rides along the riverside, even a bit of illicit drinking at Kowhai Park. He might have found himself exploring in the stand of ngaio bushes down by the river where Rob and I took our first girlfriends one afternoon in fifth form, where I got my first astonishing feel of wetness between a girl's legs, although the girl in question shut down that whole business fairly quickly.

The smell of river water. Curving ribs under a green shirt, unbuttoning her. Geneviève on hands and knees, the river water bright in the afternoon sun. The skin on our our hands rough from sanding. Her breasts spilling out as the shirt came apart, my hands on her hips, pulling her down onto me.

I shook my head, concentrated on my son.

'There are a few famous oldy things that might be worth seeing. The Tower of London, Buckingham Palace.'

'I'm sick of being a tourist,' he said. 'I basically want to go home.'

River water has its own smell, dank and clean at once.

'I just want to do normal things,' Aaron was saying.

'Home?' I said.

'What's so bad about that?'

'Well that's great.'

I felt Moira's hand on my arm. I must have sounded angry. Perhaps I was angry.

'Great.' I leaned back in the seat.

'I miss home a bit,' Moira said. 'That's normal on a long trip.'

'Still,' I said, 'you might try to find something positive

to say. You ever heard the saying "Don't look a gift horse in the mouth"?'

Aaron was shovelling his dessert into his mouth at a great pace. He spoke through a mouthful of caramel. 'What's horses got to do with it?'

'A bit of gratitude goes a long way. That's what it means.'

'That's stupid.' His face was going red. 'That doesn't even make sense.'

Moira sighed.

'Right,' I said. 'Well, what's actually stupid is—'

Moira kicked me under the table.

Aaron pushed the dessert away. 'Mum, can I go back to the hotel and watch that Michael Jackson thing now?'

'Sure.' Moira put her hand on his. 'Let me just finish my wine.'

'I can go by myself. It's real close.'

I felt, rather than saw, Moira brace for the debate. Then the eye-flick, quick-check look between us. We were efficient parents.

'No, I don't think so.' I stood up. 'Come on, Aaron. Your stupid dad is going to walk you over.'

That got a smile. I hunched into my jacket, kissed Moira on the cheek. 'Back in ten.'

He was thirteen, and it was a foreseeable enough complaint. I don't know why it infuriated me so much. What I wanted most of all that afternoon was an hour or two alone with Moira. I wanted to walk with her down the Schiavoni and watch the watery sun depart over the churches. I was sick to the heart that day and all I wanted was to talk to my wife.

But when I returned from the hotel, she had company. The couple opposite her were young, damp-haired. New wine glasses had been set out and filled.

'Peter, you know Sangeeta?' Moira reached for my forearm.

Sangeeta had a bob of black hair cropped to show off her black eyes.

'Of course.' It felt awkward to kiss her cheek, easier to shake hands. 'Stella's wedding. Excellent speech, by the way.'

Her face was fine-boned, well balanced. She was an attractive woman. Moira always seemed quite bewitched by Sangeeta. I'd watched her grow giddy and flushed in her company within minutes whenever we met up with her.

'Really?' Sangeeta laughed now. 'That memorable?' Her hand was small, dry, bare of jewellery except for a wedding band.

'No, you were funny,' I said. 'You got Moira's family down brilliantly.'

She'd been seated at our table and I'd chatted with her about her own family. Her parents ran the Four Square opposite Waterloo Station, near where Moira and her sister went to primary school. Stella had met Sangeeta at school, and the two girls were inseparable from six years old onward, in spite of what Moira later described to me as Claudia's 'nasty campaign' to dig away at her younger daughter's affection for the skinny Indian girl who spent most of her evenings and weekends behind the till, ringing up milk, cigarettes, ice creams. Sangeeta told me her parents both came from the Punjab originally, but had met in Delhi and had emigrated to New Zealand as a young married couple.

In spite of Claudia, Sangeeta had remained Stella's closest friend. They started at med school in Auckland together. Sangeeta's speech at Stella's wedding *had* been memorable, theatrical, witty, sailing close to the wind but landing on the right side of good taste. She couldn't have been more than twenty-two at the time. I had imagined her robed, devastating a jury.

Moira slapped me lightly to get my attention.

'This is Adrian.'

The man wore a brown oilskin coat which, together with his red cheeks and vast black gumboots poking out from under the table, made him look as if he had come in directly from docking lambs. Had the boots travelled with him all the way to Venice, or had he stumbled across some useful Bata rubber type shop up by the Rialto? I reached over the table and took his hand.

'Sorry.'

It wasn't clear whether he was apologising for the awkwardness of the handshake, for taking the attention away from Sangeeta, or just for being Adrian. His face loomed large and butler-like above hers, so that both heads appeared wrongly scaled. He hadn't been with her at the wedding two years previously. They didn't make for an obvious couple. I wondered how the marriage sat with Sangeeta's parents, who Moira had once told me were traditional Hindus.

Aaron was in his last year at intermediate the year we went to Venice. A few years later, Sangeeta's older brother, Maneesh Gupta, would become his music teacher at Rongotai College. I remember a conversation I had with Mr Gupta at the fifth-form parent–teacher interview night. I had gone alone due to some appointment clash that Moira had. I was struck by the man's insight into my child, his understanding of Aaron's temperament. Aaron had started to complete his piano practice each day with application and diligence, a change in behaviour that was due in no small part, I felt, to his schoolteacher. When I told Mr Gupta this, it seemed to move him almost to tears. He was a genuinely kind man. I told Moira about the meeting later that evening, and my account of the conversation seemed both to infuriate and intrigue her. I think she would have liked to have been there speaking with Mr Gupta herself, catching up on his family news, and Sangeeta's life. There was something quite compelling to Moira about those people.

The particulars of our journeys were laid out. Sangeeta and Adrian were en route to the UK, having spent time in Delhi with Sangeeta's extended family, then down to Goa, giving wide berth to what Adrian described as the 'general debauchery' of the coast, involving themselves instead in such worthwhile activities as biking through cardamom plantations and administering hepatitis vaccinations at local orphanages. Both were midway through medical training, and had given themselves the summer as a sort of escape valve.

'You get narrowed down at med school,' said Adrian. 'It's all the same kind of people.'

Moira and Sangeeta were soon deep in shared history. Moira's sister had recently given birth to her first son. The obstetric details were bandied about: induction, epidural, engorgement, latch. I turned away, and Adrian attempted to engage me on the failing USSR. He had a way of muttering into his lip and it was hard to make out his words against the background hubbub. His big chest heaved over the table.

'The Americans are going to push the Soviets from Afghanistan,' he said. 'Pakistan's on-side now that Bhutto's in charge. Have you seen what they're up to at Jalalabad?'

I didn't really know where Jalalabad was, let alone what was happening there.

'Bhutto doesn't give two cents about Afghanistan, but she wants to punish the Soviets for supporting India. You should hear Sangeeta's father on the topic. His mother, she lived in Lahore as a child. The bitterness between those countries.'

'It's surely best for Afghanistan,' I ventured, 'to get the communists out.'

It baffled me how those on the hard left kept clinging to it, even some of my old friends, this nostalgic belief that there was still something good in Marxism, even after Solzhenhitsyn, after the Khmer Rouge. I couldn't work out if Adrian was in that category. He seemed too young.

'You can see what will happen. The Soviets flee Afghanistan, and the whole Eastern Bloc goes, down, down, down.'

He tapped his finger three times on the table.

'Poland,' he said, 'Czechoslovakia, Bulgaria.'

'Liberation,' I said. 'They'll be dancing all over Europe. What's the problem?'

He looked at me.

'It's delicate,' he said. 'It's the most dangerous time of all. There's still an arsenal.'

'Détente,' I said. 'Glasnost. Surely it's safer than ever.'

'Ah, but no one accounts for backlash. Who's to say Mikhail can keep hold of the reins? That button's still there to be pressed. That's all I'm saying. You'll have some mighty fucked-off ideologues in the Party. What if they go berserk, want to make a statement about Mother Russia, the glory of the Socialist Brotherhood? *Bhush*.'

He gestured a mushroom cloud with both hands. Moira turned to look and shifted back against me, a field of warmth on my flank. I felt a bolt of tiredness. At the hotel a white bed waited.

'Let's hope it doesn't come to that.'

'Hope,' Adrian repeated. It was a scoff, a swallow, a cry all at once.

What else could I say? My childhood had been washed

159

through with the fear of nuclear war. It hadn't happened, and it seemed perverse to grow anxious about it now, at the optimistic end of the eighties. We fell into a stranded, broody silence while the women talked. Outside dark had come down, over the water, over the churches.

It was six when we left the restaurant, and the air was damp and cool. Sangeeta linked her arm through Moira's.

'Shall we explore?'

She put it to her conspiratorially. I thought of the narrow cot in the train from Lyon. I had rocked all night between the metal wall and the protective rail, breathing in the dry air. In a chance meeting in Wellington or Auckland, we would barely have stopped with Sangeeta and Adrian for ten minutes.

'We should check on Aaron.'

'He'll be fine.' Moira was three steps ahead, her jacket zipped up. 'I thought we agreed we weren't going to fuss over him?'

'Is it fussing,' I muttered, 'to see if the boy needs dinner?'

She stepped up onto a small bridge in the corner of the piazza.

'Sangeeta,' she called, 'look!'

She led the way to a bead shop on the far side of the bridge. In the window, beads were scattered in a dazzle of colour against white boards, under glass, under hot lights. They glowed and pulsed, the crimson and azure and gold, and I felt they were awful somehow, pulling on the women's attention, gaudy. Moira went inside, took up a thick string of vermillion and silver and tried it against her neck.

'What do you think, Peter?' She tilted her head in the mirror.

'Too heavy.'

'A bit Claudia-ish?'

160

'Precisely. Save it for when you're a grandmother.'

Although right now you are a *mother*, I thought. You might like to start acting like one.

It was bullshit, of course, the feeling I was trying to work up. Aaron's first priority on arriving at each new hotel was to inspect the room service menu and nut out, with the precision of a lawyer and the speed of an auctioneer, which items he had permission to order. He liked nothing more than to kick us off into the night and settle in for foreign TV and pizza. Such arrangements would be his chief boast to his friends when school started back.

'Come back to the hotel.' I took the heavy beads from Moira's neck and put my hand on her bare skin, laid a kiss on the knobbed bone beneath the nape. She smelt of her favourite perfume: spicy, floral. 'Glass of wine. Early night.'

It was too late for talking. I just wanted to erase all of Lyon the best way I knew how. Moira's generous breasts, the pout of her stomach and the warm slide into her had long been the way home, my safe harbour and my deepest consolation whenever the past started up its dangerous flicker. My best girl. *This girl.*

'Petey.' One finger came up to stroke my forehead, the side of my cheek. 'We're on the train tomorrow.'

What I have in mind is not going to work on the train, I thought.

'You're shattered.' She understood that much. She always understood that. She let out a breath.

'It's my last night.' She was looking about the shop now, trying to find Sangeeta. 'I'll never be here again, you know?'

That line felt manipulative at the time, although it turns out she was right.

'Forget the beads.' She pointed up to a shelf. 'Glasses?

What do you think of these, Sangeeta?'

She bought a half dozen, packed in a cardboard box, the same goblets that Aaron would pack and ship to London years later. I carried the package, taped heavily and stamped with the name of the shop, *Lumière*.

Ten minutes later we stumbled into the yellow blaze of Piazza San Marco, where the sky was neatly squared off. It was the first time we had seen the moon that holiday, a pretty crescent hanging in the corner as we walked west. Adrian spent long minutes trying to line up the shot with his old Lubitel.

'This calls for champagne,' said Sangeeta. 'Don't you think?'

'Here?' I asked. 'It's a bit—'

'Obvious,' laughed Adrian. I nodded in agreement.

Moira took his hand. 'You're overthinking this.'

We ordered bubbles at the Caffè Florian, where the paper doilies boasted of a 1720 opening date. There would be an extra couple of thousand lire on the bill for each decade of that, I supposed. A musician in a white tuxedo sat sipping a glass of chilled water, his cello resting against his shoulder. The whole thing was a vanity, the red velvet seats, the cherubs in the frescos, the scoop of pistachios on a silver platter, the po-faced, silver-haired men with white linen draped over the arm. No Asian cooks here to upset the famous oldness of La Serenissima. The cellist raised his bow and played Vivaldi, and I caught Adrian's eye and smiled, but within three bars the notes tore free of fakery and coiled into my body. *I'm sick of being a tourist.* I was sick of the unending day, sick of the alcohol unpicking me stitch by stitch, sick of sitting like a damp, agitated ghoul at my wife's side. A deep, unhelpful buckling was underway, in my soul or bowel.

'Excuse me.' I pushed out past the group.

Across the square, the Basilica was lit up like a cruise ship. I leaned against a pillar and concentrated on the globe of light that hung from the archway.

Adrian emerged. 'Stuffy in there.'

A group of girls with expensive shopping bags hanging from their arms passed along the passageway. American voices echoed around the stone.

'1720, eh?' I said. 'Long time.'

Adrian laughed, and rubbed his hand over one of the outside tables. 'Long time.'

People drinking coffee here, sixty-odd years before the French and American Revolutions, one or other of the Hanoverian Georges on the English throne; back home the long dream of distance unbroken, all those iwi busy with wars and migrations, generations since the white apparition of the Dutch boat sailed up the West Coast, generations more to come before young Nick in the crow's nest of the *Endeavour* would rub at his eyes and cry out 'Land!' Bit players, all of us. One lost scrap of a child. What does a private sorrow more or less count for in the long sweep of things? There is no starting point to go back to, no single moment of origin out of which everything springs.

Geneviève and I sanding down the deck of the *Lychorida*, side by side on our knees, penitents, beasts, her shirt green in the green light of a sycamore branch, the *whirr-scritch* of the sandpaper and clud of river water on the hull, then down on the mildewed mattress, taking her nipples in the mouth, one, the other, the first, the other. Her weight on me. *Show yourself to me, Peter. Show yourself.* Her hand placing my palm against her throat, the up and down switch of her swallow. *I feel you in here.* The weight of her on me.

'It'll all be annihilated in a few decades, of course.'

Adrian looked down into the viewfinder and clicked at the church.

I recaulked each seam of that boat myself and the deck did not leak in any of that winter's storms.

'No, it's a definite thing.' Adrian wound the film on. 'They've done the maths. The sea will take over.'

We stood in silence and together imagined the café chairs and tables, the American girls, the hopscotch white lines on the ground, the Basilica and the Campanile slide down under the black water. He looked pleased, as if the destruction were part of some personal project he was working on.

'The engineers will come up with something,' I said.

A pigeon fluttered up onto the table in front of us.

'She told me she's delaying medical school.' He blurted out the words. 'She told me she's not going back next year.' He was staring into the air, surprised at himself.

'Sangeeta?'

But who else could he mean?

'She's a bright girl,' I said. 'She'd make a great lawyer.'

I almost wished I'd said so at Stella's wedding. Sangeeta might have taken an entirely different path. Adrian looked irritated.

'I thought she was going to do obstetrics?'

'She was. But she wants a year off.'

'What does she want to do instead?'

'Care for her mother and father.'

'I see. Do they need a lot of care, then?'

'Emotional support, mainly. But what would I know? I'm on the outside. They treat my mother-in-law like she's made of china.'

'It has implications, I suppose, if she delays.'

'It has implications.'

The fog was coming in thick from the sea, and the lights

in the square blurred. I buttoned up my coat.

'My sister-in-law Stella was very close to Sangeeta,' I said. 'Back in Woburn.'

'Woburn? Waiwhetu, I think.' Adrian took a step back. 'And Moira? She must have been part of that.'

'Moira's thirty-seven.' I gave it to him bluntly. 'Just turned. So there's an age gap. She was friendly with Sangeeta's brother, I believe. He teaches music now?'

'Maneesh is in his forties. Moira looks like she's in her twenties.'

There was something like a quiver in his voice. Why should Moira excite such admiration? Was he coveting my wife? Moira's body was as handsome and well-proportioned as it had been a decade previously. It was stirring to spy her through the café window now, standing up and taking her handbag from the chair, *mia donna italiana*, my inconstant one, *mia donna mobile*, seduced away from me tonight by her girlfriend, her glass beads, her champagne, the rattish vapours of the Canal Grande. I wouldn't grovel for her company. Just beyond the square the Adriatic slapped at the flagstones. I had the Venetian night to myself.

'Mercy drops as a soft rain from heaven,' I said. 'That's from *The Merchant of Venice*.' I sounded like a professor in an English literature class. Is it debt or gift or mercy to care for our parents in their decline?

The women came out through the café doors. Moira came to my side and put her hand on my arm.

'I'm going for a walk,' I said, handing her the package of goblets. 'I'll see you at the hotel.'

She found my hand and squeezed: apology, pity and dismissal. She had just applied lipstick and the red line jerked out onto her skin at the corner of her lip, turning her face into something clownish, unhinged. I lifted my thumb to smudge it off. Adrian had stepped away and was

165

focussing on an unpromising portrait of the Campanile against the early evening sky. I felt that things would turn out well for them.

Geneviève had been writing to me off and on for the decade and a half since Amsterdam. She had been happy for a time, had met a man called Claude and they had bought an apartment in old Lyon between the Saône and Rhône rivers. She wrote about the hope of having children with him, but then the relationship ended abruptly and her letters took on a darker tone, circling back to a set of questions about what I had been doing, who I had been with, those days on the *Lychorida* when she had gone to Chavanoz with Abigail. I had sent her more or less perfunctory responses. That seemed to be all I could manage through those years.

In the mid-eighties a new tone and urgency came into her letters. She asked, if I were ever to come to the northern hemisphere, would I visit her. I had the sense that she wanted to tell me something face to face.

That warm April morning in 1989 I stalled for an hour at the station in Lyon, drinking coffee and fiddling with sugar sachets, watching people alight from trains and fall into one another's arms. I came close to panicking, thought about taking the next train out, to Paris, to Spain, back to Italy, to anywhere else. But I held my course, and showed up at her flat, as arranged, at ten in the morning. She had a pale blue poncho around her shoulders, and her hair was bobbed short and full around her face in the style of the time. We couldn't stop looking at each other, the surprise of it, the face known, and forgotten, and known again. She was warm and easy towards me, and after a few minutes of delicate politeness we found ourselves able to talk.

We left her building and walked through the streets together. She showed me around the neighbourhood where she had lived as a child, Vaulx-en-Velin, to the northeast of the city. Tall housing developments loomed at the north end of the suburb, and when we cut through a park there was a large group of teenagers gathered who, I thought, must have been from those projects. North African kids, gathered around a ghettoblaster, breakdancing. A boy of about Aaron's age rippled himself from chest to toe backwards along the ground, then flipped up onto his hands, then onto his feet and back down again. He was a wave of motion, always toppling, crumpling, never falling. I suggested we go to a café, but Geneviève said she wanted to stay in the park, so we bought pastries and came back to eat them on a bench, and watched the kids dance.

We spoke about her father, who had died a year previously. She said she had not wanted to stay with him until the end, but there was no one else. Her mother had left the farm some years before, and would no longer have anything to do with him. Her uncle, a doctor, helped with the nursing during the day, but would not stay for the nights.

It had felt like a shameful demise to her father, who had always been so capable, and who had always been in charge of the farm and of his family, to grow frail to the point where he depended on his daughter to be fed, to be kept clean, and to be taken to the bathroom. He felt the insult of it sharply, and grew ashamed, raged about everything, about his hatred for the army, for de Gaulle. He spoke about massacres that happened in Algeria at the end of the war, about his lieutenant, an Algerian whom he had illegally smuggled into France, but whose wife and children had been left behind and were slaughtered by nationalists. He had raged about this, the failure of France to protect those Algerians who had fought for her, who had depended on her. Geneviève became exhausted by him. It was a relief, she said, when he finally slipped into a coma, and she could put a cloth to his brow and speak to him sweetly and remember him as he had been when she was six and seven years old, and she had sat on his knee at the dinner table or climbed up onto his shoulders to touch the kitchen ceiling. Her uncle, the doctor, had come and helped through the last days, and, in the end, she had watched him inject enough morphine into his arm to cause his heart to stop.

We talked, finally, about Abigail. I asked Geneviève whether the doctor had seen the baby before she died. I had never had that clarified. But she told me I shouldn't interrogate her about that. Her voice grew sullen, and she wanted to talk about why I had sent her to Lyon. She wanted to talk about the *putain*. She had heard me up on the deck, she said, she was humiliated. *Six days after I gave birth*. And so on. I knew all this already. She had written to me about it many times.

Mary from San Francisco, her thin, keen body, her narrow hips. Under the shelter that Rob and I had rigged up in the summer at the stern of the boat, a tarp lashed to the balustrades, two mattresses underneath, a nest of blankets. That had happened once, it was true, that autumn. Mary was incidental, irrelevant, and I told her this again now, as I had in my letters.

Geneviève stared off at the teenagers. She was thirty-eight and I was thirty-seven. Her skin was taut and pinched. She looked older than she was, perhaps older than me. Her face, in spite of these changes, was very familiar to me and still beautiful.

'It wasn't Mary.'

'Who was it, then? Why did you want me to go? Why wouldn't you come with me?'

That squat where we used to bathe, the boy and girl

from Paris lying under blankets with track marks on their arms. *That shit destroys everything I hate that shit.*

Did it matter now that my intentions were for the best?

The ancient Greeks took the view that the length of a life is preordained, that the Fates cut off a measure of thread and that's that. I don't in any way understand why Abigail's thread was so very short. In the years that had passed since Amsterdam I had made my peace with it and got on with the project of caring for the people I had. Moira, Aaron.

'I'm sorry,' I said. 'It was a long time ago.'

I was sorry about Mary, because it had upset her, and I was so deeply sorry about Hendrik, but there was no point going into that now.

Geneviève sniffed.

'I don't even know where she's buried,' I said.

I had been thinking about this on the train journey from Venice. I wasn't sure whether I wanted to know, but I supposed that I should take the chance to go there. After all, I had no plans ever to come back to this part of France.

'Is it far to Chavanoz?' I asked. 'Perhaps we could go there now?'

'I don't know where.'

'What do you mean?'

'I was sick, I caught her fever. It was attended to. We didn't baptise her, do you remember?'

'What does that matter?'

'They have places for those ones.' She used her hands to gesture pushing something away from her. 'Outside the churches. That's what my father told me. That's part of it, do you see? How could I be sure of anything? My mother, she lost three at birth. That was something I found out. My mother suffered. I never understood that.'

It didn't matter. Perhaps I was relieved. How could it

possibly play out well, a scene like that, Geneviève and me standing together at our child's grave? That thick brew of mutual accusation, guilt and just the sheer stupidity of it all, brought to a keen point: it would be enough to make anybody feel ill. It was my fear of such a scene that had stopped me from coming to Lyon at the time. The important thing, at that stage, was not to disturb Geneviève. Clare, who kept in touch by phone, had let me know that Geneviève was in a mentally fragile state. Bringing my own suffering to her would only have made that worse. That was simply how it was.

Across the park, the music from the ghettoblaster changed. Michael Jackson blared out, *got to be starting something.* Two girls came into the centre of the circle and stood side by side holding hands. A spasm, like a hiccup in the muscle, passed from the left of the first one to the right of the other, and then travelled back through their bodies to the start again.

Geneviève laid her head on my shoulder. She pointed out a young girl who had left the dance circle and was now flopped down, legs sprawled on the grass. The girl lifted her hair, dozens of tiny braids, over her shoulder and lit up a cigarette. I put my hand on Geneviève's knee and we sat like that and watched the girl lying in the grass beside her friend. Her laughter was high and clear, and we could hear it over the music, over the birds in the branches above us.

'Do you remember *L'Étranger?*' she said. 'Do you remember I was reading that book?'

I did remember.

'Albert Camus,' I said. 'I remember we talked about Algeria.'

She told me that several items of the baby's clothing had gone missing from her mother's house: cardigans, jumpsuits, nappies, also the sportsbag in which she had carried her clothing to Lyon. The novel, *L'Étranger*, had been in an inside pocket of the bag. I knew the exact photograph that she was using as a bookmark, the one she had taken of me standing on the deck of the *Lychorida* late the previous summer.

On the cover of *L'Étranger* was the figure of a man suggested by a few blobs of paint, red bleeding into the green and black against a larger swirl of yellow paint, the dominant colour of the cover, like a child's sun. As we spoke of that cover, I felt as though Geneviève and I were falling into the same precise square of memory, as though by sheer force of mind the book was made present in front of us. I wanted very badly to see that book. I felt all that I had put up between me and the time of Abigail's death coming down, and I felt myself mentally scrabbling, scrambling to stay upright.

No one could tell me where those clothes went, she said. Her mother had been vague when asked. Her father had been broody, silent. She had ransacked all the cupboards in the house to find them.

'Why would anybody need clothes,' she asked me now, 'unless there was a baby?'

She also said that she had heard crying at noon on the day of Abigail's death, crying from inside the house, Abigail's crying. At noon, Peter, she kept saying. At midday. I didn't understand the significance of this, and I watched her look up into the branches of the trees as if checking for some kind of surveillance, and I wondered about the state of her mind. She pulled a sheaf of papers from her handbag, collected in a brown manila folder, and tied around with string. She flipped through and handed me a copy of the death certificate, signed by her uncle, the doctor. I already had my own copy, which had been sent

171

to me in Amsterdam. Geneveive leant over me and laid her finger on the place where the time of death was recorded: *0937 hr.*

'My father was appalled by way I lived in Amsterdam. And she was sick when we arrived. He said that if I couldn't look after her properly, then other people would.'

I could feel her body next to mine, the agitation in her. I didn't really understand her logic. I wished that we could be soothed together, and lulled, and talk now about something else. I pulled her in towards me. Her hand came up to rest on my chest, and I lifted her chin with my fingers, the sun pouring hot over us, and we were dissolved, there was laughter peeling out over the park, we were absolved, the colours were bleeding, red, green, yellow, black behind my eyes, I kissed her, lips, mouth, tongue, I put my hand beneath her skirt, across the skin of her thigh, skimming over her, I wanted everything back, I wanted to be innocent, I wanted to be inside her for the first time, I wanted to be Daphnis with Chloe. I wanted to fuck her in her own place, in her own bed, I wanted to feel her skin.

She pushed my hand off her leg. I laughed hard, pulled away. When I looked at her face, she was blinking back tears.

Oh chrissake, don't start that up.

'Where were you?' she said. 'Why didn't you come?'

'It's all right,' I murmured. 'It's all right.'

'Yes,' she sniffed. 'Everything has changed, or nothing.'

'I didn't mean to upset you.'

She gave a weak smile and blew her nose.

'Peter, listen,' she said. 'I think my father was capable of anything.'

I stood up and found a tree to lean against. On the far side of the park, the kids were packing up their music, starting to drift off.

'There's something you can do.' Geneviève reached down for her bag. She wrote down an address and told me to go and see her uncle, *Docteur Gabriel Barreau*, who lived on the other side of the city in the ninth arrondissement.

'Ask him what he knows. He signed the certificate. He won't talk to me. He might tell you something.'

'What is he going to tell me?'

She told me then she had had certain doubts about what happened over those few days in Chavanoz, that over time these doubts had led her to suspect that Abigail had been lifted from her, and placed, she did not understand by which mechanism, with another family, perhaps with the complicity of her uncle, who was the doctor who had come to the house on the day of the death and signed the certificate. *Elle est très belle ta fille*, this uncle had whispered to Geneviève on Christmas Eve, almost a year after the event. Your daughter is beautiful. Those exact words. Why had he not said *elle était*? A small mistake, but unusual.

Outside her apartment we made our farewells, and she kissed me on both cheeks. I held her hand for a moment, the veins and knuckles and tendons that stood out against the thin skin. The desire for her that had come over me in the park had completely dissipated, and it was a relief to think about the train ride though the night towards Venice, towards Moira.

It was only after we parted ways that I comprehended what Geneviève had been telling me. I was in a tram back to the Gare de Lyon, with the late afternoon sun pouring through the glass. It was like the dull thud of a tennis game, *dead, alive, dead, alive*, and I felt myself jolted from one state to the other. My daughter existed in the world somewhere. Or, she didn't. I couldn't quite work out, on that tram, the smells of sweaty bodies all around me as the carriage filled up with men and women returning home from work, which was the more terrible thought.

I got off the tram at the station. I stood by the flowerbeds, looking at throngs of tulips that had heaved and groaned and shoved themselves up into a muscular display of red, and sliced my hand through the air in a cutting motion, lopping off their petals, until an elderly man sitting on the bench opposite exclaimed, *Monsieur, mais qu'est-ce qu'elles vous ont fait ces fleurs?*

I did what she asked me to do. I went into the station and changed my ticket for a train leaving at midnight. I took a taxi across the city. We drove east, over the Saône. It was fiercely cold now that the sun had gone, and when the driver set me down, and I opened the door to the evening air, I hesitated. *C'est bien ici*, he said, and he handed me back the scrap of paper. He pointed to the house, a cream door set against a stone porch, the windows above dark except for one on the first floor, which was lit up by an orange lamp that stood close to the glass.

I sat on a step on the far side of the street and watched the house, jiggling to keep warm. It was a quiet, narrow street, barely wide enough for two cars to pass. There were a few passersby, and one or two bicycles. I watched for ten, twenty minutes, but no one came to or left the house, and the lights in the rooms above didn't change. At last, an older woman came into the room with the lamp, her figure round and soft. She came close to the glass and looked out, and then left again, and a short time later the lamp went out.

An hour went by before something, a police siren or a change of light in the sky, forced me towards the pavement in front of the house, but I found I couldn't do it, and I

turned and walked south for a block. I felt embroiled in
Geneviève's sticky logic, in her bad imaginings. I couldn't
see what possible benefit could come from asking questions
of the people in this house, and I couldn't imagine how on
earth I would frame such questions of strangers. I wanted
now, badly, to be on my way back to Venice, to step off the
train and see Moira waiting for me.

I went back and knocked on the door. Docteur Barreau
answered. He was elderly, resting on a cane. When I
explained that I was the father of an infant he had treated
seventeen years previously, and that his niece Geneviève
had sent me, he raised a cool eyebrow and said, in perfect
English, That child was very unwell when I examined her.
Could you tell me, I asked, *exactly what happened?*

Sir, he answered, *I am sorry for your loss but the
paperwork was all in order*, which struck me then—as it
does now—as no kind of answer at all. Docteur Gabriel
Barreau had nothing further to say, and did not invite me
in. I walked back up towards the main road, found a phone
booth, and rang for a taxi to take me back to the Gare de
Lyon.

When she slid out of her mother, we were all astonished.
What a wet, crusty, bedraggled thing a newborn human
is. The midwife laid her on Geneviève's bare chest, and
I put my hand on her back, the tiny haunches, the swirl
of black hair at the crown of her blood-smeared head.
Against the heat of Geneviève's skin her limbs splayed out
and she seemed to soften into sleep. The midwife draped a
towel over the two of them, and called me down to where
she was working between Geneviève's legs. I didn't want to
look. Here, the woman said, and handed me a pair of silver
scissors, small and sharp, like the ones my mother used for
embroidery. The woman lifted up the cord which lay across

Geneviève's belly, pulled on my wrist and placed it in my hand. A fat rope with solid twists of blue coils. I thought of the coiled cord of a telephone receiver. The thickness and strength of it were a surprise. It pulsed lightly in my hand. The midwife put on a clamp up by the baby's stomach. Here, cut, she said, and showed me the place. Then I made the cut, sliced through arteries and vein and tissue, and the two ends of the rope fell apart, although we left the baby lying on Geneviève's skin for a long time, and it was hours before we dressed her.

After Venice, Moira, Aaron and I would go on to London, and spend several nights staying with Rob and Clare at their elegant white-furnished home in Richmond. Late one night, after a full bottle of Sancerre, I would tell Rob that I had spoken with Geneviève. I would mention how she raised certain doubts about what had happened in Chavanoz, and Rob would laugh at the idea at first, saying that maybe someone had floated the kid down the Saône in a basket like Moses, and I would think of her lying in the washing basket on the floor of the boat, the way I found her, exposed to the night air. Why was there no blanket on her? I had left her wrapped in a blanket. It was already November, and so cold on the river by then.

Were they credible, Rob would ask, these doubts? I would take a swallow of wine. I would say that Geneviève basically seemed unhinged to me, paranoid, and that in addition I had spoken to her uncle, the doctor, who had dismissed me. Rob would press me for details, and I would describe the exchange at his house. Rob would look troubled and say to me that, frankly, if it were him, he'd go straight back to the old guy and ask a few more questions.

In the years that followed, I don't think the topic ever

came up between us again. Not until his call last week and this business about the waitress.

I haven't done a great deal of criminal law, but I do know that motive isn't especially important before the law. *Mens rea* obviously has to be established, the guilty mind, the intention to commit a crime. That would hardly be difficult to prove in a case where a death has been faked. If you think about it, that's not something that can be done by accident.

Nevertheless, lawyers do look for motive. My hunch is that, for juries, and even judges, motive tends to weigh in more than the law says it should. It is human nature to look for patterns, to hold to the idea that behaviour has a logic, that we can reason teleologically, inferring active, reasoned intention from whatever we see happening at the end.

Let's pursue the idea that Geneviève's father had a hand in this. If I were prosecutor, if this were my case, I could attribute various motives to him for the crime of faking a child's death. It would depend what evidence I had to hand. Of course, you'd want to be careful. Some motives might work against a prosecutor, setting up, if not a defence, then at least the kind of mitigating factor that might result in a lesser sentence. *My client had an honest belief, your Honour, that the child was in danger. He had an honest belief that he was acting in the best interests of the child. I submit that he should not be punished for any subsequent suffering, neither on the part of the child, nor on the part of any other party.*

The test, at least under New Zealand law, would then become: would a reasonable person hold such a belief? If a child of six weeks came into your care, hot with fever, her mother loose with weeping, her father absent, without a phone number, without a permanent address, if the child had other marks of neglect on them (I don't know, now, if we had washed her, if we had bathed her before she went to Lyon), what would you, a reasonable person, believe? Does it excuse illegal and harmful actions, if you had someone's best interests in mind? The correct course of action would of course be to alert the authorities, but perhaps if you didn't trust the authorities, perhaps if you thought you could do better, you could make out your defence.

I was her father. I don't care what he thought he saw, or how noble his intentions might have been. That man had no right to take her from me, if indeed any of this happened. It remains an untested hypothesis.

I wandered through Venice alone. The sea air was cold, and the fog rolling in thickly, and so I walked fast in order to stay warm, taking turns without any sense of a destination, left around a building, right past a small canal. In a tiny *campo*, I passed a doorway where a bouncer stood guard. The door opened and a waft of heat and light gave out onto the dark square, and a couple came out laughing, the woman in furs, the man in a tuxedo. The square fell dark again, and I listened to the report of the woman's heels against the flagstones as they retreated. Moira was in a bar somewhere, I thought, drinking with Sangeeta and Adrian. Aaron might be asleep by now in his bed at the hotel. I thought about the trees scraping at the window in Hataitai, and the sun breaking over the Rimutakas at that hour, and I understood Aaron's desire to go home. I felt ashamed that I hadn't been kinder to him about it earlier.

I walked on and on. At last, I realised I had no idea how to get back home. I wasn't sure whether the Canal Grande was ahead of me or behind. I went into a bar where everyone was speaking Italian, and I asked for directions. An animated discussion ensued and I was given many contradictory instructions. When at last I got back to the canal I found the water taxis had stopped for the night and so I had to pay for a gondola to take me back to San Zaccaria.

The hotel room was dark. I brushed my teeth and pissed by the cold light in the white bathroom. A sigh rose from the bedroom. I slid out of my clothes. Aaron's bed was empty.

Moira must still be out, I thought. Aaron lay curled in our double bed. In the half-light, my hand found his damp hair and I stroked it. I took off my glasses and made ready to lie down, placing them on top of a cardboard box on the bedside table. Moira's purchases from the glass shop.

I scrabbled for the lamp switch.

Lumière. And the hair on the pillow was sandy blond, shot through with silver threads. It was my wife.

'Where's Aaron?'

In the lamplight, the other bed was most definitely empty.

Moira muttered and rolled onto her back. A fug came from her mouth, sweet, seedy. I pressed my hands to her shoulders.

'Wake up, Moira. Aaron, where is he?'

She wrenched her eyes open and gave me a grizzled, inchoate look.

'You. With you.'

She flipped back over.

'Sangeeta really married that man,' she mumbled. 'Can you believe it?'

I hauled her up to sitting and fought the urge to slap her.

'*Concentrate*, Moira. Aaron is not here, not in this room. It's, what'—I checked my watch—'eleven o'clock at

179

night, we're in Venice, and we don't know where Aaron is. Again. Where the hell have you been?'

She looked at me coldly. After a pause, she flipped back the bedcovers and stood up. She wore one of my T-shirts, inside out and back to front, the little black tag hanging at her neck like a dog collar. She stumbled to the bathroom, bashing her hip against the wall on the way. The white lights spluttered on.

'You.' She hoisted the shirt up with one arm, sat on the loo and stabbed her finger at me. 'Jealous. So jealous.'

Her urine sluiced loud against the water, then trickled. She dabbed a wad of paper against her nest of brown hair, her legs spreading wider, head bending down as if to check something. I stepped out of the room and waited. Instead of a flush, I heard a gulp, and an animal retch.

The sink was pooled with pink vomit. Moira was wiping the back of her mouth, the T-shirt damply patched. I rinsed and wrung out a flannel under the bath tap for her, then started to run cold water down the sink, but the sour smell grabbed at my stomach, and I went out to sit down on the bed.

'Always want me to yourself.' She had got one leg into her trousers, and stopped to look for the other opening. 'Well, I'm not just your *wife*, you know. I have an existence of my own. I don't just sit around on pause while you go about your business.'

'Sorry, what? What's going on here?'

'Why are you bawling me out for spending an evening with a friend? A beloved friend.'

A thought struck me very hard, very clear.

'Moira,' I said quietly. 'Are you having an *affair* with Sangeeta?'

'Oh, good lord, Peter.' She did up her belt, mumbling. 'Calm down.'

I moved to the windows and stared down at the tiny courtyard below.

'What time did you get in?' I asked. It was six hours since I'd dropped him off. I'd read somewhere about the probabilities involved in finding a lost person, the chances shrinking over time by an exponential quotient, a half-life lost every hour.

'His jacket's here,' I said. 'He's probably somewhere in the hotel.'

'You really don't know where Aaron is?' Her voice at my back became pleading, appalled.

It was the second time we'd lost him in one day. We didn't panic. He can't have gone far. You can't kidnap a thirteen-year-old, can you? And after half an hour, a stretch of time sufficient for further insults and recriminations that our marriage never quite recovered from, we found him sitting in the hotel bar wearing the Adidas cap, drinking Coke in the company of two nineteen-year-old Canadian girls who were tolerating, even encouraging, his imitations of Kermit the Frog and Miss Piggy. It was like Mary and Joseph finding the boy Jesus back in the Temple: *Did you not know I would be about my father's business?*

*

Word of Geneviève's death came to me in Wellington four years later, by blue airmail, from Clare in London. She had kept up her connection with Geneviève in all the time since Amsterdam and had been phoned by a nephew. I read her letter over at the breakfast table. On the radio, farmers were complaining about the floods in Northland. Aaron sat opposite me in his grey college shirt, spooning his routine four Weet-Bix into his mouth. Some noise in my throat must have alerted Moira.

'What is it?'

181

I passed her the letter. She read it and laid a hand on my shoulder. Aaron looked up at the shift in mood.

'What's happened?'

'A friend of your father's. She died.'

'Well that's bad. How'd she die?'

Renal failure. There was something in Clare's tone, an inflection in the sentence, that made me think perhaps too many pills were taken. I knew I would never ask.

'She died, son,' I said. 'People do that. She just died.'

'Is there any more milk?' Aaron tipped the bottle over his bowl, shaking it about to get the final drips.

Moira passed him a bottle from the fridge, and the pips sounded for the 8am news.

Seven

My son is twenty-five and occupied with some business of his own. He is twenty-five and if he wants to keep parts of his life private from me, his father, well, that is his prerogative. When I was just twenty, and my girlfriend was only two months away from giving birth, I still hadn't made the effort or summoned up the courage to tell my parents about it. I think even now I only dimly appreciate how painful the whole matter must have been for my mother.

Aaron is an adult, and if I lie awake at two in the morning with a bad tape running through my head: *drink, drugs, grief, debt*, then I suppose that's my problem, not his. Suicide? I don't think so, I really, absolutely don't, but the tiny possibility pulses like a sick beat in the air. Just the thought, the word, is enough to send me reeling from bed, flicking lights on all through the house, opening the door on the deck to let the cold air pour through, great mouthfuls of it, the moths fluttering in and the sound of a car choking to a start down on the street below. I put Mozart on the stereo and stand under a hot shower while the music pounds through the house. *Kyrie eleison. Christe eleison. Kyrie eleison.* Have mercy, have mercy, have mercy.

When I wake again, it's past ten. I'm due back at the office today, but instead I drive to Woburn. Thick cloud sits low on the harbour, blocking out the hills. Claudia steps out from her back door, moving solidly down the steps towards me, the breadth of her drawn in by a red silk blouse, beads, lipstick, pressed pants all in place, her yellow hair fluffed into an obedient halo. With any other woman, I would assume she was expecting company, or was on her way out. But Claudia would have dressed like this, down to shoes and makeup, at six-thirty this morning. Barring extreme sickness, perhaps a couple of days off for childbirth, she has comported herself with this much care each day of her adult life.

She stands at the bottom step, hand still steadying on the rail, and waits. Her eyes are bright, and although her makeup is thick, I can't see any shadows on her face. For a moment, she peers back at me and I think she's about to announce what must be written there—*I don't know where he is, I don't know where he is*—but she blinks and turns away, walking up the steps into the kitchen.

'The girl down the road brought round another carrot cake. I told her the freezer was full and she should take it home, but she's gone and left it on the bench. It's the last thing I need, but as you're here we may as well eat it.'

The front room of the house is always sunlit, and even with today's cloud, by some trick there's a wash of yellow. Three stained glass pendants, gifts from Stella's children in Seattle, I suppose, hang on the windows: a billowing ship, an albatross, a nativity star. The fractured pieces of colour they throw dance madly over the walls and ceiling. I fall into an armchair and Claudia waggles her library book at me. On the cover is an etching of George Grey as a young man, curling sidechops, rather thin, sweet lips, large hooded eyes. I will say for Claudia that she's a great reader, eclectic in her interests. She follows my gaze.

'Sir George Grey. He started off in Australia, you know.

184

He was very conscientious about the Aboriginals,' she said. 'He thought that native children should be properly educated. He built all these boarding schools in Australia.'

I'm pretty sure Claudia would have sent her own daughters to boarding school, given half a chance.

She goes back into the kitchen, and the fat Persian jumps onto my lap. I pick up the book and flick through it. Grey, it turns out, set up the hospitals in Wellington and Auckland, New Plymouth and Wanganui. Hospitals would, he thought, be useful for introducing European habits and culture to Māori. A fatherly concern for the local people, a set of clean, well-run institutions. Is it worth anything now to say he seems to have meant well?

The cat moults white hair all over my clothes every time I'm here. I scoop it up from under its belly and pour it down onto the floor. It leaps back up and starts kneading claws into my thigh.

Claudia comes back with two plates, cream and a slab of cake on each, serviettes and forks.

'What'll you do with this one when you go to Europe?' I unpluck claws from my jeans.

She looks up sharply.

'She's been very out of sorts lately,' she says. 'It could be the change of season. I'm thinking of getting her a companion. There's a new litter up in Featherson. Though I'm not sure I could tolerate a kitten again.'

I lean forward in my seat.

'*Are* you going to Europe, Claudia?'

She swallows, wipes her mouth with a serviette.

'Oh, such a distance. You can't imagine what it's like to undertake a trip like that on your own when you're seventy-eight.'

'Have you spoken with your doctor?'

'He's very good. He wanted to know what arrangements

185

the family would put in place for me.'

'What arrangements would you like put in place?'

'The tour people look after you very well, of course. Just the way to travel, I think, no need to worry about itineraries or tickets, or even meals particularly. It's an enormously relaxing way to go about it, I think you'd find, Peter.'

And then, much to my surprise, I just come out with it.

'Aaron's gone missing.'

But what is that look? Her face is twitching, working to arrange itself.

'Missing?'

'I don't know where he is. He's not answering my calls. I've had a friend check on him. It looks like he's moved out of his flat.'

She looks at me with intense concentration. I've shocked her, I think. She's reeling. She holds her silence for half a minute, longer.

'He's a grown man, isn't he?' She starts to fiddle with her wristwatch.

'Have you heard from him?'

She looks up sharply.

'Of course not. He's just left.'

The cat leaps back onto the armchair and starts sniffing at cake crumbs.

'His flatmate said he went out all night when he first arrived back, then packed everything up and left.'

I can imagine how the interview would go if I went to the police about this.

'Aaron has friends everywhere.' Claudia takes a mouthful of her cake, chews and swallows. 'He'll be off busy with some project.'

Airy denial. Well, that's one way to avoid high blood pressure. And it's a seductive thought. *Friends, projects.*

What a beautiful scenario in comparison to the one I woke up with in the middle of the night.

'You're probably right, Claudia.'

The cat makes a soft leap up to the windowsill and stares out at the trees.

'I wouldn't worry too much, if I were you,' she says. 'The chickens will come home to roost.'

'Yes. They always do,' I say. It's not until I'm driving home that I realise she has invoked the wrong saying. But Claudia is pedantic on language and grammar. Whatever she meant, she meant it quite precisely.

Shed 5, white linen and candlelight and long glass, windows looking onto the wharf, is raucous at six-thirty, with all the patrons two or three drinks in. Richard is the first to see me.

'Welcome,' he says. 'Glad you're here.'

'You know Alistair?' Richard has elegantly manoeuvered himself so that we stand face to face in a well-formed circle. Alistair is a lawyer from our opposition, a great bear of a man.

'Of course,' I say, extending my hand.

'How are you doing?'

'Reasonable,' I say. 'Reasonable.'

Richard catches my eye. I could add something, of course, but I don't have the inclination.

'What will you have?' Richard asks.

'I'll get it,' I say. 'What are you having?'

'No, no,' Alistair says. 'My round. Another pinot'—he pushes Richard's glass over to the bartender—'a Gewürztraminer for me, and what'll it be, Peter?'

'Vodka, I think. Yes.'

There must be something Russian, fatalistic, in me tonight.

'Spirits?' Alistair sucks in, winks. 'Good on you. How do you take it?'

'Neat.'

'A shot of vodka for this man. Make it two.'

The bartender turns two shot glasses up onto the bar.

'I wasn't sure if we'd see you tonight,' Richard says.

'Ah, well,' I said. 'It's as good a place to be as any.'

He looks at me with the concerned, attentive expression that makes clients trust him.

Alistair hands over his credit card, and slides the drinks towards us one at a time. He takes the shot.

'God,' he says, pulling a face. 'That's hairy. I haven't had vodka for twenty years.'

I laugh, take a sip and hold it on my tongue, letting it set fire to the roof of my mouth.

'It's good.'

Richard's hand rests, momentarily, on my shoulder. Alistair flicks his eyes between me and Richard, reading the gesture. He doesn't inquire, instead slouches down at the bar in order to bring himself closer to my height.

'You've heard about the massive land sales in Northland, have you?' he says. 'Whole lot of Americans been buying up in the last few weeks. Fascinating times.'

'Disaster capitalism.' I'm not really sure where the phrase comes from or if it signifies something more than the obvious, but it rolls sweetly off my tongue.

'Too right. I'll tell you what, defence stocks will be on a bull run.'

'The military–industrial complex stands to make a killing.' I think of Matthew at the Law Centre, the guard, his broken jaw, which must—in the end—have hurt. 'As we used to say.' I think of Clare, her eyes shining, arriving home to Earl's Court on Mayday with a line of purple bruises up her arm.

188

Alistair furrows his brow at me, taps his credit card on the bar.

'Another of those?'

'My round.'

Laura comes through the door in a shimmy of turquoise, a mermaid sort of sequined dress over black pants. Several seconds pass before she is adopted by a group of new graduates, seconds during which I have an urge to march over to her, bring her here and organise her a drink.

A new line of clear shots trembling in the yellow light. I take one, and a short while later they're magically replaced. Another. I get a bad vision of Aaron lying on a concrete pavement, stone cold drunk, and I shake my head hard to get rid of it. It's 7am in London, and two days into November. *Call me, son.* Just pick up the phone and call.

Dylan taps my shoulder, offers his gentle hello.

'How's things, Dylan?'

'Pretty good. Well, mixed, to be honest. Quite a rough patch at home, actually.'

Now that I look at his face, he does in fact seem exhausted.

'What's been happening?'

'Both of the kids caught measles. The rash and fever came on just after I saw you last week.'

'*Measles?* Don't they get vaccinated for that?'

'Usually. Eleanor was against it.'

'Goodness. How are they?'

'They're coming right. Oscar might be able to go to school next week. They've been quite bad. Although not in hospital.'

Dylan sighs, seats himself on the barstool beside me, orders us both pinot noirs.

'We've had some pretty black looks from health professionals, let me tell you. Why didn't I take charge of

189

it, I ask myself? Why didn't I overrule Eleanor? I always thought vaccines were something you just did. Routine. The guilt is terrible, Peter. Do you know you can go blind from it?'

'Really? I think I might have had measles, as a child.'

'Well, that was Eleanor's logic. Her mother and father had it and it was no big deal. Roald Dahl's daughter died of it.'

'A busy week.'

'Dreadful. My mother-in-law's with them all tonight, so I've come out. Woman's a saint.'

How extraordinarily heroic of you to fit in twenty-seven billable hours for BioCom this week, Dylan.

On the far side of the room, Laura is standing on the fringe of a circle of women, talking to another girl, shifting her weight from one hip to the other. She has not removed her bag, which is orange vinyl, slung over her shoulder like a cycle courier; the bag and her constant, restless changing of posture suggest that she is here temporarily, that she has other places to move on to. She has an easy sway in her back as she shifts from foot to foot. It occurs to me that she had her company law exam today. Perhaps she's come straight from it. She's laughing, tipping her head back. She looks relaxed, and so I'm guessing it has gone well. Good for her.

To call it lust would be badly reductive. Laura has the unselfconscious loveliness of a woman not far from her childhood. She is all openness, all movement, all quivering energy. She is a fledgling, not even twenty yet. It does my heart good to be near her.

'The minute they're better I'll be marching them down to get the rest of their jabs,' Dylan is saying. 'Just one bad decision. The younger one was running at forty degrees for days.'

He has that haggard, haunted look. He may need a priest. I think he's going to be telling this story for some time.

I put a hand on his shoulder. 'You poor bugger. Could have happened to anyone.' The distinct impression that my voice is slurring. 'You can't make them invulnerable, do you see that, you can't cover for every possibility in the end.'

'Right,' Dylan says, frowning. 'Right.'

'Go easy on yourself, mate.' Patting his shoulder.

A buzzing sensation at my hip, my phone ringing.

'Excuse me.' Shouting over my shoulder at Dylan, 'I have to take this,' pushing to get out of the room.

Battering my fingers at the buttons. Under the awning, the rain sheeting down. It's a long number, one I don't recognise.

Aaron, Aaron, Aaron, Aaron, Aaron, Aaron, Aaron, Aaron, Aaron, Aaron, Aaron.

'It's Hamish here.'

'Hamish? Oh. Hamish.'

'Got a bit of a question for you, Peter. About your property.'

'Right. Sure. Fire away then.'

'We've just looked up the LIM report. Your boundaries. You're aware of where they're drawn, are you?'

It's a cool, slightly shocking air out here.

'Well, at the fenceline.'

'Ah, it seems they're not, mate.'

'Not at the fenceline.'

What's he saying? That green paddock beyond, those grazing horses. My land extends out into it?

'The LIM report shows a boundary about ten metres out from the house on the south side. I don't know when those fences went up, but, well, they don't reflect the legal

191

ownership of the land.'

Ten metres out. Three, four, strides. Then *thwack*, bang-end of the property.

'I think you're wrong,' I say. 'I think someone's got muddled up here.'

Laura coming out through the door, popping up an umbrella.

'Let's talk about it,' I say, 'in the morning. There's been an error. Someone's misfiled. Look, I'm a lawyer. We'll sort this out.'

Hamish clicks off.

'Still torrential. Can I offer you a lift somewhere?'

'I'm up in Khandallah,' she says. 'But there's a bus.'

'Come on,' I say. 'It's on my way, more or less.'

Laura is holding her umbrella over both of us, chatty on the short walk from the wharves to the office. She doesn't want to jinx it, but the exam was straightforward, she says, far easier than she'd anticipated. She tells me that she lives with her parents and two younger sisters, that she's studying art history alongside her LLB, and that she intends, at the end of summer, to set up house with her boyfriend, who is undertaking a Masters in history. But before I can ask about any of this she starts questioning me.

'You volunteer at the Law Centre, don't you?'

'I was there on Tuesday.'

'Any interesting cases?'

'A couple. It's always an unpredictable mix.'

She sighs. 'Actually, my boyfriend?'

We're paused on the corner of Featherston Street waiting for the signal to change, and the rain is pelting onto the umbrella. I feel her body leaning forward as if to step out onto the road. I grab her arm and pull her back, instinctively. A car accelerates fast past us.

'That was close,' I say.

We carry on towards Lambton Quay, walking in step.

'Your boyfriend.'

'I sent him down to see you that night. I mean, I suppose I knew you were on duty. Did he show up?'

'Sent him?'

That parade of faces at the Law Centre, seven or eight different cases. I can't think which of the people I saw would make Laura a plausible boyfriend, a Masters student. The elderly gentleman with the outstanding power bill? The fifty-year-old with custody issues?

'His name's Matthew.'

'Oh. God. *Matthew.* Really?'

Which immediately throws my professional ethics out the window. Laura's demeanour on my left perceptibly shifts, and I feel it, the way she is concentrating now, the little silence that has gathered between us, the precise spot where her hand is on the umbrella stem, holding it over my head.

'Obstinate kind of a guy,' I say.

Which doesn't help.

'Brave,' I say. 'Determined.'

Which is a sort of overcorrection.

'He's being an idiot,' Laura says. 'He's going to end up in jail.'

My laugh comes out as a half-choked snorting sound, which I'm hoping is largely swallowed up by the batter of rain.

'I knew you'd be the right person to talk to him.' Laura's voice, bright and certain. 'I knew it.'

In the carpark, I pop the car boot and slide in my briefcase.

'What's that?'

She's gazing at something behind me. The white sheet

around the canvas has fallen off slightly, so that a square of yellow-pink skin and a bit of white wicker chair and blue background are showing.

'Oh.' I yank on the sheet, trying to pull it back up. 'Something I brought back from the Wairarapa.'

'A painting,' she says. 'Can I have a look?'

'It's. Well. Something my wife did.'

'Your wife? I'd love to see.'

She's reaching past me, pulling down the white sheet.

The vodkas are still singing on the top of the brain. *Why this hesitation? Show yourself.*

'All right,' I say. 'Take a look then.'

I pull the sheet right off, and stand the portrait upright on the edge of the car boot. Laura's face, under the white lights, is contemplative.

'She's good,' she says, and comes in closer to inspect the surface. 'Skin is so hard to do.'

Laura drops into the front seat of the car and makes herself at home, kicking off her flat shoes, reaching for the handle to slide the chair backwards. She struggles, her neck craned. At last the seat catapults back.

'Can I ask you something personal?' she says.

'Fire away.'

'Has it worked out for you?'

There is a palpable tension in her posture, her hand pulling on the seatbelt, her torso turned to face me.

'The profession?' I turn the car out onto the Terrace. 'Lawyering?'

She sighs, sinks back in the seat. 'This time next year I could be summer clerking with you guys. I mean, maybe. If I'm lucky. If I even *want* that kind of luck. Is it true you have to have straight As to keep your CV in the pile?'

Our firm is the best in the city. Each year there is a

mountain of applications which are whittled down to forty interviews, fifteen placements. I sat on the panel two years ago and was greatly cheered by the parade of promise.

'Marks come first, it's true,' I say. 'Then gumption: Is this someone who sticks at things? Amiability and common-sense. It's hard to quantify that stuff, but it matters.'

And beauty, I am tempted to add, not that this is strictly true, or at least no more true in law than it is always and everywhere. Laura has above average chances on this count. Presuming, that is, she learns to dress properly.

'I've thought about taking a year out, going overseas. I want to drive across the States. I could, of course I could, but it's about timing. Do you ever feel like you've got to *listen*, you know, listen out really hard for something?'

At the top of Bowen Street the water rushes down the clay banks from the playing field above. Around the corner, Tinakori Road is choked up by cars outside the restaurants and pub.

It's a road originally designed for horse and cart, the breadth between oncoming traffic and the parked cars leaving no room for error. Just past the pub, a broad four-wheel drive bears down on me from the north. I scrabble though a light fug in the head to find and hold my course, sensing, as the vehicles flicker past one another, that I might have come quite close.

'I guess I better stick at it.'

She sighs. I hear exhaustion in it, and fear as well, a bare millimetre below that chirpy surface. Has Aaron been anxious in these ways, these past few years? He seemed from very early on to know what he wanted, and to know exactly how to get there. Although he has chosen what looks to me like a highly precarious path, he's certainly been devoted to it. He shucked off any dependence on my guidance or advice in his teens, although he still needs money, he still needs praise, he still needs applause for his accomplishments. Needed. Perhaps he doesn't need anything from me anymore. Perhaps that's what this vanishing is about.

My own career didn't come into focus until my twenties, until I came back to New Zealand, until I had a woman and her child to provide for, *a second woman, a second child*. I plotted out the steadiest, most reliable course I could think of, and applied myself to it. I am a capable lawyer, and I'm proud of the work I've done.

At the next set of lights, I lean back in the seat, cross my arms and look over at Laura.

'You want a good job. You want to do well for yourself.'

She shrugs.

'I admire that.'

'You have to focus,' she says, 'if you don't want to end up as a waitress.'

'I don't see you as a waitress.'

But I get a clear picture right then of Laura carrying cups of coffee and paninis out to tables on a waterfront, a cool wind coming off the sea. The *whirr-scritch* of a coffee machine. Geneviève's face, a row of buttons on a green shirt, her nipple a hard pebble under my tongue.

Kapos. Kipos.

I give myself a shake, tighten my hands on the wheel.

'You'll be filthy rich,' I say. 'I've got an intuition for these things.'

The road tilts down an incline to the main road. Turning into the traffic, I notice a blockage ahead, just under the railway overbridge.

'I don't want to be rich,' she is saying. 'It's not just about the *money*.'

Up ahead, a pulse of red and blue, a snake of cones.

'There's something revolting, really, about owning too much.'

In front of me, all the power of the state laid across the road, before which even the most docile and obedient citizen quails. The heart banging *da-dof, da-dof* in the chest. This is the moment, hand steady on the wheel, when one counts back through the evening, calmly—*you're fine, of course you're fine*—but the maths is making me sweat. I have drunk far too much to be driving tonight.

Laura is rambling on about property, putting forth vaguely socialist sentiments as I peel the car left into the only side street before the bridge, and press down on the accelerator. The road weaves and narrows, bottlenecks down to one lane, and I reel close to the clay bank, correcting wildly.

There is a gasp beside me. *Stop.* It's not clear to me whether Laura has said this, or whether it is the clear part of my mind trying to regain control. *Stop. Stay still.* I park the car, turn off the engine, the lights, hunch down. We will wait here, inconspicuous, let them pass by if they come. The street is ill-lit. Even a sharp-eyed cop would be hard pressed to confirm, in open court, the Legacy as the same car that turned off the road.

Laura's breath beside me comes heavy, hard. I could have hurt her. I've overreacted.

'Sorry.'

It is quiet, and wetly dark.

'That was a bit rough,' I murmur.

The car ticks as it cools. I hold my hands still in my lap. Her voice comes, from far away.

'This isn't the right way.'

'That's true,' I say. 'It's not the usual way. That is true.'

She places her hand on the door handle. I check the rear vision mirror. A pair of headlights are roaring up behind, seeking out the dark corners of the road.

'Perhaps don't get out, Laura.'

At this, she clicks it open an inch. The yellow light in the door flicks on. Her shoes are back on her feet.

'I'd rather you just stayed in the car.'

She has her mobile in her lap. She picks out a number, holds it to her ear. The car, not a cop, sashays past, and growls up the hill.

Not, of course, that I'm trying to stop you. *Oh, lord.*

She steps out onto the road, but leans her head in so that I can hear her speak.

'Mum.' She looks directly at me. One of the bobbypins in her fringe has worked loose and is about to slide out of her hair. 'I'm on my way home. Just letting you know. I'm getting a lift, with Peter, from work. Peter Collie.' She holds my gaze. 'Just letting you know. I should be ten minutes, perhaps, fifteen at the most.'

I put my head in my hands, appalled, admiring. Do they teach them this in school?

'See you soon.'

She hangs up, sits back in the seat and slams the door shut.

'You can keep going.' She points ahead. 'There's a road to Khandallah through here.'

There is no quaver, or hesitation, in her voice.

I cough and start the engine.

'Do you drive, Laura?'

She shakes her head. I would cheerfully hand over the wheel to her. We traverse the ridges and valleys of the northern suburbs in a nervy silence. I drive at the speed and care of a cortège.

'I'm normally better on directions,' I say as we pass through Crofton Downs. 'My wife died recently.'

She looks at me, startled.

198

'It's good that you called your parents. That's the thing to do. Good girl.'

At her house, she flies out of the car. A young girl, her sister, I presume, opens the front door to her, and a spill of white light washes over the stairs and pathway. She doesn't turn to wave; she is halfway into the house already. The door shuts out the light before I drive off.

*

The months after Abigail's death, trying to sleep on the mattress in the dark corner of the *Lychorida*, the water of the Amstel slapping at the boat, voices rising and falling up on deck, turning, turned on. Geneviève, the things I have done to you, Geneviève, the things I could do to you, *you failure you ruin you thief*, your body a gap, an absence, my hot hand, the locked loop of self on self, the whimper, the pulse, wet want spilling everywhere.

Was I ever so lonely as that again?

I kept to myself. I didn't see Mary again. In those terrible days I would walk in the afternoons around the streets behind the Oude Kerk. At about two, girls would start to appear in the windows, perched on stools, paring their nails or brushing their hair. They were languorous, the weak sun pouring through the glass and pooling on their skin. I watched for days, and then started to visit a slight girl who had a tattoo of an eagle across the small of her back, three sharp talons pressing into the skin about the level of the kidneys. For several days in a row she pulled the black curtains across the window and we lay together on the bed with its synthetic red sheet. She called herself Crystal. When I try now to see her face, it's almost blank to me, a vague indication that melts together with other, similar types. I can make out, clearly, the stretch of the eagle's wing around the flank of her waist, a lick of dark hair growing upwards from the base of her neck, the spill of long hair, and the hollow of her navel, which I found myself paying particular attention to, returning to with fascination, giving attention to. I had never been obsessed by that part of a woman's body before, but I lingered over it. I asked her once about her mother and father, and she told me their names, and that they lived in Suriname, and I imagined a cord connected to her there at the navel, unravelling across Germany, France, Spain, Portugal and away over the Atlantic to the Dutch colony on the knuckle at the top of South America, where her parents might stand outside their home holding it as a rope, a withy, between their four hands. It troubled me and it obsessed me, this vision of these others to whom she belonged.

I always visited in the afternoon. There was a seam of light where the curtains didn't quite join, and the dust spun in the shaft. She was older than me, in her late twenties, I think. I always left her a large tip. I had money to spare at that time. I had plenty of money.

*

I take the car up a sidestreet off the Aro Valley and park outside a house on a steep blackberry-covered bank, washing drying on racks on the balcony above, all the windows cracked open three inches. It's a big house, all students, I suppose, situated right below the university.

Akenese answers the door, dressed in grey trackpants and a T-shirt, her dark hair knotted around in a large bun at the back of her head. She remembers me from the time I ran into her and Aaron at the café. She's friendly enough, entirely unsuspicious of me, bringing me down the hallway where the dull beat of a stereo is playing, into the kitchen. The window behind the sink looks out onto a damp courtyard with boxes of herbs growing, and a lichen-covered sycamore with some kind of bird feeder hanging from a branch.

As we talk, Akenese stands at the bench, cutting green apples into slices and layering them in a dish. She is using a corer, a round red circle with set-in blades, which she presses down on the top of the apple to core and slice it in one movement. The pressing takes some effort. Each time she cuts an apple she rises up on the balls of her feet and gives a little huff.

'You must be wondering why I'm here.'

I have the lawyer's instinct to check her reaction. There is very little to read, either way. Her expression is even and easy, and she doesn't change posture or pause in her work.

'The thing is,' I say, 'I don't know where Aaron is.'

One hand on either handle of the corer, the slight rise onto the balls of her feet, the *swush-shush* of the blades passing through the fruit, and the segments of apple collapsing out into a circle. She gathers the pieces quickly in her two large hands and scatters them into the glass dish.

'Have you heard from him?'

Akenese looks up and nods, which seems to acknowledge my question, but not answer it. She pulls out a bag of sugar, takes a spoon and begins sprinkling the apples.

She rolls the top of the bag closed and puts it back in the cupboard.

'He was going back to London,' she says.

'Ah, yes,' I say. 'He did that. He is, most probably, still in London. Or perhaps not. I really don't know. I thought you might have some insight. I know you're a good friend of his.'

Or lover. I don't say it aloud. Her face opens into a smile, though, so I've said something right.

'I need to ask you. Was he all right?' It feels shameful

to ask this about my own son. 'When he was here in Wellington, was he in any kind of trouble? Was anything upsetting him?'

She rinses her hands under the tap.

'His mother's just died,' I say. 'So, I mean, obviously he was troubled, obviously upset. But beyond the ordinary, do you think?'

She shrugs. 'What's ordinary?'

'Do you think he was okay?'

She pauses, wipes her hands dry on a towel.

'It was like something had got hold of him.'

'Right,' I say. 'Do you want to hazard a guess as to what it was?'

She cuts some butter into a pan to melt on the stove and clears her throat, but doesn't speak. After a minute the silence grows loud. It seems she'd rather not hazard at all.

'Really, anything would be a help,' I say. 'I'm grasping at straws. I don't know what to think. When he left he was upset. I'd upset him. I'd made a decision he didn't like.'

She looks up sharply from the stove. The expression on her face suggests she too has had some experience with Aaron's displeasure.

'His grandmother always said he wore his heart on his sleeve,' I say. 'I don't know if that's true. He's quite a complicated person.'

The muffled beats of the stereo from the room down the hall grow louder, then abruptly switch off.

'I got cross at him,' I say. 'I wish I hadn't been so cross.'

Akenese flicks off the gas knob on the oven and pulls out a chair beside me. There's something soothing about her silence, as though there is no rush, as though the purpose of my visit is not quite the point, the point being that we are two people sitting in a room. Akenese is quietly breathing, and I feel, for the first time, that all these puzzles will resolve themselves, given sufficient space, sufficient time. If we sit here for an hour or two, if we talk until the sun is high in the noon sky, perhaps we could lay it out in a set of propositions, a line of reasoning with the elegance and purity of a mathematical proof that would make this tangle clear, so I might know for once and for all who Aaron is, and what he wants most from me, and how I might best make up for what I have done, or what I have failed to do.

'He did talk about travelling,' she says at last.

'Did he say where?'

'He was pretty vague. Pakistan, maybe? He's got that flatmate. He talked about India.'

Ahmed. I knew Ahmed had something to do with this.

'He's got a part in a play,' I say. 'Did he tell you that? I suppose he'll show up for that, don't you think?'

'I doubt he'd let *them* down.' Sourness in her voice.

Aaron lets—has let—Akenese down. Recently? Dreadfully?

Out in the hallway, a door clicks open. Footsteps, the toilet flushing, water running.

'You gotta relax,' she says at last. 'No point in freaking out. He'll show up when he's ready, sooner or later. Its only been two weeks since he left.'

'Fifteen days.'

She shrugged.

'I'll leave you my numbers,' I say. There's a pen lying on the bench, a piece of scrappy card in my wallet. 'If you hear from him at all, could you? Or even if you think of anything that might help me find him. Any small thing.'

Akenese slides the card into her trackpants pocket. I'm not confident that it won't get lost.

'I'm sorry about your wife.' Her eyes lowered.

'Oh. Thank you.'

'I'd hoped to meet her.'

'I wish you had,' I say. 'Where's your family based?'

'In Auckland. Aaron came up to my grandma's birthday in September. He didn't say?'

I hesitate.

'Nah, I didn't think so,' she says. 'We're too Samoan for him. He looks like he'd fit in, but he's pretty coconut, I guess.'

She's a great girl. Why didn't he bring her to meet Moira, to meet me? Ashamed of his dying mother, of her emaciated, wasted body? I know he has a bigger heart than that. Ashamed of you, Akenese? *Ashamed of me?* Perhaps it was just too difficult, too many pieces to reconcile.

'I was meant to go to London with him. I had a plane ticket.'

I sit back down.

'You were serious, you two.'

Akenese shrugs, picks up a teatowel and starts drying the dishes in the rack.

'Yeah,' she said. '*Were.* That's about right.'

'It sounds as though he might have been . . . well, unkind.'

Her eyes stay blank.

'I'm sorry. On Aaron's behalf. Can I help in any way?'

A raised eyebrow, a hint of scorn in her look.

'It's all good. I hope you find him.'

Emily Skelton. At three in the morning the name flies into my mind. I call Clare, immediately. It's a reasonable hour in London.

'Where are you?' she asks.

'Home. Just at home.' On my couch, under a blanket, staring out a black window. 'Listen, I've got a name for you. Skelton. Ring any bells?'

'There's a castle, I think. In the north.'

There's a static sound on the line. It sounds like she's outside. Wind, walking.

'Can you ask your father about it? Lord Skelton. Died in a car crash. He had a daughter called Emily. Aaron was friendly with her last year.'

'Yes, I can. I'll see Daddy tomorrow. Rachel's got her school sports day.'

Rachel. The youngest.

'Oh, lovely. Egg and spoon races?'

'She's twelve now. She's made the relay team this year. We're on the Heath right now practising baton changes.'

'I won't keep you.' I pull up the blanket around my neck.

'Shelton,' she says. 'I do know there's a Lord *Shelton*.'

'Could be. I'm pretty sure it has the k.'

'I'll follow up.'

There's a dog yapping somewhere in the background.

'No word from him at all?'

'His grandmother's not too worried. She reckons he's off with friends somewhere.'

'But not contacting anyone. Is that plausible?'

I can only imagine the kinds of conversations she and Rob are having about me. I'm like a walking Oscar Wilde joke. *To lose one child may be regarded as a misfortune; to lose two looks like carelessness.*

'Emily Skelton. Shelton. And tell Rachel it's all in the fingers. Grab on hard. Fingertips.'

*

I have seen for myself the magic that Clare's family connections can work. She left Amsterdam a few days after Abigail's birth to return to London for her friends' trial over the Mayday riots at the Old Bailey in 1973. It was an unfortunate decision to go home. Once she was back in London she too was arrested, charged and eventually convicted for incitement of violence. New photographs of the riots had come into the hands of MI5, and were used as evidence in the case. As a result the City University of London expelled her from her degree. She was briefly in despair about this, but I was to learn there is very little that will disbar a child of the English upper classes from getting ahead if the will is there.

Her family had a connection to the Chancellor of the University of Warwick through the Chancellor's wife, Antonia Roby. Antonia was the daughter of Lord Charnwood, or Godfrey, as the family called him, a man who had formed a friendship with Clare's great-grandfather at Oxford almost a century before. The two men had stayed friends until their deaths, and the families had become socially entwined.

Clare was called in for a private meeting. Discussions were held. However it was accomplished, in the autumn of 1973 she arrived at Warwick campus with long clean hair, a leather satchel and a stack of new textbooks, ready to start her third year.

I drove up to Coventry to say goodbye to her on a day in late September. I was a week shy of flying back to New Zealand. The events of the past year were drawing to a conclusion. The days were growing cool and bright, chill coming on in the morning and evening, and the leaves were starting to turn. I knew now that when autumn came in the northern hemisphere it came down hard. I wanted the mornings of light and warmth, I wanted silver beaches and bare hills. I wanted my mother's face, my father's voice. I was sick of being in Europe. It was coming up to a year since Abigail had been born, and I was still reeling and lurching through the days, prone to long hours of brooding and bad thoughts that circled around. I thought going home might improve my state, which in fact it did.

At Warwick that autumn day, Clare and I walked under long columns of poplar trees. I don't remember what we talked about. We walked past the glassy block of the new library. It was hot, and the streams of students moving along the concrete paths wore summer clothes and sandals. They looked like the kids we'd been with in Amsterdam.

As we passed the main entrance, Clare pulled on my arm. A man, stocky and bald, with a pale, protuberant forehead, was stationed ahead in our path.

'It's the Chancellor,' she murmured. 'I'll have to speak to him.'

She gave herself a tiny shake, and I sensed a tightening in her, a drawing up as we stepped forward.

'Miss Rochford,' said the man.

'Sir Cyril.' Clare bobbed slightly, almost a curtsey, then rose up and smiled brilliantly. 'What a pleasure.'

'You'll read in history, I believe?'

'Yes, I will. And this is my friend, Peter.'

The Chancellor turned and blinked at me, but in the next moment his attention was taken over by a man in a blue suit who appeared at his shoulder, and we were released.

'You heard of the Radcliffe Line?'

Clare and I had gone to drink stewed coffee in the student cafeteria.

'Nope.'

'Well, so, when we left India'—Clare used her hand to draw a horizontal line in the air—'they split the country into India and Pakistan.'

'*We*,' I said.

She shrugged. 'Our Chancellor was in charge of the border. They had to sort it out within a matter of weeks.

They named it after him.'

'That old man back there?'

'The very same. Sir Cyril Radcliffe. He was furious about it, Grandad said. It was an impossible task. He never forgave Mountbatten and the prime minister for the position they'd put him in.'

'Your Chancellor personally decided where the border of Pakistan would be?'

'It was complete pandemonium. Just extraordinary, the things that happened,' she said. 'Poor man. Dad says he's quite haunted.'

I watched Clare's mouth as she spoke. She was always more beautiful when she was animated. Her hair fell loose over her shoulders in reddish-brown waves. All the girls wore their hair like that back then.

She reached across the table and took my hand. 'And now you are going to the other side of the world. Will I ever see you again?'

'Perhaps. Probably. You could come to Wanganui. Imagine that.'

'And Geneviève?'

'What about her?'

'You should go and see her.'

'What use would that be?'

Clare sighed and let go of my hand. She looked out the window.

'Every time I phone her,' she said, 'she asks about you.'

'Are things getting any better, do you think?'

'I don't know.'

'It's too late now. I'm leaving next week.'

'You could delay, if you wanted to.'

She looked hard at me, searching for something. I don't know how I looked to her then, or what my expression said.

'I stayed in Amsterdam for months,' I said. 'She could have come there to see me.'

Well, that was a weak thing to say. I knew perfectly well it would have been too difficult for Geneviève to come to Holland.

Everything Clare had told me about her phone calls to Chavanoz suggested that Geneviève was falling apart catastrophically in the months after Abigail's death. I already knew how bad things had been after the birth. The weeping that went on and on. It was clear to me that if I turned up in France it would make her situation worse. There was her distress over Mary, for instance, and other complications. Leaving Geneviève alone was the least I could do. I didn't want to intrude. But I didn't explain myself well to Clare. I suspect she's always held it against me.

*

At work on Monday, there are various emails to deal with. Hamish has called about the boundary of the section at Castlepoint. *Could we meet face to face?* There's correspondence to do with structural changes to Air New Zealand's financing, none of which I feel equipped to deal with this morning. Nothing from Dylan. Nothing from BioCom.

I walk past my office, past Richard's, past the open-plan area, and into the library, a piece of the building that faces north, with a view over the train yards and the docks, where everything gleams in the morning sun like children's toys.

'Have you got an atlas?' I ask the librarian.

It seems most likely that Aaron is in fact in Colchester with Emily Skelton. Or is it Shelton, after all? *Shelton, Skelton, Shelton, Skelton.* If he's upset, and if Emily has a car and knows Aaron well enough, she may well take him on a drive through coastal Essex: Walton-on-the-Naze, Clacton-on-Sea, Mersey Island, West Mersey, Bradwell-on-Sea, Southend-on-Sea. I can breathe best when I think of him somewhere in the borders of the United Kingdom. Eating greasy fish and chips, staring out at the North Sea on a grey November afternoon, is as cheerful a vision as I can muster. Rather than grabbing at outlandish possibilities and weak leads, the best approach is to start with the probable, the local, the last known place where Aaron was.

So that's how Richard finds me, with a double-page spread of the United Kingdom open on the low table. I shut the book and look up at him.

'Peter, we should get together today. If you have a moment.'

His eye seems to fall on the closed atlas. Of course I have a moment, Richard.

'When suits?'

'Now, if you're free? Coffee across the road.'

'Great.' I push the book to one side, shoulder into my jacket. Informal, then.

We sit for half an hour over flat whites and cheese scones, and an amiable, meandering conversation. It appears that Richard has no particular purpose in mind beyond a general managerial catch-up. I manage to make several reassuring noises in regard to potential new clients whom I have begun gently romancing this week. But when Richard finally asks about Aaron, in his usual genial manner, I just want to lie.

'He seems to be going through a rough patch,' I say.

'Hardly surprising. London is so miserable in the winter, too.'

'He's got a part in a play in November.'

'He is? What's the play?'

'Ah. Something I hadn't heard of before. It's some kind of critique of capitalism. Rampant consumer madness. Acquisition fever. Credit cards at their limit. Life on the seedy side.'

'You must be very proud.'

'We are. I, that is. Am. Yes.' Richard screws his face into a mild grimace of sympathy. My teaspoon scrapes around and around the empty base of the cup.

'Peter. Can I ask something? Do you have any professional support?'

'Support?'

'Counselling, say. Do you think it could perhaps be time to access that? I'm mentioning this more as your friend than as your manager.'

The adrenalin through my arms announcing, before I know it, that something has gone wrong.

'The firm covers it, of course,' Richard sighs. 'You're one of our top people.'

'Could you be a little more precise about your concerns, Richard?'

He swallows.

'I'm worried that your attention is compromised. I'm worried about your judgement. There's things happening in your team that you don't seem to be in control of. What's going on with Dylan? BioCom are threatening to walk without paying their bill.'

'Dylan works hard.' I don't blink. 'He's put in some huge weeks for them.'

Richard's tongue work around his teeth. He seems to be considering his next words.

'We've had a complaint.'

He holds my gaze, measuring my response.

'A complaint?'

He nods.

'From whom?'

'There's a process that will kick in. I want you to be in the best possible position, Peter. I want to know you have support.'

What in Christ's name is the man talking about?

'What is this?' I say. 'Some kind of rumour, what?'

Richard leans back in his chair, folds his arms.

'You know how we work, Peter. Natural justice and good faith; the firm operates, we always do, on those two principles.'

Faith. Justice. *If you've done nothing wrong, you have nothing to be afraid of.* There is a thin film of distance over Richard's eyes though. It's not just his professionalism that's making him reticent. Richard doesn't know what to think about me anymore.

'This,' he says, his hand swirling in the air to indicate our table, the two of us talking, 'is just a heads-up. An informal conversation.'

I drink wine, watch TV late into the night. The 10pm news reports that the Northern Alliance is pushing towards Kabul. The Taliban appear to be fleeing. Tomahawk missiles are still arrowing in from warships in the Arabian Sea. Explosions over Kabul, Jalalabad, Kandahar. There is animated talk of precision targets, smart bombs. The television screens a blur of hallucinatory green, night cameras, bursts of fire, an incomprehensible commentary. *They're firing, there's a great deal of firepower here.* The image cuts to Bush. *We will not waver.* The president stares unblinking at the camera, seated at a desk in front of a window, a backdrop of lush grass, trees in full leaf. *We will not falter and we will not fail.*

There's footage, old footage this, surely, it must be

Vietnam, of a B52 disgorging a load of bombs, droplets, droppings, released as a person might open up his fist and release a handful of seeds. They waft, lofted through the air, they scatter in a chain behind the aircraft and the plane flies ahead, empty, while behind it the ground lights up again, and again, and again. A field of fire. The ground the bombs fall on is dusty, blue-grey rock and there are jagged lines of bare mountains in the background, and so this is happening in Afghanistan after all, and now.

I wake at four in the morning, and it's cold in the room. I fell asleep on the couch. Tight bands gather around my chest, and I am not sure how to breathe. Calm down, I say over and over, calm down. Soothe and panic, soothe and panic. Is it happening, the thing itself? To die of a massive coronary alone in a cold room and *who is going to tell Aaron because where.* Seconds pass and then minutes. My fingers warm on the couch fabric, so apparently alive for the time being. I'm terrified that Moira is going to die, *which she has,* I'm terrified I will not see her again, *which I won't.* I saw something cold and single-minded in Richard's face yesterday. I have lost his favour. It's cold in the room, but there's already blue light coming in at the large windows, and no chance now of going back to sleep.

Friends, projects. I have cocooned myself in Claudia's assurances. I have delayed, I have hesitated, I have waited, I have bided my time. Each morning I have woken up and thought: *today.* He will call me today.

He's not going to call. He isn't calling.

The sky is steely grey shot through with summer light, and the harbour is a millpond. The sailor is already on deck, although it's barely seven in the morning, uncovering the mainsail, checking the winches.

'You here for the lesson?' he asks.

I shake my head, swig at the takeaway coffee in my hand.

The sea is sliding up onto the hard. I wander ten metres south to the deep slipway, where they bring the boats up to be scrubbed and fixed. There's some kind of king tide going on today. The water is thigh-deep here, no way through. There's a bit of debris caught in it, floaty pods of seaweed, twigs of driftwood, a plastic milk bottletop. The blue disc rises and falls on the swell.

The sailor looks at me quizzically. 'You came and checked out my boat the other week, didn't you?'

'Yeah.'

'It's gone, sorry.'

I look over. Out past the boats on the breakwater wall the sign has been taken down from *Te Haunui*. I have a huge sense of relief that I wasn't foolish enough to buy it. I am no sailor.

So I walk off, north towards the band rotunda and Point Jerningham. The sun is creaming up into the sky and burning off the cloud, the hard summer water brightening into deep blue. Four kayakers split the surface of the water like a series of zips. Joggers and bikers and rollerbladers pour down the Parade, taking the morning air. A silver-haired gentleman in a suit stares at me intensely as he approaches from the south, and when we are almost abreast, he nods and raises a hand in a tiny greeting. I know the face—an Indian man, he's connected to Moira's sister, but I can't, in the moment, fish his name out of my mind or any context, so I give a curt nod by way of answer and charge on, gazing out at the water. *Gupta*, I think, twenty metres on, *Gupta*, but my pace is stalled now by a young couple strolling in front of me, the girl with a glittery blue skirt and a vinyl bag slung over her shoulder, her partner tall and lean, the

214

back of his green Swanndri tight-fitting, with mud-blond curls falling to his collar, running his hand up and down her back, and I'm about to manoeuvere past them when the girl gives out a loud laugh. *Laura!* I say it aloud and they turn, boy, girl, in towards one another, pivoting like a pair of dancers, Laura *and* Matthew, and I have no desire to speak to him, so in the half, quarter, tenth of a second that their faces come around to face me I have already turned to the south, and I am walking away.

Back past the silver-haired gentleman, past the Norfolk pines, past the swimming pool. Down the steps again, to the water, the water. The first sailing school boat is chugging free of the marina, and *Te Haunui* glints bright in the sunlight, another man's boat. Good for him, whoever he may be. May the wind be always at his back.

The tide lapping on the concrete. The blue milk bottletop, still bobbing, floating.

Orpheus, after everything, gets torn limb from limb by women, women who some say are jealous because he loves boys more than them, women who some say are driven mad by his music, women who some say are pulling things apart simply in order to get some relief from ceaselessly having to keep their households together. All that is left of Orpheus at the end of the story is his head, carried off by the ocean currents. It washes up, disembodied, on the sands of Lesbos, singing.

These broken wings da da da dum, dum come and heal me da da dum.

'You know, I saw you back there.'

Matthew. Coming down the concrete steps.

I keep my hands in my pockets.

Two, three more steps and he's almost level with me. I crane over his head at the gap at the top of the stairs where he's appeared.

'Laura's carried on up to varsity. She's got summer school.'

He cracks a wide grin.

'She wasn't really into your porno paintings.'

He steps down, on the level now, on the hard.

'Just stay where you are, I think,' I say.

'I told her to go and talk to the bosses.'

'Do not,' I say, 'come any closer.'

'Are you threatening me?'

He's blocking the stairs, hands on hips. The boy thinks he's in a Bond movie. I could walk away to the left, up onto the pathway underneath the swimming pool, but then he and I will have to wrestle to the death on the precipice above the sea. All of a metre or so above the sea, and more of a shallow marina, but still.

'You're one of those guys, aren't you?' he says.

'One of those guys.'

'Everything and everyone is just there for the taking. That's how it looks from inside your skin, hey?'

My blood is going hard in my chest. If he comes any closer there is some risk I might actually try and deck him.

'I hope your hearing goes well,' I say. 'All you can really hope for in your situation is a sympathetic judge.'

Then I'm walking away to the right, along the front of the white boatshed. I reach the edge of the slipway. Step down into the water. I've come out in jeans, running shoes, what does it matter. Wet pours into my shoe, grips around my shin, rises almost to my groin. Wading, slow, heavy, sludgy, three, four metres of water but *what what*. Under now, submerged now, face, head, wet, wet, feet, *where feet?* Break the surface, breathe huff, breathe huff, *did that bastard push me?*

He's standing back at the corner, watching.

Balance gave out on the slimy bottom is all. Lost it for

a second is all.

Heave ho, up. Onto the concrete, drips piddling like something from a bog. Kick off shoes, yank off jersey.

'Oh god. You all right?'

Matthew has the grace, at least, to come and check.

'Fine,' I say. 'I'm fine.'

Jog the flight of stairs up to the Parade, press the car keys *shump shump* in my pocket, wet gear tossed in the boot, lay an old blanket on the front seat of the Legacy, and away, damp, panting, salt on my lips.

There's a smell in the boardroom which has something to do with morning, with the cleaning product they use on the long table, and also something our bodies have brought into the room, the layered effect of a dozen hair products, perfumes, aftershaves, the hot singe of ironed cotton.

When I stepped through the doorway, I felt a slight sideways shift in the air, a tiny shriek-rattle of anxiety rising off the skulls of my colleagues. It arrives in my chest as a hard fact: I am a problem to these people, this morning. Richard will not meet my eye.

'Coffee, Peter?'

Natasha works her way clockwise around the enormous table. Her lipstick is the colour of fire trucks, alarms, emergencies. I fix my eyes on her silver necklace, and the splash-bubble of brown liquid into the cup. The teaspoon titters against the porcelain.

'Thank you. That's good. No sugar.'

'Let's get underway, shall we?' Richard pegs his glasses out to the bridge of his nose, presses his index finger to the paper in front of him. 'We have several apologies today.'

A big case is running in Auckland, another in Christchurch. The government's contract to buy back Air New Zealand has several people tied up in a meeting across town. We are fourteen people seated around the table; we form a quorum. Binding decisions may be taken. Natasha taps the details into her laptop.

'Do I have seconder for last month's minutes?'

I nod, raise my hand. Let the record show I was an active member of the collective. On this day. Mozart starts up in my head. *Dies irae, dies illa.* Day of wrath, day of doom.

After the early agenda items have been dealt with, Natasha will rise from her laptop and bring plates of pastries, large silver dishes with the buttery, excellent Danishes and croissants that the firm buys in from Bordeaux Bakery. Fruit, iced water. Peppermints. There will be a ten-minute break to endure, inconsequential chatter about January plans for the Coromandel, Hawaii, Fiji. Richard, the meticulous manager, will hold off on his most difficult piece of business until as close as possible to the meeting's end.

Above Richard's head I can just make out the faint impression of the square where the Hotere used to hang. In their wisdom, the guardians of the art collection have left that wall blank, and have hung, instead, a vast Bill Hammond on the opposing wall, a painting I cannot stand to look at today, the birds' heads having taken on a vulturish aspect, their green-gold feathers dark with menace.

They begin with a discussion on recruitment policy, which promises to be long and circuitous, as no one can agree on hiring criteria. Natasha's nails are painted the same violent colour as her lips. Her hair, very black, spikes down to her biceps. She raises her hands from typing at intervals and casts her eyes around the room. She seems to look at me briefly, repeatedly, then away.

'Before we break'—Richard removes his glasses to the table—'there's a partnership issue we need to attend to. Peter, do you mind if we speak to this matter now?'

Natasha leaves to fetch the pastries. The smell of fresh ground coffee swirls into the room. No record of our conversation will be taken, so the matters that are about to unfold before these fourteen partners will be set down only softly in memory, open yet for shaping, interpretation. This is Richard's kindness; this is also his caution.

'If I may?' Even now, he waits for my permission.

'Of course,' I say. 'Please, go ahead.'

I am, essentially, pissed off. There's a line in Euripides' *Medea*: 'It's not at all clear whether all the work you put in produces good or useless children.' I read that play at university when Aaron was about eighteen months old, and keeping us up all night, and smearing his food over all our surfaces, and delighting us, his busy little chimpanzee hands, and toddling, and climbing all over us and bestowing bitey, licking kisses on our faces. It was slowly becoming clear to me that I had embarked on something that would take first call on my strength and care for many years to come. I never got to that stage with Abigail.

Where's the payback? Call me a bean-counter, but show me the parent with grown children who doesn't feel it from time to time. Here I am, with a son who has taken himself off-radar completely, given no thought, not a winkle of consideration, as to what this might do to his father, struck low as I already am.

He's flicking me the bird just for the sheer thrill of it like an angry twelve-year-old. That was how old he was when he tried that pithy line, the one we'd been waiting for, the one he was doomed to deploy from the first moment I told Moira I wanted to marry her: *You're not my real dad.* It was almost a relief when he spat it at me, in the middle of an exhausting back and forth about whether he should be expected to carry the rubbish bag out to the kerb.

I don't know why you treat me with such contempt.

When it's 2am and the branches are scraping on the glass and there's hours to go until the sky lightens, little scenes come back and I think, Yes, I can see how that might have played out differently.

You didn't really get Moira at all.

What the hell does that mean?

What can we expect of each other, anyway? Perfect sympathy, boundless availability? I am not at my best these days, I'm simply not at my best.

There's Mum, up in Wanganui, her hands trembling on the teapot. Every now and then I get a glimpse of it, what it will be like when she slips off. It feels like dropping into a void, even three months shy of fifty, which is a good long time to have had a mother. To be halfway to orphanhood at his young age, that is hard indeed.

What is it that you think I didn't get, son? Maybe I could have just asked that at the airport. Maybe I could have spoken gently. Maybe none of this needed to happen.

Aaron operates, as he always has, in a whirl of his own needs and emergencies. I just wish he would look at me, from time to time, and ask, *How are you, Dad?* I wish he would see something in me other than my usefulness: my hand to reach for my wallet, my voice to sing his praises, my arm to steer him round in the car wherever he wants to go, my energy to plunder whenever he's down and wants company. He will reappear, I just know he will, at the precise moment that he needs something from me.

Four weeks now since I saw him. What a gnawing misery it is to have produced a useless child.

When I think about the man in Perth, Mark, this is what I think: that he helped himself to Moira. That he preyed on her, offering drinks, shifting his chest in closer to her, sliding an arm around the waist, over her hips, chipping away at her resistance.

Moira was twenty-one at the time, and she was no child. I remember her clear, greedy confidence the first night we slept together. But this man, I think he just saw her as game. I don't think she had any choice. She was drunk and she couldn't consent. Those are simply facts.

Once, many years ago, Moira and I were talking about a case I had studied at law school.

'When it happened to you in Australia,' I asked, 'did you ever think of reporting it to the cops?'

We were washing dishes in the kitchen. She was rubbing the teatowel around the edges of a dinner plate.

'When it happened?'

'When you were raped.'

I felt the difficulty of the word in my mouth.

She stopped drying and stared at me.

'I never said that. That's not what happened.'

'No? Take me through it again.'

'*Through* it?'

'Can you explain it to me?'

Moira placed the plate on top of a pile in the cupboard. It didn't make the slightest clink.

'Not really.'

I fished a dozen pieces of cutlery from the sink, ran them under the tap and put them in the drying rack.

'Okay, let me start again,' I said.

'Right.'

'I just want to understand. If you could explain it to me.'

She turned away and wiped crumbs from the table with her hand.

'Because,' I said, 'you know, this Mark. I think Aaron's going to want to know one day.'

'This is about Aaron?'

I peeled the green rubber gloves off my hands, laid them on the bench. I reached for her waist, spun her towards me. Her body was stiff, reluctant, but she allowed me to kiss her forehead.

'I'm sorry,' I murmured. 'I know these aren't easy things to talk about.'

'It wasn't rape.'

'Look, I don't want to go on about it.' I looked her in the eyes, spoke as quietly as I could. 'But honestly, Moira, I think it was. Technically. Legally.'

I don't know what I expected. Some kind of breakdown perhaps, tears, catharsis. She pushed me off and stepped backwards.

'There's no shame in it,' I ventured softly. 'It wasn't your fault.'

Her eyes narrowed.

'Technically,' she said. 'Legally. What is this, *LA Law*?' I was taken aback at the venom in her voice. 'You think you're Arnie Becker?'

'Hey,' I said. 'It's just a conversation.'

'Tell me,' she said. 'Why do you need this so badly? Why do you *want* this to have happened to me?'

I didn't think that was very fair, but it was clearly hopeless to keep asking about it. I did keep wondering, though, down the years, about Aaron, about his temperament, about this dark, forceful man he had come from. Wouldn't anyone?

*

What I've been sentenced to, although no one has dared to use the phrase in front of me, is gardening leave. Time to tend the flowers and vegetables, to grow fat and idle, to hum out the days. A sweet euphemism. *Pending investigation,* as Richard put it at the meeting. But he could barely bring himself to make eye contact with me.

*

The office is dark except for the safety lights that gleam at floor level, casting complex soft-edged shadows on the wall.

The boardroom is never locked. There's nothing valuable, nothing confidential in here, only the bare sweep of a walnut table the size of the deck of a small yacht, the twenty black leather chairs. Empty, the room feels twice the size it did yesterday. It's warm, too; they appear to heat it all night long, little breezes playing out from the central heating ducts low on the walls. From the long windows the clustered lights of the city blaze out. The harbour edge is rimmed with orange, the staircase of the motorway over the Wainui hill, and in the middle the gap, the black bowl of the sea. The red light set on the rocks of Somes Island pulses, waxing, waning in warning. Sailor, plot your course away, don't attempt to make land in the night. Better to drift with the tide till dawn than to come a cropper on these rocks. *Keep it in a holding pattern, bide your time.*

Bugger that. Burn a bridge, cross a Rubicon. Set fire to things. Join the Angry Brigade, throw a bomb. Don't hesitate.

I heave Moira's canvas in through the double doors, prop it by the windows. Keep the lights off, work in the half-dark, just in case someone is down there on the pavement watching. A security guard, monitoring cameras? No matter, I'm doing no harm. Stand on the swivel chair, arms at full reach, bring down Hammond's birds. Unwrap Moira's painting, hoist up, jiggle around to square it off. I take a seat near the head of the table. It'll be face on to Richard when he next sits down here. If it lasts that long.

'Le pape est mort,' I say.

My voice reedy in the empty room.

'But you're not.'

I wheel about. An audible hallucination? No one's here. I stare intensely at the lips of the painted man.

Outside the window, the red light, pulsing.

'That's true,' I venture.

'Stand up, Peter.'

I do what I'm told.

'Dance.'

'Do what?'

'Go on, dance.'

I try out a tentative tap of my left foot. Then the right. The rib cage swaying side to side. Tupac starting up in my head. *Chukka chukka chukka chukka chukka chukka.* Little fist pumps. Hips rolling. Take a spin. *These broken wings da da da dum, dum come and heal me da da dum.*

He's staring down at me with his frozen, open face, the man in the canvas. How did Moira capture that gaze, fix it hard in the paint? It's like he doesn't even know he's naked.

It feels vaguely obscene, what I'm leaving here. But it's out of my hands. Let them figure it out. I shimmy and groove through the door, down the hallway, into the kitchen, where I swipe myself two bottles of milk, and exit by the lift, out into the windless night.

Laura! I wake at dawn thinking that. She'll be the first one to walk into the room today. One of her jobs—I know, I've seen her do it—is to set up the boardroom before meetings. Check the number of chairs, check the data projector is working, check the blinds are pulled up or down to the right degree depending on the brightness of the day.

Truly, it's not meant for you. It has nothing to do with you. I can see how this is going to play out. Laura's going to startle, then walk backwards, very slowly, out of the room, go get her supervisor and whisper to her, and the supervisor will raise an eyebrow and go and look for herself, make a discreet decision to lift the painting down and get it into a cupboard, while Laura hangs back, outside the door, a little pale, shaky, threatened by the aggression of the painting set there like a trap, a threat. That's how the boyfriend, Matthew, master of symbolic action, planter of white carnations, will see it.

Or. Like this. Laura will laugh aloud. She'll go closer to inspect the brushwork, the layering of colours. She'll hold up a little finger, very gently, and touch the shin, the greyish patch of shadow on the ankle that rests on the floor. Laura's face, without intending to, will gather into the same expression of concentration the artist wore when she made this work, and, for a moment there, she will be Moira, gazing at the picture she has made, wondering how on earth she did it, and wondering whether the smallest spot more of bluish-grey might fill that ankle out and bring it into better proportion.

Part Two

Eight

I have had some news that I am struggling to comprehend.

This evening there was a knock on the door. I was downstairs in the study sorting through the finances: bank statements, old chequebooks, invoices. I thought it must be Claudia as I walked up the stairs, although she would rarely turn up unannounced, then I thought of the nextdoor neighbour, a young, tidily dressed woman who has been known to come and complain when I don't park the car far enough into the garage, blocking the footpath, meaning that when she goes walking with her toddler and baby, they have to bump down off the pavement and make a little semicircle out onto the road. I have listened with great seriousness and forbearance while she explained this problem. I can appreciate that with a buggy there would be some slight inconvenience in having to go down off the curb, that perhaps, with a lively imagination, you could even paint some shadow of risk over the toddler on this suburban street where a car or two rolls by every half hour. But the truth is I can't take the problem seriously enough to change my parking habits. Moira used to roll her eyes and say the woman was neurotic. I thought, last night, if it was her at the door again, perhaps I'd offer her a glass of wine to just upset the whole dynamic from the outset.

It wasn't her. I opened the door to a tall Indian man with silvering hair, wearing a blue suit and glasses. It was Mr Gupta, Aaron's old music teacher from Rongotai College.

'Good evening. I'm sorry to bother you.'

The full evening sun poured in through the door, and I had to squint to take him in. He was wearing a suit. I was in my shorts, barefoot. I felt a little caught out, somehow.

'Not at all,' I said. 'Please, come on in. Can I get you a drink?'

He came through into the hallway, and the lounge, and remarked, as people always do, on the openness and light, the green canopy of the trees below the window.

'Now, let me get this right,' I said. 'You're a teacher.'

I thought about the parent–teacher meeting where I felt I was talking with someone who knew my son, who brought an extraordinary degree of insight and care to his work.

'Ah.' I saw the slight embarrassment on his face. 'I'm Maneesh Gupta.' He extended his hand. 'We've met once or twice.'

'Of course,' I said. I signalled to the sofa. 'Maneesh, I was about to open a bottle of wine. Will you join me?'

He waved his hand in refusal.

'No. Well, tea?'

'Yes, thank you.'

I vanished into the kitchen to make a pot, and laid out a plate of Shrewsburys from a container in the pantry.

'You're a lawyer, Mr Collie?'

'Peter, please. A lawyer, yes. That's my background.'

'I know this comes somewhat out of the blue,' Maneesh said, his eyes firmly resting on me, 'but I've come here to talk to you about Aaron.'

'Oh,' I said. 'Well, that's excellent. Good. I'm having

some difficulties with Aaron at the moment. To be honest, I don't know quite where he is.'

Maneesh sat immensely still and didn't speak for some time. I thought I'd gone overboard.

'Please don't worry,' I said. 'A slight blip in communication, that's all. He's fine, he's completely fine. He's in London.'

Maneesh sighed.

'Actually,' he said, 'he's in New Delhi. With my aunt.'

Here's the link: Maneesh Gupta is Sangeeta Gupta's brother; Sangeeta Gupta is Stella's friend; Stella is Moira's sister; and Moira is Aaron's mother.

In fact, it's simpler than that. Maneesh Gupta is Aaron's father.

Maneesh brought out a photo of himself at twenty-five, a formal studio shot of him posed in a chair against a pale blue background, wearing a suit and yellowish tie. It was, without doubt, one of the oddest moments of my life, this man who had just entered my house for the first time ever, taking out from his jacket pocket a photo of someone who could have been Aaron's brother, laying it down on my coffee table, and saying, in faintly embarrassed tones, 'Perhaps you can see a resemblance?'

The sun had tilted low to the west, and cast across us where we sat. I looked at the photo, and I looked at Maneesh Gupta's hands lying flat on the table in the hard light, the squared-off nails, the gold wedding ring on his left hand, his deep-brown skin, the sag and wrinkle around the knuckles, the protrusion of tendons and veins. There was a slimness to the wrist, a small scar on the thumb.

Moira, drunk to the point of oblivion, in the back of a ute with this man.

'But what,' I said, 'were you doing in Australia? Why

were you in the Northern Territory? I thought your family were from the Hutt.'

Maneesh took a slow sip of tea and swallowed. He placed the cup slowly down on the saucer. He seemed to be waiting for me to understand something, and, in due course, I did.

'Oh,' I said. 'That's not how it happened, is it?'

So, in fact, Moira flat-out lied to me for twenty-six years.

When I first met her she was a couple of months pregnant. She told me on our fifth date, drinking coffee at the Matterhorn on Cuba Street. I was a few years home from Amsterdam, at law school, dating girls who kept turning out to be hopeless in one way or another. It threw me, of course, it felt like the universe was making a bad joke, but the girl was gorgeous, her wide brown eyes, the way she wore her clothes and our easy flow of talk and laughter. Nothing she had to say stopped me wanting to be with her.

I stayed my first night with her that night, and fetched her crackers and ginger beer from the kitchen first thing in the morning when she felt queasy. I stood barefoot in her cold kitchen with the bottle of gingerbeer in hand, the spring light pouring in at the window and the scent of daphne from a sprig in a blue jug on the bare wooden table, and suddenly I understood the arrangement we were going to come to. A woman, a child. I could make it right. She was busy trying to get her socks on when I came into the bedroom and told her we should get married.

She told me about the man from Perth and the back of the farmer's ute. She repeated the story a few other times over the years. The details never changed. Mark, she said, I just know he was called Mark. He never said his surname, she said, and I never asked.

Well, Mark never existed. He's a worked-up piece of imagination. She definitely did go to Australia with her friend that year, that much was true. I've seen the photos.

Maneesh wasn't particularly interested in a discussion of the past, and neither, really, was I. He mumbled over a few quick facts. He knew Aaron's date of birth.

'I was with Aaron's mother,' he said, 'for a year. Neither of our families were aware of this.'

'Because?'

He shrugged. 'It was easier.'

'I see.'

'And then we stopped seeing one another. I had no suspicions, none at all, until Aaron came into my music class. I have a son who is five years younger than him. When Aaron answered to his name, and I looked up at him sitting at the desk in the first row, I thought, for a confused moment, I was looking at Jayesh.'

The spitting image.

Wait.

'A year?' I said. 'What, a whole year?'

He swayed his head. 'The best part of a year.'

I had several questions. Maneesh, I wanted to say, could you please state how long the fucking between you and Moira went on for, whether it was for the entire twelve months or somewhat less than that, and how often it occurred, and under what circumstances, and at which addresses, and in which beds, and also, if there were other places, on which floors, couches, cars, tents or grassy banks did you lie with her, and did you intend in all this to get Moira pregnant, or did you take precautions not to, or did you assume that she was doing so?

I became hypnotised by his hands. I had no choice but to imagine those manicured fingers on Moira's body, and it gave me a profound dismay, as if he'd just walked in and

233

told me he'd been sleeping with my wife non-stop for the twenty-six years of our marriage.

Moira had had a handful of lovers before me. There was her high school boyfriend, who she told me had 'broken her heart'. We came to one another with pasts. But to have spent a year with this man, an entire year just before we met, Maneesh Gupta present in her mind this quarter-century past, and walking around the same city, running into him, and to have him teaching her son, *his son*, and not a word to me in all this time of any of it? No tiny slip-ups, no accidental revelations. What kind of crazy self-censorship does that require?

You didn't really get Moira at all.

Did she cry out, with Maneesh? Those long fingers, on her skin. Did she arch her back?

'Delhi,' I squeaked out. 'Is that where you're from?'

'From the Punjab,' he said.

Maneesh is tall and slender, but so very . . . well, an Indian man. I wouldn't have picked that.

'Which part?'

'My parents came from Lahore, but they met in New Delhi. My aunts and uncles live there too, their children, some of them have grandchildren. My sons have gone back to visit several times.'

There is a slight shaking in his hand as he pours more tea into his cup. That gold band on his left hand.

'But how many!' I leapt to my feet.

Maneesh looked alarmed.

'How many children do you have? You mentioned a name. Jay?'

'Oh. Jayesh.'

'Because, I mean. Well. How many are there?'

'I have three sons.'

'Three.'

I slumped back down in the chair, exhausted. There's something awful about the number. I can't explain it. Aaron has three brothers.

'And now he's in Delhi,' I said. 'You're sure of this?'

Maneesh bowed his head slightly. 'I spoke to my aunt on the phone this morning. And I spoke briefly to Aaron. He's had a little stomach trouble'—Maneesh allowed himself a smile—'as first-time visitors often do, but he's coming right.'

'What a relief,' I said. 'What a great relief.'

I spoke briefly to Aaron. This morning.

Then I very badly wanted to pin this handsome, lean man hard against the wall and put my hands around his elegant neck and choke him.

'I'm sorry.' Maneesh's brow tightened, and he peered into his teacup. 'I wasn't sure whether I should come. When Aaron admitted that he hadn't spoken to you at all, I thought, well, I must take this upon myself. But perhaps I should have left it to Aaron.'

I waved my hand in the air to brush his comments away.

'They're in the Hutt, your parents?' I remembered Stella and her friend Sangeeta zooming around Claudia's driveway with pockets full of Pineapple Lumps and Toffee Milks. 'Didn't they own a Four Square out there?'

'Yes. That's ended, unfortunately. They lost the franchise under difficult circumstances.'

Aaron's grandparents.

Maneesh sighed. He looked around the room, took in the art on the walls—an Albrecht, a Matisse print and two of Moira's works—and sighed again. A forlorn expression came over his face. I thought, for a moment, that he was about to offer his condolences on her death, or make some other comment about her absence, and I thought I would probably dock him for real if he did.

'My wife has been badly upset by all this,' he said.

'I can imagine. So why now?'

'Sorry?'

'Why spill the beans now? Why upset your wife? And in the middle of everything Aaron's going through. It seems, well, poorly thought through.'

'Oh, I see.' Maneesh looked miserable again. 'No, it didn't play out like that. Aaron came to my house shortly after the funeral and told me bluntly that he knew who I was. His mother had apparently talked to him.'

'Moira told him.'

'It seems so.'

Maneesh couldn't meet my eye. It occurred to me that he hadn't used Moira's name once through our entire interview. *Aaron's mother* was his preferred formulation.

He stood up and prepared to go, but before he did, he pulled a business card out of his suit pocket, and bent over the coffee table to write on it.

'My aunt's phone number and address in New Delhi.' He handed me the card. 'I can only imagine how worried you must have been.'

I pour a large glass of wine and stand out on the deck with the trees curving in all round and the heat going out of the sun. He's in Delhi, with nothing worse than traveller's runs. What more could I ask for? But I am gasping for air, and glugging back the drink, and holding on to the rail of the deck as if I might fall down. There is a black hole of tiredness at the base of my neck that I want to collapse into. I want to fall asleep for a week or a year.

In the morning I pick up the phone and call Rob.

'*Delhi?*'

For a moment I consider holding back the details,

but there's really no way to explain any of it except by explaining it all.

'What's he like then, this bloke?'

'He's Indian.'

'As you said. Any other characteristics?'

I sigh. 'Look he's a perfectly nice man. Intelligent, amiable. Musical.'

'Must be hard on your boy,' he says. 'Gutting, I suppose, learning that your dad didn't bother coming to find you. I mean, all those years.'

'Well, I'm his dad,' I say. 'I'm still his father.'

'Course you are. Genetics, though, powerful stuff. Kids want to know.'

'Yeah?' I say. 'I would have told him myself, obviously, if I'd known.'

Rob doesn't answer for a bit. Then, 'Don't you ever feel like the karma's trying to tell you something?'

'The karma.'

'It's odd, right? First Clare and I spot that girl in Greece, and next thing your boy's off finding his old man.'

'Something metaphysical in it, do you reckon?'

'I reckon you should get off your arse and do something, that's what I reckon.'

'I see.'

'You don't know what happened to that kid of yours. You still don't know.'

'Yes. You've made that point.'

'Have I, though? Mull it over for another decade or two. No rush.'

'Fine. Well, as you mention it, *are* you going to Mytilene soon?' I ask. 'I can't come to Europe. That's just not possible. But if—'

He cuts me off. 'We are, as it happens. But I'm not doing that, Peter. I'm not doing that shit for you. I've got kids of my own, you know? Rachel's in some kind of London-wide athletics meet next week and she's training fit to bust a boiler. Three times a week we have to drive her to Clapham. And Clara's a right mess. She's taken up with some deadbeat Metallica-playing stoner and she's having screaming fights with her mother about staying nights with her. She's fifteen. Bit young to decide you're a lesbian, don't you think? So yes, we're taking them to Mytilene the minute school breaks up, but frankly no, I'm not going hunting for anyone on your behalf.'

'I wasn't asking you to do anything.'

'It's great to hear that your boy's all right,' he says. 'I've had a few bad moments, wondering.'

'It's been rough on everyone,' I say. 'I'm sorry.'

Later in the morning, I ring Delhi. Maneesh had written out the number in full: country code, area codes. I take the phone into the study, press the eleven digits down in sequence. There are a bunch of clicks and hums. After an interminable pause, telecommunications companies connecting around the globe, a foreign ringtone starts up.

'*Namaste.*' It's a woman. The aunt?

'I'm looking for Aaron Collie. From New Zealand.'

I don't give my name. It occurs to me that if I announce who I am, he might not, even now, come to the phone.

The woman fires off a string of words I don't understand. Then silence.

'Hello?'

My heart had been going like the clappers. Now it slows to a disappointed trot. It isn't him.

'Aaron,' I repeat. 'Aaron, Aaron, is he there?'

'You are looking for Aaron?'

Am I not making myself abundantly clear?

'Phoning from New Zealand, is it?'

'It is, New Zealand. He's from. And I'm calling from. His father,' I say, helplessly. 'Aaron Collie. I'm Peter. Collie, also. Peter Collie.'

'Aaron's father, what an honour. But Aaron has actually left us.' The man's tone grows sorrowful. Something collapses in my chest.

'Left you?'

'If you'd only phoned yesterday. Oh dear.'

'Please.' In what sense has he left you?

'My brother and I drove him to the central bus station early this morning. He's travelling, yes, right now, arriving into Lahore. There was unexpected traffic around the Moti Barg and he almost missed the bus. Special service, of course, it only goes three times per week. My wife was absolutely correct, you know, we should never have taken the RK Puram Road and the flyover. As it happened, were stalled there for close to an hour.'

'Lahore.'

'Indeed. Even my wife has never been back to Pakistan. She has not seen her brother in fifty years. Aaron wants to find him. He is a bold young man.'

'Can he get into Pakistan? Can he go there?'

'Ah. Well, of course there's complex paperwork involved in applying for the visa, triplicate copies and so forth. And so his stay here has been longer than expected. But, he's lucky. For Indians, it's much worse, impossible. He should have applied from New Zealand, in fact. No one can go to Pakistan on a whim.'

'He's stayed with you, all this time. Over a month?'

'I will say this: I was suspicious of the young man in the first instance. It was, I admit, a shock to learn of his unexpected nativity. But, you see, we have no children. To have Maneesh's son in our house, for Amrita this has been nothing short of a miracle. She misses her family very

239

badly. What I have come to understand is that this burden gets worse as a person gets older. She is, my wife . . . how can I explain it? The sorrow of the past overwhelms her at times.'

Maneesh's child.

'Amrita considers Aaron her own grandson, almost. She loves him as if he were the son of her own child. The Guptas, I don't know, they are perhaps upset about the circumstances. You could say they have not completely welcomed him. You know, when they come to India, Maneesh and his sons, they make extremely short trips. The girl, Sangeeta, has never, not once so far, brought her daughters to visit us.'

I had the sense the man could continue in this vein for quite some time.

'It's a long way,' I ventured. 'It costs a lot.'

He went on. 'My wife's sister, she has never travelled to India either. And now, Aaron, he has formed an intention to locate Salaa-ji. He has been writing letters, making approaches. It's been over fifty years. Extraordinary. I can't tell you what it has all meant to my wife. Until now, she was reluctant so much as to speak of her brother. She is nervous to see Aaron going to Pakistan, of course, but as he begins to conduct his enquiries, we have some hope of hearing news. She is happy, and so I am happy.'

So Aaron turns out to be a one-man family reunification SWAT team. All boldness, clarity, action, firing off letters, lodging his visa applications. Not a bone of fear or hesitation in him.

'Well, I'm grateful,' I say. 'And a month is a long time. Can I send you, perhaps, some money? Can I reimburse you in some way?'

There is a long pause. Akenese's face, the offence in it, when I tried to help in this way.

'Sir. Please do not speak of money.'

'How can I find him?' I say. 'Who do I call?'

'We have no phone number, actually. We will just wait. But shall I contact you, if I hear from him?'

'Please,' I say. 'Yes.' And I give my phone numbers and email address to this unknown man in a city I've never been to, and hope that he will bring word of my son.

Karma. Did Rob mean the John Lennon instant kind, or the slower variety? The four-volume dictionary in the study lists it as a Sanskrit word. Sanskrit comes down from the Proto-Indo-European language from which Greek and Latin, Bengali and Urdu, Russian and Persian all descend. The etymology of karma is from a root word in that ur-language, meaning to make or to form. The Lithuanian *keras*, to charm, is a close cousin.

Karma, to act, and in acting to make and form the next hour, the next day, the next lifetime into which we will step. To act, and in so doing to cast a charm over the future.

Does karma mean that everything comes back to me, everything returns, that whatever suffering I go through is at my own hand? If that is its essence, then it's a pitiless doctrine. What did Moira do in any of a thousand lifetimes to bring the cancer on herself? I would punch anyone who said she deserved it, as I wanted to punch her long-lost second cousin from Kaikoura when she turned up at our house one evening with some kind of miracle-cure fermented milk drink, and said we needed to have faith that God would heal her, in the very week it was rapidly becoming apparent that God was not at all inclined to do so. No. Just give me the implacable, impersonal Fates, measuring out the thread and making their arbitrary cut.

Was there something I did that caused Aaron to stop speaking to me? Now that is a simpler yet more difficult question.

I dial my parents' number, hang up, dial again, hang up again. *Mum, he's in Pakistan. He's safe.* The plain fact is, I haven't even told her that I had lost track of him. Always this instinct not to alarm, not to upset. And now that he's found, explanations seem weary, unnecessary. But I would like to see them again, face to face.

'Peter.' That tightness in her voice. Is it two weeks since I've called?

'Listen,' I say. 'I was thinking, what about a trip for you and Dad? What about a few nights away?'

'A trip? To Wellington?'

She sounds surprisingly open to the idea.

'Come up to Castlepoint with me,' I say. 'The real estate agent wants to meet me. I'll go up Friday afternoon. I'll swing by and pick you up.'

'It's hardly a swing by.'

'Close enough, once I'm in the car.'

'Do you think we'd manage? Dad doesn't walk far these days.'

'No walking required,' I say. 'Door to door service. Views over the bay, cooked breakfast. Go on, Mum. It might be your last chance to stay there.'

'You're really selling it?'

'I'll be signing off on the highest offer on Saturday morning. Time to get it off my hands.'

'Perhaps we could.' There's something like wonder in her tone. Why have I not made this happen before?

'I'll talk to Dad,' she says. 'I'll see if I can convince him.'

*

242

I do need to get away, to the big air, the open road. It's turning me into a shut-in, the lack of employment. Agoraphobia: *fear of the marketplace*, and indeed the unedifying truth of the matter is that, since I have been put on gardening leave, I have found myself reluctant to go into the city, or even, some days, as far the Hataitai shops. I have hunkered down in the house for most of the past fortnight, set up base in its smallest room, the study. I take mugs of coffee and plates of honey toast downstairs and conduct my little errands, the phone calls, the emails. The books are a solution of sorts. There is the lower shelf of dictionaries and atlases, also the outsized *Daphnis and Chloe*, and above three shelves of volumes, mostly on Greek topics, but other histories as well, now organised back into order. I have begun methodically reading my way through Arrian's *The Campaigns of Alexander* by way of a project.

On the wall is a series of line drawings which Moira made of Aaron as a young child, my favourite among her works. There is an eastern window that gives on to the lower garden. I have a view from here of the washing line, my shirts and underwear still and limp in this unnerving lack of wind. There are tiny ticks and creaks all day through the house, as the wooden planks make their minute adjustments, swelling in the heat of the afternoon, cooling later in the evening.

Even on days when I conduct all my business from inside these four walls, I am determined not to let myself go. I observe the morning ceremonies religiously: the hot shower, soap, a bowel movement, an ironed shirt. My father once told me that on Crete and in Egypt, Colonel Kippenberger instructed his troops that, no matter what happened, they were to shave each morning. If they found themselves in confused retreat, if their commander had been shot in the night, if they had started to doubt in the

Empire and the faithfulness of their wives, water and a razor came first. Such rudiments can hold a man together.

My own face reflected back in the dark window.

You selfish bitch woman, you conniving, lie-orchest-rating, cowardly, idiot woman.

I went to bed hoping to fall again into that sweet, deep sleep, but I'm awake now, somewhere in the early watch of morning with a rage in my chest, I'm out of bed, in the lounge, pouring out profanities.

You mind-screwing, shit-strewing, diabolical, deceitful ruination of a woman, what did you think was going to happen to the rest of us after you detonated your little time bomb from your *while-I-lie-here-dying* bed?

Well, it's not all that satisfying, shouting at the bare glass. I fetch my ragged copy of the order of service and prop it up on the bookshelf. A little three-inch-square shot of Moira smiling in a sunhat on the grass at Castlepoint.

Did you talk to a child psychologist?

Did you consult your horoscope, read tea leaves, talk to a priest, talk to your God, consult your conscience, did you toss a coin, ask an oracle, did you ever put the question to a stranger on a train: Well, what do you think I should do?

We'll never know. Did you ever ask *me*? On one of those hundreds and thousands of nights that we slept together in our bed, foot grazing toe, hand cupping breast, forearm flung over stomach, did you ever wake up in the night and think: There's the symphony orchestra tickets to buy, and the new curtains to measure up, and a paint sale on at Resene, and when did we last clean out the gutters, and, golly, there's another piece of business outstanding that I really ought to attend to—What do you think, Peter? Is it time I told Aaron, now that he's five years old, or ten, or fifteen, or twenty, that his dad is his music teacher and his grandparents are selling K Bars and packets of Rothmans twenty kilometres away on Waterloo Road?

And did I turn away, and mumble something about the electricity bill and getting the car traded in, and slide back into foggy sleep, and forget by the morning that you'd spoken at all?

Claudia is sorting out clothes to give to the Salvation Army: some kind of spring-cleaning project. A plastic bag gapes open on the lounge floor, a dozen parrot-bright scarfs and tops strewn over the chairs.

'How many scarves does a lady need, do you think?' she asks.

'Three?'

'That seems mean.'

Claudia takes a yellow silk scarf, folds it into a small bundle and places it in the bag. She straightens herself up with some effort.

'This one's gorgeous.' She holds up a rose and teal swirled scarf. 'I bought it in Florence, all those years ago. I was so terrified to tell Donny, I thought I'd dashed our budget for the trip. I spent thousands of lire. Turned out it was worth about three pounds. I should have bought a dozen of them.'

'Go and make up for it this time.'

'You're right. I plan to take an enormous suitcase.'

'You'll regret that when you're trying to pull it along a train platform. You need to be able to lift it.'

'Lift it? They have boys for that kind of thing. Donny and I never had to lift a finger in Italy.'

'When did you go to Italy?'

'Oh, it was the sixties. Sixty-four, it would have been. Moira was in her last year of primary school, and I was pregnant with Stella.'

'Almost forty years ago. Things might have changed a little.'

'Someone will help. There's always help, as long as you tip them enough.'

It's so easy to summon Moira into this room right now. She would be animated, fretting and fussing over the clothes with her mother, cheerfully appalled at her comments about the boys, bossing and ordering Claudia as best she could. Claudia, in later years, had started to enjoy being taken in hand by her daughters, and had allowed herself to abdicate control from time to time.

I take a seat in an armchair, steeple my hands up and fix my eyes on my mother-in-law.

'You remember the Guptas, Claudia?'

She looks up. There is a definite sharpness in her eyes.

'The Guptas?'

'Sangeeta?'

'Oh yes, Sangeeta's been a wonderful friend to Stella. She's a doctor now. She has two daughters. The parents ran the Four Square down the road. Wonderful business people, they were. It was a tidy, well-kept shop. Nice people.'

'Maneesh?' I lick my lips.

Claudia takes hold of a pale pink T-shirt, shakes it out, holds it up to the light and then lays it flat on the bed, folding in the sleeves.

'Yes.' The body of the shirt in half, then in half again. 'They had an older boy.'

'He came to visit me yesterday.'

Claudia pauses in her folding but doesn't look up. She gives out a little breath, then resumes a determined rolling-up of the T-shirt.

Her eyes stay fixed on her hands. There's perceptible pinkness in her saggy neck. It seems proof enough.

'So maybe you could help me understand,' I say. 'After

246

they'd been sleeping together for a year, and, you know, once she was knocked up, why didn't Moira marry him?'

I'm taking a risk. Claudia's blood pressure is fairly well controlled with the medications, but there was that minor stroke five years ago that put her in hospital for a few days and left her with slurred speech for months afterwards. I'll keep my eye closely on her, make sure my mobile is ready in my pocket.

She doesn't flinch or look up. She continues her business with the T-shirt, placing it into the bag with great gentleness.

'I don't know what you're talking about.'

I burst out laughing. 'Yes, you do.'

She sniffs, stands up straight and looks at me. 'It's an awfully long time ago, Peter. Why would anyone care now?'

'Did you *tell* her to break it off?'

'Oh, come on. You know Moira. Who could tell her anything?'

'Did you ever think what it would do to Aaron?'

She sits down in the armchair opposite me, and crosses her arms.

'They're very traditional in their views, those people. You understand that, don't you? They don't take kindly to mixed-race marriages, Indians. Of course people think, nowadays, that those sorts of things aren't a problem, but the fact is, if you try to spend your life with someone who doesn't share your values and customs, it's very—well, it's extremely difficult. They had a strong sense of that, the Guptas. They had an Indian girl all lined up for him. I can't say they were wrong.'

I cross my arms over my chest. 'I suppose Aaron could have ended up working in the dairy.'

It's bait, and she takes it.

'Ah, well.' She smiles, shakes her head as if shaking

247

away a dream. 'He probably would have enjoyed that as a child, ringing up the till.'

'Unpacking the chippies,' I add. 'Stacking the turmeric.'

She looks up at me. There's a snicker of laughter in her face.

'A near miss, all in all,' I say.

'He's had a marvellous childhood.' She stands back up, crosses over to the table and lifts up a white linen shirt to the light. 'Everything turned out for the best. Just look at that. How on earth did I do that? Oil spots all over.'

'The thing I can't believe, and I'm not sure how to put this, the thing that astonishes me most—'

'Yes, go on.' She lays the shirt flat on the table, and peers down at it, scraping her fingernail over a stain on the front pocket.

'I can't believe Moira obeyed her prejudiced batshit mother over something as important as this.'

She stops the business with her fingernail, looks up and stares at me.

'You rude bugger.'

'For god's sake, Claudia. It was 1975.'

'Obedience didn't come into it. Moira made up her own mind. She always did. I didn't know a thing until the baby was born, and then it was startlingly obvious what had gone on. He's the spit of his grandfather, Aaron is. Have you met him, Mr Gupta?'

'Did neither of you spare a thought for Aaron? How myopically dysfuctional can one family be?'

'I think you might keep your insults to yourself, Peter.'

'*You* could have told him.'

'It wasn't my place. In any case, it was mere suspicion. Moira never told me, and I never asked.'

'Sort of like the US Navy.'

'I'm sorry?'

248

'We all know, and we all pretend we don't know. Except Aaron *didn't* know.' I sigh, and sit down in the armchair. 'It was cruel. I can't understand why Moira was so cruel.'

'Oh, I don't think so, not really.' Claudia tosses the linen shirt into a rubbish bag and picks up another one, patterned in paisley. 'Look at how Aaron fell in with those Islanders at college. No interest in anything but rugby, but such lovely manners. And they went to church, those boys. Christian values. They were a jolly good influence. Aaron was perfectly happy to be included, anyone could see that.'

No interest in anything but rugby. I think of Isaia Lemalu, who has just finished his Master of Fine Arts, and George Faletau, who at sixteen saved all his paper run money for a year to buy himself a ticket to the Three Tenors. But I'm too tired to argue. Claudia will be Claudia. And the fact is that in those early days, behind closed doors, Moira and I spoke of Aaron's new friendships in more or less exactly these terms.

My real dad's Rarotongan. Why contradict him, once he'd made up his mind? It wasn't the most rigorous way to think, but I can see how Moira might have ended up there.

None of which explains why she didn't tell *me*.

'I've been such a sucker,' I said. 'I fell for everything.'

'You can't possibly take that view of matters. Everything turned out well for you.'

'That's how it seems to you?'

'But, it did! Except for—'

'—the bloody cancer?'

Claudia stops. She sits down hard in a dining table chair and gazes out the window. The cat leaps into her lap and starts to pound at her stomach, and she absently strokes its back.

'Moira was a very private person. I sometimes feel that I hardly knew her at all. My own daughter.'

It's a heavy feeling that settles over the room. Misery, which might connected to *misericordia*, mercy. The quality of mercy is not strained; it drops as the gentle rains from heaven. It's really not necessary for me to be mean to Claudia.

'And where is Aaron?' Claudia shakes herself a little, as if surfacing from a dream. 'Do we know yet?'

'Yes. He's in India. Or perhaps Pakistan.'

'As I thought. Well, it'll be fascinating for him.'

When I leave, Claudia heaves herself down the three steps, although I tell her she should stay up on the porch. There's the handrail I installed last summer, which she leans on heavily. She offers me her cheek before I get into the car and I land a dry kiss on it.

'Did she love him?' I'm asking before I can stop myself.

'Love who?'

'Maneesh. Moira. Did she?'

'Love.' Claudia bites down on the word and gives me a scornful look. 'What on earth could it matter now?'

A full week after my midnight break-in to the office, I feel mortified to remember what I did with Moira's portrait. Yes, it's not too strong a word, mortified: *mortalis* again, dragging all her children behind her, morgue and mortuary, immortality and moribund. To mortify the flesh as the ancient monks did, *to put it to death* with scourges and whips and pins and hairshirts. The subduction of desire, the beating out of the devil. Perhaps pale-skinned punk kids I see up Cuba Street are modern day monks, their various piercings and tattoos a visible badge of the body transcended. I have no idea when mortification first entered common usage as meaning embarrassment or shame, but there's a natural emotional logic to it, as I have, in literal fact, been walking around the living room striking my own forehead with my palm and groaning aloud as if in pain when I think of the painting of my naked body hanging in that room of professionals. What was I thinking? It wasn't thought, it was possession, or abandonment, I don't know. I am not and never have been keen on self-exposure of any kind. What I did with that painting is a most unaccountable aberration, and my sense is that I have opened myself up now to a strange and rare scrutiny, and to the great likelihood of being misunderstood.

Gardening leave or no gardening leave, the Community Law Centre still expects me to front up for my monthly duty, and so, in the spirit of Kippenberger, on Wednesday evening, I do. There is something quite cheering about being useful, and the time passes quickly. After a productive consultation with a young couple who are being ruthlessly screwed over by their landlord, I step out of the interview room and find Laura seated in the waiting room, black Doc Marten boots swinging, arms folded over her cycle bag. The administrator hands me a sheet for my next interview, with Laura's name scribbled on the top of the page.

'Ah, I can't actually see that client,' I say. 'Conflict of interest.'

The administrator, an older woman who takes quite a stern approach with the volunteers at the Centre, frowns.

'Really?'

'Yes, really.'

'I'll see if Mai's available.'

When the administrator walks off down the corridor to find her, Laura comes right on in to where I am and pulls the door shut behind her.

'I need to talk to you.'

Her satchel is over her shoulder, both hands gripping the strap. There's something very determined in her face.

251

'Open the door, please.'

'I have to tell you something.'

'Open the door.'

Laura sighs, pulls on the handle and swings the door open. The waiting room is full of clients, who are now all watching us. Well, good.

'That complaint I put in,' Laura says, 'at work.'

Witness tampering, my brain begins to shriek. *Coercion.*

'Laura,' I say, 'legally, I cannot talk to you about this. This is simply not a conversation we can have.'

'I've withdrawn it,' she blurts out.

Such an endearing desire for approval in her face, like a child who smashes her plate on the floor then rushes to find the brush and shovel. What does she expect from me: *Good girl, never mind*?

She flops herself down into the administrator's office chair.

'You *were* drunk when you drove me home, right?'

Due process requires me to walk out, remove myself from the room. But I give a very small nod.

'What happened was, I talked it over with my boyfriend. He thought I ought to put in a complaint.'

His goblin face swims up in front of me. The swing of dark blond curls on his shoulders. *You're one of those guys.* The breadth of his body, blocking me at the marina.

'I wasn't too sure. He, my boyfriend—'

'Matthew.'

'Yes. Matthew.'

'Go on.'

'He said I was downplaying it. He was all like, What do you think predators do? As if I've never had creepy arseholes try it on, you know?'

Matthew with his distaste for technicalities, Matthew who thinks his testimony will bring ethical clarity to the

252

court, to the world. If I were properly strategic about things I would organise right now for Laura to sit in with Mai, get an affidavit from her detailing Matthew's tactics, his insinuations. Signed and witnessed. Admissible evidence.

'As if I can't judge for myself,' Laura is saying. 'When I told him about your wife's painting he hit the roof. He wanted me to accuse you of hitting on me, but there was no way I was going to put that in the complaint. You're not a sleaze. So I just said about the drinking.'

'Laura, I don't understand what's gone on, but I actually don't want to talk to you about it, without—'

'Without a lawyer?' She smiles.

'Exactly.'

'So, go find one,' she says. 'We're in the right place.'

'Why did you come here tonight?'

'I felt weird.' Something almost whiny in her voice. 'I wanted you to know what happened.'

Neither of us spoke.

'Then I heard you lost your job and everything. It seemed like it had all got out of proportion, you know?'

Her dark eyes gazing up at me from the chair. Her hair mussed up and a long ladder down the front of her black tights. I turn my head away. None of it matters now. I'm never going back to the firm.

'You should go now.'

The administrator comes striding towards the office frowning, with Mai behind her.

'Can I help?' She stares down at Laura in the chair. 'We don't usually use this room for clients.'

'She's going now,' I say.

'Yeah.' Laura stands up and swings her bag over her shoulder. 'I'm going.'

*

This morning I found Sangeeta's phone number in Moira's black leather address book, and made an arrangement to meet her at the café opposite Wellington Hospital.

It's a fairly gruesome business, returning to the hospital precinct. The neoclassical pillars of the hospital loom over the main road, recalling endless appointments and consultations, radiotherapy and chemotherapy, and returning to those same rooms later, nerves shredded, waiting for the oncologist to pull up the examination results and give his most recent verdict. Moira and I ate many meals in the café where I plan to meet with Sangeeta, both before and after such appointments. As the months wore on, we largely stopped discussing the immediate medical situation and began to talk about the past. Moira told me stories from her childhood and her girlhood, and we sank deep into shared memories of various trips and holidays we had taken together, in Venice and London, in Pelorus Sound and Castlepoint. And always, we talked about Aaron. Moira's extraordinary capacity to remember everything, everything about him: *he must have been six that year, he must have been nine, he'd just started school, he was taking karate lessons, we took him to see* Star Wars, *he'd broken his arm that summer, he wasn't allowed to swim. Remember?*

I don't know how to comprehend those conversations now. They were delightful, among the warmest and sweetest of my marriage. But now I think they were just gossamer cobwebs over gaping holes.

Sangeeta, to my surprise, arrives with Adrian. I take them in as they come to the table, Adrian's lanky figure, Sangeeta's short and fuller than I remember. I never spoke to her at Moira's funeral. She and Maneesh appeared to me that day as such peripheral figures, incidental to the central events of my life, and Moira's.

254

'It's seems we're more connected than we thought.'

I want to set a light tone, to take the awkwardness out of the encounter, but Sangeeta's smile looks forced, and Adrian immediately pulls an ugly, pitying face.

'You too?' I lean in towards him. I can hear the bark in my voice. 'That night in Venice, drinking champagne in San Marco square, did you know back then?'

Sangeeta's eyes widen.

'I'm sorry.' I pull back into my seat. 'I'm getting ahead of myself.'

'Basically, no,' says Sangeeta. 'Of course Adrian didn't know. Neither did I.'

Adrian watches me. He sips his Coke and pushes himself back from the table, his ankle resting on his knee and his hands behind his head, so that his body is an arrangement of triangles, spread large, inhabiting as much of the air around him as he can.

I can't think where to take the conversation after such a bad start, and I can't, in fact, remember why I wanted to talk to Sangeeta so desperately. But I do want to look on her face. The palimpsest of Aaron's features pressing through hers is clearly visible now. The shape of the eyes. The cheekbones. Hiding in plain sight.

'I did know it was a possibility,' Sangeeta says. 'Stella and I, we talked about it once. We were only teenagers. Maneesh and Moira, we found one time, a letter—' She breaks off, presses her lips together. 'We knew that my brother and her sister had been lovers. We found that pretty funny.'

Maneesh and Moira, two syllables each, the matching consonant. It has a good ring to it. I'm glad to hear it spoken aloud.

Sangeeta, I want to say, she died a block away from here, in her small room in the hospice. Sangeeta, there are still days, many days, when I cannot accept that I will not see her or touch her again.

'Have you talked with Stella about all this?' I ask.

'I haven't been in contact with Stella for a long time,' she says. 'I don't have a phone number for her in the States.'

'I have Moira's address book here.'

I thumb through the little pages, find the number, write it on a serviette and pass it across the table. I have no idea how that phone call will unfold, but that's not my business.

'The whole situation does have a funny side,' I say. 'I will admit that.'

'It would be fair to say that it's put the cat among the pigeons in your family, hasn't it, Gee?' Adrian lays his hand on Sangeeta's shoulder.

Sangeeta's face turns icy. It's time to get the conversation onto safer ground.

'Look, it's been years,' I say. 'What's happened since we last met? You're in medicine, are you, Adrian?'

'We both are. I'm a consultant paediatrician over the road. Sangeeta's working as a GP now.'

'Children?'

'Two daughters.'

Aaron's cousins.

'Wonderful.'

'You know, your son will love it in Delhi,' says Adrian. 'Fantastic city.'

'In fact, he's in Pakistan.'

Sangeeta looks up, surprised.

'I know,' I say. 'It's hard to keep up.'

Adrian looks out the window to where the red buses are stacked up at the lights. There is a twitchiness in him; he is keen to return to his patients. Moira and I occasionally saw children on the oncology ward. I always found myself avoiding the eyes of the parents. I remember Adrian's

256

combative arguing in Venice. He must draw on some deep seam of gentleness in himself, invisible to my eye, in order to minister to those kids.

When we stand to go, Sangeeta tells me I should get in touch if there is anything further she can help with. This seems like a sincere offer.

Nine

My mother lowers the blinds in the front bedroom, while I put the kettle on to boil in the kitchen. My father, on the other side of the door, makes use of the toilet. We are at such close quarters here in the bach. I hear the stop-start sluice of his pissing, the hoick and spit as he clears his throat. I don't mind the intimacy. I've given them the front room because it has the best bed in the house. Also, I don't want to sleep there myself. I'll doss on the couch, because the back bedroom with the shaky metal bunks is full of insect corpses, and because this way I'll hear either of them if they up in the night and need the loo. The last thing I want to deal with way out on this remote coast is a fall, a broken hip.

'Tea, Mum?'

I poke my head around the bedroom door. She has lifted folded sheets out of her bag, thrown the pillows down off the bed.

'I'll do that,' I say. 'Come and sit down.'

'Won't take me two ticks.'

With both hands, she billows the white sheet out over the bed. It releases the smell of lemon Persil into the air, which is Wanganui, and falling asleep as a child. But I grab hard at the two far corners, straighten and tuck, hoist the duvet up and give it a hard shake. My mother starts peeling off the old pillowcases, which is in fact a good idea. I can't think when they might last have been changed: possibly the last time Moira stayed here.

No, I do not want to sleep in that bed.

'Shall I make tea?'

'A bit late, love. Think we'll turn in.'

It has been a long day. We didn't get to Palmerston till lunchtime, and then the roadworks on the Manawatu Gorge slowed us to a crawl. We stopped for toilets and drinks in Eketahuna, and then again in Masterton, so it was almost six by the time we were winding the last few miles towards the coast, the light cooling over the hills. I abandoned my plans to cook a meal, and pulled in at the Whakataki pub instead.

That was a good decision. Dad was pretty tickled. It was just his kind of place, a country pub with a pool table, an eclectic mixture of deer-heads, beer flags, rusty saw bits and black-and-white photos of the lighthouse on the walls. The bar was tended by women in their forties or fifties, unfussy, their creased faces and smoky voices putting him at ease. He tucked in to his food, fish with an inch of batter on it, a slab of apple crumble slathered in cream: everything he shouldn't be having.

The whole time we sat over our meals, my mother watched the two kids at the table next to us with hungry eyes, small boys, perhaps three and five, concentrating hard on their red fizzy drinks. At last, her need overtook her. 'Beautiful children,' she said to the young mother. 'Aren't they good.' The young mother smiled absently and stroked the older boy's hair. Later, when the jukebox started up and the room grew crowded, we heard the kids' shouts float up from the swings at the back of the garden, and the grandparents, who couldn't have been much older than me, took their beer and cigarettes out to sit on the deck and watch. I bought Dad a whisky, and he knocked it back in a few sips, leaned back with his arms over his chest. It was good to be there, right there.

I'd told them about Aaron as we'd headed out of Wanganui. I explained about Maneesh. It had essentially been a monologue. I was surprised, and also infuriated by their lack of interest, although I suppose I should have expected it. My mother, the way she came into Moira's room in the maternity ward of Hutt Hospital twenty-five years ago and gazed down at Aaron. Didn't miss a beat, not a blink. 'What a healthy-looking boy.' Which he was, astonishingly so, given his early arrival. Every time she saw him, she repeated these terms: healthy, chubby, strong, a real little man. But she couldn't bring herself to say anything about the way he was so plainly not mine. I had made that clear to her from the first, but she simply partitioned it off, that history of Aaron's, never spoke of it, never enquired. In the car this afternoon, Mum had one or two questions about Pakistan, how he got there, which city he was in, and then that was pretty much the end of it.

After my parents are in bed, I take my cup of tea down to the front section to drink it while looking over the bay. It's one of those calm, sultry nights that will give way to a breathless morning. The wind blows a gale five days out of six up here, but that sixth day is enough to make you forgive all the rest, a sabbath, a reprieve, when the afternoon light hits the yellow rocks and the sky turns to lapis lazuli behind. But tomorrow I'm selling, no matter what the weather does. I'm a veteran here, and a single gorgeous Saturday won't fool me.

There was a newspaper clipping on the wall down at the pub tonight, a headline from nine years ago, sailors who underestimated how furiously the wind rakes this coast all the way up from Palliser to Cape Turnagain. Colin McAndrew, a dough-faced, red-headed fellow, was the lone survivor from a yacht that had been making her way up towards Auckland, crewed by four friends from Carey's Bay in Dunedin. It was July, and when they realised the winds were dangerously high, they pulled in to Castlepoint Bay in the dark rather than try to sail on. As the men laid anchor, the boat swung around and was rolled by the huge waves. *They literally stepped off the yacht into a boiling sea*, the journalist had written. Colin was hours in the water, churned and tossed as if he were in an enormous washer, holding his lifejacket together with his hands. He finally struck sand, and crawled up to a house where he broke in. Finding no telephone, he collapsed into a bed to sleep until he could warm up. He woke hours later, broke into another house and, from there, phoned the police. What dreams came to him that night, hypothermic and alone, an intruder, lying in a stranger's bed in a stranger's house? What a painful dawn that must have been for him. The gradual reconstruction of events, the realisation that, from a single mistake, a mistake anyone could make (did they check the weather before setting out?), from a series of mistakes, none in themselves serious or unforgivable, the very worst of consequences can unfold.

Early morning Saturday I drive to Masterton to meet Hamish at the real estate office. He leads me into a room with a bare blue table and beige walls.

Hamish places a stack of brown envelopes and a ringbinder down on the table. His white shirt cuff is pinned together, and I watch how he makes use of the forearm to shove the chair back. He scatters a pair of company pens onto the table, and we both sit down.

'We have three offers here.'

'It only takes one,' I say. 'If it's good enough.'

His eyes go blank, and I suddenly realise that Hamish has very little interest in this sale.

'Before you take a look at these,' he says, 'you need to understand that the LIM report that I mentioned was verified as correct.'

'A report which would be confidential to that party, I assume.'

He pulls a quizzical face.

'This was a substantial factual matter about the property.'

'Should we be checking the realtor's code of conduct here, Hamish?'

He looks at me, very level, very steady.

'The three offers that have come in,' he says, 'are in line with what you'd expect for the size of the section.'

We remain there in a stand off, more or less. Hamish keeps his arms folded across his chest, which could be a defensive posture, or just a desire to hide his weak spot, his missing hand. In the end, he slides the ringbinder across to me, and I open it. The top page is a chart with three entries, names, conditions, figures. I scan down the column. They are low, pitifully low numbers.

'Not much in it for you, is there?' I say.

Hamish leans forward on the desk, still keeping his arm hidden. 'Did you know about the boundary?'

I shake my head at him. 'That's not relevant. The real question here is what to do with this set of indifferent offers.'

'I doubt that going back to the market at this point will get you a better result,' Hamish says quietly. 'In fact you might find you get worse.'

I could just keep hold of the place. Aaron, after all, views it as a shrine. If or when he ever comes home he will want to come up and stay the night with all the old fixtures around him, the flyblown mirror in the bathroom, the orange rocking chair, all the details he has sanctified to his mother's memory. But Aaron is not here, and he's certainly not offering to help me with the maintenance.

Hamish waits. The neutral, tea-coloured paint on the walls, the cheap, hard-wearing carpet. This room could be a counselling room or a medical room, any one of those thousands of servicable, uninflected spaces, a room in which a patient is given her diagnosis and then her prognosis, her range of options, and then fewer options, and finally no options at all.

'Fine,' I said. 'Fine.'

I lay my finger down on the highest offer, from Miranda and James Tyson of Masterton. I will sell Aaron's precious reliquary for less than the price of a good European car.

'Where do I sign?'

Hamish produces a contract.

'Right here,' he says, gesturing with his empty cuff. 'And here, here and here.'

Back at the house, my parents are reading the newspaper on the couch. I propose a walk to the lighthouse. My mother looks up.

'Do you want to?' I ask.

She gives the slightest nod. I don't know if she gives herself permission to do much, these days, without him.

Then Dad wants to come down and see the sands, so we leave him in the passenger seat of the silver Legacy, parked facing the wide skirt of Deliverance Cove, the windows open for air, his crossword and biro to keep himself busy.

'Get a photo of the view from up there with the two of you in it,' he says. 'I wouldn't mind seeing that.'

My mother is fitter than I would have expected,

scaling the steep steps up the cliff face without difficulty. She keeps her hand hovering over the rail, and grabs at me once or twice when a gust comes over the crest of the rock, but she manages well. When we make it up to the plateau of the lighthouse, we rest our backs against it and take in the view to the east. There's a complex sky out to the horizon, streaks of purple slicing into the roiling blue. Below, a wide shelf falls away to the sea, the water slapping and sucking against the sedimentary rocks, a mish-mash of fossils and crumbled shell eaten at night and day by the ocean. A sea-cave runs right beneath the lighthouse, which we used to clamber around to from the beach at low tide for the thrill of showing Aaron the keyhole of blue on the other side. It would black out whenever a high wave came through. Once or twice we found seals sunning themselves on the pebbled shoreline there.

'Do you want to go further, Mum?'

The path carries on over the knoll and down to the rock shelf, but the terrain there will be more difficult.

'What do you think?'

The cars on the beach glint in the sun. We can make out Dad, leaning against the bonnet, but he doesn't see us waving.

'He's all right, isn't he?' I say. 'Let's go on.'

My mother's face is full of trepidation at the top of the knoll. It strikes me that I could be taking the adventure a little too far. But I hold her arm on the way down the narrow steps, and when we drop to the flat of the shelf, the wind falls away. There is nothing but the bare red rock, and pooled salt water in the hollows, and the sea slopping around below.

'It's like being on the moon.'

My mother has her hands on her hips, her chest out. It's

a youthful, vigorous posture, and I haven't seen her in it for some time.

'Odd, isn't it?'

There's a wooden bench set into the rock, grey grasses growing around it, and we sit down. My mother produces two barley sugars from her pocket, and offers me one.

'The size of that ocean.'

'Nothing between here and Chile. Perhaps an island or two.'

'Do you think so? It would just be the Pitcairns, but they're further north.'

'I suppose you're right.'

My mother's expansive general knowledge often takes me by surprise.

'Funny thing,' I said. 'For a while there I didn't actually know where Aaron was.'

She doesn't answer.

'He doesn't much like it here, does he?' she says eventually. 'Finds it a bit quiet, he told me once.'

'Well, now he's on a subcontinent with over a billion people,' I say. 'So that'll be different.'

'How's he getting on?'

I look out at the water. 'I haven't spoken to him. He hasn't been in touch.'

My mother takes my hand in her two, pats it gently. 'It'll come right.'

A seagull slices through the sky, circles and lands near us, shrieking. My mother sucks on her barley sugar. After a while, I stand up from the bench.

'Shall we go down?'

We start our way towards the steps that lead back to the sand. Up on the main path, the wind hits hard. My mother finds the descent more difficult than the climb, and I take her by the arm. Her frame so thin, as if she could be lifted entirely off her feet in a heavy gust. I hold on until we step off the concrete path onto the yellow sand.

On our last evening in the bach, we stay up late over a glass of sauvignon blanc. Dad falls to talking about the war, his quiet war. He was stationed for two years in Fiji, where the threat of a Japanese invasion did nothing to dilute the pleasures of lagoon swimming and scaling coconut trees. He describes how his unit arrived in Venice at the end of the war under Freyberg's command, and the travels he undertook through Italy and Austria afterwards, searching for news of his brother, who had been taken prisoner by the Germans in 1944 and was presumed dead. He never did find his brother, any trace or story of him. I knew about my uncle, but I didn't realise that Dad had been in Venice, and I hadn't appreciated the extent of his travels afterwards. My mother and I listen, and I pour more wine. It occurs to me that there are certain tracts of my father's life that I have never fully imagined.

When my father goes out to perform his ablutions, my mother and I are left alone in the lounge. There is a scatter of moths on the sliding door, wings pressed flat against the glass.

'Why didn't Moira tell me, Mum? Why didn't she ever say about Aaron's father?'

My mother, who is working on her knitting, finishes her row, lays it aside and looks at me in silence.

'You know, you do think the world of that boy.'

The peculiar weight in her phrasing. The *world*.

'Of course. I do.'

She picks up the knitting, flips it over and starts a new row. 'Reason enough, isn't it?'

When they go to bed, I pull out the sleeping bag and make my arrangements on the couch. The beam from the lighthouse will be swooping through the blinds in the front room, just as it did whenever Moira and I slept there. *Et lux perpetua luceat eis.* I think of how the broken stutters of the beam will lick over their bodies all night long, perpetual light, shining upon them.

Tomorrow I will drive them northwest across the width of the island and deliver them home. If I then tipped slightly westward, and travelled tens of thousands of kilometres further along that trajectory, I would arrive at Lahore, and Aaron. Who is this man he is looking for on that vast continent, and what does he imagine will happen if he finds him?

Ten

Down at the marina, skitters of breeze play away from the shore. The sky is bright and open with a light northerly. The sailor is on the training yacht, fiddling with the winches.

'Not a bad day.'

He startles, looks up from the deck.

'A beauty.' He rubs his hands clean on his jeans. 'Set to stay good for the weekend too.'

'Here's hoping.'

'Look.' The sailor climbs over to the floating dock, and walks up to where I am on the concrete. 'I remember you. You had your eye on my cruiser.'

'Peter.' My hand shoots forward.

'Gavin.' His handshake is quick and firm. 'Still looking?'

'I am,' I hear myself say. 'Yeah, I'm looking to buy. Something smaller.'

He sniffs, shadows his eyes against the light.

'Racer? Cruiser?'

'I don't race.'

Does he genuinely not remember the kite failing that day of the race, the red waft of it sliding under the skin of the water?

'You see over there?' He points out to the clutter of boats at anchor in the middle of the marina. 'Third one in, closest to us.'

'Green hull?'

'That's the one. Tidy little Alan Wright. Twenty-two footer. My mate's boat.'

The boat is, on first glance, scruffy. The paint looks flecked and faded. She's pint-sized, not a whole lot more boat than the trailer sailer.

'You've sailed her yourself, have you?' I ask.

'Yeah, plenty. She's set up for single-handed sailing, if that's something you're after. All lines lead back to the cockpit. Four berths.'

'What's her name?'

Gavin looks vague. 'Can you read it?'

I peer over the silver water, try to decipher the black letters against the green.

Cronus.

I should have taught Aaron to sail. That is something I regret. The confidence that builds when you must rely on the other man to execute his part, or risk finding yourselves both upside down in the drink. We could have done with that, Aaron and I. Out on the water every Saturday together, working the wind, the tide. It might have been the making of us.

'Look,' Gavin says, 'if you're at all serious—'

'I am serious,' I cut in. 'I could sail her alone, that boat, is that what you're saying?'

'You sailed much?'

That moment, just around the Ngauranga buoy, when I let the kite unfurl. I was waiting on the hard *whump* that should have come when it filled with wind, and I imagined how beautiful we would be on the homeward leg, gliding on the breath of the northerly, the red sail plump, a woman's belly in her ninth month. But instead there was the sick judder and flap of the thing as it twisted itself around the rigging, a skinny, knotted, hopeless piece of rag, and then the shouting of the crew behind me.

'Nothing to it, a boat like that,' Gavin is saying.

'You got a price?'

'You better talk to my mate. Not really my place.'

'Give me a ballpark? Compared to that crusier, for instance. *Te Haunui.*'

'Ah. Well. Maybe a quarter. A third. Not sure.'

Why *shouldn't* I buy a boat? On the one or two occasions I considered it, Moira talked me out of it, which, on reflection, feels like a certain meanness on her part. I can't think now why I ever took her objections, along the lines of *Would you even use it anyway* and *Why don't you just borrow one when you want to sail,* seriously. Reason, not the need! Moira knew nothing about sailing. And, at the risk of sounding reductive—it's distasteful to make calculations—the fact is we invested a lot, certainly by way of opportunity cost, into her painting. Did she listen to me at all, when I tried to tell her how it felt to be out on the water?

'How much time you got?' Gavin asks. 'I can take you out now if you like. My mate keeps a key here.'

The breeze is stronger out on the water than in the shelter of the boatsheds. Just outside the marina Gavin cuts the motor and calls me up to the cockpit, where the ropes all run down.

'Jib halyard and jib sheet here,' he says. 'Main halyard, this one.' He lifts a green-and-white rope in his palm. 'And here, the mainsheet's this one, the kicker's here.'

'Right.' I touch each rope in turn, trying to memorise.

'She's got a jib fitted right now, but I know she comes with a couple of genoas too. Go on, take the wheel.'

I put my hand on the tiller while he climbs up to unfurl the mainsail. I find a spot to steer towards, a pile of red and blue containers over at the container terminal, and experiment with a tiny turn of the tiller to the left, an overcorrection back to the right. We're barely moving through the water and bouncing around on the swell, so it makes little difference. It's a good feeling to have the tiller in hand.

'Okay, go for it,' Gavin shouts. 'Hoist the main.' He has taken off the lashings, and stands up by the mast. He peers upwards as I pull hand over hand on the green and white rope, and to my relief the sail starts to run cleanly up the pole. I know enough to cleat the halyard on, and the sail starts to fill out as the wind hits it, although now I can see something's gone awry at the top.

'She's not there yet,' Gavin shouts. 'Point up!' I give the tiller a wrench to starboard, lining the bow up with Somes Island, and the sail lies back down, obedient and limp. I uncleat the halyard, yank the sail up the last metre, cleat it back on, and slide the tiller to port. As the wind comes over the side of the boat the sail starts to fill out quickly again, but this time I have the mainsheet in my hand, and I winch it in a little, and a little more, until the boat has a slight lean on, and soon we're moving steadily forward under sail. Gavin drops down into the cockpit beside me.

'Nicely done.'

It's absurd, how good it feels to hear that.

We glide on, and there's time to turn around and take it in, the view of the city from the water. The big black tower of the BNZ stands out, *Darth Vader's pencil case*, as the kids used to call it. We keep going on the reach, past Point Jerningham, on towards Point Halswell. I can make out the white marble of the Massey Memorial through the trees.

'You want to try a tack?' Gavin asks.

'Sure.'

271

'You're going to put the bow through the eye of the wind, right?'

By the time we're motoring back into the marina, I'm exhilarated. We've tacked and reached down towards Queen's Wharf, close enough that I can make out children playing up on the toy lighthouse. Gavin shouts, 'Gybe, gybe!' We're going at a fair clip by now, and I get a rush of terror that I am too late, the wharf is dead ahead, but the motions come instinctively, pulling the mainsheet in, thrusting the tiller to starboard. The boat comes around, the wind catches the sail, the boom swings over and I duck. I hear the thwack as the boom hits home, and the boat gives a light judder and carries on.

'Nice,' Gavin says. 'Well controlled.'

The thrill of it is feeling the way the boat responds to me, how I'm able to channel it all—wind, momentum, the water running past the bow—to hold still at the centre of it and imagine a path, and it opens. I should have gone back to this years ago.

'Can you get your mate on the phone?' I ask as we're rowing back to shore. Gavin's pulling on the oars, checking over his shoulder.

'Absolutely. Look, I don't think you'll regret it.'

She's bobbing skittishly at anchor. If I can talk to a broker today, I might be able to get the transaction through tonight, get back out on the water tomorrow.

'You could change the name, I suppose. Although the old sailors will tell you that's bad luck.'

'I wouldn't do that,' I say. 'I wouldn't interfere.'

There's no mistaking the approval in Gavin's face.

Later that afternoon I write a cheque for a deposit, and make a phone call to organise the sale of some shares. Peter Collie, age forty-nine, first-time yacht owner. Well, it's a little disingenuous of me to blame Moira. After all, I held the chequebook all along, and if I have hesitated to take this plunge, that must have been for my own reasons.

Money was never really the problem. A boat like the *Cronus* is small beer in the big scheme of things, even now with my career going down the tubes, even with the miserable purchase price for Castlepoint. My salary swooshes into my bank account each fortnight, although the hiatus can't last much longer. Richard knows, and I know, that I am not going to come back, but as of yet no one has taken the final step.

Dad would be baffled by this whole situation. I'd be ashamed to tell him. In his world, if the washing machines were fixed, the money came in, and if they weren't, it didn't. Quite often—too often for my mother's comfort— it didn't. When I was six or seven, and before Mum got her job at the library, we had weeks when she'd make a cheap cut, mutton neck or pork hocks, stretch out for days on end, and after that was gone we'd have an egg for tea. There was no such thing as gardening leave for the men at the Gonville meatworks, a kilometre down the road from us, and not for those at the superphosphate plant at Aramoho either. I suppose it's the children of children in our neighbourhood who work at those places now. If those factories are even still open and operating.

Eleven

I've been avoiding going into town. It's the thought of being stuck in a coffee queue, or standing waiting for the lights, and being accosted by someone from work—a junior solicitor, one of the partners. There's the possibility that every last person in the office has seen the portrait, that gossip about naked Peter Collie has flown from the boardroom to the mailroom and everywhere in between. How excruciating the little bobs and noises of social exchange would be, the ordinary phatic communion of the moment, while I stand wondering how much of my skin is showing, what curves and lumps my inquisitor imagines he can make out beneath my clothes.

But this morning I woke up and thought that one cannot indefinitely avoid entire swathes of geography out of mere anxiety. The Legacy needed a service and that was a good enough reason to get going. I checked it in to the garage in Thorndon, then walked down Tinakori Road, and down onto Hill Street.

NZ Out of Afghanistan Protest Noon Today Cenotaph. It was written in block letters, done in pink chalk outside the Parliament gates.

The roses, which get pruned back over the winter, were starting to bloom. From the slight rise under John Ballance's statue I watched the suited bureaucrats cross the concrete concourse in pairs and threes, sliding into the little tunnel that takes them straight to the Beehive, and the tight clusters of civil servants did in fact have the appearance of worker bees, their hip-satchels and leather clutch-cases like pollen sacs weighed down with data and numbers and policy papers gathered from government ministries up and down Molesworth Street.

Protest Noon. I carried on down towards the city, past the pōhutukawa, the flags clattering on their poles. By the time I was near the iron gates at the bottom I could hear the sound of the crowd. People were up on the steps, climbing onto the lions, waving banners and shouting. There were only about forty or fifty bodies in total, but there was something fortifying about the energy of it, the bright squares of the placards hoisted skywards under the marble column, the white stone stained with green copper streaks from the statue, far above, of the man on the horse. I was standing back and gazing up to the top of the column and back down to the roaring mouths, young faces, peppered through with a few grey heads, when a man pressed a yellow flyer into my hand. I looked up at his face the same moment he looked at mine, and we both startled. It was Matthew.

'Oh, hello.' He looked stricken.

'You,' I said.

There was something that looked like shame in the slant of his shoulders, in his crestfallen face. I felt a certain vindication, seeing that. I made to push on. The traffic was pouring down Bowen Street, and the crowd were starting to carry a chant.

One two three four, we don't want your imperial war.

'Hey, so I had my hearing.' He was calling out from behind me. I turned around, and he stepped forward. 'They let me out on bail. I've got to keep my head down.'

275

I wasn't really sure what he wanted. I was concerned he might start shouting at me again.

'Gotta keep my hands off the carnations.' He made a little weave of his head, as if to say, Come on, humour me. 'Also, I broke up with Laura.'

That surprised me. 'Oh,' I said.

'Or, really, she broke up with me.' He glanced up at me, tentative. 'She finds me too *idealistic*, I think.'

Or controlling, perhaps, Matthew? But I couldn't really bear to talk about it. My hands, almost involuntarily, made a dismissive gesture.

'So what about this?' I flicked my chin towards to the crowd. 'Are you even supposed to be here, on bail?'

He smiled, looked around. 'Probably not. But good turnout, right?'

'What do they want?'

'You heard of Donald Rumsfeld? He said we're going to bomb them back to the Stone Age. With Helen Clark's backing. With our spy bases. Our SAS troops are going in this week.'

'Do you know anyone in New York?'

Matthew's expression grew cloudy. 'What does it matter? It doesn't bring anyone back.'

'I heard a story on the radio last week,' I said. 'One man, just last week, his wife was sure he was working in the North Tower and then he turned up. He'd been standing outside on the street when they fell, but he got knocked on the head and lost his memory. And then he just shows up at home, three months later.'

He looked irritated at this. 'Right.'

'By the way, Rumsfeld didn't come up with that line,' I said. 'That's what the Nixon administration said about Cuba.'

He frowned. 'Really?'

276

'Or maybe about Vietnam.'

'Vietnam? You see, that's the point, isn't it? That's exactly the point.'

'What would you ask the Americans to do, then? Out of interest.'

'They gave the Taliban, like, two weeks. And then, *ptshwww*.' He opened up his hands like starfish as he made the noise. He looked like a child, a six-year-old playing a game at the tea table.

'You expect negotiations, patience, diplomacy. After such horrors?'

If he had been in that city, if the terrorists had harmed one hair of my son's head.

Matthew held his gaze, and his eyes burned into me. I saw he had no patience for realpolitik, or for the limits of ordinary human forbearance.

'It's illegal,' he said. 'Your type should care about that, at least. Helen's leading us into an illegal invasion.'

Those worker bees hiving into the prime minister's office with their recommendations, their cautions, their carefully freighted paragraphs, would have thought of that, would have made a note among their papers.

'Perhaps,' I said. 'But which court? Which judge?'

Matthew's face was starting to take on a haggard, tired look, and I felt exhausted too. There were only so many ways this conversation could play out, as it was playing out over and over again in streets and living rooms and cafés across the globe.

Behind us, the chant shifted. *What do we want? No more bombing. When do we want it? Now.*

Ptshwww. I saw a bomb bursting in the middle of the air, a sharp-shooter's bullet arrowing in a line, a column of utes full of men touting Kalashnikovs rattling past. I saw yellow packages falling from the sky, hundreds of them, peanut butter, cluster bombs. *Cowboys, criminals.* How far is Lahore from the Afghanistan border?

Yes—Aaron, if he were here, would come and protest too.

'You know, it's weird.' Matthew was leaning in, confidential. 'The thing is, I've been getting fairly paranoid lately. Kind of jumpy. The court case has put a lot of pressure on. Everyone's always telling me to play it safe. I guess they mean well. But, man. I know I've been a bit rough on you.'

I think this was meant as an apology. His hand came to rest on my shoulder, and I glanced up at him. He had deep-set eyes, Matthew, very large. The goblinish look of him.

What do you think predators do?

'You might want to sort that out,' I said, 'the paranoia. It can get people into a world of trouble.'

But he was already looking away, losing interest. Whatever it was he'd wanted out of the conversation, he seemed to have been satisfied.

I read up about Mughal emperors and Punjabi cuisine and I look up photos of Lahore on the internet. I imagine him visiting the Wazir Khan Mosque, the Shalimar Gardens. I see him go to street vendors, eating tandoori chicken and rogan josh and lassi, I wake him before dawn with the muezzin call, I serve him sweet chai, I take him to the market to buy a woollen coat for the cool evenings, I lay him down to sleep at night with a friend because I don't want him to be alone.

But the internet has no answers and the only details I can imagine for him are banal, and all I am left with is his silence and my fury, *oh thankless child*, waking up and going to sleep inside the echo chamber of the one-sided conversations I have all day with Moira, and, now, with him.

After a week, I give up and ring Delhi again. Yes, he is in Lahore, yes, they have heard from him. Yes.

'Oh, such a rigmarole for him, terrible.' Again, this tone of mourning. 'There has been a nasty deception with the hotel he booked from here in India. They were offering him a room on the roof, no hot water, no electricity, and, worse than that, I believe some kind of extortion has been taking place, as they were charging many thousands of rupees per night for this inadequate room, and holding his passport until his booked nights were complete.'

My heart batters out a tattoo. Aaron, separated from his passport in some kind of dodgy gangster hotel in a Pakistani city. I don't even know which language. Urdu, Punjabi? Sanskrit? How will I negotiate?

'What do we do?' I said. 'How can we sort this out?'

'Yes, it was a bad situation. But don't be alarmed. He's now moved to a home.'

'To a home.'

What kind of home? He's a twenty-five-year-old man.

'This is due to a contact of mine, a connection at my work. My wife was so happy that we could arrange this for him. They are a very good family, a Sikh family actually, four daughters.'

'A family,' I said. 'That's great news. Four daughters. Gosh.'

'Children, sir.'

Do I imagine the note of reproach in his tone? *I have no improper thoughts about your friend's daughters, sir, let me assure you.*

But I am warmed by the thought of the hospitality of these strangers, with their large household, welcoming Aaron in. It has nothing to do with me, nor Moira. A bed has been offered to him because he belongs to Maneesh, or because he belongs to Amrita, or because he belongs to the Punjab, or because of some other web of loyalty and debt that I cannot guess at. Still, from my living room in Hataitai, so many thousands of kilometres away, it feels like a wild and unexpected generosity that my child should be cared for in this way.

'Thank you,' I say. 'You're doing so much for him.'

'It is no trouble, no trouble at all.'

'I've been waiting to hear all week, you know,' I blurt out. 'You did say you'd contact me.'

'You are Aaron's good father, of course we have not forgotten you would be concerned.'

I bite my lip, will myself to be quiet. It's not actually the fault of Aaron's somehow-uncle that I have no line of contact with my son.

'I don't know why he's not writing to me,' I hear myself saying next. 'Why isn't he calling?'

It is hard to tell whether the noises I hear next are static on the line, or Amrita's husband making a sympathetic kind of tsking sound with his teeth. I get the feeling he is reluctant to weigh in on our quarrel, in any case. It's possible that Aaron spoke freely and confessionally about me during the month he stayed with them. Whatever that might consist of.

'Did he say when he's coming back?' The wistfulness in my voice.

'He's going to find my wife's brother. He is a very single-minded young man. You can be proud of him.'

'And will he find him? Will that be easy?'

A long sigh. 'There is a problem with the Guptas, actually. My wife has been longing to find her brother for, well, over fifty years now, but her sister, my Didi, well, how shall I say this? There is a great stubbornness in the family. There has been some breach, I suppose you might put it that way, in the relationship. For a long time I believed if I could only bring them face to face, two sisters together, one from New Zealand, one from Delhi, the difficulty would come clear. But Didi has never come back to India, and of course we are all too old for such an arduous journey now.'

His wife and Maneesh's mother, two sisters. Their missing brother. All three of them must be in their seventies by now. I am an only child. Sibling relationships mystify me. The festering irritability, the eruption of subterranean jealousies and old quarrels, and then, when you least expect it, utter, bottomless loyalty.

'Aaron has little information with which to commence the search. There was a shared understanding, back at the time the family was separated, about the city of Rawalpindi, a supposition that Salaa-ji had gone there. If he makes no headway with finding him in Lahore, Aaron will take a bus north. That's a journey of five to six hours. Pakistan has no modern train system, of course.'

'North,' I say. 'Further into Pakistan.'

'Yes, basically due north,' he says.

'But why?' I say. 'It makes no sense. What could this man in Pakistan possibly matter to Aaron?'

There is a silence for a moment.

'He seems to feel, I don't know, you might say an affinity. It's as though his great uncle is a part of himself. He has been undertaking various spiritual practices in India. He has been perfectly diligent with his yoga, morning and night. A serious boy. I would say he feels it very closely, that Salaa-ji has been cut off from us.'

I would never talk to Aaron in such a way. We don't seem to have the language between us.

'One impediment to his quest is that my wife was a mere child of seven when she left Lahore. Names, dates, addresses, everything you need to trace a missing person, my wife has no recollection of these details. Her sister,

281

Maneesh's mother, was the elder sister.'

'You think she knows more. Facts. Things that would help Aaron.'

'I can only imagine Didi knows a great deal that would help in finding Uncle. Amrita, she is quite badly affected by all this, actually. Is this good for her heart? I don't know. It gives her hope, but it pains her. Her digestive system has been most out of sorts this past week.'

She lives in Lower Hutt, Maneesh's mother, Mrs Gupta. A twenty-minute drive from where I stand, looking out at the green canopy.

'What does Aaron need to know?' I say. 'How can I help?

It seems an unlikely coincidence to bump into Matthew twice in the space of one week, but that is what has happened. I was walking through Manners Mall this afternoon, in search of a longer internet cord for the computer, as part of my plan to rearrange the study to make better use of the light. The streets were full of shoppers and workers, the windows already festooned in tinsel, piped carols pouring from the doors. Purchase completed, I rested for a moment against the fountain and surveyed the mall. A young guy came up and rested his hips against the marble in the spot to one side of me, opened up a McDonald's cheeseburger, and bit into it voraciously.

I knew his face. Lean, rangy bloke, black hair buzzed down to a number two, a sports backpack, tramping boots, a faded plain T-shirt. Harry? Henry? Perry. Perry, who had summer clerked for us several years back, stayed on part-time while he did his last paper, and worked hard with my team on a data-mining case. I'd helped him prepare for his last exam. I heard he'd gone off overseas after that. He was a highly promising young lawyer, and I was pleased to see him back around town. Perry. Something different about the body shape. Thinner? But yes, it was definitely Perry.

'Perry.' I said it aloud. 'Perry.'

The guy turned his head towards me, and gave an apologetic smile.

'I'm his brother.'

'You're Perry's brother? Uncanny. You sure you're not Perry?'

'Twins.' Perry-not-Perry swallowed his food, wiped at his mouth. 'How do you know Perry?'

I said that he'd worked with me, and gave the name of the firm.

'What's your name then?'

'Peter Collie.'

Perry-not-Perry's face seemed to go gentle. 'Perry *talked* about you,' he said. 'You were his mentor, right? He told me you were a totally generous guy, gave him hours of your time. I'm Lucas.' He offered his hand.

The unexpected upswell of the heart. *A totally generous guy*. It's true that I did put a lot into Perry that summer, as I always try to with the summer clerks. Perry had a rare talent though.

'Perry's a top man,' I said. 'What's he up to now?'

'He's, ah, in Canada. You didn't hear? He—'

But Lucas broke off, because there standing in front of us was Matthew. There was a moment of confusion when I thought, or assumed, that it was me whom Matthew was approaching, and then suddenly the two young men were hugging, slapping each other on the back. They were relaxed in one another's space in a way that suggested a longstanding friendship.

'You know this guy?' Matthew poked his thumb towards me. 'Wellington, eh?'

'I know Lucas's brother. We worked together.'

283

Matthew was looking at his feet.

'So, what's happening in Canada?' I turned back to Lucas. 'Is Perry with a firm?'

'He had an accident,' said Lucas.

From the look on both their faces, I knew he wasn't talking about a broken leg.

'He was skiing. Major brain damage.'

'My god.'

Lucas shrugged. 'He's making some progress.'

I had no idea what that might mean, what might constitute progress for Perry, where his new starting position was.

'When did it happen?'

'Two months ago.'

Right around the time that Moira was dying.

'The doctors say he'll be able to fly soon. Then he can come home. He won't be back working though.' Lucas swallowed. 'Like, probably ever.'

'I had no idea.'

'Yeah,' said Lucas. 'Well.'

Matthew appeared to be half listening, half staring out towards the crowds of shoppers.

'You working today?' Lucas asked. Perhaps he was wondering about my jeans and sneakers.

'Between things.' I lifted up the plastic bag in my hand. 'Getting a bit of shopping done.'

'You want to come for a beer perhaps? Matt and I are going nearby.'

'What, now?' I said.

Matthew gave a neutral grin. If he was alarmed by Lucas's sudden invitation, he did a good job of hiding it.

'I guess I want to know more about Perry's work,' Lucas said. 'When he gets home I want to be able to talk to him about all the things he used to do. I've been thinking it might help, I don't know, wake up that part of his mind or something. Only if you're free.'

'I am, certainly. All right. Why not?'

We ended up at the Irish bar at the top of Courtenay. The wizard with the lank ponytail was there, working the tables as fast as he could, thick with Friday afternoon drinkers. We found a table on the upper level, out on the balcony, wedged up hard against the wrought-iron fence, with a view down to the street.

I asked Matthew and Lucas how they'd met, and Lucas laughed, and Matthew said, 'You don't want to know.' But, in fact, they wanted to tell me. They'd spent a night in the cells together after a protest action against the Indonesian Embassy, during the years when East Timor was straining towards independence, when the Indonesian military were using force against the population of that island while the New Zealand military were continuing friendly relations and joint training exercises.

'Someone had vomited in the cell and they never cleaned it,' said Matthew. 'That smell. I'll never forget it.'

'Why do you do it?' I asked.

'Do it?'

'The protests. The actions. Why put yourself on the line? There's a thousand useful things a person could do.'

Lucas seemed to bristle at the question, but Matthew looked thoughtful.

'I hate the way they do it in my name,' he said. 'With my money.'

I was struck by the way he seemed to feel this personally. He spoke about a hospital in the west of Afghanistan that had been damaged by British and American bombs, patients and medical staff killed. He was animated, agitated. It made me wonder why I hadn't asked him this question when I interviewed him at the Law Centre. I didn't see it as relevant, I suppose.

After that, I spoke with Lucas about some of the cases I'd worked on with his brother, and then, when we'd exhausted that, Matthew started into a description of his Masters research. He told us he had been investigating lines of influence from Martin Luther King back to Gandhi, from Gandhi back to Te Whiti at Parihaka. Lucas was nodding intently at all this. It sounded like engaging material. Parihaka, I knew, was a place in Taranaki, the site of a disagreement between the British Army and the local Māori that had unfolded along rather different lines than the usual colonial wars.

Later, he and Lucas began to talk about movies and music, and I ordered a second beer, and a third, and sank further down into my seat and stopped talking, letting their enthusiasms, their articulate, intensely held opinions, wash over me. And then my bladder started to pain me, and I went off to the gents.

When I came back, fresh pint in hand, the two boys were side by side in conversation, Lucas with his fuzz of black and Matthew's tangle of dirty blond ringlets, leaning in towards one another, and I realised that it was long past time for an old codger like me to push off home. I thought I'd just finish my beer quietly and leave without saying much more. I propped myself up behind them, leaning on the balcony railing, and looked down on the people walking a few feet below. The wind had dropped away, and the balcony was empty except for an entwined pair in the far corner, hands exploring one another's thighs.

'What about a firebomb?' That was Lucas. 'A small one.'

'A small bomb?'

'Thow it into the embassy. Through a window.'

286

'How? You're not going to get anywhere near the US Embassy. British, same thing.'

I was trapped there like an awkward butler, looming behind them, listening. I could have interrupted, or I could have scooted down the stairs and gone on my way. I don't know quite what pinned me to my spot on the railings.

'Okay,' said Lucas. 'What about blood? Blood poured over the pavement. Outside Government House. Insinuating basically that there's blood on your hands, Helen. You could spraypaint that on the fence. *Blood on your hands.*'

Lucas was surely Catholic. The symbolism came to him as naturally as breathing.

'Blood's filthy, frankly. You don't want to spill that around.' A fastidious streak in Matthew.

And then I couldn't stand it any longer, and I made a small harrumph sound, and Lucas caught it, looked up and smiled. Matthew shot a guarded look at me. I saw his face cloud over and flush, as it had in the office at the Law Centre.

'Got any ideas, Peter?' Lucas craned around to look at me. 'Direct action? Something newsworthy.'

Matthew was narrowing his eyes, weighing me up.

'Not really my thing,' I said. 'It's probably time for me to go.'

Matthew gave a curt nod, but Lucas, who'd had several beers and seemed to be feeling even more extravagant towards me, pulled on my arm and got me sitting back down. 'Finish your drink. What's the rush?'

It was vertiginous, the way he looked so exactly like Perry. Those afternoons in my office several years back, the pleasure of proceeding through legal thickets step by logical step, his spectacularly sharp intellect, always able to keep up the pace, at times moving beyond me. What parts of that excellent mind were still working now, what parts

287

had gone dark? I resolved that I would go and visit Perry, when they brought him home from Canada. His parents, what they must be going through.

I thought about arriving back at the empty house, the balcony with the trees dark all around. I thought about waking in the morning, which stretched out like a desert of time with no appointments, no temporal markers at all.

'All right,' I said. 'What's the rush?

Matthew pulled a pouch of tobacco out of his bag, rolled and lit up. He said, 'Do you want one, then?' Maybe I looked hungry to him, desiring.

'I wouldn't mind.'

He rolled me one, passed it over, and gave me a light. The sweet taste of the tobacco in the throat, and the third beer, loosening the knots in the deepest parts of my shoulders. I stretched back, felt the *pop, pop* of vertebrae releasing. The wind had almost completely dropped off, and a full moon was faintly showing in the pink sky above the Embassy Theatre.

'You ever thought about the warships?' said Matthew. 'They dock here in Wellington from time to time.'

'Mess with an armed ship?' Lucas's chin retracted. 'They'd shoot first, ask questions later.'

'When those boats come to Wellington they sit there with all that grey flank exposed to the harbour, to everyone on the shoreline,' Matthew said. 'Think of it as your own personal billboard.'

What, I wondered, were the statutes pertaining to damaging military equipment? It wouldn't surprise me if there was something on the books that made it an entirely separate crime, with higher penalties. The state gets touchy about its hardware.

'Afghanistan is landlocked,' I said. 'The navy aren't even involved.'

Matthew flapped his hand dismissively. 'Army, navy, it's still the armed forces,' he said. 'One of those frigates will get sent to the Persian Gulf sooner or later.'

'Well, technically—'

'Who gives a rat's arse about your technicalities?' The glowing point of his cigarette, smoke dispersing above his head.

An hour later we were sitting in a dim Turkish place eating kebabs that barely held together, onions and parsley and bits of chicken and sauce oozing out of the wrap and into the plastic wicker basket in front of me on the table. We had cosied down into a booth, and a television on the wall was playing a quiz show with women in sparkly bikinis. Matthew and Lucas were working through a number of details.

Matthew thought you'd send one person in, that you'd get alongside the vessel by kayak because it wouldn't show up on a radar, and I mentioned that you'd want a decoy distracting the onboard watch team with some kind of display further out in the harbour. Lucas was preoccupied with types of spraypaint, and how much noise the can might make, how you might tape it to a long stick to achieve the height needed, and the question of which colour would stand out best against warship grey.

It was all hypothetical and good fun. They were boys looking for a thrill. And when I left them for the night and got on a bus home, the person who I thought about, as we went into the dark of the bus tunnel, was Clare.

I remember Clare's uneasy mood, that May morning in our flat in Earl's Court, when she came home with her legs and arms covered in bruises from the police baton. I heated her up shepherd's pie and wrapped a bag of frozen peas in a teatowel for her to hold against her knee. She sat on a wooden chair and was at once elated and terrified, describing the rushing forward of the protestors at Grosvenor Square. She felt herself important, her body a weapon, her voice a source of power, and yet she was also in pain. I fixed her up as best I could and left to work my late shift at the nearby pub.

I don't know why I never joined her and Rob on any marches or demonstrations in London or in Amsterdam. I was as disturbed as everyone else by the images from Mỹ Lai and by the young girl running from napalm, but I came from a home where no one spoke of politics. Wellington was far from Wanganui and the decisions made there inscrutable, Washington and London unimaginable. My dad fixed washing machines. If he held opinions about wars overseas, about the decisions of Holland and Holyoake, what did it matter?

In August of 1981 I stood towards the front of a crowd in Rintoul Street, in Newtown. The call came, *Brace, brace*, and so we linked arms hard, elbow locked with elbow. I was between two men, although there were women in our line too. The call came, *Push, push*, and we heaved forward and became a wall of force, and at my back there was the pressure of the body behind me, and at my chest there was the pressure of the bodies ahead of me. I kept my legs splayed out for balance; we were shuffling forward, gaining a little ground, another five steps towards the park, the blue hats of the police line visible ahead of us, and sweat falling into my eyes, but I couldn't wipe my face. There were a hundred people trying to force their way forward, a scrum, a phalanx, a formation. We were close enough to Athletic Park to hear the roaring and shouting as the Springboks came onto the field.

We never made it to the Park. That match played out

without interruption. After the final whistle we unlinked, drifted off, like so many pieces of confetti.

When I fell asleep that night in the wide bed, Moira's foot touching mine, I wanted to feel it again, that crush of bodies, the way energy passed through and out of me, the way my borders dissolved. I have never experienced that in quite the same way before or since.

The jab of a limb kicking in utero late in pregnancy. I felt those punches once when Geneviève (or was it Moira?) lay spooned against my back. I jerked up in the bed. Is that the baby or is it you? I asked. But she was already asleep. Tap, tap, all night, the child's morse code playing through the screen of its mother's skin.

Twelve

'Maneesh. It's Peter here.'

How I hate voicemail.

'Look, it's a strange thing to ask, but Aaron's on a family history hunt in Pakistan. Your mother may have some information that would help. Happy to follow up directly if you have her number.'

I imagine myself conducting an interview with Mrs Gupta. How would I even begin?

'Or, if you could ask your mother. Your uncle's birthdate. The address where your mother grew up. Ah, and . . .'

The next bit is odd, personal, there's no way around it.

'Any identifying marks likely to be on his body. Tattoos, scars and so forth.'

I can see that it's a grisly request. The association with a morgue. I'm asking a man I barely know to interrogate his elderly mother on explicit details concerning the body of her brother. How did we get here again?

'Look, Maneesh, if you could just call me back?' I say. 'When you get a moment.'

A postcard arrives in my mailbox. A nondescript photo of lilac trees laden with blossom, a concrete path running through the grass. It could be a park in any city of the world. The cursive inside the black border reads *Spring*

Season in Rawalpindi. Tattered corners, a scrawl of blue biro, an inked postage stamp. Twenty-one words.

> Hunting for Great-Uncle Omar Chaudhry about as bad as looking for a Patrick Murphy in Dublin. May take me some time.

And then his name, and an affectionate breezy *x*, tiny, but definite. A kiss. I think of him sitting down to write this, after so many weeks. So I write him back, a long email, in which I speak of my relief at hearing he is safe, give my blessings for his Indian relatives and make a very handsome offer of cash, and tell him he only needed to say the word and I would have it transferred immediately. *So you don't need to do anything desperate.* I don't write that. I say nothing about the gardening leave, because I don't want to bore him with it, or let it concern him. The letter comes to several paragraphs, and once I've finished I make tea, and read it over, write a postscript, *Honestly I mean it about the money don't hesitate,* and at last, with my heart bashing about in my chest, I fire it off.

It occurs to me I don't need to wait for his permission to give him money, and I ring up the bank and have a substantial sum moved to his account. Then I fetch the atlas from the study, and run my finger up to the dot on the map.

Aaron won't be walking beneath flowering lilacs right now. Rawalpindi is the same latitude north as Sydney is south, and we're already into December, so, late autumn.

> <aaron.collie@xtra.co.nz>
> Dad, I can't explain how badly I want to find him. It's all I think about. I walk around the streets of Rawalpindi and stare at all the old men. I'm searching for a face. Would I

recognise him, just a little bit? I wear shalwar-kameez because I want to blend in. I think, if I'm dressed like a local, maybe Uncle will recognise me. Who ever bothers to scan the faces of tourists in case you know them? But in a kurta, I get nods, glances, sometimes smiles. Well, there are two million people in this city and I'm not going to run into him by accident. My flatmate from London has put me in touch with his cousin. He's Pashtun, he speaks four languages, and he's helping me look through government records. If I can't get any further here in Pindi, I'll head to Peshawar with him, and stay with his family there.

I call Sangeeta and ask her to meet me for a coffee. I tell her it's about Aaron, and she says, *Of course.* When I arrive she's already seated inside the café on Oriental Bay, talking on her mobile. She waves her hand at me and keeps talking, her red bracelet fluttering in the light.

'Sorry.' She clicks down the lid of the phone. 'Sahana can't find her hockey gear.'

'Oh, team sports,' I say, 'such a hassle.'

She gives a laugh.

'Shall I get straight to the point? Aaron wrote to me from Rawalpindi. He's looking for your uncle.'

Her face rapidly closes over.

'I don't know how he found out about him,' she says. 'The relatives in Delhi never speak about him. No one does.'

The waitress arrives with a coffee in each hand. 'Two flat whites?' She places them down ineptly, so that the brown liquid sloshes into the saucer.

'They do speak about him,' I say. 'They spoke to me. This man, he's still your uncle. If your mother has any kind of contact with him, she could write to him. She could write and arrange for him to meet Aaron.'

294

'Write to him?' Sangeeta lifts up her cup, and mops the bottom of it with a serviette. 'No.'

'Her own brother? Of course she can write to him. Whatever the quarrel between them.'

'The quarrel between them?' Sangeeta places her cup back down and looks up with a sceptical expression.

'Whatever your mother and her brother have spent half a century fighting about, whatever this'—my hands flutter upwards—'protracted intergenerational falling out is about, can't they get over it for a moment?'

Sangeeta stares at me.

'Aaron's very determined,' I say. 'Chances are he's going to locate your uncle, and then your mother will have to speak with him.'

'If my mother were to speak with her brother at this late stage of their lives, it would be, well, astonishing.'

I sigh. 'This is ridiculous,' I say. 'This is an absurd state of affairs.'

Sangeeta checks her watch. 'You know, I have to take Sahana to hockey in half an hour. Is there actually something specific I can help you with?'

'Okay,' I say. 'Can I back up a little? Your mother and her brother, they were separated, what, in the'—I count back the decades—'fifties, forties?'

'1947. August.'

Clare at Warwick University, the stocky Chancellor, his eponymous line on a map. *Poor man. Dad says he's quite haunted.* I knew this. The migration from the Punjab, Partition. I had talked with her about that at Stella's wedding, years ago. At the time, details had floated past me as so much general chit chat, as background noise.

'I do know that your mother grew up in Lahore.'

Sangeeta looks at me, as if weighing something up in her head.

'Yes, in the south of the city,' she says at last. 'The family were well off. They owned a house, quite a large house. My grandfather died when my mother was about ten, but they still had their house. When the rumours about independence started, my grandmother didn't sell early enough, or she couldn't.'

'Go on.'

'Her older brother was seventeen. He didn't want to leave.'

'But your grandmother felt she had to leave.'

'Oh, she had to leave all right.'

How had Clare put it? *Complete pandemonium.*

'Your uncle. What happened to him?'

'My mother's brother stayed in the village. He must have found a way to stay in Pakistan. No one knows if he's even alive.'

'Your Aunt Amrita in Delhi. She seems to think he's alive.'

'I see. It's good of you to let me know.'

I would like to move on, at this awkward moment, to some other topic of conversation. Her daughters, perhaps, their hockey teams. But I have come for a purpose, and so I press ahead.

'It must have been dreadful for your mother. Leaving everything behind.'

'Yes. Of course.'

I sigh. 'Sangeeta, I don't want to pry. I am genuinely interested in this.'

'I see. And what do you plan to do with this information?'

Well, I can hardly answer that.

'There is one story,' she says, 'that I could tell you, if you want to hear it.'

'Please. I really do.'

'My grandfather was a sitar player. That was the one

object that was able to be salvaged when they fled. When they walked to the border, my grandmother slept with one daughter under each arm, and the sitar between them. Maneesh has it now. One of his sons is learning to play it.'

'That's a good story.'

'The only one my mother would tell.'

'She had nothing else from the house?' I say. 'Any photographs, perhaps?'

'The house was lost. Amrita and my grandmother attempted to get compensation for it once they got to Delhi. They paid an agent in Bombay to deal with the paperwork and he swindled them, and when the money came through he took ninety percent of the value of the house. They were dispossessed. But everyone must have been so bewildered in those years. My father's family had also come down from the Punjab.'

Aaron's grandmother, Aaron's grandfather.

'So they came to New Zealand.'

'Yes. Here we are.'

'Did they miss India?'

She shrugs. 'They were already away from home.'

'And then two children. Life in the Hutt Valley. Nappy valley, they used to call it.' She smiles. 'A typical migrant success story. A deputy principal, a GP. Their efforts paid off.'

'So now a peaceful retirement.'

She gives a rueful smile. 'That hasn't been plain sailing. Two years ago, my father lost the franchise for their shop. It was stolen out from under them, to be honest, by a young employee, a boy from Rajasthan. He bad-mouthed them to the franchisor, told lies. It seemed to bring everything back for my mother. That betrayal in Delhi, the way they were cheated out of the money from the house, how they lost her father's inheritance, that's all she wanted to talk about. She stopped eating, she couldn't sleep. It was as if all that she and my father had built up here for almost fifty years counted for nothing. I couldn't comfort her, or really do anything, and neither could Maneesh. It was terrible. I'm sorry—' She breaks off. 'Now I'm telling you far too much.'

'Not at all,' I say. 'What an awful time for you.'

'It was.'

'Has your mother *met* Aaron? I don't even know—'

'No. Maneesh didn't want them to. My parents have been, after all, quite shocked to find out about all this. Maneesh has always been the obedient child of the family.'

'How is she, your mother?'

'She's a little better this year. She comes on outings now, at least. We took her to Paekakariki last week, and she walked on the beach.'

Sangeeta's voice lifts. Small victories.

My father's heart. My mother's anxiety.

Last night I met Maneesh's wife at his home in Khandallah. He had made a cordial invitation by telephone to come and meet his wife, and my sense was that this was some kind of open acknowledgement of Aaron, perhaps the first time his name would be spoken aloud in his household.

The bizarre and yet true fact is that I had to drive up Punjab Street to get to Maneesh's house. Khandallah street names are a dislocated echo of the Raj: Burma Road, Rangoon Street, Simla Crescent, Agra Crescent, Calcutta Street, Cashmere Avenue. Back when I used to walk around these streets with my aunt and mother in the 1960s, we never saw a single Indian face. We wouldn't have expected to.

The suburb itself was named for the nostalgia of Captain Edward Battersbee, an army veterinarian who retired to

New Zealand after years of service with the East India Company. Battersbee built his homestead, Khandallah, on the northern hills of Wellington. The early settlers picked up the theme and ran with it. Even the English-sounding Nicholson Road, where my aunt used to live, was named for Sir John Nicholson, officer of the East India Company and administrator of the Punjab. Nicholson ferociously put down the Indian Mutiny, scornful of the leniency of his fellow British officers towards the natives. He died, still young, of a wound inflicted in the storming of Delhi. The Victorians called him 'the Hero of Delhi' and immortalised him with ballads and books. I know all this because in the fourth form our cranky old English teacher made our class recite a dramatic poem in which Nicholson meets with Mehtab Singh, a man with rubies in his turban, who refuses to take his shoes off for the British. My job was to read the bit where Nicholson chastises Singh:

Have ye served us for a hundred years
And yet ye know not why? We brook no doubt of our mastery,
We rule until we die.

Even back then, we thought that was pretty revolting. The teacher, who came from Leicester and was colloquially known to us as Pommy Dick, lost his last shred of authority with our class with the introduction of that poem. Whenever he tried to give any one of us a detention, a theatrical whisper would start up across the back row, *we brook no doubt of our mastery, we rule until we die*, and we'd all crack up laughing.

There is one street name in the suburb that has nothing to do with India. Box Hill is part of the main arterial route, the slight rise and dip that separates Ngaio from Broadmeadows. There's a train station at the bottom by the same name, a park and swimming pool at the top, a children's playground with an old red engine that I used to climb on when my aunt took me there. It's a common enough name around the world: there's a Box Hill in Surrey, and another one in Australia. This small, local hill, though, according to the local history signs that have recently gone up in Khandallah village, was named for a stockade that Governor George Grey built in 1846 at the end of the first leg of his military road north. It was known then as Sentry Box Hill. The signs don't go into any detail about why Grey was building his road, and my knowledge of local history is too patchy to come up with an answer.

Praneeta brought out a silver tray laden with sweets and tea, and sat down in the chair opposite me, her gold-and-pink tunic glittering in the light. She wore her hair in a long plait and there was barely a thread of silver in it, although she couldn't have been much younger than me.

'Peter's a lawyer,' Maneesh said to Praneeta. He names my firm. 'One of the top companies in Wellington, isn't it?'

I decided not to quibble about the details.

'Praneeta is a senior lecturer at the university.'

You should take my wife seriously, he might as well have said. This job would account for the BMW parked in the driveway, and the size of the house, a new build on a subdivided section, not in any way the modest ex-state bungalow I had mentally conjured.

'What's your area?'

'Biomechanics,' said Praneeta.

It gave me the most terrible wince on Moira's behalf. Was she just not ambitious enough for him, not academic enough? I wanted suddenly to speak up for her, defend her. A baby grand piano sat proudly in a corner of the lounge. I thought about the sitar that had travelled from Lahore to

Delhi to Wellington, I thought about Ravi Shankar playing with the Beatles in the sixties, about Maneesh's mother as a young girl lying with the instrument resting between her and her mother. None of this seemed a useful direction in which to take the conversation. I reached for a sweet from the tray, a sticky ball lying in a pool of syrup. It tasted of cardamom and nutmeg. A small silence gathered.

'Is there any word on your uncle?' I asked. 'Has Aaron found him yet?'

Maneesh didn't answer.

'I was trying to work out his age,' I ploughed on. 'If he's four years older than your mother, that would make him—'

'Sixty-seven.' Maneesh crossed his arms.

'Not so old.'

'Yes. And not so young.'

'Do you have any photos of him? I'm curious.'

Maneesh stood up. His fingers worked themselves into a knot. 'No photos,' he said. 'Nobody has photos. You are curious, Aaron is curious, but for us, this is not a matter of curiosity—'

Praneeta was looking at her husband. I saw worry on her face, but also satisfaction. She doesn't actually want me in her house, I thought. Well, why would she? Nevertheless, here I am.

'Well.' I drained my teacup. 'About Aaron. He emailed me from Rawalpindi. You might, I suppose'—then suddenly I couldn't quite manage the clutching sensation in my throat and chest—'you might have heard from him more recently than I have.'

Maneesh sat back down in the armchair. 'Yes. Aaron called me. He's arrived in Peshawar.'

'Ah.' I swallowed. 'So he's gone up there, has he? He did mention he might. Nice city, is it? You ever been yourself?'

I ended with a barking laugh.

Maneesh looked baffled. 'Peshawar?'

'It's not easy for an Indian national to get in to Pakistan,' Praneeta said. 'Maneesh has had no reason to go there.'

'Fair enough. Why would you? Quite reasonable. Home's best.'

'It's a concern, to be honest,' sighed Maneesh. 'Travelling alone in such places, at such times.'

'He has a friend,' I said. 'He's with a local.'

'This Pashtun,' he said. 'Yes. It sounds to me like a commercial agreement. I don't know how much use such a person would be in a jam, unless you keep paying.'

'There's no problem with money,' I said. 'There's plenty of money.'

'You wouldn't want Aaron's companion to know that, I would think.'

I leaned in. 'The bottom line,' I said, 'is that Aaron will leave that country just as soon as he finds your uncle.'

Maneesh looked at me levelly.

'You could help with that,' I added.

He ran his tongue over his teeth, and sucked. Praneeta reached down for the teapot, lifted it and swirled it round gently, gauging how much was left.

'How do you think I can help?' Maneesh asked.

'I've told you. Talk to your mother,' I said. 'A birthdate, a photo. She must have something.'

Maneesh stood up. He went over to the window, and looked out at the garden. A pair of cabbage trees poked up into the ribbon of blue harbour visible from this part of the hill. A single white yacht moved, a fleck of white, across the water.

'*Have* you talked to her?' I pressed on. 'Have you raised it with her?'

Praneeta stood up too, then, and lifted the silver teapot,

supporting it on the bottom with one hand. I imagined the warmth of it against her palm and chest, held in that way, like a rabbit or a cat. Maneesh turned around, and wobbled his head to and fro in a gesture that might have meant yes, or no, or both at once.

'Actually,' he said, 'we will leave my mother's privacy undisturbed.'

'I understand this is sensitive.'

He gave me a hard look.

'I realise'—I fished around for the right way to put it—'that there's some distress in talking about this. What if I were to go and talk to her myself?'

A beige phone, fixed to the wall by the window, started ringing, a soft electronic burr. Nobody paid it any attention. Maneesh crossed his hands over his chest. Praneeta stayed frozen on the spot, still nursing the teapot.

'As I said. We will not be resurrecting such matters with her.'

I felt like one of his fourth formers. *Yes, sir.* But also, *I will if I have to.* And Maneesh probably guessed at that too, because he remained standing, staring me down.

Praneeta left the room, and we heard the low rumble of the kettle starting to boil in the kitchen. Maneesh sighed, shook himself and sat back down in the chair.

'Why not simply go to Pakistan?' he said. 'That door is open to you. Just go over, bring him home.'

'It's not that easy.'

'No? Why not?'

I once went to pick Aaron up from a Blue Light disco when he was thirteen. It was supposed to be well managed, run by the cops, but some of the parents had reported glass bottles being smashed on the road outside, so Moira sent me down early to take a look. There was in fact a fair amount of mayhem happening outside the hall, yobbish kids carrying on, and I thought it best to take him home. But the expression on Aaron's face when he saw me pushing through the crowd of teenagers to find him, his arm slung around a girl, slouching in the scooped plastic seats at the side of the hall. *Go away*, he hissed, standing up and raising a hand in front of him. *Go away.*

'I doubt he'd come back with me. Your lot'—I swirled my hands around the living room, meaning to implicate all of Maneesh's people—'is the only thing he cares about right now.'

'It's a fool's errand he's on,' Maneesh said. 'I've told him to stop.'

His tone was airy, dismissive.

'Your uncle's dead. Is that it? Is that what you mean?'

Again Maneesh gave that wobble of the head, not a shake or a nod.

Equivocating bastard. Is this how he was with Moira, a quarter of a century ago? This not-quite-yes, not-quite-no carry on. Who walked out on who, in the end? Oh it's always complicated, but it's not really, is it. Finally, one person decides. Did he hurt her, did he insult her? The man was playing me like he played her. I wanted to shake the answers out of him. *Is Aaron chasing a phantom? Why won't you help me?*

In a bedroom upstairs a stereo started up. A series of thuds sounded through the ceiling. Praneeta, coming back into the room with a fresh tray of sweets, raised her eyes up and Maneesh smiled.

'That's Jayesh,' said Praneeta. 'He loves to dance.'

'He does? Aaron dances too. And Sangeeta.' I turned to Maneesh. 'Genetics, eh?'

Praneeta turned her head away, and placed the tray down on the table. Wife of the man my wife once loved. Well, people got in these situations all the time, especially in this small city. It's just that it never happened to me. It's probably a common enough feeling, this hot rush of gratitude towards her, capable, accomplished Praneeta, simply for existing, for holding Maneesh's attention, for having held him all these years in a home, in a marriage that appears to have been consoling, companionable, content enough to have prevented him from turning into the kind of drunk, nostalgic, self-pitying arsehole who would seek out Moira for a late last fling. The mother of your child? That's someone you might go to in a tight spot. I guess I know that. But he never has. As far as I know. And I would know, I think. I'm sure I would.

'The simple matter is,' said Maneesh, 'you and I, we must convince Aaron to come back to Delhi.'

'Well that would be nice, wouldn't it?

'We must work together,' he said. 'We must strategise.'

I spent the entire day today at the public library. I read into the evening, the lights flicking on at the library, the summer light melting away in the town square below.

The Earl Mountbatten of Burma arrived in Delhi in February 1947, charged with overseeing a transfer of power which, despite the splittings and rumblings emanating from that vast nation, the British government yet hoped would unfold as a gentle and decorous withdrawal of the Empire from the subcontinent. What did they want, the King, the prime minister, the cabinet? Their hope was that Britain would leave India as one might leave a grown son, full of paternal pride, handshakes, a round of self-congratulation, perhaps some last words of gratitude from the newly independent state for the railways, democracy, the education system, for giving India her liberty.

At this point, the history books employ words like *vortex, acceleration, chaos, panic.* Mountbatten's response to the sectarian violence that was now erupting across the continent was to get Britain out fast, and then faster still. In June of 1947, he announced that independence would now, suddenly, come in August. At a stroke, eleven months of planning were collapsed into two. What started as an orderly retreat became an ungainly pell-mell race for the ports. Bungalows and hill stations were abandoned as rumours thickened and grew. Pakistan, shimmering in the air, that imaginary nation first conjured by Allama Iqbal, began to solidify and become substantial. Sir Cyril Radcliffe was flown in from London and, under the baking heat of that summer, was tasked with drawing his line within three weeks, through the Punjab and through Bengal, a border that sliced through the homes of Muslims and Sikhs and Hindus and Christians. At midnight on 14 August 1947, fireworks were lit. The Indian Army were released from British command. Mountbatten, dressed in full naval uniform, read out a message from the King: *transfer of power, consent, fulfilment of a democratic ideal, peaceful change*. The maps of Radcliffe's border were kept under lock and key until after the celebrations were complete.

I couldn't bring myself to read the details of the killings. Trains, villages, streets, fields. There seems to be no clear accounting of the dead. One million? Two? Towns and villages went up in flames. Accounts of rapes and atrocities on girls and women on both sides of the divide. Fifteen million people poured east, poured west, the largest mass migration the world has ever seen.

*

In May 1941 Chagall and his family were forced to walk over the Pyrenees to the border of Spain in order to get out of Vichy France. There were no transports out of Marseille, or any other port in France, and the overland route to Portugal was the only possibile means of escape. I imagine Chagall, fifty-four years old, winding up through the vineyards and bare rocks, under the late spring heat. Was he registering the beauty of the Costa Brava, seeing colours and forms he might later want to paint? I doubt it. There would have been only the urgency of moving forward through difficult terrain towards a line on a map that was at once arbitrary, and absolute.

Six months earlier the German philosopher Walter Benjamin, frail with a heart condition, had made the same journey, crossing the mountains with a small company of fellow refugees. When the party arrived, weak and exhausted, at the town of Portbou on the Spanish Mediterranean, the authorities, following a new order from France, refused them entry and informed them that they would be delivered back to the border the next day. That night, in the hotel room under guard, a depleted and despairing Benjamin took morphine pills and died. Within a matter of days, the Spanish authorities would once again start accepting refugees from France, but on that single day, they were barred entry. Chagall, walking that same route, would have known of Benjamin's fate the year before. He must have been anxious about the border, the capricious authorities, as he trudged upwards to the ridgeline of those bare mountains, step by step by step. A Jew, an artist, but on that day just a human body trying to get itself across the line to a safety that always lay ahead, precarious and with no guarantees.

*

The image of that baby grand in the lounge, the Rachmaninov sitting on the stand, has been nagging at me for days. Finally, standing in the shower this morning rinsing soap off my chest and groin, I realise that I already knew about Maneesh. Moira told me the whole story, coded lightly, so I wouldn't hear a thing. That supposed high school boyfriend of hers. Night-long fumblings in the school music room. Well, I ask you, how likely is it that a pair of randy schoolkids would have access to their school music room after hours? That love affair never happened at secondary school.

I might fire off an email later tonight. Aaron, for the record: your conception occurred in the music room at Teachers' College, Donald Street, Karori, a prime example of the new brutalist architecture, all hand-chipped concrete ribbing and open pale pine staircases. You might note that it took place *weeks* before your mother's trip to Australia, the ostensible date on which you began life, which explains why you were the fattest premature baby any of the midwives had ever seen.

Maneesh rejected her. I believe her about that. Nights spent in the dark beneath his window, listening to him playing piano. My Moira, her instinct to protect herself. If she tells him about her circumstances, she will evoke in him pity, and grave obligation. But what use to her is that? She wants to be loved. So she sits in the dark outside his house, abased and alone, but she won't burst in and hurl insults, she won't throw a rock through the window and, *fuck you*, she won't ever, ever tell that boy, practising his scales over and over again on the other side of the window, the one thing that might convince him to take her back.

Even if she had told Maneesh, if they had married, how then to accommodate Claudia, with her caustic tone, her barbed *noblesse oblige* commentary condescending to every race other than the Anglo-Saxons? I don't know how Aaron ever made sense of that. Perhaps he didn't.

For all these reasons, in the spring of 1975, Moira was to go to Auckland. The arrangements had been made. Her mother, who had been 'surprisingly sweet about it', would travel with her.

I had been meeting Moira at the Matterhorn for several weeks when she told me she would be heading north the next day, and would be back in two weeks.

'What's in Auckland?' I asked.

That would have been a small, easy lie to tell. She could have gone to Auckland the next day, and come back and told me then, or not told me at all. Something might have unfolded between us along an entirely different trajectory from what did.

But she said she was going for an abortion, and she told me about Mark. I asked her if she wanted me to come along, which seemed to surprise her. I stayed over at her flat that night, the first time I'd done so. There was cut daphne in a vase on the wooden table, and in the morning I brought her gingerbeer from the fridge. I took the bottle into the bedroom, where she was sitting up in bed pulling her socks on. I told her she should marry me, and she laughed.

'Shall we save this conversation for when I come back?'

'What if you didn't go to Auckland?'

She frowned and pulled her legs into her chest. 'Oh, I see. You're one of those anti-abortion people. Well, fair enough.'

'No, I'm not.'

'If I don't go to Auckland—this week, actually—then I will give birth in July and sign papers and hand it over, which is not really how I pictured things unfolding, as a girl, when I did think about it, which I suppose I did, to be honest. I know you're going to say I should just give it away to some loving, stable parents, and I have some sympathy for your argument but actually, also, I don't, and I can't. Sorry.'

'Don't go to Auckland. Don't sign the papers.'

'What do you mean?'

'You should marry me.'

She took a long drink from the bottle, reached over and placed in on the bedstand. 'And have it,' she said.

'And have it.'

'You *are* one of those anti-abortion people. Isn't this taking your point to an extreme?'

'I'm not. Go to Auckland, or don't. I'll still marry you. Why would this be difficult?'

'You hardly know me. Also, it's not yours.'

'From what you've told me it's not really anyone's, at this point.'

'And me?'

I took the bottle and drank. The sweet flavour, the tang of the ginger.

'I feel like I know you. I know the important things.'

'You're mad.'

'Yes,' I said. 'But it could work, don't you think?'

*

In the study, the light on the answer machine blinks wildly. There's a single message, which I play over several times before ringing back the person in question, a young curator from the City Gallery who, she tells me, occasionally contracts herself out as an advisor on corporate art collections. She has been working with my firm recently, she explains, and they passed on my phone number. She came across Moira's painting in the basement, *just a lucky find*, and she has a request to make. I listen to the details of what she's asking with much astonishment, and a good deal of trepidation, but in the end I agree. *Show yourself, show yourself.*

*

In Plato's *Republic*, Socrates tells the story of Er, who, after death, is taken to the place where souls migrate, to witness the spectacle—*sad and laughable and strange*—of souls choosing their next life, a choice they seem to make on the basis of what they have learned from their last life. Orpheus chooses to become a swan, because he does not wish to be born from woman, the women of Thrace having murdered him. He would rather hatch from an egg. Thamyras chooses the life of a nightingale, and Agamemnon the life of an eagle. *And not only did men pass into animals but I must mention also that there were animals tame and wild who changed into one another and into corresponding human natures—the good into the gentle and the evil into the savage, in all sorts of combinations.*

Plato's conception of the universe seems to be more or less a karmic one, which is a remarkable thing to consider. The *Republic* was written at about the time that Philip II of Macedon was born. More than fifty years were to pass before his son, Alexander the Great, arrived in the Indus Valley and entered the Punjab. On the banks of the Beas River, Alexander's men sat down and refused to go any further, terrified by Porus's war elephants, by rumours of thousands more of the horse-trampling monsters on the other side of the river. Alexander's army forged a road through the Khyber Pass, from present day Kabul to Peshawar, but I doubt that before that time there was any way that Indian religious belief could have been available to the Greek mind. It's true that there was the cult of Orpheus to draw on, the mystery schools with their teaching of death and rebirth, of a soul imprisoned in a succession of earthly bodies, but still, it seems astonishing to me that Plato would arrive at this quintessential Eastern philosophy. Perhaps reincarnation, like meaningful distribution of reward and punishment, is just an idea that arises naturally out of the human condition. Who has never wondered what it would be like to be a seagull?

If I got to choose, I'd come back as a sheepdog, and I'd work the station at Tinui or Castlepoint, riding on the back of the ute out to the far paddocks. I'd eye the flock, herding in the lost ewe and her runty lamb. Possum for dinner, stars overhead. Just the thing. What this says about what I have learnt so far, and what I have yet to make sense of, I don't exactly know.

*

I read Aaron's email from Rawalpindi over most mornings. *I wear shalwar-kameez because I want to blend in.* I'd love to see a photo of that. This email, and the postcard with lilacs, are the only things I've had from him since his leaving Wellington airport six weeks ago. Most days I type a little something to send him, some odd story from the newspapers, a family anecdote or something about Moira, some moment from the past or habit of hers that's been visiting me. I try to get it down accurately and then I flick it off to him.

Of course, I keep hoping that I'll see a new message fly in from him, hoping to hear that he's heading south, hoping there will some kind of outpouring as in that one letter. *Dad, I can't explain how badly I want to find him.* It's astonishing how much of a consolation it is to have had that one message. I feel as if we have it underfoot; a bridge, even if slightly shaky. So when Maneesh phones me to say that Aaron has arranged a time to call the following evening, and I should come to his house at that time, I hesitate. It feels like I'm being asked to play a trick. I am, too. Maneesh is too much the diplomat to point blank tell me that he hasn't told Aaron what he's up to, but we both know it's a conspiracy to dupe him into getting on the phone to me. At which point, once I have his ear, Maneesh is expecting me—*real Dad*, at the end of the day—to tell my boy to let the uncle business go, and get his arse back over the line to India. Outflank him. Triangulate. Present a unified front.

Well, there's no way in hell I'm going to tell him to do anything. I just want to hear his voice.

'Sure,' I say. 'I'll swing by.'

I wake from a dream in which Aaron is shouting at me from behind a glass window, and I can't hear his voice. I try to get up but I feel *rent*, as though something has been ripped from me, as though part of my own flesh has been torn away, and I fall back into bed and weep for the sheer physical pain in my chest. I sleep again, and when I wake later the rain is sheeting down from a low flat sky. In the afternoon it lets up and I drive down to Lyall Bay and park at the surf end by the airport. The sea is empty, limp and grey, fist-high wavelets breaking and sucking quietly at the sand.

The beach is criss-crossed with dogs making their overtures to one another, the arse-sniff, the play-bow, little darts away, then haring off into frenetic games of chase. Their owners stand in clusters, calling the dogs back from the edge of the sea, reining them in when exuberance threatens to give way to aggression. I watch as a huge dog, grey-brown, leggy, long in the face, runs down the sand and barrels right into a knot of tiny dogs, who start to yap ferociously. A man steps forward and puts his hand on the large dog's back, speaking to him in a low tone, and I realise it is Dylan from the office, with his Great Dane. She's a truly enormous dog, table-high. Dylan puts her on the leash and pulls her away from the fray, and then he notices me watching, and comes over.

Dylan's warmth is genuine. He has come into Wellington for the afternoon, he says, checking out property in Miramar. He gets into a conversation about schools, asks where we sent Aaron.

'Rongotai College,' I hear myself saying. 'It was good, perfectly sound. He made wonderful friends there.'

'My wife's obsessed with zoning,' Dylan says. 'She's keen on the northern suburbs. But it costs. The kids need a big section to run around on. This one'—he slaps the dog's rump—'needs a lot of space.'

That annual bonus must have come through, after all.

'Tell me, Dylan. Did you actually do all those hours for BioCom?'

He can answer however he likes. The sky is grey overhead and we watch a plane roar up off the tarmac, tipping around to the north. We are simply two men on a beach.

'I did.' His brow furrows. 'Do you want to know the details?'

'Not really'

'They're a fascinating company. Don't tell Richard, but I've started working pro bono for them in the evenings.'

'Generous of you,' I say. 'How do you manage that with the kids?'

'That's where it started, actually. Oscar's been in and out of hospital with complications from the measles. Seems to have affected his hearing. Terrible. Then we met this family in the hospital, also from Titahi Bay, and their girl, a twelve-year-old, has had rheumatic fever. You heard of that? Permanent damage to her heart.'

'Nasty.'

'This is what got me involved with BioCom, funnily enough. Turns out they're researching an improved antibiotic for exactly this problem. This kid, right now she has to get a painful injection in her bum every month for the rest of her life. So I'm doing the legal legwork on that.'

'For free.'

I have never seen Dylan so animated, so driven.

'It speeds things up. They're hoping to get to the testing stage early next year.'

He pauses, calibrates himself. 'But how about you?' I watch him mentally fish for a tactful question. What portion of an unemployed, widowed man's life can you politely enquire about? 'How's your son getting on in London?'

'He's in Pakistan, in fact,' I say. 'He was in Delhi for about a month.'

'Did you watch the news last night? You'll be glad he's left.'

'The news?'

'You didn't see? Terrorist attack on the Indian parliament. Could have been large-scale. Just luck that the bomb didn't go off. Quick-thinking security guards, it seems.'

I don't know whether Maneesh's relations live anywhere in the vicinity of the parliament. 'I hadn't heard.'

'Well.' Dylan ruffles his dog's ears. 'I better give this girl a run.'

The big droopy chops on her. Soulful, doggish eyes.

'Yes,' I say. 'You'd best. Good luck with the house-hunting.'

His face seems to sag. 'I like Titahi Bay,' he says. 'I don't really know why we're leaving.'

Back home in the study, I discover that the *Times of India* has its own webpage. I find out that Dylan has accurately reported the facts to me, that none of the fourteen dead in yesterday's attack in New Delhi was a member of parliament, although, had the plot succeeded and the bomb gone off, India would have lost her entire elected leadership in one hit.

The new information today is that the Indian government is laying blame for the attack on a Pakistan-based Kashmiri separatist group. In response, there is talk already, today, of the government mobilising their army towards the Punjabi and Kashmir borders. The *Times of India* runs an editorial that is largely approving in tone of such military escalation. The papers in New York and London, on the other hand, worry aloud that both sides have nuclear weapons, and make plain-speech appeals to India's restraint.

I think of Adrian in Venice, and his fears, which I found lurid at the time, of Soviet generals with their fingers on the nuclear button. How he gestured a mushroom cloud to me, the way the movement of his hands was reflected in the mirrored wall of the booth in that cheap-end restaurant, with the women next to us speaking of birth, *the obstetrician didn't even realise she was breech until a foot appeared.* I had dismissed such talk as the anxieties of another era. Now Pakistan is fighting America's war on one border, preparing for their own on another. How calm, how level-headed, are their generals? Aaron, a human speck somewhere in the middle of it all. *Let's hope it doesn't come to that.*

Praneeta met me at the door, took my coat and brought me into the dining room. The table was laid with food, rice, breads, bowls of sauces. It was late, and I'd already eaten, but protesting over this only made Praneeta smile.

'Are we expecting others?

'You, and ourselves. But don't worry, my sons have a good appetite.'

She handed me a plate and, although there was no one

else in the room, seemed to expect me to make a start.

'Just as you want,' she said. 'Please help yourself.'

I took a little and she pulled out a chair for me to sit at the table.

'Maneesh will come soon,' she said. 'He's had to take his father to the hospital.'

'Oh. Nothing serious, I hope?' At nine at night, it was clearly not a routine appointment.

'He fell,' said Praneeta. 'But they have had the X-ray. Nothing is broken.'

'Has this happened before?'

Praneeta placed a silver mug of water in front of me. 'Yes, it has. That's why they're running some extra tests.'

'Your own family, are they nearby?'

'My parents live in San Bernardino. I have a sister in New Delhi.'

'I heard about the attack on the parliament.'

'Yes, it's a bad situation. And now they've closed the border to Pakistan.'

I blinked. 'Really? What does that mean?'

Before she could answer, the beige phone on the wall started to burr. I leapt out of my seat and stood beside it, useless as a dog, waiting to lift the receiver if Praneeta gave me the nod. My heart was battering about. *Hello!* I wanted to answer it and I didn't want to. But Praneeta gave her head a little shake, warning me off, lifted the receiver and launched into a rapid-fire conversation in Hindi, peppered through with English.

I sat back down at the table and listened, snapping tiny corners off a papadom, placing them on the tip of my tongue.

'They're on their way now.'

'Can I ask about the border?' I said. 'Is no one allowed through? Because you see, my son—'

317

'Yes, I know,' she interrupts. 'He'll have to fly out now. To Bangkok or Dubai, then he can get a connection onwards.'

Then Praneeta walked out of the dining room, and I saw her down the hallway with an armload of sheets. She was preoccupied, agitated. I was a stranger in her house, and a burden to her tonight. I ought to go, the circumstances had changed, and I didn't need to be sitting here eating when her frazzled husband and fragile parents-in-law arrived back from the ordeal of the ER. I stared at the beige phone, imagined the smooth plastic of it in my hand and pressed to my ear, and the sound of his voice clicking, echoing, arrowing down through the lines, *Hello Ronny, it's me.* That's all I'd planned to say. I'd got no further.

I stood in the lounge, the big windows with the view of the Rimutakas and the chinks of harbour. It was a melancholy time of day. The house was quiet except for the thump of music coming from upstairs. Those boys, I supposed. I thought about the strange chain of events that had brought me here to stand at Maneesh's window, to look out at his view, as if I had consumed him, or he had consumed me.

It's now a week shy of the solstice. There was blue light in the arch of the sky last night, the harbour water black. It's a drawn out performance, the play of the light and colour at this time of year. I'd forgotten about December, the year tipping relentlessly into summer and the flax flowers opening their sticky orange-black fingers and the pōhutukawa white-grey fuzz starting burst into red stars. I felt exhausted by it. It's intolerable, summer ahead, all the days fat with beauty, useless. *I want her back.* She won't. *Come back.* I want her. Back, come back. *She won't come back.* The chug of it, on and on.

Sangeeta appeared in the room, bouncing in red spiky heels and tight jeans, and with her two willowy girls in their early teens, long black hair, sparkly T-shirts, studded belts, immediately squashing themselves side by side on the couch and pulling out a pocket videogame. Nobody looked surprised to see me there, and neither did Adrian when he appeared a moment later, pushing an elderly man in a wheelchair. The man's ankle and the wrist were heavily bandaged. What had Claudia said? *Have you met Mr Gupta? Aaron's the spit of him.* But I couldn't see it, really. Adrian steered the grandfather to a spot beneath a lamp, while Praneeta came to his side with a glass of water and a hot facecloth, and knelt to tend to him. Maneesh came in last with a woman who had to be his mother, a thin, erect woman wearing a rich emerald sari. She paused at the doorway, scanned the room, met my eye, and nodded. *Shrimati Gupta, Mata-ji?* I didn't know what I was supposed to call her.

'Good evening.' I walked across the room, made ready to shake hands, then retracted. It felt like the wrong gesture. A kiss would be far too intimate. Finally I just nodded. 'I'm Peter.'

'Yes.' She held herself very calm and still. She seemed younger than I might have imagined. She looked at me in a way that suggested she knew most of what there was to know. 'Hello.'

That seemed to be sufficient. The family settled down to business, piling up plates with food, coming and going from the kitchen. Adrian came up to me and pulled a little face of commiseration, or pity, I wasn't sure which, but I bridled at it in any case. Was I expected to take the phone call from Aaron, if it ever came, in front of him, in front of everyone here? Was there not a private phone somewhere in the house?

'These are your girls?' I nodded towards the children on the couch.

Adrian nodded, his mouth full of bread.

'Yep.' He shouted, 'Rashi, Sahana!'

Neither of them looked up. 'They're a little annoyed,' he said. 'We were on our way to the movies tonight when we got the call to come to the hospital.'

It's surprising to me that it would take five children and grandchildren to help Mr Gupta at the hospital. I've taken care of my parents more or less on my own. Perhaps I should have involved Aaron more, perhaps I should have had higher expectations. Perhaps it takes a bit of inconvenience to knit a child to their kin. I do find that Aaron is cool and cavalier about my parents, far less adoring than he is of Claudia.

'He's going to be all right?' I nodded towards the wheelchair.

'Bruised, shaken up.' He leaned in towards my ear, spoke quietly. 'Maneesh thinks his sister's not looking after them properly. He's insisting they stay here tonight. Poor Baba-ji, he just wants his own bed.'

Sure enough, Mr Gupta looked done in. His head was tipping down onto his chest. Praneeta had laid a blanket over his knee, and stayed sitting by his side. Mrs Gupta was sitting between her granddaughters, handing them out sweets, and stroking the hair of the younger one. She heard the phone first because I saw her startle and look towards the wall, and it was only then that I heard the burring, almost buried under the soft voices in the room.

Maneesh glanced at me, then walked over and lifted the receiver. I saw him stretch the cord around the doorway so as to get into the dining room where it was quieter. He beckoned me over.

'Excuse me,' I said to Adrian, and I put a hand on

his arm, which was supposed to be an apology but was actually a way of steadying myself. Of grabbing whatever, whoever was closest.

Maneesh held the receiver out. 'It's him.'

I took myself around the corner and half buried my face in the wall before I spoke. 'Aaron,' I said, cupping the receiver. 'It's me. It's Dad.'

'I didn't expect this.'

'I know, right? Surprise!'

'Ha,' he said. 'Well, it's okay. In fact it's good.'

There was a certain amount of static on the line. It wasn't as clear as I might have hoped, and it was hard to make out intonation, but it was him. *In fact it's good.* Yes it was, oh yes.

'Where are you, Ronny?'

'Do you remember I said about my flatmate in London?'

'Yes,' I said, 'I do. Rob went there to look for you, Rob spoke to him.'

'So, I'm staying with his cousin.'

'Okay.' A known person, good, that was a good start.

'In a house,' I said. 'You got an address for that place?' I realised I was twisting my finger into the coils of the phone cord, looping them around and around my skin.

'Ah, yeah. Sure. You're really there with Maneesh, Dad? That's weird.'

'Well, so, funny thing. Everyone's here. Sangeeta, Adrian.' I paused. 'Your grandparents too.'

'Wait. You're saying Maneesh's mother's there?'

'She's, ah, yes.'

I poked my head around the doorway and looked into the lounge. Mrs Gupta was sitting on the couch with her hands folded in her lap, and beside her, his head inclined towards her, was a boy who was perhaps Aaron. I felt my breath draw in. Aaron, sitting beside the woman in an emerald sari, dressed in a sports-jock polo shirt which he would normally never have been seen dead wearing.

'Ah,' I said faintly. 'Where are you?'

I heard voices far off down the phone, talking in the background. I could make out some sort of exchange, excitement.

I couldn't take my eyes off the couch. Now the grandmother said something, and the young boy laughed.

'I'm in Peshawar. Dad, it's wild. There's thousands of refugees flooding over the border. But Maneesh's mother. Is she really there? Can you get her? Can she come to the phone?

I stared at the boy's face. His face was slimmer, darker, younger, and when he smiled it wasn't quite familiar. He wasn't Aaron. He was so much like Aaron, I felt my body ache to move towards him, to put my arms around him.

Jayesh. The eldest brother.

'Dad, listen. My great-uncle is here. He used to be known as Sanjay. I've found him. He's here with me. He wants to talk to my grandmother. Can you get her? Say it's her brother? Can you put her on?'

'Brother?' I said. 'A brother?'

'Tell her,' he said, 'it's Sanjay.'

The uncle was there. *Home, my boy's going to come home.* I'd book the flight, Bangkok, Dubai, whichever direction he chose. Mission accomplished, over and out.

'All right,' I said. 'I'll try.'

'Tell her,' Aaron said. 'Just tell her.'

I covered the receiver with my hand and spoke up, into the room.

'Mrs Gupta.' It came out as more of a shout than I'd intended. 'It's your brother on the phone. Sanjay. Calling from Pakistan. He wants to speak to you.'

The room went very silent. Mrs Gupta didn't move.

322

After a moment, I lifted the phone to my ear. 'Ah, Aaron,' I said. 'This isn't straightforward.'

'Neema. Where is Neema?'

But it wasn't Aaron. It was a clipped, curt voice, the voice of a stranger.

I looked straight at Mrs Gupta. 'Are you Neema?'

Her mouth opened a little, then shut again. I waited for some gesture, some answer, but she didn't move.

'Maneesh?' I held it out. 'Will you speak to him?'

Maneesh crossed his arms.

'Stop this!' Sangeeta hissed loudly.

'Hello,' I said into the receiver. 'I'm sorry, she won't, ah.'

'Looking for Neema,' the man said. 'Neema.'

'I know you are,' I said. 'Look, what can I tell you? She's well, she's very well.' I felt the stares of the entire room hard on me. 'They're all well. Fantastic family, just great. Thriving. Grandchildren, several of them, just beautiful.'

'Who are you?' said the voice. 'Neema, please. Sister.'

'Can you give me Aaron?' I asked. 'Can I have him back?'

But then the call was suddenly cut off, and the toneless pips started beeping in my ear.

Sangeeta saw me out of the house. We talked quietly on the driveway.

'What happened there?'

'I told you. I warned you. It would have astonished me if my mother had spoken to him.'

'Aren't you at least pleased to find out he's alive?'

'It makes no difference to me. But my mother is upset.'

'Her brother is alive. He wanted to speak to her. *Why* is she so upset? Just because he stayed in Pakistan, and she left?'

Sangeeta looked down at the concrete.

'I imagine my mother when she was young, you know. She was twenty when she arrived here. I always imagined her as an adult. But now I think, twenty. What's twenty? She came with my father, and already pregnant with Maneesh. I can see her walking around Woburn, all those fenced houses, hearing this new accent. The light must have been strange to her. I can sense the weight inside her. Her baby growing, and then alongside him this heaviness, this dead weight.'

'She would have been homesick.'

'No. Not that. It's everything that was invisible. I don't know what my mother witnessed when she fled her village. I don't know what they went through. A woman at that time, on that road, alone with two daughters? My mother was sixteen. I don't know.'

'You've never asked about it?'

'I'm not sure I could bear to know.'

I sighed. 'Aaron's worked so hard to find that man. For Maneesh, you. For all of you.'

She gave me a level look. 'We didn't want it though.'

'Well, he didn't know that. He couldn't have known that.'

'He didn't ask, actually.'

Thirteen

The towers touched everything in Moira's last two weeks. The nurses, the visitors, the newspapers, the TV all dragged that jittery, shocked, changed world into her room, a room where we were trying to accomplish something like prayer, or just breathing in any case. I wanted to seal off the room, keep it all away from her, but it seeped in everywhere.

One night at the hospice Aaron played me something on his laptop, a reverse slow-motion film of the North Tower's collapse. How everything moved upwards and inwards, shards of debris rocketing home into place, the brief flare of the explosion, metal and glass molding into place beneath the flames. I wanted it to keep going, to run it all the way backwards, the bodies flying up the towers as if pulled by a smooth string, the plane exiting from the building like a knife backing out of butter, flying backwards across the Manhattan sky, across New York State, across Massachusetts, landing backwards on the tarmac in Boston, the passengers reversing out of the airplane, the box cutters unpacked from the backpack.

*

I don't know how I appeared to Geneviève the last time I ever saw her, on that day I spent with her in Lyon in 1989. In her eyes, was I defensive? Aloof? I put my hand on her knee and she started crying, and then I moved away from her. Where were you? she said. Why didn't you come?

*

Hendrik, the steel cutter from the shipyards, gave the impression that he was a man with contacts, a man with projects. When he spoke to me in the locker room, I knew that whatever deal he was offering me would almost certainly be illegal. I didn't think I wanted to get involved. One Friday, a fortnight after he had first spoken to me, he spoke to me again after work, again in the steam and the hush of running water, and, under the yellow lights, he asked me if I'd thought about it. He mentioned, in an offhand, forgetful way, a number of guilders. It was a very large number. It was equivalent to five hundred pounds sterling. It was a number that would cover two years of rent on a flat in the Jordaan or Oud-Zuid.

It was around this time that I left Abigail with the Irishman on the boat, and came back to find her set down in a basket in the corner with no blanket, blue from cold. Perhaps a week later, I said I could clear the boat, and he took me outside the gate and explained what was involved. I went past Centraal Station on the way home that day, and booked Geneviève a ticket to Lyon.

Hendrik volunteered almost no information about what I would be taking onto the boat, and I asked for none, and in this way I could remain ignorant, or innocent, and I cultivated this ignorance, or innocence, deep in my bones and gut so that, by the time it was five in the morning and I woke alone on the *Lychorida* and came up on deck to a clear, frozen night, and I had winched up all four boxes—each weighing about ten kilograms, each wrapped in waterproofing—from the rubber dinghy that had pulled up alongside our vessel and was gone again within ten

326

minutes, and by the time I had stored the boxes beneath a blanket down the hold, in the space where Geneviève and the baby had been sleeping, I could genuinely say I had no knowledge of what I was involved in.

*

Yesterday I got back out on *Cronus* for a couple of hours. It was hot, and almost still. The sheets of rain that had come down over the weekend left a mist sitting on the hills, and the water was pale, eggshell blue, streaked and dappled with pockets of cobalt where the slight wind blew offshore.

I was mucking around in Evans Bay, enjoying the easy glide towards Shelly Bay, when I noticed a huddle of boats sitting off Point Halswell. I tacked up into the wind, almost as far as Somes, and saw what was underway. A grey ship, a naval vessel, progressing slowly past the Seatoun shore, a massive piece of military equipment under the escort of two red tugboats, like jolly bath toys mixed in with some kid's army set. As she turned the corner and made her way in towards the city, the yachts sitting off the coast of the Miramar Peninsula came in to glide behind and alongside her, a welcoming flotilla, all of them, I noticed, keeping what would have to be an officially appointed distance from the ship. I sailed down into the inner harbour before taking *Cronus* back into the marina, past Queen's Wharf where she was moored, the HMNZS *Canterbury*, ready for public admiration, all flags flying.

*

There was snow in the air the day I stored contraband on the *Lychorida*. The sky roiled in from the sea through the morning, and a cold bite came on the wind. A few loose flakes fell around noon but didn't settle. I lay all morning on a bed in the top cabin, and tried to read. The collect was

327

due at 4am, exactly twenty-four hours after drop off. The slush of the river beneath the hull caught at me, the thrum of passing boats, the distant trills of bicycle bells on the bridge and along the banks. Around two in the afternoon there were a series of bangs and shouts from the shore. My chest contracted. I came out on deck and saw a truck outside the Carré Theatre, back doors flung open, a ramp set out in preparation for unloading, a quarrel unfolding between the theatre staff and the driver. Nothing to do with me.

Around four, I ate a meal of rice, sausages, thought about a cold beer, thought better of it. I needed my wits about me. I rugged up with a coat, a hat, and sat on deck in the dark. The lights of Magere Brug danced in the black river water.

The arrangement was that a bicycle with a small box trailer would pull up beside our mooring. There was a password to exchange, and the driver would pass me three hundred guilders in cash before receipt, by way of an advance. I would be held responsible for the boxes, *Your life on those goods*, Hendrik had said, until the bicycle departed. After that, there was a one month stand-down period for whatever machinations needed to take place, then the rest of the cash would be paid out.

I thought of Geneviève and Abigail arriving at Chavanoz. I thought about the heat in the baby's forehead the morning before. I hoped that a doctor had been called. I had convinced myself that it was reasonable to do what I was doing. With Hendrik's deal, I would gain the power to change our circumstances entirely. Renting in Amsterdam wasn't the answer. It would only prolong our problems. I had no career here, no future, and sooner or later we would get hungry, or need something, and I would be tempted back into this racket. I was a father now. I would buy the plane tickets with the money, and we could all three be in New Zealand by March. I held on to the image of my mother taking Abigail into her arms.

It started to snow thickly at nine, and I worried that the pavements would become unpassable. I had seven hours to wait. I slept fitfully for an hour or two around midnight. At about two in the morning the sky cleared and my breath grew steady. I felt that I had come through the worst of it and was safe, that the business was almost accomplished. From half past three, I sat up on deck and kept watch. The snow wasn't deep. But no one came. I heard one bicycle slide by in the slush, but it didn't stop. By quarter past four, my head was full of electricity, and at half past four I thought I might throw up. The rubber dinghy had pulled up against the stern of the *Lychorida* on the stroke of four the previous night. There was no contingency plan. Sometime tomorrow, any time from mid-morning onwards, my flatmates on the boat would drift back home. I stared at the shore, at the dark gaps where the buildings stood, at the empty pavement punctuated by orange streetlights.

The sky stayed dark until close to six, when the first hint of indigo, an almost imperceptible lightening started to give shape to the shoreline. I had gone below to count the boxes again when I heard a tread on the boards above, the weight of a person stepping over the rail from shore to deck. No one was supposed to come aboard. I wanted a gun, or a knife, and I had neither. I wondered if it was too late already to jump ship, get on a train for France. I had my passport in my pocket.

It could end, I supposed suddenly, in murder. Already I heard steps coming around to the companionway. I rushed forward through the galley. Would I shout? To whom would I shout, who did I think would help me now? My judgement, I saw in an instant, had been terribly poor.

Rob's face appeared, smiling at the top of the ladder. I swore. I had a kitchen knife in my hand. His brow furrowed for a moment, then he swung himself down the steps and poured water into the kettle.

'Tell me.'

I took him down to Geneviève's bed and lifted the covers to show him what was stashed underneath. What was I hoping for? *Rightio, let's get this sorted then. Pete, you're in over your head all right, but no drama.* I remember the dreadful paleness of his face. He stared at the boxes, took a few steps back.

'They haven't come,' I said. 'They're late.'

'What the hell is in those?' He pointed at the boxes, came no closer.

'I don't know.' I shrugged. 'Weed, maybe?'

Rob made a slight snort. 'Weed. You think?'

I sat down on the bed and put my head in my hands. 'They might still come,' I said. 'They could still come.'

'Is it Hendrik?'

That was clearly the one name I must not, under any circumstances, divulge. But I nodded anyway. Rob whistled and shook his head.

'Does he have you over a barrel, this guy? What have you done?'

'I wanted the money.'

'I could've got you money. You stupid arse. You stupid arse.'

I could hear traffic on the bridge, and the light was strengthening minute by minute. I checked my watch.

'They're three hours late. I don't know why. I don't get what it means.'

'I could kill you, you know that? I don't need to, though, because they're going to do that.'

'What if we throw it overboard?'

'Yeah, well they'll kill you. Do you think it's a game?'

I swallowed.

'I don't want to be here. I don't want to leave you, but I don't want to be here.'

'I know,' I said. 'Go, go on. It's okay.'

Rob stroked his fingers over his lips for a minute.

'Here's what we're going to do. I'll come back and stand outside the theatre at noon. If nothing's happening by then, we'll talk. But you come over to me, got it?'

'Leave the boat?'

'Ten metres away. I'm not coming back on board until those boxes are gone.'

'Fair enough,' I said.

'You really don't understand who you are, do you? You're a kid from Wanganui. You haven't got a clue. You don't even speak the language. This business, it's not your world. It's not mine either. *Money.* What in blue heaven do you need money for anyway?'

'You've made your point, Rob.'

'Guess I have.'

He came back, put a hand up and squeezed my shoulder.

'See you at noon. If it's gone by then, I'll buy you a beer. Idiot.'

In the middle of 1973, *Time*, or perhaps it was the *New Yorker*, ran a story about the sudden surge in the volume of heroin coming out of Afghanistan. Over the winter of 1971, US aid workers, abundantly funded by the Nixon administration in the hope of fending off any nascent Soviet sympathy in the populace, had laid down extensive irrigation systems in the southwest of the country. In Kandahar, the poppy farmers were rejoicing over two years of bumper crops. 'We'll never go back,' farmer Ali

Mehrzad was quoted as saying. 'Now we have found a way to live.'

I read the story on a layover at San Francisco Airport, on my way home to New Zealand, flying on a ticket I had paid for in full, in cash.

*

Laura knocked on my door this morning. There was an awkward moment when I couldn't decide whether I should invite her in or not. In the end, I opted for staying on the doorstep.

'I need your help.'

She came out with it bluntly. She was wearing the glittery blue tunic she'd worn at the drinks, the night I drove her home. I think she must have walked up the hill to my house, because she was puffing, red in the face. But she did also look upset, agitated.

'It's about Matthew.'

'Oh?'

'I shouldn't be telling you this.'

Well then, darling, don't.

'He's going to do something.'

'Something?'

'Illegal. You have to talk to him.'

Being informed about intent to commit a crime would certainly put an ethical, perhaps even legal, responsibility on me.

'Perhaps stop there,' I said.

'It's happening tonight,' she blurted. 'Can't you talk to him?'

She pulled out her mobile phone.

'Ah. No. I don't want his number. At all.'

Laura lowered her phone.

'He's not a child,' I said. 'He's a grown man. You didn't

like it, did you, when he tried to tell you what to do?'

She sucked on her lip. 'Okay, well,' she said, 'I'm thirsty. Can't I have a glass of water?'

I still didn't invite her in. I padded back into the kitchen, poured her water from the jug in the fridge.

'If he gets caught, it'll be serious.'

'Well, it's his decision, isn't it? He has his reasons.'

She took a long drink of the water. 'I really can't convince you to help.'

'No, you can't.'

She handed me back the glass, slung her bag over her back. 'Well, thanks for nothing.'

I watched her walk down the hill in the sunshine, her dress gleaming and winking like a sapphire.

Just after midnight, I pull up the Legacy in the carpark behind Freyberg Pool. The sky is clear, the wind slightly blustery, and there's no moon that I can make out, which has to be part of Matthew's calculation. I shump the car lock, walk around the back of the pool to the boats. On the walkway under the overhang, I trip over a sleeping bag which has a living body in it, a face and voice emerging to grunt at me, a swallowed shout. A smell rises up, the rank stink of homelessness, fetid sweat. The face, half seen by the marina lights, is young, a headful of dreadlocks.

My first instinct after Laura walked away down the hill was to see if I could track down Matthew after all. There was a part of me that wanted to talk him out of it, to lay out the risks, to make sure, at the very least, that he planned to wear a lifejacket. *Everyone's telling me to play it safe. I suppose they mean well.* I got a beer out of the fridge, sat on my hands, fried up a chicken breast for dinner.

By 10pm, I was restless. I put Mozart on the stereo, tried to settle with the newspaper, but I kept pacing, checking my watch. He will have planned—anyone sensible would—for the quietest watch of the night, three or four in the morning. It's only a week off the solstice, and the sky starts to grow pale as early as four, which is a detail I hope he's considered. I thought of him making his preparations, duct-taping a spraycan to a long stick, figuring some system to keep the button on the can pressed down. Whose kayak does he have, and where will he put it into the water?

By eleven I'd packed a bag with waterproofs, warm clothes, food, binoculars. My intention was to motor *Cronus* to a point halfway between the end of the Overseas Terminal and Queen's Wharf, and sit there. I'd be two hundred-odd metres away from the action. Even in the dark, I might be able to make out something. Then, if I saw the need, if the situation warranted it, I would motor *Cronus* upwind, due east from the *Canterbury*. If I puddled around with my sails a bit, drew attention to myself, the naval watch would keep their binoculars trained on me out in the water, and Matthew would have the cover he needed.

It would be easily deniable, any whiff of collusion. Why I chose to go sailing in the middle of the night, that might take some explaining, but no doubt people do stranger things. I doubt it will come to that in any case.

It's a fine night to be out, still warm, the white lights rimming the harbour reflected in the black water like a string of glass beads. I putter *Cronus* out of the marina, and round the tip of the terminal. The *Canterbury* is still lit up on deck. The wind's getting up, which is going to be a help to Matthew, even if it makes the paddling tricky, because it scatters the tiny sounds that would otherwise echo and magnify in the dark. I'm guessing he's going to paddle over towards the ship some way out from shore, away from any pedestrians, his profile too low to register on a radar. In theory.

I sit just outside the breakwater at Chaffers, where *Cronus*'s mast, for now, is going to blend in with the thicket of moored yachts but where there's enough space around me to bob about without fear of hitting anything. At 1am I make tea by torchlight, and bring the cup up on deck and scan the shore. The lights have gone down on the ship. I flick on the VHF, listen for a while to the talk, open a packet of mallowpuffs and crunch up mouthfuls of marshmallow and biscuit. By two, I'm starting to feel woozy. At three, I get sick of it, kick the motor on and decide to nose in closer.

There is something moving over the water to starboard, maybe a hundred metres out into the harbour. I cut the motor and listen. Every sense strains towards it, and I get the impression that someone's there, even though in the rising wind it's hard to say whether it's sight or sound or some other kind of knowing that tells me. I suspect he's painted the kayak black.

Matthew! It would be stupid to shout out. And yet, it also might stop him in his tracks. Maybe we could wrap this thing up before it starts, be reminded that there are other avenues, plenty of other avenues, to put forward dissenting views. Because the ground rules matter, because whatever political opinions we hold, we should first agree not to damage property, not to hurt persons. Is Matthew not entering into the grey zone where terrorism begins? There's a light plash as the kayak cuts in front of the bow, a flash of orange where the stern is, and then he's gone.

At some point I lose sight of him. The shorelights give off a decent glow, and it takes me five, six, seven minutes of scanning the black sea to see what's happened. The kayak has flipped upside down, and draped across the top of it is a figure like a seal, black on black on black, with a small nub of orange at the stern of the kayak. Matthew is maybe a hundred and fifty metres from the *Canterbury* and the wind is now starting to push him out into the harbour.

Aaron, when he was only two or three years old, used to climb up on my back whenever I was down on the floor or sitting on the couch, and fasten his hands around my neck. I would stand up and heave him around the room to thrill and terrify him, while his arms gripped me with a ferocity that I have never felt from another human body before or since.

*

Rob didn't get to buy me a beer that day in Amsterdam, even though the collect did show an hour later, at quarter past eight in the morning, a plain pedal bicycle with a tarp-covered trailer pulling up alongside the boat, just as promised, powered by a man whose face was almost entirely covered by a hat, a scarf, dark glasses and a fat jacket. He stood quite still onshore in the thickening sleet while I lifted up the boxes one by one, and he deftly slid them under the tarpaulin. Our neighbour on the next boat downriver, Thomas from Brussels, stood watching the entire process, his hand shielding his eyes from the sleet. I felt the collect take this observer in, and angle his bike and face away. He passed me a wad of notes, and I knew I shouldn't count it out right there. There seemed to be no jitters, no hiccups, and there was no apology or explanation for the lateness either. Other than the exchange of passwords, neither one of us spoke.

Once empty of its cargo, the boat felt instantly lighter on the water, the wind sweet across the decks. I would sleep exhausted tonight in her hollows and the river would run below me. I had done it.

When Rob approached the Carré Theatre at noon, I skipped over to him. He carried a bag with ham and fresh bread. He was elated. We went down below. I had just cut a chunk of baguette and opened it, spread on a slab of yellow butter and taken a bite, the salty butter, the soft chew of the bread, when two policemen appeared at the companionway ladder. Rob had vanished into the bathroom. I stared at the pair of blond Dutch cops, one taller than the other. The gush and splatter of Rob's piss hitting against the tin bucket came from behind the bathroom door.

Thomas, from the boat downriver. Or was it all a sting? Jail, I saw, was another possibility I had failed to properly imagine.

The taller of the two cops read out my name and date of birth. When I nodded, the shorter of the two slid his face into a horrible softness. He asked if I had a daughter, and I answered yes, and felt astonished that this would be their first concern. It occurred to me that perhaps it was part of the Dutch system, that maybe there was a built-in leniency in the way I would be dealt with because of my paternal responsibilities. I felt, in fact, that I deserved that, because the entire situation had come about due to trying to meet precisely those responsibilities. Or, perhaps they intended to take my daughter off me because of my actions, but here too I felt smug, because they couldn't, pleased that I'd had the foresight and care to remove the baby and Geneviève from the country. I was so far down this chain of thought that I didn't register anything that was being said, until Rob slung his arm around my shoulder, and nudged me down to sit in a chair, and held in front of me the piece of paper that the taller cop had handed him.

'How did she die?' Rob asked. It wasn't until he said that that I realised the arrival of the police had nothing to do with Hendrik's boxes.

*

By the time I can get in close, the wind has pushed Matthew further out into the harbour, well away from Queen's Wharf, out almost to a point level with the shoreline hulk of Freyberg Pool. I flick on as many lights in the cabin as I can, casting seams of yellow light over the choppy sea. I carry the large flashlight to the rear of the boat and train it on Matthew's body, twenty metres away, still draped over his kayak. Black wetsuit, no lifejacket. He gets a hand up in the air to show me he's all right, and I drop the ladder down the aft of the boat, fling the life-ring out to him. He strikes out for it, swims two, three, four feet and gets the ring over his head, and I haul on the rope, pulling him in towards me.

He reaches the foot of the ladder. 'Matthew,' I say.

Well, it's dark. He has no idea who his rescuer is.

'Matthew.' Tenderly, gently. 'It's me.'

He's peering up blindly. I spin the flashlight back on myself in order to show my face.

'What the fuck are *you* doing here?'

Neck-deep in cold water, with my life-ring around him, swearing at me.

'Are you stalking me?' he says.

I lay the flashlight on deck and start descending the ladder. I step down onto the lowest rung so that I'm ankle-deep in the water, and with one hand fast to the boat, help lift the ring off his neck.

'This isn't your scene,' he says. 'You're not even supposed to be here.' Such a cold voice.

'How about we just get you out?'

Matthew takes my hand and pulls up on it, and I'm on the verge of getting him up out of the sea, so it's a shock to us both when I let him go, when he plashes lightly back into the water, and when my foot comes square onto his back, *I'm here to help, can't you see I'm helping you*, when my foot presses down on his body with some force, so that I see, or half-see, in the dark under the stern—

Matthew going face down into the water, his dirty curls floating up around him, limbs churning under the water, is it ten seconds is it a minute, the sea swallowing him

—then hauling him up for real, dragging on his form, getting him onto the deck. The weight of him on me. Into the rescue position. Coughing, spluttering.

It's me, I am beside him, bent over his body, my fingers wound into the curls of his hair, my hand on his. Spit it out, I say, spit it out. Gagging. A croaky sound from the throat.

Matthew, I whisper, Matthew. My face lowered to his, my cheek pressed to his, salt-wet between us: his sea-skin, my wet eyes.

Coughing. On and on. Finally, he rolls onto his back, and looks up. 'My god.' He looks at me, his face open. 'I slipped right under.'

'You did.'

'I got stuck. I got caught on the boat or something.'

My hands are shaking, and I lift them away from his chest.

'You're crying,' he says in wonder.

'You frightened me.'

'Thank god you were here.'

*

I stayed on the boat in Amsterdam for the rest of that winter and into the spring. The money from the deal came through, a significant amount of cash, and I could have moved into a flat with it, but I didn't want to leave the *Lychorida*. Rob went back to London after Christmas, and a bunch of boys from Dublin moved in. That New Year's Eve I lay in my bed below deck and listened to them singing and playing guitar up on deck, Dylan and Hendrix and the

Doors. After midnight they started into old Irish songs. *And I wish the Queen would call back her army, from the West Indies, Amerikay and Spain.* I lay still in the hold, on the sheets of our bed. *And every man to his wedded woman in the hopes that you and I might meet again.*

I quit my job at the shipyards, and I paid cash to sleep beside Crystal from Suriname, and sometimes I wandered up to the train station and thought about buying a ticket to Lyon. I had made the decision not to disturb Geneviève, as I have already explained. I did feel that was the best way to express my care. I admit that from her point of view this might have been indistinguishable from a sort of callous abandonment.

Once I did buy a ticket to Lyon, and I travelled some distance too. It was early spring, I think, March, the light opening up, and I had been feeling that perhaps it would be fine to go after all. I wanted to talk with Geneviève about Abigail, I wanted to remember certain things about the baby that I felt I was forgetting. I fell into a doze as the train rattled over the Dutch countryside and then I dreamed of water, a terrible dream of a river in full-flood, of the Amstelsluizen failing, of headwaters rushing past, of water lapping up onto the land and pouring over the pavements, a wall of water coming downriver in a torrent, pushing down bridges and swirling over the boats. In the dream I was drowning beneath the weight of all that water, unable to breathe. A customs officer startled me out of sleep at the Belgian border to ask for my passport. I reached for it in my bag, and showed it to him, and then I looked out the window and knew I would not go to Lyon. The weeping, the way it went on and on. I got off the train at Antwerp. I had lunch and went to an art gallery, and that evening I took the train back to Amsterdam.

*

The sky is grey, the laced, ragged edges of nimbostratus bouncing up over the headland, the wind picking up from the south ahead of the rain. We probably should have bought property at one of the beach hamlets that pepper the West Coast on the main route out of town: Waikawa, Hokio Beach, Tangimoana, Foxton Beach, detours that Aaron and I used to veer onto on impulse on our trips to and from Wanganui. We'd turn east from State Highway One, drive down several kilometres to the groin where a river or stream hit the platinum sand, piles of driftwood, silvered trunks of uprooted trees, the long curve of the sea's edge trailing all the way up to Mount Egmont, which you can see through the haze on a clear day. Better weather on that coast, and much closer to Wanganui, too.

But instead we bought here, at Castlepoint. I take the last few turns past the Whakataki Hotel and slide along the beach road. Always, the punctuation mark of the lighthouse, drawing you on to land's end, the reef, the sea.

I've come out on impulse. Settlement day is fast approaching. The bach has been cleared out, grotty furniture picked up by the Salvation Army, the last bits and pieces boxed up and stored in Hataitai. There's not even a bed there to sleep in. It's an unreasonably long drive for a daytrip, and I'm not sure I fancy a night sleeping on the floor, but the city has loomed over me all week, the glass towers tightening on my head like a vice, and I just want this, the wide air and the rearing cliffs, the long scoop of the lagoon.

Driving over the Rimutakas I thought I might come back over later in the summer to check out what Miranda and James Tyson do with the house. I wouldn't mind spying one of them out on the lawn, Miranda in her sunhat, James in his shorts, sipping gin and taking in the view, their children, which I hope they have, scampering chirpily about in the grass, tumbling and nipping like kittens. I would like to see them happy in that place. It would give me a sense of avuncular pleasure to see that, a restorative tonic to wash down the bitter pill of having failed to check, when I purchased it twenty years ago, the legal boundaries myself. That still rankles, and I suppose it always will.

Odd to think of us making use of the section all these years. How strange to think that the land was never ours. To all intents and purposes it made no difference to how we lived there, our sunbathing, games of cricket, those smoky barbecues in the gusting wind.

Before driving north this morning, I visited the City Gallery Wellington. I'd seen an advertisement in the paper for the curator's talk, which I didn't want to miss. I had a certain trepidation about the event, and so I went to peruse the shelves on the nextdoor library's second floor to put it from my mind.

Deep in the New Zealand shelves, I found the biography of Governor Grey that Claudia had been reading. It might even have *been* Claudia's copy, for all I knew, read and returned. I got absorbed in a piece about Te Rauparaha's arrest in 1846, which took place at the old chief's pā in Porirua, thirty miles from Grey's main military base at Te Aro. Grey's men marched for two days in order to reach Mana, the route taking them on a new military road through the northern hills, a road commissioned by the Army specifically in order to track down Te Rauparaha. When they arrived at Mana a hundred and fifty armed men seized the chief at dawn, and brought him aboard a man-o'-war. He was taken to Auckland, where he was held without trial under martial law in the British naval vessel *Calliope* for twelve months.

I don't know much about Te Rauparaha. People talk about his cunning, and I've heard that he sold Kapiti Island several times over to various Pākehā. According to these dates, he must have been in his eighties by the time Grey came to arrest him. The biography doesn't say anything about the conditions onboard *Calliope*. It does say that Grey let Te Rauparaha come home to his people in Otaki two years later, when he had ascertained that he was no longer a risk to the settlers.

Box Hill, that little rise in the northern suburbs, its namesake railway station at the base, a quadrant of streets full of pretty villas and well-tended lawns. That's where Grey built his sentry, a military base to guard and provision his men on that march to the Ngāti Toa pā, at a time when the northern hills above the harbour were wild, open land, without a house in sight.

A decade later Captain Edward Battersbee would retire up to those lonely, empty hills after his long, and no doubt rewarding, career tending the battle horses of the Bombay Light Cavalry. Mutinies quelled, order restored.

A lesser man might choose to huddle down on the foreshore in the growing settlement, rather than up on this exposed spot. But Battersbee is not afraid of natives. Look at the old Captain up there in the wind, hammering in the first planks of his homestead. His house will be the first in the area, with a commanding view over the harbour, and he names it Khandallah: the resting place of God.

When I think of Matthew on the boat, I wonder about myself. I am not a violent man, and yet I did hold him down in the water. Matthew believes I saved him, and the next time I see him, I don't expect I will correct that belief. On the face of it, I should be mortified. And yet whatever

343

shame there is in me seems to be amorphous, dissipated, weak as an emotion from a dream.

The fact is, I was glad to shut him up. I wanted to see the gratitude in his face. I went out there to save him that night, and I did.

I drive to the end of the road, and bump down onto the beach. There are tractors sitting up on the wet sand, a dog turning circuits in the dunes. On the sands, just below the lighthouse, the silhouette of an extraordinarily tall figure casts a line into the surf. The giant fisherman is so curious, so inexplicable, that I lock the car and trudge down, tripping over a carcass of mullet as I go, blue flies rising off it and dispersing.

Drawing closer, the figure wobbles and breaks into two parts, and I realise I have been looking at a man with a child on his shoulders. They share the same mass of tightly curled black hair, the girl's falling loose down her back. Put down on the ground, she scuttles away like a wound-up toy, scribing a line parallel with the surf. Eventually she slows and looks around, alarmed by the distance between them, and her father, watching, beckons her back. As he lowers his hand his body jolts; the line grows taut. He reels in the catch as his child returns to him.

By the time I reach them they are crouched over the bucket, and I can hear the slap of the thing against the plastic.

'Looks like a beauty,' I say, peering in from above. It's a glimmer of rose, a hand-length long, with wide blue paddles on each side of the body that it collapses against and crushes as it flips. Soon nothing is moving except the tail and the whiskers beneath the head, which continue to claw faintly at the air. 'Good for eating?' I ask.

'Yuck,' says the child. 'It's got eyes.'

'Not bad,' says the man. 'Quite decent for a gurnard. They're not a big fish.'

'Is it alive?' says the girl. She pokes a finger into the bucket.

'Oi,' says the man, yanking at her arm. 'You want to get yourself bitten?'

She pouts, keels back on her haunches and sits down on the sand, strews a handful towards the water, but the sand sifts into her eyes and she starts to rub at them.

'You ever tried gurnard?' the man asks me.

The girl is pulling on her father's arm, one fist digging into her face. He stands still, waiting for me to answer.

'Never,' I say. 'At least, not to my knowledge.'

'Daddy,' shouts the child, 'I can't see.'

'Bloody hell,' he says, 'keep still.' He tips her chin up towards him, his other hand cradling the back of her head. His wide finger arrives on the slight, blue skin beneath her eye, firmly pulling it down. He kneels and squints in, and she balances there, compliant, holding her breath. In the next instant she blinks and writhes away from him, turning belly-up on the sand, arms and legs flailing, a thin uneven scream releasing from her lungs.

'Jesus, what a performance!' The man stands up, leaving her thrashing. 'You got kids?'

'A boy,' I say. 'But he's twenty-five.'

'Is that right?' says the man. 'Hard to imagine. They stop this eventually, do they?'

'More or less,' I say, laughing.

'I've got older two boys,' he says. 'But I reckon girls are another game altogether. This one's a right handful.'

The belligerent roar drops back to a whimper.

'I just wanted a day's fishing,' he says. 'Hey!' he shouts to the girl, 'you want to get sent home?'

He flicks a knife from his pocket, picks the fish from

the bucket and, holding it in one hand, slices a line from tail to head, blood pouring through his closed fingers like juice from a squeezed fruit. The girl falls silent and shuffles close, dazzled.

'You visiting?' says the man, holding the fish in the palm of his hand, digging at the innards. He wipes his brow with the back of his wrist, the knife pointing away from his eyes.

'Just over for the day.'

'Here,' says the man, holding up the heel of clean flesh, 'why don't you take this?'

'Oh no, really,' I say, 'I couldn't.'

He drops it in the margarine container. 'Go on,' he says, handing it to me. 'You'll enjoy that.'

About a dozen people in all came for the curator's talk. I hovered at the back of the art gallery, and kept my sunglasses on and my hat lowered. The curator spoke about the exhibition, which was entitled *Self: Portrait*. She had been tasked with chosing portraits from collections across New Zealand, curated only on the principle of her own interest and affinity. I believe the underlying notion was that the exhibition would indirectly 'portray' the curator herself. She had made an eclectic choice of both famous and unknown works, each of which she began to talk about in turn. When she came to stand in front of Moira's painting, I turned away and made an intense examination of a Goldie painting of a young Māori girl.

We might imagine that the artist here has chosen to peel off the man everything that defines him, she said. Her voice was melodious, authoritative. A person of this age must have a history, must have a role. And yet here the figure is not father, not husband, not lover, not worker. He has no context around him, only that bare white chair. I see it as a thought experiment, she said. I see it as the artist

346

putting the question to us. What would happen to this man if he were stripped of all his titles? It's an entirely unknown work, but it's become a favourite of mine, she said.

She moved across to a Rita Angus, and that was it. I walked out of the room and out of the gallery, out into the wide square of sunlight, and I threw my arms up, and the pigeons around me startled and flew off.

Inside the empty bach, I walk over to open the curtains. Always, the theatre of this moment, unveiling the view, taking in the particular way the light is working the water and the headland today.

The water is steel and the sky thick with the coming rain. And, right here in front of me, a horse. Two, three horses, a bay and two blacks, blue tarpaulin covers on their backs. They're standing ten feet away from the window, and startle at the movement of the curtain, clop a few feet backwards, register my presence at the glass, resume grazing, although the bay is keeping her eye on me, her tail flicking around a little.

Why are there are horses on my back lawn? Why, in fact, is there is a fenceline running between the house and the horses, the fence is not where it should be down over the slope, *somebody has moved the fence.*

I screech open the glass doors and stamp out to investigate. The horses look up with clear suspicion, and the two blacks trot off towards the slope. Ten metres out from my front door the posts are newly dug in, piles of clayish dirt still visible at the base of each. The top wire doesn't look electrified, but I check with the back of my hand first anyway, before hopping up and over. The bay stands her ground, but looks a little skittish.

Moira's studio floats off like a piece of nonsense stuck in the middle of the field. It's locked up. It doesn't look like anyone's bothered with it, and the windows are intact. There are piles of horse manure to swerve around on the way down to the old fenceline, here, where the slope steepens and starts to fall away, the holes filled in roughly, dirt stamped down. Do the horses hesitate when they get to this line, at the edge of their old estate?

Inside the studio the air is cool and nothing has changed. There's the gap where the portrait was sitting on the easel. If he'd have been left here, if Hamish hadn't asked to look in the shed. Marooned, solitary, fading slightly through the summer with the hot light battering in all day at the window. Staring blankly back at the horses as they amble over to use the walls of the shed as a pissing post.

Something else you failed to mention, Moira, another loose end you failed to tidy up. I could have brought it into town for you, could have hung it for you on the wall of the room where you lay dying instead of those fucking awful geometric abstractions they specialised in at that place, that monstrosity that glared at us from the end of the hallway each time we arrived to see you, its off-centre golden circle like a bad eye. Who chooses those things? I suppose it's too disturbing to put up paintings of bodies— *it's all I'm interested in, the human form*—in a place where bodies are at the centre of everyone's concern, seeping, disintegrating, falling away.

But I'd never have brought it in. It would have frightened you to have that painting there, to look with dreadful clarity at what you saw when you made that work. That naked man, stripped of all his titles, you may have been curious about him at certain moments along the way, but in the end you chose to lock him in the shed. *Who the hell are you, if you're not his father?* You too, you most of all, you wanted to draw a veil.

When I sat beside you in that room, and your spirit was

quailing, you wanted me steady and certain. Certain, like a father must be certain when he says to a child, *That type of spider isn't poisonous*, says to a child, *It's extremely rare for a plane to fly into a building, that almost never happens*, says to a child, *I will catch you, I will help you, I will save you.*

I couldn't save you from any of it. On the day of your death, all I could do was stay close. *I'm here, Moira.* I said it over and over. The smell of the rose lotion, the tiny flinches your fingers made inside my fist. *I'm here.* What else could anyone say? *I'm here*, and I tried to be, to summon as much presence as I could into those hours, that little room. When your breathing became shallower and smaller, Aaron left the room. He's only twenty-five, Moira, he couldn't bear it. So there we were, you and me, and I sat with you, and I stroked your hair back from your forehead, stroking and stroking, damp heat under my hand, your skin sweating, and I knew you were on the cusp and that soon you would be gone, but still, I couldn't imagine it would ever happen, because you were with me, the breath still coming into you and releasing, the blanket drawn up to your chest, and your mouth fallen open, and when a long pause came, I waited with you and held my breath too, and then after a few seconds you drew again, once more, another sip of air, and I felt that I had never loved you more, or more plainly. Everything's fine, I said, don't be frightened. A gust of wind outside made the window vibrate loudly, and when it fell quiet again I saw that you were not breathing. *You're beautiful*, I kept saying, *you're beautiful*, and after a few minutes I heard Aaron come in behind me, he put his hand on my shoulder and I held it to my cheek. *She's gone now*, he said, and I nodded and we stayed with you for over an hour, for hours, and you were ours.

*

In the middle of the night, the phone rings. I fumble for the receiver, press it to my ear in the dark. 'Hello?'

'It's me, Dad.'

'Aaron?'

There's a gasping, shuddering sound coming down the line that I can't place for a moment or two.

'Are you okay? Wait, Aaron, are you crying?'

'Dad. Are you there?'

'I'm here, Ronny. Talk to me. What's going on? Are you hurt?'

'Dad, I saw this kid today. I mean, I didn't just see him. I—'

'Where are you?'

Son, you've got to fly out to Dubai or to Bangkok, you've got to get to Islamabad or Lahore or Karachi, you've got to get on a plane. I bite it all back, the answers I have, and the worry and the bile too.

'I'm in Peshawar,' he says. 'There are people coming over the border, thousands of people. Every day, every single day. Ahmed's family, they tell me to keep out of it, but I've been going down to the Red Cross tent, trying to be helpful or something. I'm not that helpful though. I don't know how to do anything useful. And today, there was this kid. His brother was pushing him, he had him in a kind of wheelbarrow.'

I flick the light on, sit up. 'Go on.'

'He was in a bad way. He'd lost maybe part of his leg.'

'Right.'

'Well he died. The kid died. Fuck, I was right there beside him, and he died. '

Big loose sounds start coming down the line. He's sobbing, hard and full and uncontrollable, and it goes on for minutes.

'I wanted to tell you that.'

'Did he have a name?'

'I don't know his name. I don't know anything about him. I didn't do anything for him. Except I was there, that's all.'

'I don't know what to say.'

'I just wanted to talk to you, I guess.'

'Well, I'm here.'

'I miss you, Dad.'

My heart stands completely still.

'Anytime,' I say. 'Anytime.'

Fourteen

Mytilene, February 2002

The sea is milky blue all around the yacht. It seems to breathe and exhale, as if we are gliding upon a lung. Rob stopped chatting shortly after we left the shore, and is now holding the tiller, the tea I brewed half an hour ago perched on the deck beside him. We've navigated around the northwest corner of the island, and from here, smack in the middle of the Mytilene Strait, I can see the purple hills of the Turkish coast on one side, the Lesbos beaches on the other. There's barely a few kilometres between the two countries, the same distance, the same colours, the same perspective as you get when you look east from Ngauranga over to Eastbourne. If you were trying make landfall in Europe from Asia, this would be the place to make your crossing. I'd asked Rob if we could land in Turkey and go for a ramble, but we'd need a visa. It's a quiet stretch of water, and there's certainly no one out here today.

The day after I flew in, Clare brought me to the waterfront, and we went down the café. Kipos. The girl, Lisette, was there working tables and, I will admit, as soon as I saw her I could understand why she had startled them so much back in August. She was taller and darker than Geneviève, but she had a similar look about the face. I launched fairly directly into my enquiry. The dates were wrong. I think I alarmed the girl by asking for evidence, which may have come across a bit heavy on my part. Still, she indulged me and produced her French identity card, which showed a 1978 birthdate. She was born six years after Abigail. She was only twenty-four and, in any case, she came from Brittany, which is about as far away from Lyon as it gets. She was a warm, confident girl with a beautiful smile. She went back to her work, and Clare pulled a little face at me and apologised. I told her I really hadn't expected anything, that my whole purpose in coming to Greece was to see her and Rob, and to have a holiday. The coffee at the place was pretty awful, although the paninis were just fine. Well, I would have been foolish to expect it to be otherwise.

Afterwards we drove up to the Tériade museum in Vária, on the hill behind the harbour. It was just a small house, and no one else was there. The weather has been cool and there are hardly any tourists at this time of year. The walls were lined with Chagall's lithographs, a whole series of Bible illustrations as well as the ones from *Daphnis and Chloe*. What struck me while inspecting them was just how good the reproductions in my golden book are. The colours are very close, and the scale of the pictures is similar to mine. It was quite reasonable for the bookseller to charge me the price he did, even though I had to wait a month to drink Dutch beer, saving up for it.

I inspected the picture of the infant Daphnis exposed on the hillside. A goat stands above the baby while, cresting over the brow of the hill, haloed and raising his hand like Christ, comes Lamon, the goatherd who will shortly find the child and take him home. The sun is coming up, a double-yolked splotch of yellow at the edge of the hill, contradicting the text which says it was the hottest part of the day. For Chagall, then, this was the morning, and the point of the illustration was that the child had survived the night. How does it feel to be abandoned and helpless in the dark, to cry out for warmth and food, and have no one come? A goat or a sheep, even a cat or a dog, would have known what to do, would have laid themselves, warm-blooded, beside her on the boat.

Last night, I did a Yahoo search for private investigators in France. I've gone so far as to put a couple of phone calls through, and I'm waiting to hear back. There was something so easy, so energising, about putting the questions to that girl at Kipos: Where are you from? Who are your parents? I could ask those questions again, I think. I could ask them many times over.

Aaron, when I last heard from him at Christmas, had flown out to Bangkok, and from there back into Delhi. The stand-off between India and Pakistan continues. *Like some terrible divorce.* That was Adrian, back in Venice, but I'm not sure it's the right metaphor. Amrita and her sister on one side of the border, their brother on the other. Neither nation has said categorically that they would not make a nuclear strike, if provoked.

Aaron said was he was planning to meet up with a contact of his in Chennai, and teach English for the year. I asked him about his play, *Shopping and Fucking*, which is opening this week in London, and he seemed vague, blasé, as if he could no longer remember the person who had got that part. Claudia, oddly, has decided to go and see the play in any case, as the tour group are stopping over in London for three days on their way to Rome. I'm sure she'll give me a full report.

Aaron has no plans to go back to the UK in the

meantime. I can't imagine he'll be rushing back to New Zealand either. That's fair enough. He doesn't owe me anything, except to live his life. If this state of affairs feels intolerable to me, that doesn't make it any less reasonable. *Cronus* is moored at Chaffers Marina. I'll maintain it and keep it in good order, in case he comes for a visit, in case one day he wants to make use of it.

Orpheus's head, severed from his body, is said to have washed up somewhere along the coast of this island, still singing. His head and his lyre were buried by the islanders and music has risen from his oracle ever since. *Lyre, lyric, lyrical.* Orpheus is ancestor to the poet Sappho, whose statue stands in the square on the Mytilene waterfront facing out to the harbour, carved in contemporary white stone. I noticed her standing there after we farewelled Lisette, high on her plinth among the cafés, her hair loose, lyre on her shoulder, hand crooked out in a gesture that looks like an invitation to dance.

The bedroom that I'm occupying in the house over in Molyvos has a peacock-coloured rug on the floor, a beautifully appointed bed with plump cushions, an art deco lamp and a corner window that looks out to the sea. On the bedside table there is a handful of carefully selected volumes: Plato's *Republic*, Euripides and a new translation of Sappho. These details speak of Clare and Rob, the excellent care they take of the place, their solicitousness towards me. I have slept well in that room, and I have woken early in the morning and sat in the yellow armchair with the window open, reading over Sappho's fragments, scraps of language which somehow are more vital still for having been torn away from the body of the work.

O Evening Star, bringing everything
that dawn's first glimmer scattered far and wide—
you bring the sheep, you bring the goat,
you bring the child back to the mother.

Rob noses the boat into the Mytilene harbour as the sunset
starts. The hill above the water is topped with a radio
mast, blinking its red light. The sky starts to flood orange
and pink, and the gulls are circling and crying as we come
into the mooring.

Clare is standing on the shore, waving both arms at us.

'What's she up to?' says Rob.

I'm tying up, looping coils of the blue-and-white rope
around the cleat, making sure it holds the boat fast against
the pier, when Clare presses a mobile phone into my hand.

'It's your mother,' she whispers.

I take the phone and greet my mother.

'It's Dad,' Mum says.

I knew this, though, because why else would my mother
call so urgently, on Clare's phone? I knew what had
happened when I saw her standing on the shore, and now I
know it. I feel it hit my body: solar plexus, stomach, bowel.

'I don't know how to tell you,' she says.

You don't have to.

'Will you come home?' There's a tremble in her voice.

'Yes, I'm coming, Mum,' I say. 'I'm already coming. I'm
on my way.'

Notes

The New Ships spells Aotearoa placenames as they were when the book was set, in 2001, meaning macrons have been omitted, and Whanganui city has been spelled Wanganui.

The quote on the poster in Peter's London flat comes from Raoul Vaneigem's *The Revolution of Everyday Life*. Copyright © 2010 by Donald Nicholson-Smith and published by PM Press (www.pmpress.org).

'Sappho Fragment 104a' translated by Gillian Spraggs and reproduced from www.gillianspraggs.com/index.html. Copyright © Gillian Spraggs.

The lyrics on page 53 are from 'Chains' by Che Fu, from the album *2b S.Pacific* (BMG, 1998).

The quote on page 90 is from Mustafa Kemal Atatürk, the first leader of the Republic of Turkey. It is inscribed on the Ari Burnu Memorial at Gallipoli, and also replicated on the Atatürk Memorial at Tarakena Bay on Wellington's South Coast, a place where the New Zealand landscape is considered to strongly resemble that of Anzac Cove (Ari Burnu) in Turkey.

The newspaper article on pages 260 and 261 was published in *The Dominion* on Friday 24 Juy 1992. While the yachting tragedy is real, I have changed the names.

The quote on page 299 comes from 'A Ballad of John Nicholson' by Henry John Newbolt.

The quotes from Plato's *Symposium* on page 311 come from the Benjamin Jowett translation.

Acknowledgements

I am grateful for the generous support of Creative New Zealand (the Louis Johnson New Writers' Bursary); the IIML at Victoria University of Wellington; the Robert Burns Fellowship at the University of Otago; the Massey University Visiting Artist Scheme through the School of English and Media Studies; and to Dianne and Peter Beatson for periodic use of their writing retreat in Foxton.

Thanks to my editor and publisher, Holly Hunter and Fergus Barrowman, for your expertise and attentive work on the manuscript.

This novel was completed as part of a PhD in Creative Writing at Victoria University of Wellington. I'm grateful to Bill Manhire for encouraging me to join the programme. I had innumerable conversations about the novel with my supervisors Damien Wilkins and James Meffan. The novel also benefitted from the expertise of examiners Emily Perkins, Kim Worthington and Chad Wriglesworth; of members of my PhD class, too numerous to name here but all generous with their engagement and encouragement; and of the many people who have fact-checked and answered my questions on matters as various as Indian and Pakistani history, classical Greek beliefs on reincarnation, languages, Orpheus, Punjabi names and corporate law culture—thanks especially to Wajeehah Aayeshar, Sekhar Bandyopadhyay, Suman Puri, Timothy Smith, Geoff Miles, Brannavan Gnanalingam, Josh Blackmore, Babette Puetz and the New Zealand Translation Centre.

A particular thank you goes to Rajorshi Chakraborti, who drew my attention to the obvious connection between the material I was writing, and the suburb of Wellington in which I grew up.

To Elizabeth Knox, Sarah Laing, Kirsten McDougall, Susan Pearce, Emma Martin, Pip Adam, Anna Smaill and Tina Makereti: thank you for keeping me reading through these busy years.

To friends Bronwyn Davies, Amy Austin, Dion Howard, Dianna Thomson, Simone Drichel, Fiona Eason, Rachel Smith-Robb, Sabine Fehrmann, Tim Corballis, Ingrid Horrocks, Anna Sanderson, Lena Tichy: thank you for the conversations, the company and the unstinting support. Bottomless appreciation goes to my parents, Sally Munro and Patrick Duignan, who helped in every possible way. All my love and gratitude to my partner, James Hollings.

To my children, Esmé, Phoebe and Leo, with love. This novel, started long before any of you began, is done.